Praise for Della Borton's previous Gilda Liberty mystery, *Fade to Black*

"Borton's memorably wacky characters and . . . Hollywood references add up to a fun read."
—*Publishers Weekly*

"If you're hooked on the American Movie Classics channel, you'll welcome Gilda Liberty and her crazy movie-loving family. . . . Just relax and enjoy the glitter and the glitz. Hooray for Hollywood!"
—*Meritorious Mysteries*

"*Fade to Black* is a lighthearted mystery with some weight to it, and unlike some Hollywood movies, sequels to this debut will be highly welcome."
—*Rock Hill* (South Carolina) *Herald*

By Della Borton
Published by Fawcett Books:

FADE TO BLACK
FREEZE FRAME

FREEZE FRAME

Della Borton

FAWCETT BOOKS • NEW YORK

A Fawcett Book
Published by The Ballantine Publishing Group
Copyright © 2000 by Lynette Carpenter

www.randomhouse.com/BB/

Library of Congress Catalog Card Number: 99-91513

ISBN 0-449-00408-2

Manufactured in the United States of America

First Edition: February 2000

10   9   8   7   6   5   4   3   2   1

To James Naremore and Murray Sperber,
who transformed all my nights and days in the dark.
When my students complain that nobody
will watch movies with them anymore,
I tell them:
it's all your fault.

Acknowledgments

My thanks go first and foremost to Murray Sperber, author of *College Sports Inc.*, whose groundbreaking work on the business of college athletics was a major resource for this book.

Thanks also go to Kathy Amato, owner of the Strand Theatre in Delaware, Ohio, for her lesson in film projection, and to the late Cindy Johnson, my other instructor. I am indebted as well to Sergeant Russell L. Martin of the Delaware Police Department, who cheerfully answered my questions about search and seizure.

Finally, I'd like to thank my dialect consultants, Brian Sweeney and Laura Zebuhr, for their careful editing.

Prologue

FADE IN
Ext.—Columbus, Ohio—Night
MONTAGE: Cityscape, Columbus, Ohio. A series of shots of sites unrecognizable to the average moviegoer: the riverfront, the courthouse, City Center, and finally, the Buckeye State University Union, as shot from across a busy street on a lively Saturday night. The details may not be familiar, but the ambience is. The sidewalks are crowded with young people, the bars are overflowing. It has started to drizzle, so the crowds are huddling together, and a few umbrellas pop up. A couple dashes through the street traffic, jackets held over their heads. There are several hints for those who know their collegiate iconography, including the name of the nearest establishment, and a flag flying from the union building, visible by a streetlight. One or two umbrellas feature the same logo as the flag: a collegiate *B* against which leans a jaunty scarlet rodent of indeterminate species. This is the heart of Groundhog country.

Ext.—Columbus City Street—Night
Faint sounds of TRAFFIC NOISE.
LOW-ANGLE SHOT of street sign, showing that we are at the corner of Sixth and Hess. CAMERA TILTS DOWN to a FULL SHOT of a MAN in a trenchcoat, glistening with the dampness of the night. He is an attractive man who might be any age within the range of AARP eligibility. His eyes are shaded by a forties-style fedora, but he shows a broad smile beneath a bushy, white, Mark Twain mustache. He is looking in the direction of the CAMERA.

1

He extends one hand, holding out a rectangular package or box of some kind.

CAMERA TRACKS BACK to a LONG SHOT. A GLOVED HAND enters the frame from the lower right, and reaches for the package. The Man's smile widens. We catch a glint of light reflected off his eyes. He pulls back his extended arm, and instead offers the other arm, hand empty, palm up. The Gloved Hand drops. Another Gloved Hand appears in its place, and this one is holding something. We see a flash of light, and hear a GUNSHOT.

CLOSE SHOT of Man. As he looks down, the Man's face registers surprise, then shock. His empty hand gropes in the folds of the trenchcoat, just above the belt. A Gloved Hand reaches out and snatches the package from him. He crumples to his knees, then falls forward.

In the sudden silence, we hear the unmistakable sounds of HIGH HEELS TAPPING WET PAVEMENT.

                                                          FADE OUT

1

I've always been a night person. There is something about the sights, sounds, smells of night, the *feel* of night, that appeals to me. For one thing, darkness concentrates the mind and senses. Daytime floods my senses with too many impressions, creating a sensory soup in which no ingredient is distinctive. At night, there is less competition. What light exists is more particular about what it chooses to illuminate. Night is the time of silhouettes; you can appreciate the shapes of things in a way that is impossible on even the cloudiest of days. In darkness the scent of a lily or hyacinth can expand to fill the universe. The slightest brush of a breeze against the skin is more sensuous. The rising and falling hum of crickets and the sounds of other night creatures are more noticeable. Weather events are more dramatic—snowfalls more luminous in moonlight, lightning more dazzling against a night sky. And when the stars come out on a cloudless night, they are like a net of diamonds flung across black infinity. Who can look at them and not feel some elemental stirring in her soul, whether astronomical or astrological? Night is the time to breathe deeply and think deeply.

And now, after years of living like everyone else, my days revolved around my nights. No more rude awakenings, no more sleepy showers. While other women my age, other middle-aged middle managers, were stuffing their legs into pantyhose tight as sausage casings, ironing blouses, applying makeup to bleary eyes, and stumbling out the door with briefcases hanging from their arms, I was sound asleep. While they were power lunching or power walking, I was just getting up. And about the time they were starting to check their watches, I was on my way to work.

The theater business has its advantages.

On the downside, I only saw stars on my way home, and my nights were filled with the scent of popcorn, not lilies. The weather had taken on a significance previously unknown to me, not least of which was its potential to wreak havoc with the electrical supply in my small Ohio town. I saw no one on my way home at one A.M., at least, no one who was willing to speak to me. And I didn't even have time to watch the movies I was showing.

That last remark is meant to be taken figuratively. As owner of the Paradise Theatre in Eden, Ohio, a property reluctantly inherited from my recently deceased Aunt Maesie, I could be said to be "showing movies." In actuality, the technical side of the operation, including the showing of movies itself, was handled by my business associate, theater manager, and head projectionist, my cousin Duke. My reluctance to involve myself in that aspect of the business had become a source of some tension between us.

What I liked about movies, I maintained, was the magic of those stories, unwinding in the darkness on the silver screen. I wanted to continue believing in that magic, perfectly focused, perfectly framed, without doing any of the mechanical business of focusing and framing myself, which would spoil the illusion. I also have the manual dexterity and mechanical aptitude of a platypus. I pointed this out frequently to my cousin. Duke wouldn't buy it. No daughter of a Hollywood song-and-dance team, not to mention all of the other industry people I was niece, aunt, granddaughter, sister, and cousin to, was permitted to be that naive.

That's how I came to be standing in an overheated projection booth on a May afternoon. What the weather was outside, I couldn't tell you; there was a soundproof booth and several layers of building between me and it.

"Now, you take this like so," Duke said, eyeing me through

thick lenses to make sure I was paying attention. He had seized one end of the film between thumb and forefinger. He was a big kid, even for seventeen, and looked squashed by the ceiling of the projection booth like Orson Welles in all those low-angle shots from *Citizen Kane*.

"And then you—" He held it to his mouth and licked it.

"You're putting me on."

"I'm *not*!" he said indignantly, opening his eyes.

"That's gr-r-ross!" I said. "No way."

"You *have* to, Gilda! It's what they do!"

"You don't know where that thing's been," I said.

He heaved an exasperated sigh. "Well, look, if you don't want to lick it, you can just—" And he held the thing to his mouth and rubbed it across his bottom lip.

"Well, that's a relief," I said. "That looks so much more sanitary. Why, in the name of Louis B. Mayer, would anybody do such a thing?"

"Look, one side is slick, and the other is kinda sticky. That's how you know whether the film's been wound on the reel with the right side out or not. Just because we do things right around here doesn't mean everybody does. Half the time these multiplexes got some flunky on projection who could care less whether he's got things right side up or not, and wouldn't know how to tell if he didn't."

"Like me," I put in. Ignorance is bliss.

"But you," he said, extending the film to me, "will know better."

When I had first started working with Duke, in those early days after Aunt Maesie's funeral, he had struck me as a painfully shy, awkward teenager. His stash of science fiction novels and computer equipment in his private digs upstairs tagged him as a classic nerd. He seemed, in fact, a complete contrast to the actor he'd been named for. But now that he was more comfortable with me, now that we'd officially become partners and I had gained some experience in working with him, I'd discovered a more confident, even commanding, side

to him. Within the walls of the Paradise, he wielded as much
authority as John Wayne in the saddle. He had run the theater
on his own those last months while Maesie was ill—no small
feat for a high school kid. Maesie had taught him everything
she knew so that he could take care of the theater they both
loved after she was gone. I figured she'd left the place to
me because I was a grown-up, and because I was the least in-
terfering member of my highly meddlesome family. I had
certainly never wanted to interfere with the projection equipment in any way; the ticket dispenser was almost more than
I could handle, and the popcorn machine terrified me. But
Duke had insisted that I become a projectionist.

"The art of projection," he'd said, in the serious voice that
signaled a quotation from my Aunt Maesie, "has a long and
venerable history."

We had the projectors to prove it. The one I was con-
fronting right now was a Century behemoth that looked like it
had been hanging around since the day after Al Jolson said
"You ain't heard nothin' yet."

"So why would you want to screw it up by getting me involved?" I'd asked. "Would you want to be a terrorist's junior
high chemistry teacher? Or the Roman senatorial knife grinder
on the fourteenth of March? You want to follow in the footsteps of the United Artists executive who greenlighted *Heav-
en's Gate*?"

But he refused to be distracted or deterred.

"Anyone can project," he'd said on another occasion in
the same voice, "but not everyone who can project is a
projectionist."

I thought he was probably half right. I'm suspicious of all
statements that begin "Anyone can."

Seeing me hesitate now, he turned to the makeup bench,
picked up a pair of scissors, and snipped the end off the film.

"See?" he said. "No cooties."

Intellectually, I knew he'd only cut a piece off the leader.
But I was still enough of a novice to experience a cardiac flutter when the plastic fragment hit the floor. After all, this film

was somebody else's property. What if he'd just eliminated the hundred-and-first dalmatian?

I took the film from him and tentatively rubbed first one side, then the other, across my bottom lip. He was watching me like an anxious chef.

"Okay," I said. "One side is stickier than the other. But how am I gonna remember which side goes out? At my age the brain cells are kind of worn. Will you write me a note?"

He made a face the way he always did when I made a point of my creeping senility, and said, "Sure, if you want me to."

Actually, every surface in the room was already covered with enough diagrams and cautionary notes to intimidate Dr. Strangelove. Most were in Maesie's neat hand, some were in Duke's scrawl. Some of them were so yellowed with age I wondered whether they were still applicable, or if they were mementos of some bygone piece of equipment.

"And while we're on the subject, could you also write out some instructions for that new cappuccino machine? I get so flustered when we're crowded, I can't remember how to work the damn thing."

"We're not," he said sternly, "on that subject, but okay, I will. Now, pay attention, Gilda. Once you know you've got the film loaded on the platter right, you thread it through here like this."

I watched him with a sinking heart as he threaded the film along its intricate path, pointing out various potential hazards along the way. Menopausal women, even those without kids around, shouldn't be expected to acquire new technical skills that demanded a lot of short-term memory. And then thinking of kids reminded me of the ones I'd lost in the breakup with Liz, and I thought about how I was going to miss Paulie's graduation from junior high, and then about how we weren't supposed to call him "Paulie" anymore but "Paul," and I teared up a little, so I forced myself to think about when my own son, John, had made the transition from "Johnny" to "Jack" after reading *Profiles in Courage*, and I wondered how

John's latest gig was going out in L.A., and how long his current band would last, and—

Duke was looking at me.

"What did I just say?" he asked.

I blinked at him.

"Gilda, you've got to pay attention!" he admonished me. "If you don't, you're gonna scramble the brains and break the film!"

"My brains are already scrambled!" I moaned. "I'm sorry," I continued contritely, "but it's too confusing! Look at all the opportunities I have to screw up! What if I break something? What if I break the film in the middle of some big romantic scene, and we have to jump cut right in the middle of a Michelle Pfeiffer kiss? It'll look like we're back in the Production Code era. With my luck, that's just when it will happen, too. Or the sound will go funny, like they're speaking in Chinese, and I won't know what to do about it."

I could hear the rising panic in my voice. Much as I'd disliked being an insurance executive, I could swear my hair had turned grayer in the few short weeks since I'd become a theater owner. Frizzier, too, from all the pulling, and, of course, longer, because I didn't have time to get it cut. If I didn't do something soon, I thought, fingering my split ends, I'd fall into the clutches of my aunt Gloria, former hairdresser to the stars.

I wrenched myself back to the present crisis. "I mean, you said you were going to train Todd, didn't you? He seems like a quick study, don't you think? I just think it's a big mistake to trust me with heavy machinery. Or even light machinery. What we need is another projectionist—a real projectionist, not a technophobe with a diagram!"

"You could hire me," said a voice from the doorway.

We both turned in surprise.

In the doorway stood a slender young woman in black— baggy black pants riding low on what passed for her hips, black T-shirt under a black leather jacket. She wore a heavy silver chain around her neck, as if padlocking her head to her body, and a matching chain looped from one hip pocket. The black set off her bright red hair, so bright as to be practically phosphorescent, cut military short on both sides, and spiked at the top. She had large brown eyes in a thin face, an eclectic collection of earrings hanging from both ears, and a nose ring. She had a small rose tattoo at her throat, and I happened to know that underneath all that black there was a goddess tattooed on her right arm who bore a suspicious resemblance to Wonder Woman. She looked as out of place in Eden, Ohio, as Flipper in a bathtub.

"Cousin Faye," I said in astonishment. "What are you doing here? Aren't you in school?"

Faye McCadden was in film school at USC. I had seen her at Aunt Maesie's funeral, and at another funeral shortly afterward when her father's stepfather had been murdered. Her father, my cousin Spencer, was a photographer in L.A. and official still photographer at the family's funereal gatherings. For a fleeting moment, I wondered if someone had died whose death I wasn't aware of. We have a large family, and I don't always tune in to their gossip.

"School's out for the summer," she said. "I'm spending the summer with Mom, and helping out with Grams, and, like, working on my own stuff. So I need a job."

Her mother, Carol, Spencer's ex-wife, lived in town and worked at Eden College.

She strode purposefully over to the projector and looked it up and down like a casting director's assistant vetting an extra. She gave it a firm nod.

"Have you projected before, Faye?" Duke asked her, getting down to business.

"No," she said, "but I'm sure I could do it. It doesn't look hard."

Her confidence elated me. Duke, who articulated this view himself when he wasn't pontificating about the venerable art of projection, looked offended.

"She's a filmmaker, Duke," I pointed out encouragingly.

"She's a videographer," he rejoined, a little disparagingly.

She turned and studied us. "Look," she said, "do you need a projectionist or not?"

"You're hired," I said.

That night, walking home, I breathed the night air contentedly and admired the beauty of the stars. I had needed a projectionist, and a projectionist had been provided me. What I didn't know was that I could've used an astrologer as well.

2

"She's making a movie," Duke informed me a few days later, as the two of them set up the concession stand while I took inventory in the adjacent storeroom.

Who isn't? I was tempted to say. But I realized that what was true of our family might not be true of families in general.

"A documentary video," Faye corrected him, dumping a load of ice into the bin beneath the drink machine. Everything she did was done energetically and seemed to produce a lot of noise. With her punk look and high energy, she seemed an unlikely match for Duke, but they were getting along famously.

"On women in sports," Duke added. "Do we have any more Twizzlers?"

I handed him a box.

"Women in college sports," she said. "That's one reason I'm here this summer. I needed some Big Ten material."

She disappeared into the room where the ice machine lived, and we could hear the explosions of ice against metal.

"She has a contact on the Lady Hogs," Duke said, a little awed.

"Berta Homans," Faye called. "Forward. She's, like, a friend of a friend. You know her?"

From inside the storage closet, I called back, "I don't really follow college sports." The conversation was making me lose count. I started over on the Milk Duds.

"What?" she shouted over the din from the ice machine. "What'd she say?"

"She said no," Duke reported in a loud voice.

Faye was back with another tub of ice, which she sent crashing into the bin. "You never heard of her? She's the shit! She must average a kazillion points a game. She's gonna be a hot recruit in the WNBA."

I went on counting.

Faye appeared in the doorway.

"In fact, now that I have all that money from Maesie, I'm going to invest in my own equipment—a new camera, an editing deck, the works! I'm so stoked!"

My aunt Maesie, in addition to her one real estate holding, the Paradise Theatre, had accumulated a small fortune in her eighty-three years and had left her family well provided for, down to the last great-grandniece and -grandnephew.

"I mean, I think Maesie would have approved, don't you?" Faye added. "She always told me how she loved fooling around with the editing equipment. The physical process of editing— splicing film and all that. She loved that."

I gave up on counting.

"The thing is," Faye continued, "I don't really have a place for this stuff. My apartment's miniscule."

"I thought you were at your mom's," I said.

She shook her head. "Too many kids, too much confusion. Can't deal with the 'rents on a day-to-day basis."

"Your mom charges you rent?" I asked.

"What?" She looked blank.

"She means parents, Gilda," Duke translated. " 'Rents are parents."

"Oh."

"Yeah, right, and there's no space at her house for the equipment. That stupid boat takes up practically the whole garage. And anyway, I don't want the kids getting into my stuff and trashing it. So I was wondering, Gilda. You have so much empty space here. I mean, Duke showed me all those dressing rooms over the stage and all. So I was wondering if I could keep my equipment here. You know, like, use one of those empty rooms and set up my editing stuff and my computer."

I opened my mouth to voice an objection, but she kept talking.

"I know there's a problem with the wiring, but Duke said Uncle Val put in new electrical lines for him, and I know he'd do the same for me if I asked him. I'd pay my share of the electric bill, honest! It's just—you have all this empty space, and space is what I need."

I noticed that Duke had conspicuously dropped out of the conversation. I began to suspect a conspiracy.

"And if you're worried about insurance, I'll pay anything extra. But your insurance probably already covers lots of equipment anyway, right? So it probably wouldn't be that much, right?"

As a former insurance executive, I was being beaten at my own game. And I couldn't even criticize the nonchalance with which she offered to pay for everything; I myself had been one of the biggest benefactors of Maesie's largesse, and I had noticed a similar shift in my own attitude toward money.

"What about security?" I asked. "Your equipment will probably be more portable, and more appealing to the average burglar, than mine."

"Come on, Gilda," she said. "This is Eden, Ohio. Half the town doesn't even lock their doors at night."

"You're thinking of the old Eden, Ohio—the way it was before Megaverse moved in, the downtown closed down, and crime went up."

"Okay, so I'll get a deadbolt installed on the door upstairs," she offered. "But I still think this place is pretty secure. Duke stays here most nights, and if I work here, I'll probably be around late at night, too."

"Well, okay," I said. "I guess."

That was how I became a patron of the arts and investor of sorts in the production end of the movie business. But that was only the beginning.

3

"Gilda, help! I'm *desperate*!"

Who isn't? I thought crossly, giving the phone cord a petulant yank.

I'd just rolled out of bed after lying awake for a good half hour, chastising myself for making no progress on my vow to move out of my aunt's house by Memorial Day. Like Faye, when I'd moved back home, I hadn't wanted to deal with my 'rents, either, so I'd moved into the family mansion, Liberty House, where my Aunt Lillian lived with her housekeeper-cook-companion, Ruth Hernandez. It gave me space to move around in, but I still felt like I was watched all the time, probably because I *was* watched all the time. I felt my family breathing down my neck like the Egyptians before the Red Sea parted. When I was emotionally stable, it drove me crazy. Now, when I was still fragile from my breakup with—okay, let's be frank here and call it my abandonment by—Liz, the love of my life, my family's surveillance, even when sympathetic and well-intentioned, drove me to distraction. I had to go to my room to cry, like a six year old, knowing that by the time I emerged, phone lines all over Los Angeles would be hot with discussions of my mental health. Yet today was Friday, Memorial Day Weekend was upon us, and I was still residing in the bosom of my family. It was anything but restful, especially in my current condition, and if I felt burdened by my family's concern, I was also tired of playing referee, interpreter, go-between, therapist, adviser, and hand-holder to the vast tribe of Liberties, whose lunacy was no doubt intended by some wag of a deity, played by Groucho Marx, to take my mind off my troubles. I got no thanks for all this help, I thought sourly, just more unwelcome advice on how I ought to be living my life. My relatives saw my life as a bad script in need of doctoring.

My family's life, as I saw it, was a long-running soap opera, so desperate calls for help were a daily occurrence.

"What's up, Faye?" I yawned.

"Something's come up," she said. "I need to shoot tomorrow."

"Well, call one of the others and see if they can fill in for you," I said. I refrained from pointing out that she'd only had this job for two weeks, and that so far I'd probably given more than I'd gotten in our employer-employee relationship. Arguments against self-interest didn't cut much mustard in my family.

"That's not what I mean," she said. "I'm not scheduled to work till tomorrow night, and I can do that. What I mean is I need somebody to crew for me."

"You want to take Duke? Is that it?"

"Not Duke, *you*! I know Duke can't leave the theater."

I, on the other hand, was superfluous. She had a point, but in my present mood, I was offended anyway—offended and astonished.

"Me! I don't know anything about shooting video!"

"I know that, Gilda, but we'll think of something easy, like holding the fishpole or something," she reassured me. "I have a photographer, so most of it's schlepping anyhow. It's just that I have this great opportunity to film something, but I need help."

"What about your mother?"

"She and Chuck are going to the lake with the kids."

"Your grandmother?"

"Come on, Gilda! Grams is seventy-one!"

"Clara's in good shape for her age," I said. "Anyway, how heavy is this equipment I have to schlepp?"

"It's not bad, but Mom would disown me if I asked Grams to carry it."

"Would she disown you if you asked your Aunt Adele to carry it?" I asked. "You know she'd be thrilled."

"Be serious, Gilda!" she said. "Aunt Adele would try to redesign the set, and she'd start a fight if they tried to stop her."

Adele Liberty had been a set designer in Hollywood before she retired. Nowadays, she devoted her talents to decorating and redecorating the Studio Inn, a local hotel owned by her and operated by her daughter, Greer.

"Your Aunt Gloria?"

"She'd rag on everybody's hair, and then try to redo it."

This was true. Gloria Liberty Wilcox, the former Hollywood hairdresser, had never made her peace with retirement, as indicated by the frequent, and often startling, changes in her own style and color.

"And don't suggest Uncle Ollie!" she warned. "This is brand new equipment. He'll break it if he comes anywhere near it—you know he will!"

Oliver Wilcox had once directed comedies, the slapstick kind. He had never permitted a pratfall to go untaken.

"What about—" There were enough Liberties to fill the credits for *Star Wars*.

"Gilda, please!" Faye interrupted me. "I've thought of everybody. I want you!"

The few Liberties who were locally available and mentally and physically competent must have made other plans for the weekend. In my own judgment, I did not belong in this category, as witness my adventures in projection. But theater owners didn't make plans. The logic was not lost on me.

"Besides," she added, "I use an all-woman production crew on principle."

"On the principle that you can't talk any men into doing it?"

"On the principle that the technical side of filmmaking has always been one big men's locker room, except for editing, and even there—" She interrupted herself. "Look, why do you think I bought all this new equipment in the first place?"

"Because you could afford to?"

"Well, sure, but that's not the point," she said, a note of exasperation in her voice. "You can have a hard time renting equipment if you're an independent without a track record or a Sundance showing or an Academy Award nomination. And if you're a woman, forget it. Filmmaking is just like athletics in that respect, only talent counts for even less. And all the money and the perks go to the boys. So, how 'bout it, Gilda? Can you help me?"

"I have a matinee to cover," I pointed out. "How long will this take?"

"I called Sandy and asked if she'd work for you," she said. "Sandy said it was okay with her."

"Well, all right," I said grumpily. "But remember I'm not Arnold Schwarzenegger, or even Martina Navratilova. I'm middle-aged and out of shape and my hair is turning grayer by the second."

"Gilda, you're the phattest!" she enthused.

"I said I was out of shape," I rejoined tartly. "I think 'fat' is a slight exaggeration."

"No, no, not 'fat' with an *f*, 'phat' with a *ph*! It means you're cool!"

"Well, in that case— So where are we going? What are we shooting?"

"You'll see," she said mysteriously. "Pick you up at eight. Gotta run. I've got a zillion things to do. I didn't get much notice on this."

She hung up before I could express my horror at the proposed time of departure and retract my promise to help.

* * *

She showed up at Liberty House the next morning in a dark blue van driven by a tall young woman with black-and-purple hair, and fingernails to match. They looked like a colorized version of two of Dracula's girl group. On the side of the van, it said FAST FLUSH PLUMBING.

Aunt Lillian, the matriarch of the Liberty family, spotted it coming up the circular drive.

"I believe your ride is here," she observed, "unless you've called a plumber."

I came and stood next to her at the window.

"In my day," she commented, "the studio sent a limousine."

"I'm not an actress, Lilly," I said, giving her a kiss on the cheek, "just a grip."

"Natalie borrowed the van from her dad," Faye explained. She gave me a hand up as I clambered in, eye to eye with the goddess tattoo that set off her biceps. She was clearly in a good mood. "Isn't it phat?"

"Totally phat," I agreed wryly. Even with Faye's help, I had dented my shins on the way up.

I shook hands with Natalie, who nearly opened a vein in my wrist with one of her fingernails. One word, I thought. She says one word on how she can't lift heavy equipment because it will ruin her nails and I'm outta here. Gazing in dismay at the back of the van, I saw enough equipment to shoot *Lawrence of Arabia* in the North African desert, along with enough copper pipe to create an oasis.

I sat in stunned silence for a minute, contemplating how I, the only Liberty with no interest in filmmaking, came to be on my way to my first shoot, and at an hour I hadn't seen in weeks, not counting the times I'd seen it on the silver screen.

"Here," Faye urged sympathetically, turning around in the front seat and pushing a thermal mug into my hand. "Drink this."

"What is it?"

"High-test java."

I took a tentative sip and felt the first jolt of caffeine flash along my nerves.

"So tell me more about this video you're making," I said.

"Okay, look," she said, settling into her topic, "Title IX has been around for more than twenty years. You know what Title IX is, right?"

"Kid, I knew what Title IX was before your mommy bought you your first pair of Winnie-the-Pooh Keds," I pointed out testily.

"Yeah, catch the clue bus, Faye," Natalie put in, grinning at me in the rearview mirror. "That was back in the day." From the neck up at least, Natalie was pierced in as many places as Faye and was as heavily adorned with silver jewelry.

"Yeah, okay, so you'd think everything would've changed, right?" Faye continued. "And in some ways it did—more women's teams in more sports than before, girls' Little League, a few mixed-gender kids' teams. But the higher you go, the less opportunity there is. We only just got the WNBA and the ABL, and there's nothing comparable in professional baseball, football, hockey, or soccer. At the college level, women get less than a third of the scholarship money men get, their operating budgets are even lower compared to men's, and the recruiting budgets even worse than that. You see that documentary *Hoop Dreams*, about the boys from the Chicago projects who were trying to make it as basketball players?"

We were on the highway now, between Eden and Columbus, and she had to shout over the road noise. My hair blew into my mouth if I opened it, so I just nodded.

"That show was killer," Natalie offered.

"Yeah, it was great, but it only told part of the story," Faye said. "What about all the girls in those projects who could have been great athletes, who maybe had as much talent and desire and persistence as William and Arthur? You think any fancy private schools are scouting Cabrini Green to hand out money to them? You think any college coaches are coming to call on them? And even if a college coach was interested in them, she wouldn't have enough money to fly in from out of state to visit, or enough money to send them even a bus ticket to come look the school over. See, the guys all want to make it to the NBA. Most of them won't, they'll crash and burn, that's what *Hoop Dreams* shows. But some guys do. Up until this year, there wasn't even that much of a chance for girls, and in every team sport except basketball, that's still true."

"So where are we headed?" I asked, raising my voice and brushing hair out of my mouth.

"Northstar Mall," she said. "See, Gilda, the problem is that people's attitudes haven't changed all that much, and they need to. People still think that even little girls who are tomboys should settle down in their teens and worry about being thin and pretty and socially acceptable, not strong and powerful and assertive."

"Your A.A.," Natalie put in.

When I looked blank, Faye translated. "A.A.—that's our abbreviation for the average American. Nat's and mine, I mean."

"And what's at Northstar Mall at this ungodly hour?" I asked. Since I wasn't much of a mall shopper, I didn't know anything about this one except that it had a multiplex cinema with which the Paradise competed, more or less, for first-run features since the Eden chain theater had burned down. But if there was a movie showing at this hour, I'd do more than lick it, I'd chew it up and swallow it. They haven't shown movies at this hour since Rosie the Riveter got fired from the graveyard shift and went home to the suburbs. There's no ante meridiam equivalent to the matinee anymore.

"Oh, we have a few hours to set up before anything happens," Faye said, glancing at her watch and then turning to look out the window as if to check our progress. "Don't worry, Gilda. You'll know what's going on and what you have to do before we roll the camera."

"But what are we shooting?" I persisted.

"Oh, sorry, didn't I tell you?" She had begun rummaging nervously in a large canvas shoulder bag. "It's a cheerleading contest—a girls' cheerleading contest. Like, one of those big promotional events that's supposed to draw people to the mall over Memorial Day Weekend."

At this hour, the mall parking lot was relatively deserted, and I was relieved when Natalie pulled into a loading zone not five feet from a door. Since I hadn't been assertive enough to decline this foray into video production, I showed my own strength and power by schlepping enough equipment to sink the *Titanic*. On the third trip to the car, Natalie read my face and said, "Once you start shooting, you can't just run out to the van when you need something, Gilda. You've got to have everything right there."

Of course, the first lesson I learned was that you never do have everything right there, something's always missing or forgotten. The second lesson I learned was that filmmaking, or video making, could be extremely tedious and boring if you weren't the person setting up and checking the equipment. My parents, who had spent years on the Hollywood sidelines playing bridge and tapping their tap shoes, had warned me about this part.

Faye had enlisted the cooperation of a boutique owner, who'd let us in through the back entrance to her store. It was mostly an earring shop, and I assumed one glance at Faye's heavily freighted ears and nose had probably told this woman she was making a good investment. Natalie and Faye ran electrical cords from her outlets, and my first big job in production was to tape down these cords so that nobody would trip over them. As the niece of a former studio electrician, I performed this task without a hitch.

A raised platform had been set up not far from the front of the store, and when we arrived, two mall employees were unfolding the last of the audience chairs. The metallic report as each chair was yanked open echoed through the cavernous empty building. The workers disappeared as another man showed up with a case as big as ours and two large speakers on a dolly and started setting up sound equipment. He and Natalie exchanged amicable nods. The other two employees, a man and a woman, returned carrying a long folding table between them and positioned it between the audience and the stage. They draped it with a tablecloth.

Natalie conferred with the microphone man, and Faye joined them. They turned this way and that, pointing, gesturing, nodding. When they were through, I was called upon to help Natalie set up some lights and reflectors. She explained that they were setting up an interview area off to the side, where they could position the lights beforehand and use lavaliere mikes. While we were talking, the mall opened, people began arriving, and I was sent off to find a cord adapter—the thing forgotten.

When I returned, they had me stand in for an interviewee, with a lavaliere clipped to my T-shirt.

"Pretend you're eight years old," Natalie told me.

At five-two, I'm short to begin with, but at eight I'd been even shorter. I scrunched down.

"Testing, testing," I said into the mike.

"Not like that, Gilda," Faye corrected me. "You're speaking *into* the mike, bending your head down. Pretend it isn't there, and just talk normally."

I reddened a little. We were beginning to attract an audience.

"So tell me, little girl," Natalie said. "Why do you want to be a cheerleader?"

"I just love sports, and I love dance, and I think cheerleading will help me with my dance career," I said, making a conscious effort to appear unconscious of the mike.

Faye was wearing a headset and watching something on the camera. She waved a hand in circles to encourage me to continue.

"I intend to study dance in college, and hopefully, if I work really, really hard, I can win the Miss America contest, and that will allow me to do what I really want to do in life, which is to help people."

Faye circled her thumb and forefinger to let me know I could quit, but I was growing inspired now.

"And even if I don't win Miss America, maybe I'll win Miss Congeniality, and—"

"She's still got that shadow on her nose," I heard Natalie say to Faye. Faye straightened up, and looked through the viewfinder. Then she came and adjusted a light.

I was starting to sweat. The audience was beginning to get involved.

"Hey, lady!" someone said. "Is this gonna be on TV?"

"Why don't you interview me?" someone else asked. "I got something to say."

"Shift that reflector over just a little," Natalie called. "That's good."

"Who's that?" somebody asked. "Is she somebody famous?"

"She doesn't *look* famous," somebody else said doubtfully.

"Say something else," Faye urged me, "now that we have some crowd noise."

"I'd just like to thank all the little people who helped me get where I am today," I said dutifully, batting my gray eyes at the camera lens. "My mother, who worked long hours into the night sewing the sequins on my costume—"

Faye pulled a peremptory forefinger across her throat. I unclipped the mike and handed it to her.

"That was great, Gilda," she said, "but we don't want to start offending prospective interviewees."

She was right: The prospective interviewees were arriving. They continued to arrive until the place was crammed to the rafters with anxious mothers, doting grandmothers, a few fathers and brothers trying to look blasé, and little girls. Everywhere you looked were girls in short pleated skirts or circular skirts that stuck out like clown collars, girls in tennis shoes and girls in cowboy boots, girls in clingy leotard tops, girls in T-shirts, girls in sequined vests. Girls with breasts and girls without. Fat girls, skinny girls, and girls in between. The combined scents of hairspray, perfume, and deodorant were cloying. Some of these girls—I'd gathered from Faye that they couldn't be older than twelve according to the contest rules—were taller than I was.

Faye pressed a smaller camera into my hand—a Hi8,

she said—and, assuring me it was idiot-proof, suggested that I wander around for a bit and shoot anything that caught my eye.

"Just point it and hit this button," she said.

"What about light?" I asked nervously.

She shrugged. "We'll see what you get with the existing fluorescents." She went up front to deal with some paperwork at the judges' table.

I found myself drawn to a munchkin who didn't come up to my kneecap, and who reminded me of Liz's niece from the back—same long, wavy dark hair, same way of standing with one hand on her barely discernible hip while her opposite foot absentmindedly rubbed the back of her calf, causing one leg of her tights to wrinkle like rhinoceros skin. I felt the same pang I always did when I was reminded of Liz and all I had lost when I lost her. I trained the camera on the little girl to distract me from the flood of memory, and as I did so, she turned around. Like many of the girls in the area, she wore makeup, even though she couldn't have been more than six. The makeup was carefully done so as to appear artless and natural, but there's no way to make lipstick and eyeshadow look natural on a six-year-old. Her mother caught sight of the camera and leaned toward her, speaking in a low voice. The little girl dimpled up at me and waved. I felt a chill, as if I were watching a budding JonBenet Ramsey.

A murmur and general shuffling of feet in the crowd alerted me to the arrival of the judges and other contest officials. Three people approached the judges' table—two men and a woman. I gathered, from what Faye had told me, that these were celebrity judges—a corporate bigwig, a local radio personality from WKLV, and the Buckeye State basketball coach. The taller of the two men grinned, waved, nodded, winked at the girls, and occasionally fired a jocular finger at a father or brother or other male standing on the fringes, watching the proceedings. The other was more subdued, in dress as well as demeanor. His complexion was pasty, with almost a prison pallor, and he didn't look as if he were having a good time. He wore the smile of a terminally ill undertaker when he smiled at all. His hairline had receded to the top of his skull, accentuating the whiteness of his skin against his gray hair.

"Hey, coach!" a heavyset man standing next to me called out. "How you feelin'?"

The pale man turned toward us and gave us a thumbs-up that lacked conviction.

"Triple bypass," the man confided to me, obviously assuming I wouldn't have this information. He was right. "Poor bastard."

"That's the basketball coach?" I asked. I'd figured him for the corporate executive.

My neighbor gave me a startled look. He'd assumed I was ignorant, but not that ignorant. "That's Creighton Hale," he informed me charitably. "Made it to the semis this year, too. Probably what did him in." He shook his head again. "Poor bastard."

I returned to the interview area, where Natalie and Faye were taping an interview with a girl of perhaps ten and her mother. The contestant wore skintight black biking shorts and a red T-shirt with the Buckeye State logo in glitter on the front. In glitter, the groundhog was even less identifiable; he looked a little like a scarlet Godzilla.

"Jennifer, did you ever play on a sports team yourself?" Faye was asking the girl.

"Yeah, um, I used to play soccer in the summer," Jennifer replied, eyes wandering past the camera. No doubt she was scoping out the competition.

Her mother stood by, brushing the long blond hair away from the girl's face. She looked up at Faye anxiously.

"How come you don't play anymore?" Faye pursued. "Do you like cheerleading better?"

"Yeah," she said, "I like cheerleading."

"Yes, ma'am," her mother corrected softly.

"Soccer's pretty rough," she observed. She flicked her head

irritably, liberating her hair from her mother's restraining hand. "Sometimes you get hurt. This one time I broke my wrist and had to wear this thing on my arm for, like, forever." Her green eyes grew large with the memory.

"Anyway, soccer's okay when you're little," she said authoritatively. "But now only the tough girls play it." She gnawed on a corner of one finger.

"Don't, honey," her mother said, brushing Jennifer's hand away. "Your polish, remember?"

Jennifer's red nail polish matched some of her sequins and her lipstick.

"What's a 'tough girl'?" Faye asked.

Jennifer looked at her and blinked.

"Oh—you know," she said vaguely.

"No, I'm curious," Faye said.

"Well, you know, like, girl jocks," she said. "There's this group of girls at school, and they're on this girls' basketball team, and they pretty much stick together and don't have anything to do with anybody else."

It was easy to imagine why, given the preadolescent attitude toward girl athletes, as expressed by Jennifer.

"They don't care how they look or anything, and they're just, I don't know, tough," she said.

"Do you think it's unfeminine to play sports?" Faye asked.

"Well, *some* sports, sure," Jennifer affirmed.

"Like what?"

Jennifer frowned. She appeared to be thinking the question over. "Well, like, in the Olympics. I mean, diving is pretty, and skating, and gymnastics—" She faltered; she'd run out of possibilities.

"What do you like about cheerleading?" Faye asked, taking a new tack.

Jennifer's mother was now distracted by a bustle around the judges' table.

"I don't know, it's fun," Jennifer replied. "It's like dancing, and I like to dance. And I like to get up in front of people, you know, and lead cheers, and get people all excited."

"Mrs. Alper," Faye said, snagging the mother's attention, "would you say that you've promoted your daughter's interest in cheerleading?"

She smiled at her daughter and then back at the camera. "Yes, I think it's a healthy interest for a girl to have, don't you? She loves all the excitement, and the attention she gets. She can hardly wait until she's old enough to attend cheerleading camp."

She looked fondly down at her daughter and made one last attempt to subdue Jennifer's hair.

"I was a cheerleader in college," she said, "and my husband played tackle on the college football team." She smiled sadly into the camera. "Young people have so few healthy interests these days, don't you think?"

4

"Healthy interests, my ass," Faye was muttering.

The contest was starting, and Natalie moved closer to the action with the camera and tripod. Faye had brought along a tape recorder, and she'd talked the mike man into letting her set up her own mike. Now she sat down on the floor with her earphones on. I was free to wander around and watch the contest. I ditched the Hi8 and ambled off.

They started with the youngest contestants, perhaps because the organizers recognized the futility of holding the attention of the Barney set for very long. For the five- and six-year-olds, who were in a category by themselves, mothers were allowed to stand in front of the platform and coach. Few of these girls were organized into teams, and most quickly developed stage fright, memory loss, or a total lack of enthusiasm. Some stood scratching a shoulder or picking at an elbow scab, staring at frantic mothers as if they had never seen these women before in their lives. Some stood paralyzed. One tried covering her memory loss by singing "Santa Claus Is Coming to Town" and was rewarded by such thunderous applause that she launched into "Jesus Loves Me." Some were carried off the stage crying, their faces streaked with a rainbow of makeup and damp hair. But a few were Shirley Temples in the making. They bounced and preened, cocked their hips, wiggled their butts, shook their pom-poms, and flirted shamelessly with the audience. These performances always left me feeling a little sick. I supposed there was an outside chance that one of these little girls might become the next FloJo, but I suspected they'd have to leap larger hurdles off the track than on, in that case.

One mother coached her daughter so enthusiastically that she knocked our microphone into the judges' table. I saw Faye's head pop up, her lips moving with words I could guess even from this distance. She stalked forward and righted the mike, and the show went on.

The little girl who won the five- and six-year-old division was the one I'd spotted this morning. She did a mean set of splits, crowned by dimples.

The crowd remained passive spectators up until five girls performed in the eight-to-ten category. These kids were dressed comparatively simply in red shorts, T-shirts, and gleaming white sneakers. Instead of a team logo or team name, they had ALVA'S AUTO PARTS stitched in gold-trimmed black over their hearts. They wore no makeup, only a decorative hair ribbon or two, and they carried sticks that looked like mop handles. I saw Natalie move closer to the stage, camera balanced on one shoulder now. With the precision of a military drill team, the girls performed a routine that was clearly inspired by the Broadway show *Stomp*. Jaws dropped, and the audience grew very still, then exploded into applause when they were done. Then one separated herself from the group and came to the front of the stage to demonstrate how they wanted the audience to clap. The others picked up the rhythm with their sticks, and once the audience had more or less gotten it right, they added the cheer, a call-and-response that engaged the crowd's lung power. Needless to say, they won their division.

The winner in the oldest division was a group from a Catholic school, who actually dragged a gymnastics mat onto the platform and built a death-defying pyramid on top of it. They had a harder time inducing audience participation, since too many mothers were doing what I was doing: holding their breaths until the stunt was over.

A mother standing near me said, "I hope to God they got their St. Christophers."

But they survived the stunt to win their division.

The Buckeye State coach had just handed the trophy to the winners when a commotion started in the back of the crowd. The crowd parted, and a phalanx of young women rushed the center aisle and stormed the stage. All of them wore shorts and jerseys. The one in the lead dribbled a basketball, and so did several of her companions. A few carried signs. The one closest to me said A WOMAN'S PLACE IS ON THE COURT, NOT ON THE SIDELINES. Another said MAMAS, DON'T LET YOUR BABIES GROW UP TO BE CHEERLEADERS IF THEY REALLY WANT TO BE PLAYERS. A third said WOMEN DEMAND EQUAL PLAY. And a fourth—WHY NOT A BOYS' CHEERLEADING CONTEST?

Some moments of general confusion ensued. There was a smattering of applause in the crowd, though whether because people understood what was happening or whether they thought it was part of the program was hard to tell. The suddenness of the group's appearance had frightened some of the younger kids, so the thumps of balls on linoleum and wood were accompanied by wails. I could see by now that all of the women in the group were wearing team practice jerseys, though they didn't all seem to be from the same team. Some were from Buckeye State, some from local high schools, and some from Eden College.

As I watched, I considered the irony of the Eden College mascot. The Eden teams were called the Angels, which had always struck me as a peculiar name for a group of sports competitors. But now it occurred to me that perhaps whoever had named the team had had in mind avenging angels. These were the Lady Angels, but it struck me that they had more in common with *The Avengers'* Emma Peel or even with *Charlie's Angels* than with traditional sentimental representations of angels.

Someone with a different sense of humor had named the Buckeye State teams for one of Ohio's most ubiquitous inhabitants—the groundhog. At football and basketball games I'd watched on television, someone dressed up in a garish, slightly moth-eaten, red groundhog suit gave a feisty impersonation of a Fighting Groundhog, but it had never seemed all that convincing to me. The Fighting Lady Groundhogs had been even harder to swallow.

My eye caught a flash of red at the rear of the crowd, and suddenly, there it was: the Fighting Groundhog. For a minute, I thought he—in my undoubtedly sexist imagination, I'd always assumed it was a "he"—was staging his own counter-demonstration. He raised a paw and threw something into the crowd, and I saw the kids scramble. Something hit my foot, and I looked down at a small brown ball. I picked it up. The Groundhog was pelting the crowd with chocolate balls wrapped to look like basketballs. As he approached the stage, I could read the sign he wore pinned to his back: GROUND-HOGS FOR EQUAL OPPORTUNITY. Onstage, the women had set up a basketball drill. The Groundhog mounted the steps to the stage and clumsily joined in.

Most of the kids who had been crying had stopped. Cheeks lumpy with chocolate, they were laughing at his antics. A few of the younger ones were still tearful in a parent's arms, eyeing the Groundhog with the same trepidation they felt for any cartoon character come to larger-than-life.

I saw two mall security guards move in on the stage from

either side, only to find their paths cut off by a couple of female players who were almost their height. From the stage, the Groundhog made belligerent gestures in the guards' directions, shadowboxing until he spun, lost his balance, and fell on his keister, to the delight of the kids.

The event sponsors had apparently been thrown into confusion. One security guard was barking into a walkie-talkie. A woman who might have been in charge tried to announce something over the microphone, but she'd dragged it too close to ours, and all she was producing was ear-splitting feedback. The judges, meanwhile, stood to one side. The coach was glaring, and an angry flush had replaced the pallor on his face. I found myself hoping that someone in the crowd knew CPR.

For the most part, the audience had decided to enjoy the show. One player had stepped forward to lead her own cheer—an old standby: *What do we want? Fair play! When do we want it? Now!*

I glanced around for Natalie, but I suspected she had been prepared for this demonstration. I caught a glimpse of Faye through the crowd: She was standing, rubbing her ears.

As soon as the mall's security reinforcements showed up, it was over. The women stopped voluntarily, and the guards' efforts to eject the players from the mall were frustrated by autograph seekers who had spotted two of the starters for the Lady Groundhogs. The security guards shrugged it off, though I could see one over by the judges' table making placating motions in the direction of the woman in charge. Admiring crowds surrounded the Buckeye State coach, who was making a visible effort to appear a good sport, whatever revenge he was plotting for the women players and the Groundhog. The Groundhog was surrounded by his own fan club, and I saw him clumping off down the mall, trailing kids like the Pied Piper.

"Here." Faye was thrusting a clipboard into my hand. "Go find the eight-to-ten winners, and ask if we can interview them. Get them to sign a release form."

On top of the papers were release forms signed by the three judges. I unclipped those and moved them to the bottom of the pile.

The winners in the eight-to-ten category were also surrounded by admirers, but the offer of an appearance on film won them away.

"See, we on the road to fame and fortune now," said one, who was lugging a trophy the size of an Oscar.

"Next thing you know, Nike be on the phone," another agreed.

"We already doin' endorsements," another told me, and pulled at her T-shirt to call my attention to the Alva's Auto Parts name.

"Yeah, how much you payin' us to be in your movie?" a snaggle-toothed girl asked, grinning up at me to show she wasn't serious.

"You shut your mouth, girl," the first one reprimanded her. "Maybe you about to be discovered."

"Is this a movie like *Hoop Dreams*?" one asked.

"I saw that picture," another said, whirling on her. "Girl, that picture was *bad*!"

When we arrived at the interview area, two of the basketball players were holding court. They were sitting on the ledge of a mall planter, and girls were grouped around, some standing, some sitting on the floor, most, but not all, wearing cheerleading outfits. One of the players was white, heavily freckled, with reddish blond hair rolled back into a pair of braids, like the Blue Bonnet margarine girl in the fifties. She had thin lips that stretched thinner and turned down at the corners when she smiled, forming deep furrows there. The other player was black, with a weave pulled back and gathered into a ponytail, and wide-set medium-brown eyes topped by thin crescent eyebrows.

"That's Berta Homans," one of the girls informed me in tones of reverence. She pointed at the black player. "And that other one, she plays for Eden. Can we go listen?"

"Be my guest," I said, hoping I hadn't just ruined the shot.

They squeezed into the crowd.

"My mom and dad won't let me play," one girl was saying. "They're afraid I'll get hurt. They let my brother play, though, even though he broke his wrist and hurt his knee last year." She absentmindedly fingered her own scab-encrusted knee.

"Well, it's good that parents worry about us, I guess," the blond player said cautiously, "but maybe you could point out to your parents that many of the diseases likely to kill or disable you when you're grown up are connected to a lack of exercise. Heart disease and osteoporosis, for example. Playing sports encourages you to stay active for the rest of your life."

"I get lots of exercise as a cheerleader," somebody objected shyly.

"Sure you do," the blond player agreed. "I mean, cheerleaders play a big role in college sports, and we players really appreciate them. We're not saying there's anything inherently wrong with cheerleading, are we, Bert?"

"Yeah, we are," the other player retorted. "No, I'm just kidding. Ain't nothing wrong with cheerleading, long as cheerleading's what you really want to do. Hard to know what you really want to do, when everybody's telling you you want to be a cheerleader. But Ms. Pigtails over there"—she indicated the former speaker—"Ms. Pigtails wants to play football. And I'll bet you her folks ain't never gonna spring for no spikes and pads, but she got herself one killer cheerleading outfit."

"Would any of you like to be professional cheerleaders when you grow up?" Faye asked my girls.

"You mean like the Dallas Cowboys cheerleaders?"

They exchanged looks of derision.

"That's just T and A," one of them said. "T and A is all." The others nodded agreement. "We got *talent*."

Faye interviewed a mother who said she wished she could get her daughter more interested in sports than in cheerleading, a mother who said that she thought cheerleading was a good way to develop character and poise, and a father who said he'd disown his daughter if she ever became a cheerleader for a professional sports team. When things had quieted down and the onlookers had thinned out, Faye interviewed a teenage boy who said that he had inspired his sister's interest in cheerleading because he was a cheerleader himself. As Faye pressed him, his gaze wavered and his voice dropped. Yes, he would rather be playing football and basketball than leading cheers for the teams, but he just wasn't good enough at either.

"I tried out for the football team," he said, "and once for the baseball team, but I didn't make either one. I don't know. I guess I'm not fast enough, or big enough. I'm a pretty good cheerleader, though, 'cause I'm good at gymnastics. And I enjoy cheerleading a lot—it's a lot like a sport, you know. But I know some of the guys call me a fag behind my back."

"Why?" Faye asked. "Don't most schools have male cheerleaders?"

"Yeah, they do, but—I don't know. Somehow everybody still thinks of it as a girls' thing. I mean, look around." He gestured with one hand. "You didn't see any boys in this contest, right? If I'd shown an interest in cheerleading when I was my sister's age, my parents would've probably taken me to a shrink."

"What do they think now?"

"Oh, they think it's okay, I guess, 'cause they know you have to be popular to get selected, and have some athletic skill. Besides," he said wryly, looking up at Faye, "I have a girlfriend now."

"Faye's amazing," Natalie confided in a low voice, shaking her head. "The stuff she gets out of people!"

By the time we finished the interviews, dismantled and packed up the equipment, and loaded it all back into the van, I was beat. It had started to rain, which made the whole job that much more challenging. Faye worried about her equipment, but I couldn't see why. It was all snuggled into its carrying cases. The equipment was dry; I was soaked. On the trip home, Faye was chattering on about calling someone in the

Channel Six newsroom to offer them some footage of the demonstration, but I wasn't really paying attention. I made it into the living room at Liberty House, collapsed on the couch, pulled an afghan over me, and fell asleep.

5

I awoke to a pungent odor of perfume that told me my Aunt Gloria was in the vicinity, though with the wind blowing in the right direction, she could have been standing on a street corner downtown. Eyes closed, I further analyzed the signals my senses were sending me. There was another faint scent beneath the cloying blanket of L'Air du Temps—the scent of my Aunt Clara's clove cigarettes. And was that barely perceptible whisper and stirring of the air against my face caused by the flutter of my Aunt Adele's false eyelashes?

I opened my eyes. There they were—the weird sisters in full theatrical makeup.

"Gilda!" Aunt Gloria started a little guiltily, and stepped back. "You're awake."

"Well?" Aunt Adele prompted me.

"Well, what? What time is it?" I fumbled frantically on the end table for my watch, worried that the early show might have started without me.

Aunt Clara perched on the arm of a chair. She wielded a ridiculously long cigarette holder like a conductor's baton. Her boyish haircut, along with her slight frame, made her look like a latter-day Anita Loos.

"We want to know how it went," she said.

"It was tiring," I said succinctly, "which explains why I was sleeping." I could see I had an hour before I needed to be back at the theater, so I relaxed a bit. I never relaxed completely in the presence of my aunts.

"Well, did Faye get what she wanted?" Gloria asked. She sat down on the couch across from me and began playing with her rings.

"You'd better ask her," I said.

"We would, but she's not here," Adele said, "and you are."

"Will she be looking at the dailies tonight, do you think?" Gloria asked.

"I don't think they have dailies in video," I said. "Not the way you mean. But you can probably see a clip on the Channel Six news at eleven."

"But how will she know if she needs to retake anything?" Gloria looked inquiringly at Adele.

"She can't retake it, Gloria," Clara said condescendingly. "It's a documentary. She shot footage of an event. They can't go back and restage the event for her benefit."

Gloria looked as if she knew better, but refrained from comment. In the old days, they could restage Pearl Harbor on the back lot of any major studio. For that matter, they could restage Creation.

"So what was it like?" Adele asked. She perched on the foot of my couch.

"I don't know," I said irritably. "We hauled a lot of equipment into the mall, set it up, filmed the contest, filmed some interviews, packed everything up, hauled it back to the van, and drove away. What's to tell?"

"Who did the makeup?" Gloria wanted to know.

Now we were coming to the heart of the matter. What they really wanted to know was whether there was an opening for them in this project.

"No makeup," I said. "It's a documentary. That means no hairstylist, Gloria, no set designers or decorators, and no actors."

"Well, there must be a narrator," Clara said in an injured tone.

"I wouldn't know," I said. "I'm only a lowly member of the crew."

"It's not as if we're trying to interfere, Gilda," Gloria said reproachfully.

"Certainly not!" Adele said. "It's just that there's a lot of talent in this family that could be useful to Faye if she chose to use it."

"A lot of experience, too," Gloria said. This from the person who envisioned Faye sitting in a small studio theatre, screening rushes.

"What there seems to be a lot of in video making," I said, sitting up and running my hands through my frizzled hair, "is equipment that needs carting around from one place to the next. So if you women want to volunteer for the crew, I'm sure Faye will be overjoyed."

But Gloria's eyes had followed my hands.

"I wish you'd let me put a conditioner and a nice rinse on your hair, Gilda," she said. "It would bring out your highlights. And maybe a perm, with a loose curl, just to give it some body. It would do wonders for you."

That was my mother's cue.

"Gilda takes no interest in making herself more attractive, Gloria," she said, strolling in, coffee cup in hand. "She's too busy being a martyr—moping around as if she thinks she can win Liz back through pity."

"And I don't think there's a single song-and-dance number in Faye's video, either," I retaliated.

Her eyebrows lifted over her coffee cup.

"I'm not interested. I'm retired," she said. She was lying through her pearly-white, razor-straight, show-business teeth.

6

My parents' career on stage and screen—and later, even television—had spanned five decades. My grandparents had been "in the business" virtually since Hollywood had been invented. My grandfather had been a cameraman, as they called it in those days before there were "cinematographers," working mostly for Fox, later 20th Century-Fox. My grandmother had worked in the wardrobe department at Metro, later Metro-Goldwyn-Mayer. My father's older sisters, twins Mae and Lillian, had paved the way for his acting career. But my father, like other song-and-dance men, had never been particularly famous for his acting. My other grandmother, my mother's mother, I remembered as a feisty harridan whom no one could please. In her promotion of my mother's career, she had made Gypsy Rose Lee's mother appear a rank amateur. By the age of six, my mother had begun the singing and dancing lessons that would one day lead to fame, fortune, and my father. Perhaps some of my discomfort at the cheerleading contest had derived from a sense of recognition—from an uncanny feeling that I was watching a rerun of my own mother's childhood, as directed by her mother.

Yet my mother had never held this early choice of career against her mother.

"It was a hard life to live when I was growing up," she'd concede, "but lots of kids had hard lives. And I honestly don't know what else I could have done with my life. In those days, girls could be nurses, schoolteachers, or wives—"

37

"Or nurses and schoolteachers and *then* wives," my father would put in.

"That's right—everything led to that. You didn't go to secretarial school to become a secretary, you went to secretarial school to become a wife. And frankly, all of the available possibilities would have bored me to tears. But I loved to perform."

"And besides," my father would add at this point, "she met me. And the rest—is history." With that, he'd make a sweeping gesture, take her hand, and twirl her into an embrace.

But it must have been hard, my mother's life as a child hoofer, living out of a suitcase and subjected to a Svengali in flowered print dresses and wide-brimmed hats. Perhaps all the success of Douglas and Florence Liberty had blunted those memories. And whatever her character flaws, my mother had never been one to wallow in self-pity, as she accused me of doing.

Yet at any given time in the Liberty family, there were plenty of emotions around to wallow in, and the nonactors in the clan were as adept at this activity as the actors were. Clara held all the aces at the moment, since her husband had recently been murdered. But every Liberty was working on his or her own private script, and they were all capable of histrionics. Moreover, they so valued this capacity for creating a scene that they chose partners who were just as bad as they were, so that the whole tribe was like one of those traveling circuses in a Fellini movie. The only Liberty who had chosen a mate with a more subdued personality was my Uncle Valentino, whose partner Tobias was a writer. I was convinced that half the attraction on Tobias's part was the endless material my family provided, and he didn't deny it. He sat in the background during every family crisis, observing the scene with his writer's eye. Needless to say, family crises were as thick on the ground as aspiring actors in L.A.

That's why I didn't react when Faye called me in tears on Monday.

Ruth Hernandez hammered on my door at eleven o'clock.

"Gilda, you awake?" she called. "Faye wants to talk to you on the phone."

I grunted, and Ruth took that for assent. I heard her retreating footsteps.

"Gilda, are you awake?" Faye's voice was clotted with tears. "Have you heard about last night? Something terrible has happened!"

"Yeah?" I mumbled noncommittally.

"I've been robbed! Somebody broke into my house last night while I was at work, and they took—" Her voice squeaked, distorted by emotion, and I couldn't understand her.

"Calm down, Faye," I said, and stifled a yawn. "I can't understand you. Take a deep breath, and tell me again. What did they take?"

I still wasn't concerned. Liberties generally believed not only in the principle expressed in *mi casa es su casa*, but also in what, to their minds, was the obvious corollary, *su casa es mi casa*—and they followed not only the spirit but the letter of the law. I wouldn't put it past any of them to waltz into Faye's apartment and "borrow" something.

"My video!" she shrieked. "I had all the tapes on a shelf in the living room, plus the footage we shot the other day in the VCR. He took everything!"

"Did he take the VCR and your other video equipment, too?" I doubted Faye had anything else that was worth as much and was as fenceable as that equipment.

"No, he just took the tapes," she said. "Oh, and he ate some leftover cheesecake I had in the fridge."

"He did what?"

"He ate my cheesecake, which I was looking forward to eating when I got home last night!" Now she was beginning to sound more mad than hurt. That's okay, I thought; mad is good. "And he left me this note! 'Thanks for the cheesecake, doll'—that's what it said! Doll! The last time I heard anyone use 'doll' was on some gangster movie rerun. I couldn't believe it! What a jerk! The cops didn't seem that surprised—about the cheesecake, that is. They said burglars do stuff like that. They said I should be, like, thankful he didn't take a dump in my toilet. They were a little surprised about the note, though. So I asked if they could match his handwriting with known felons, or run a DNA test on the fork he used, you know? Because they couldn't find any fingerprints anywhere. But they said they didn't think that would be possible, but they didn't say why not."

Because, I thought, they didn't take the case seriously, and they weren't going to knock themselves out trying to solve it. The videos weren't worth enough. I didn't blame them; I didn't take it seriously, either. I had even more reason than the cops did to suspect that the perpetrator in this case was a friend of Faye's or a family member.

"What am I going to do?" Her voice squeaked again. "That was my whole senior project! And I even got this call from this Channel Ten sportscaster who saw the contest footage on Channel Six Saturday night and was interested in my project. I don't even have anything to show him now. He probably could have got me a screening and everything!"

"Faye," I said, "have you talked to Clara about this?"

"No, but I guess she knows about it."

"How about Adele and Gloria?" I asked. "Have you talked to them?"

"No, why would I?"

"Because they've all been very curious about this film you're making."

"Oh," she said, and paused. "Okay," she continued, sounding marginally more cheerful, "I'll call them. But if they snagged my tapes and my cheesecake, tell Peachy to get the caskets ready."

The allusion to caskets I understood. Peachy Gower, one of my oldest friends, was the local undertaker. She had inherited the business from her dad. But I was again reminded, as so often when I was around Faye, that I was, in her terminology, "old skool"—in with the in crowd, and out with the current generation. That was okay with me; I didn't want to be forced by fashion to pierce any more body parts, either.

I was eating a sandwich in the kitchen when Faye called again. In front of me was a long list of Monday morning calls—to the booker, to the distributors, to the concessions supplier, to the painter.

"Grams is here," she said, "and Aunt Adele and Aunt Gloria. They said they didn't take the tapes."

I heard Adele's outraged voice in the distance.

"What I *said* was that I couldn't imagine what made Gilda think we would barge in here and steal something, much less help ourselves to anything in the refrigerator! And we certainly wouldn't have made such a mess if we had!"

"What mess?" I asked. "What's she talking about?"

"Oh, there's mud on the carpet from the burglar's shoes," Faye said dispiritedly. "That's another thing, Gilda! It's not like I don't have a doormat outside! Why couldn't the asshole wipe his fucking feet before he came in to rip me off? I asked the cops if they couldn't have the mud analyzed, but they didn't go for that, either."

"I'm sorry, Faye," I said. And I was, too, even though I still suspected a practical joke. I put one hand to my forehead and rubbed the place between my eyes where it was starting to throb. "What do you want me to do?"

"Adele says you know a detective. Do you think you could maybe call her and ask her to investigate? I know the cops aren't going to do much. I mean, it's not like somebody was murdered or anything. But that was my whole senior project, Gilda! I spent hours making those tapes! I'm, like, totally screwed!"

"Adele knows the same detective I know," I said, a bit crossly.

"I know, but she says it would be better coming from you. Please, Gilda?"

The throbbing intensified. The detective I knew would probably be as enthusiastic about a routine B and E case as Orson Welles would be about directing an Andy Hardy.

"Before I call," I said, "I want to come over and see what we're talking about."

Faye lived in a one-bedroom apartment in a complex on North Main—the kind where the only door opens out onto the parking lot. That meant a cheeky, self-confident burglar who was undaunted by security lights, neighbors, and late-night dog walkers. If he'd come while Faye was at work, he was probably gone by midnight.

Inside, the apartment was sparsely and eclectically furnished with ghosts out of my past, which means all the pieces probably came from Carol's and Clara's basements. I flushed guiltily at being ambushed by past sins; not only did I recognize some of the stains and nicks, I'd put them there. My flush deepened when I recognized an end table I'd made in high school shop. It was being propped up on one end by layers of folded paper.

The crime scene had been thoroughly contaminated. If the burglar had worn an unusual aftershave or cologne, it would have been buried under the scent of perfume, clove, and permanent-wave solution. If he'd left any fingerprints, they'd probably been smudged. If he'd disarranged the room in any way, my Aunt Adele would have tidied it. If he'd dropped anything, she would have absentmindedly picked it up and put it in her pocket. My three aunts were sitting lined up on the sofa, like a matinee audience waiting for Glenda Farrell to show up and solve the crime. They all wore pastel polyester pantsuits that matched their nail polish and complemented their hair: Clara's hair looked blonder than my memory of it, and she wore a pale yellow pantsuit; Gloria's chrome-silver hair was set off by pastel gray; and Adele's hair appeared to have been dyed to match her tangerine outfit.

I lit a cigarette.

Faye, who looked like she'd been up all night, showed me how she'd carefully preserved the mud samples by building a wall of books around them. Laid across the top was Erik Barnouw's book, *Documentary*. Wearing a Playtex glove, she solemnly presented a fork covered with fingerprint powder.

"This is the fork he used," she said.

He'd licked it pretty clean. That was significant: It told me he'd liked the cheesecake.

Again, I was assuming the burglar was male, but statistics were on my side. Perhaps equal access to training opportunities in this profession would change that someday, but for now, there were fewer lady burglars than Lady Angels and Groundhogs.

"And here's his note."

He'd scrawled it on a Wendy's bag in a messy, manic hand.

"Is this your Wendy's bag, or did he bring it with him?" I asked.

"He got it out of the garbage can over there by the refrigerator," she said.

That meant it was no good canvassing local Wendy's restaurants to see if anybody remembered a shifty-looking man who had ordered a double cheeseburger and a shake, and shown dissatisfaction with the dessert options.

All in all, he hadn't done much. There were no signs of a search that I could see. He—or she—had found the videos easily, eaten cheesecake, written his note, and left. Wait—he hadn't found the videos all that easily; he'd taken one out of the VCR. I noticed there were two machines—a Beta on top of a VHS. I looked at the eject button on the VCRs, but they, too, were covered with fingerprint dust, so the cops had already thought of that.

"Was anything else disturbed?" I asked Faye. "Anything out of place, as if he'd been looking for something?"

"No."

"How'd he get in?"

"Picked the lock. That's what the cops said."

I turned in surprise. "Don't you have a deadbolt?"

She sighed, and glanced at her audience. She'd already heard this lecture from them and probably from the cops. "I have one, but I didn't use it. I know you told me Eden had changed, but I'm not used to it yet. And I'm not used to having anything worth stealing."

I let it drop and toured the kitchen.

"Is this how you found everything?" I asked.

She nodded.

The slob hadn't even rinsed his plate. The empty cheese-cake box was sitting out on the counter.

"Okay, I'm sure the police asked you this, but have you thought of anybody who might have done this as a joke? Or even to teach you a lesson about security?"

She shook her head.

"I really can't." She lowered her voice and leaned closer. "I don't have that many friends around here anymore, and the ones I do have know I'd kill them if they pulled something like this. So the only people I know who might possibly think it would be funny, or, like, clever, would be—you know—"

Our eyes swiveled in the direction of the living room.

"Yeah," I said. Some members of our family had a peculiar sense of humor. Gloria's husband Oliver, the former comedy director, leapt to mind, closely followed by Adele's husband Wallace, retired bit player in horror movies.

"Have you talked to Ollie and Wallace?" I asked.

"Not directly, but I kind of, like, you know, hinted around, and Adele and Gloria both swear their husbands were home last night." Her voice had dropped to a whisper. "Anyway, Ollie would have clowned around and broken something, and Wallace would have been tanked and broken something."

"The thing is," I said seriously, "if I call in Styles, and this turns out to be a family matter, I'll never hear the end of it."

"Well," she said, frowning, her tone matching mine, "the only family member we know of who's ever been picked up for breaking and entering is Lillian, and we don't think she's involved, do we?"

My Aunt Lillian, Mae's twin, was now the oldest sibling, which gave her the status of family matriarch. She was eighty-two, walked with a cane, and never drove if she could help it—or we could prevent her—but all that hadn't deterred her from a small venture into housebreaking and burglary.

"No," I admitted, "I can't think of any reason why she would be." I sighed. "Where's your phone?"

She pointed to a wall phone next to the refrigerator. I punched in Styles's office number and got her answering machine, so I tried her home phone. Styles's recorded office greeting was abrupt, but her personal greeting was more like a grunt.

"Styles, it's Gilda," I said. "I've got a problem."

There was a brief silence, as if she were trying to place me among the vast crowd of Gildas she knew.

Then she said, "Sweetheart, everybody in your family's got a problem. That's why Freud invented psychoanalysis."

"This one's a burglary-type problem."

"And you forgot whether the nine comes before or after the ones in nine-one-one?"

"Boy," I said, "you must've gotten up on the wrong side of the bed."

"Technically speaking, I haven't gotten up at all," she said.

"What'd you do, go dancing last night?"

"In a manner of speaking. You wouldn't think a guy who'd sustained severe whiplash in a car accident would choose to spend his recreational hours in a mosh pit, would you?"

"You were tailing a guy who went dancing?" I asked doubtfully. "Styles, yesterday was Sunday."

"Oh, he'd barely gotten started by the time Sunday was over. Besides, Sunday isn't what it used to be."

"Well, about this burglary—" I began.

"Cookie, let me explain how you can tell the difference between plainclothes detectives and private dicks," she said irritably. "On a plainclothes detective, the socks and tie match."

"You don't wear a tie," I pointed out.

"That's another way." She yawned conspicuously into the phone.

"Styles, I have a cousin who's in film school. Somebody broke into her apartment last night and stole all the footage she'd shot for her senior project."

The pause told me I'd impressed her.

"That's even weirder than usual for your family," she said. "Anybody check your Aunt Lillian's car to see if the engine was warm?"

"Styles, what would Lillian want with seven hours of Beta video?"

"How should I know? I don't understand how any of you thinks. You want my advice? Round up the usual suspects. Lock up all your relatives in a room, and don't let them freshen their makeup till somebody comes clean."

"I don't think it was one of my relatives," I said, with as much conviction as I could muster, which wasn't much.

"Who else?" she demanded. "Quentin Tarantino? Is the competition at Sundance getting that rough?"

I wrapped the phone cord around my hand and made vinyl knuckles out of it. This was proving to be even harder than I thought.

"Look, she's really upset," I said. "Those tapes represent a lot of hours of hard work to her. They're irreplaceable. I thought you could just talk to her."

"Talk to her? That sounds a little too pro bono to me," she said suspiciously.

"Oh, screw pro bono!" I said in exasperation. "I've got money, she's got money—"

"All God's Liberties got money. But I'm busy right now, sweetheart."

"Styles, if you were busy, you wouldn't be on the phone with me!"

"It's a holiday, for Christ's sake! I'm busy taking the day off!"

"Surely you've got ten minutes to give Faye a little advice about where to start, or what to think about, stuff like that."

Styles groaned into my ear. "Okay, ten minutes," she said. "But I've gotta bring Waldo. He's going stir crazy from staying cooped up while I've been on this damned insurance case."

"You can bring all one hundred and one dalmatians for all I care," I said, and gave her directions to Faye's apartment.

She arrived about half an hour later. She wore a tank top and olive drab army fatigues that looked like they'd been deep discounted at an army-navy surplus. She walked like an arthritic gorilla and held a Styrofoam cup of coffee in a death grip. Leaning against the doorjamb with her eyes closed and a leash wrapped around her ankles, she looked petite—a word she hated. Her unlaced brown high-tops matched her curly dark hair, and her patent-leather eyes were swimming in a sea of pink.

Waldo, a bloodhound-basset mix with a nose for dirt, precipitated her into the room by making a beeline for Faye's carefully protected soil sample. Styles tripped over the leash and started to topple. I reached out a hand to steady her.

"Don't touch me!" she growled, regaining her balance. "I feel like somebody's been hitting me with a sledgehammer all night, and I've got the bruises to prove it."

Waldo had pushed his nose into the framework of books and was now sniffing at pulverized dirt clods like a pig rooting for truffles.

My three aunts greeted Styles with lackluster warmth. She knew too much about them to make them feel entirely comfortable in her presence. She nodded in their direction and acknowledged my introduction of Faye with a brief glance.

"What's Waldo got?" she asked.

"Oh, that's my mud sample," Faye explained, hovering protectively. "It's from, you know, off his shoes."

Styles gave her a blank look. Then her eyes shifted to me. I lifted a rueful eyebrow, but I was damned if I was going to act as interpreter.

"How'd he get in?" she asked.

"Picked the lock," I answered, so Faye wouldn't have to. "And yes, there's a deadbolt, but no, it wasn't on last night."

"Obviously," Styles commented, taking a sip of her coffee. "So he breaks in, steals a bunch of videos. How many?"

"Seven," Faye said.

"Seven," Styles repeated. "And they were where?"

"On this shelf here next to the VCRs," Faye said, crossing to a short bookshelf that held two rows of tapes. The top shelf was empty. "Plus one in the Beta deck."

"So he just took your film school tapes, is that it? No other tapes?"

"Just the Betas," Faye confirmed.

Styles bent over to study the tapes.

"Well, look on the bright side," she said. "He left you *Citizen Kane*, *The Maltese Falcon*, and *Duck Soup*. So either he's got lousy taste, which is nothing against you, sweetheart, but your name isn't exactly a household word yet, or he's got an old VCR that only shows Betas. Or what?"

She straightened up and looked at Faye. Waldo was straining to get closer to my aunts, but she was keeping a tight grip on his leash. Maybe she was afraid he'd sniff them, too, but I suspected that their combined scents had already overwhelmed his olfactory nerves.

"What do you mean?" Faye frowned.

"Look, what's this movie about, anyway?"

Faye told her.

"Why would somebody want your footage?" Styles asked. "You got any exes around who would sabotage your project just to get back at you? Anybody that mad at you?"

Faye's eyes unfocused. She seemed to be running the movie of her life and loves in her mind. She was fidgeting with her multitudinous rings, which made her hand look like a jewelry counter display. After a minute, I glanced at Styles, who raised her eyebrows at me.

"I don't think so," Faye said at last.

"Cookie, if it takes you that long to reconstruct, the answer is probably yes," Styles said, swallowing the last of her coffee and crushing the cup in her fist. "How about competitors? You got any of them?"

"Competitors?" Faye echoed doubtfully.

"Yeah, you know, like other film students. I don't mean

Spielberg and Zemeckis and Tarantino, or even Spike Lee and John Sayles. I'm talking about your peers—people you're competing with for grades or recs or prizes or money for grad study or jobs, whatever." Styles lobbed her fistful of Styrofoam at a trash can, banked it off the wall, and scored.

"Well, sure, I guess I have some," Faye said, still dubious, "but most of the guys don't take women seriously enough to think of us as competitors. They're too busy competing with each other. As far as they're concerned, I don't have anything they want, except money."

"Ah, money," Styles said. "If somebody held your tapes for ransom, would you pay up to get them back?"

Faye stared at her. "You're kidding, right?"

Styles shrugged. "Looks to me like it would be a piece of cake—break in, help yourself to the tapes, call you up and demand that a certain sum—say, five thousand—be deposited at a certain isolated location, no cops, no questions asked, and the next day the tapes are on your doorstep. Or not. They're not too worried about getting caught because it's relatively risk free, if they're smart, and they know that the cops aren't going to miss a doughnut break tracking down a video-napper."

"But why would they wait until I came to Ohio to do it?" she asked. "I mean, if it was somebody from film school, they'd have even more opportunity in L.A."

It was a reasonable question, I thought.

"Maybe they think the cops are dumber in Ohio," Styles said, "though you'd think they'd know better, after the O.J. case. But I'm just offering theories here. You really don't have any copies of any of this footage? It's that irreplaceable?"

"Well, yeah, pretty much," Faye said.

" 'Pretty much,' what does that mean?" Styles persisted.

"Well, there's some footage I copied for my prelims. That's where we go in and pitch the project to the instructor and show them some footage and a kind of script. And then, Channel Six has some footage they aired Saturday night that we shot at the mall. But both of those are second generation, because I didn't want to give Channel Six the original. Plus, I don't know—"

"Wait, wait, wait!" Styles held up a hand. She backed up, perched on the arm of a chair, and crossed her ankles. Her high-tops were still unlaced, I noted. "Channel Six aired some of your footage Saturday night? This same footage we're talking about? The same footage that somebody boosted last night?"

Adele spoke up. "Wallace taped it off the news, Faye," she reported. "It was a nice little segment, though I thought they could have mentioned the family heritage."

"Yes, Oliver taped it, too!" Gloria enthused. "It was good publicity for you, dear, but I wish they'd said more about your movie."

"I tried using one of Grosvenor's gadgets to tape it," Clara said, "but I couldn't get the damned thing to work, and by the time I'd found the right page in the manual, it was over." Clara's late husband had been to gadgetry what Armand Hammer was to art. He'd been driven to possess the newest and most advanced of everything, and in the end, his obsession had led to his death.

Styles was staring at each speaker in turn. Now she looked reproachfully at Faye and me.

"Okay, now would somebody like to tell me this story from the beginning this time?" she said crossly. "I mean, hey—it's your nickel, but I've got better things to do, sleeping among them."

"Where do I start?" Faye asked me, cowed by Styles and not comprehending what she wanted.

I'd been cowed by Styles at one time, but I more or less got over it in sixty seconds. I try to avoid pissing her off, but I don't try all that hard.

"We shot some footage at a girls' cheerleading contest at Northstar Mall on Saturday," I said. "At the end of the contest, some women basketball players from Buckeye State, Eden, and some local high schools staged a demonstration. Faye offered Channel Six some footage, I guess." Faye nodded. "So they copied her tape, edited it down to what they wanted, and ran it that night. Right?"

"And they identified her as a filmmaker working in Eden," Styles said.

"It must have been a slow news day," Faye observed. "I didn't expect them to use as much as they did."

"All right." Styles spread her palms. "I'm not saying it couldn't be any of those other scenarios we've been talking about," she said, "but it strikes me as too big a coincidence that the footage aired Saturday night, and the original's gone by Monday morning."

"So what are you saying?" Faye asked, her curiosity overcoming her awe of Styles. "Are you saying somebody didn't like what I did with the cheerleading contest, and so they decided to screw up my whole project by stealing my tapes? You mean, like, some bogus right-wing conservative asshole who wants to keep women on the sidelines and off the playing fields?"

"We-e-ell, I suppose that's possible, though it's not quite what I had in mind," Styles said.

When Styles's attention had lapsed, Waldo had pressed his advantage, and was now trying to clamber into Gloria's lap. My other two aunts wrinkled their noses in distaste and edged away.

"Do you think it's significant he went for the cheesecake?" Faye asked, clearly pursuing her own thoughts. "I mean, was the cheesecake, like, symbolic?"

Styles blinked at her. I thought she went a little pale.

"What do you mean, 'went for the cheesecake'?" she asked slowly.

"My cheesecake!" Faye said in an injured tone. "He ate my cheesecake!"

"What flavor?"

"What?"

"What flavor?"

"Well, chocolate."

"Did he leave you a note?"

It was Faye's turn to look startled. She went into the kitchen, retrieved the note, and handed it to Styles. "He called me 'doll,' " she said, aggrieved.

I heard Styles swear under her breath. I couldn't read her expression because her head was down. She was massaging the back of her neck with her free hand.

"I know this guy," she said, so quietly that I didn't think Faye had heard her.

"What?" Faye said, stepping closer.

Styles raised her head. She looked more tired than she had when she'd walked in the door.

"I know this guy," she repeated.

7

"You know him?" Faye echoed excitedly, and sputtered. "Well—well—what kind of guy is he?"

"He's a slob," Styles said, looking around.

"But what makes you so sure?" I asked. "Did you recognize this guy's handwriting?"

"I can smell him!" she said. "It's his M.O., right down to the fucking note! And yes, I do recognize his handwriting."

"But—but—what would he want with my tapes? I mean, can't you just, like, call him and tell him to bring them back?" Faye danced around Styles, gesticulating.

Styles shook her head. "Bad idea," she said.

"Well, why not? Do you think he's holding them for ransom or something? Will he throw them away or eighty-six them?"

Styles stood up and began to pace. My aunts watched her, fascinated. At the first commercial break, there'd be a race to the phone—I could see it coming. Waldo was snoozing with his head in Gloria's lap.

"Look, babe, the guy I'm talking about is a P.I. like me—a Columbus P.I.," Styles said. She was running a hand absent-mindedly through her hair. "He didn't come up here, hit your apartment at random, and walk away with your tapes because he's a fan of independent documentary. Somebody sent him here, okay? And he likes to get paid, see? He doesn't do this stuff for his health."

"Like somebody else we know," I put in wryly.

Styles took no notice. "Does he still have your tapes?" she continued. "Who knows? I'm betting he was only interested in one, and he took the others either to confuse the issue or because he didn't know which one was the right one. How are they labeled?"

"In time code, with some kind of descriptive notation," Faye said.

"So the one from Saturday was labeled . . . ?"

"Well, let's see, it would have been the seventh tape, so that would make it oh-seven, plus the number of minutes, seconds, and frames—I'd have to look that up. And then it said 'Cheerleading contest.' "

"So, that's pretty straightforward," Styles said. "That means if that was the tape he was after, he probably knew he had it, and which one it was. Was that the one in the VCR?"

Faye nodded, pale.

"So do you think he threw the others away?" she asked in a small voice.

"Well, on the one hand, we're talking about a guy who never throws anything away until it's in an advanced state of decomposition and he needs the space," Styles said reflectively. "That's in your favor. On the other hand, he's a lazy sonofabitch, so if he pitched them, he probably didn't go out of his way to do it. This complex have a Dumpster?"

Faye stared at her in horror.

"It would be worth checking, that's all I'm saying," Styles insisted. "So, whatta we got? The tape aired Saturday—early or late?"

"Late," I said, seeing that Faye was distracted by visions of her senior project nestled among coffee grounds and ketchup. "Eleven o'clock."

"So, eleven o'clock, somebody sees the tape, doesn't like what they see, calls in our P.I. pal the next day. The guy takes next to no time tracking you down, maybe through the TV station. Maybe he finds out you work nights, or maybe he just hangs around outside, watching your place until you leave. Lets himself in, finds the tapes, checks the refrigerator—"

"Why?" I asked.

"Oh, because working makes him hungry," she said. "Maybe there's some deep Freudian thing going on, maybe not. Anyway, he's got a sweet tooth, so he helps himself to some cheesecake, writes you a note because he's charming for an unprincipled slob, and leaves. Now what? Does he meet the client and hand over the tape right away or not? That's what we can't know."

"So if we can't call him up and ask him, what do we do?" Faye asked glumly. "Go to his place and pretend to be Jehovah's Witnesses or something so we can look around?"

I felt rather than saw a stirring on the couch. My aunts were catching a whiff of a production in the making.

"I played a Seventh Day Adventist once," Clara said casually.

"Valentino could play someone from the electric company," Gloria volunteered. "I'd have to color his hair, perhaps, and make him up to look younger."

"Nonsense," Adele snapped. "We three will go. Nobody suspects three mature, respectable women to be spies."

Styles's eyes betrayed her amusement. "Maybe we won't have to go through all that," she said. "Today's Monday, Memorial Day. Does Cleveland play today?"

"You mean the Indians?" I asked, surprised.

"Yeah, you know—the baseball team."

"I think so," Gloria said. "Ollie said something about a 'twinight double header.' I'm not exactly sure what that is, but I know it means he'll be glued to the television screen for hours."

"Could you call and ask him what it means for sure?" Styles asked her. "Ask him when the second game is likely to be over."

Flushed with importance, Gloria went into the kitchen to call. Adele was looking a little hurt, so while we waited and Styles paced, I said to her in a low voice, "Aunt Adele, this is the first time I've been to Faye's apartment. I think you could do wonders with this place."

She brightened. "I could, if Faye would let me," she said. "She says it's just for the summer, and not worth bothering about, but I think environment is so important to a creative artist, don't you?"

"Absolutely," I agreed.

"Do you remember the way I did Norma Shearer's living room in *The Best for Last*? Of course, nowadays, you see a lot of those balloon valances, but at the time—"

"But I don't understand why somebody would hire a P.I.," Faye said suddenly. "I mean, if they wanted a copy of the tape, why didn't they just ask me?"

"Good question," Styles replied. "If we had the tape, maybe we could answer it. I'm assuming they saw something on it that was significant to them. Whether it would be significant to us or not is anybody's guess. But I doubt if they want you to understand the significance, because if they didn't care, they'd approach you straightforwardly."

"But I don't get it," Faye said. "What kind of a significant something do you mean?"

"Okay, take this guy last night. He's trying to take an insurance company to the cleaners over this minor traffic accident. He claims he came out of it with severe whiplash, and he shows up in court in a neck brace. Happens all the time, right? So the insurance company hires me to follow the guy around and see just how incapacitated he is. The guy goes dancing, I follow him around with my little camera and document every move he makes that's inconsistent with his professed injuries. You could have done the same thing without knowing it. Let's say my guy has a daughter in a cheerleading contest. When she gets up to do her cheer, he's coached her so many times, he stands in the back and goes through the motions along with her, forgetting that he's not supposed to be able to move his neck. Understand?"

"Yeah," Faye said slowly, "but that means we might never be able to find out what's wrong with my tape."

"That's right," Styles said. "Our priority is getting your tapes back, not necessarily figuring out why they got snatched in the first place."

Gloria returned with the information that Cleveland was indeed playing that night, and we could expect the game to last until nine or nine-thirty—ten or ten-thirty if there was overtime.

Styles grimaced. "I don't like it," she said, "not on daylight saving time. Pray for cloud cover."

"I don't get it," I said. "If you're thinking what I think you're thinking, you want to break into his place and look for the tape, right? But if he's a Cleveland fan, won't he be home watching the game?"

"Nah, he goes to his favorite bar, sits around with his buddies and watches it on the big screen."

"You know an awful lot about this guy," I observed.

"I know where he lives, cookie," Styles retorted. "That's the important thing."

"So can I, like, hire you to do that?" Faye asked. "Break into his place and look for my tapes?"

"You'll have to come with me," Styles said. "I don't know exactly what I'm looking for, and his place is likely to be messier than the Dumpster."

"Okay," Faye agreed cheerfully. "Can I bring my camera and tape it?"

"No."

"Shall we come along as lookouts?" Gloria offered.

"No. We're staging a B and E, not casting *Gone with the Wind*. Gilda and Faye and that's it."

I was surprised to hear myself included. I did have a theater to run.

"I do have to work sometimes," I grumbled.

Styles ignored me. "Pick me up at seven," she said. She found the end of Waldo's leash wrapped around the coffee table, picked it up, and gave it a yank. "Let's go, Waldo." To us, she said, "Dark clothes, no jewelry, okay?" Here she gave Faye's nose ring a significant look. "I'll bring the gloves."

"So you don't leave any fingerprints, I suppose," Adele said, nodding sagely.

"So we don't pick up any more germs than we have to," Styles said.

She was already headed out the door.

Faye was following her. "Wait! What about the Dumpster?"

"I'll leave that to you," Styles said.

"But what if we, like, find more evidence?"

"Save it. Waldo will have it for dessert."

"Well, aren't you going to tell us this guy's name?"

"What do you want to know his name for?" Styles demanded irritably. "He didn't bother with yours. He calls you 'doll,' you call him 'pops.' "

"Is he an older guy?"

"Older than he thinks," Styles said. She suddenly grinned in apparent satisfaction.

8

"What a dump!"

Styles stood in the doorway surveying an apartment no bigger than Faye's. There the resemblance ended, since this one was littered with the debris of somebody's life. It looked like Macaulay Culkin had been left home alone during a Kansas tornado.

"What do you know from dumps?" I asked bitterly, sniffing at my arms to see if they were still scented with *essence de Dumpster*, despite all my scrubbing. We hadn't found Faye's videos, so Faye was investing a lot of hope in this mission.

Predictably, we were having a thunderstorm—the kind that makes theater owners like me think that the patron goddess of the cinema got her wires crossed when we asked for enough rain to squelch outdoor entertainment. I was grateful for the cover of darkness, but my shoes squeaked with every step from the water that was sloshing around inside them.

Styles was carrying a black gym bag slung over her shoulder. It seemed much too bulky to carry the set of picklocks the size of a doll's tool kit that she had used to open the door. Maybe she'd come prepared to blast her way in, if necessary. But I'd already noticed that detectives didn't seem very security conscious when it came to their own digs. At least, Styles wasn't.

Faye was still outside, conscientiously wiping her feet on a mat that said BEAT IT! Styles had had her call on the car phone to make sure the apartment was empty.

"Would you get in here?" I said to Faye.

"Well, we don't have to sink to his level," she retorted self-righteously.

"That," Styles observed, picking up a jock strap, yellowed and stiff with sweat, that had been draped over the front door knob, "would be a challenge."

"How do you know this guy anyway?" I asked. I'd nearly tripped over a toolbox hidden under a casually dropped newspaper dated two months back. "Did you meet him at the annual detectives' banquet? Or did you have a more intimate relationship—trade picklocks or something?"

"Let's just say our paths have crossed," Styles said grimly.

"Oh, God!" Faye had just gotten her first peek at our theater of operations. "This place has been searched already! Somebody beat us to it!"

"Nah," Styles said. "It always looks like this."

"How are we going to find anything in this mess?" Faye wailed.

I caught a movement by the bedroom door. A lanky yellow cat, a tom by the size of him and the notches in his ears, was picking his way through the debris and across the floor.

"Harry," Styles greeted him. "How's it hangin'?"

The cat stopped in front of Styles, sat down, and looked up at her expectantly.

"Give me five," she said, and extended a hand to him, palm up.

He slapped it with one paw. I exchanged a glance with Faye.

"Is the cat gonna, like, object, if we search the place?" she asked.

"Nah, he's probably got stuff buried in the wreckage that he hopes we'll find, right, Harry?" Styles scratched his ears. The cat closed his eyes with an air of condescension. "Old catnip mice, old Ping-Pong balls, old girlfriends."

The cat took a leisurely stretch, and then headed for another door—the kitchen, I guessed, from long experience with feline priorities.

"Start searching near the door," Styles instructed us, "on

the theory that he sheds as he walks in. Remember, they might be inside something—a bag, a box, a briefcase, a file cabinet."

"You think he's got a file cabinet?" I asked skeptically. "What would be the point?"

"It's where he keeps his liquor," Styles said. "I'll check his refrigerator."

"Are you going to eat something of his?" Faye asked hopefully. "Can I come watch?"

Styles shook her head. "He uses his refrigerator as a file cabinet. It's where he keeps his most important stuff—and his beer."

"Do we have to put everything back like he had it, so he doesn't know we've been here?"

"It's a good idea," Styles conceded, and I realized Faye wasn't going to get to leave her note. "Ninety-nine percent of the stuff we'd move, he wouldn't notice. But there might be one or two things he pays attention to."

"I don't know," I said to Faye, who was digging through an overflowing magazine rack. "We got here pretty fast. I think your tapes should be in the top layer if they're here."

Somewhere a phone rang, and we froze. Our gazes circled the room and met in puzzlement. The phone could be anywhere.

"You know who you called," a man's deep voice said in the silence. "I'm not here. If you're a potential client, my office number is in the book. If you're an attractive lady, leave a message. If you're not, drop dead."

After an electronic beep, a woman's voice spoke, smooth as well-aged bourbon. "I need to see you to retrieve—what I asked you to get for me. Can you meet me tonight? Call when you get in."

She hung up, and Faye and I exchanged looks.

"Jeez, Gilda, do you think she's talking about my tapes?"

"Beats me," I said.

"A woman," she reflected, frowning. "Somehow I just didn't figure it'd be a woman."

"It might not be," I cautioned. "That call could have been about anything."

"Yeah," she agreed, "but it still creeps me out."

The room was lit solely by lamps, and our burglar wasn't wasting any money on wattage. The atmosphere was heavy, thick with the accumulated effects of what smelled like cigarette and cigar smoke combined, from what I could tell beneath the generally fusty, gamy odor of the place. The smell—in addition to my nervousness—made me crave a cigarette, but I knew Styles wouldn't approve if I dropped any ash, in spite of the general disorder. The dim light threw our distorted shadows on everything—furniture, crumpled paper, piles of clothing, crammed bookshelves, grocery bags filled with miscellaneous items that may have once had a destination, the brown and stringy corpse of a spider plant. I spotted an old brown-painted desk in one corner. It sagged in the middle, the legs leaning in slightly like a quartet of drunks holding each other up. On top of a pile of papers sat a garish red-violet teddy bear. A careless glue job on his button eyes made him appear to be weeping. Perched on his dusty head at a rakish angle was a Cleveland Indians cap.

Crowded into one corner of the desk, its back to the wall, was a small photograph, a candid snapshot of a young woman.

"Gilda," Faye called in a hushed voice, "look!"

I crossed to where she was kneeling on the floor by the magazine rack. She handed me a catalog that seemed to run to protective gear and devices—bulletproof vests, burglar alarms of various types and descriptions, stun guns, automatic weapons with night-vision scopes, and other paraphernalia.

"Yeah," I said wryly. "Too bad he didn't order any of this anti-intruder equipment."

"No," she said, turning it over in my hands. "The other side."

The catalog was addressed to "J. M. Styles."

"This could explain why he's got an old picture of her on his desk," I said.

"Do you think he's her ex?" Faye asked.

I frowned, considering. I'd never thought of Styles as having a husband, even an ex-husband, or having any name other than "Styles." The Styles I knew wouldn't be caught dead agreeing to anything, much less saying "I do" to a long list of promises. On the other hand, marriage itself is a transforming experience. Was it possible that inside of her was a warm, genial, cooperative Styles repressed by bitter experience?

"Gilda, I wish you'd do your shopping on your own time." Styles had returned, her arms full of black plastic boxes.

Faye dropped the trash can she'd been in the process of emptying onto the floor, and rushed over to Styles.

"My tapes!" she breathed ecstatically. "Styles, you're the bomb!"

"Make sure they're all there," Styles cautioned her.

"They're all here," Faye said happily, and laughed. "They're cold! Did you really find them in the fridge?"

The cat had followed her into the room and jumped up on the arm of the couch. He sharpened his claws on the tattered upholstery.

The phone rang again, and again the masculine voice filled the room. A confident voice, I thought—an insolent voice, just on the border between humorous and rude.

"I know you're there," another woman's voice said, this one boozy and hoarse, "so pick up the goddamn phone!" In a slight pause, we heard a metallic clink—an answering machine distortion of ice in a glass. "Goddamn you, Jake, if you're with that redhead with the Odd Lots dye job, I'll personally come over there and pull out every perky little curl on her goddamn head!"

She waited a few seconds, then slammed the phone down. The cat flattened his ears and flicked his tail in irritation.

Styles caught me watching her expression, raised an eyebrow, and grinned at me.

"Sounds like old Jake's personal life is as messy as his personal space," I observed.

"Messier," she agreed.

The cat's head swiveled to the front door. He hopped down and trotted in that direction.

"Oh, shit!" Styles swore softly, took the tapes from Faye, and crammed them in her bag. "Come on!" She tugged at my elbow. "Fire escape!"

I heard somebody fumbling with a door lock and swearing.

She led the way through the bedroom, which was almost as littered as the living room, and threw up the screen in a back window. I could hear the traffic from High Street. We were bathed in the pink neon glow of a furniture store sign. Styles had stuffed a panic-stricken Faye through the opening before Faye had had a chance to worry about where she was landing. I followed, then took the bag from Styles as she climbed through.

Styles eased the window down. Faye was already halfway down the fire escape. I slipped on a wet metal step, and felt myself caught by the scruff from behind. Styles hauled me up and we kept going.

"What kind of baseball fan is he, anyway?" I complained, as we raced for the car in a downpour.

"The worst kind," Styles said, gasping for breath as she flung open the car door. "If they're playing lousy, he can't bear to watch."

The car was an old, dark blue Pontiac, well endowed with rust, which Styles had borrowed from a friend. I presumed from this that Jake might have recognized her pickup if she'd driven it. I was dripping all over the seat and the threadbare carpet under my feet, but one glance at the floor persuaded me that the car had good drainage.

We looked up through the rain-streaked windshield at the building we'd just left, the Belvedere Apartments. It was a sturdy, unornamented red brick building from the forties. The Short North, as the neighborhood was called, was a transitional neighborhood known for its art galleries, but Jake's building hadn't made the transition. It was stolid, unpretentious, and worn, a respectable widow of a building suffering a slow decline into a poverty that was not especially genteel. It had seen its share of cat fights and other altercations, and could no longer pretend to be shocked by them.

"Will Harry give us away?" I asked.

She shook her head, spraying me with water.

"I paid him off," she said.

I didn't ask her who the guy was, though I could guess. After all, I'd known from previous experience that Styles had a relative with the same last name working as a P.I. in Columbus. She hadn't volunteered any information then, and obviously didn't plan to now. She had a right to her privacy; I respected that. I also might want her help again some time, and I didn't want her holding grudges.

"What will he do when he finds the tapes missing?" Faye asked from the darkness of the backseat.

"He may not find out," Styles said. "I left some dummies in their place."

"Labeled like mine?" Faye asked, clearly impressed.

"Yeah."

"So he'll deliver the dummies to his client," I said.

"Do you think that woman on the phone was his client?" Faye asked. "The first one, I mean."

"Don't know," Styles said. "Don't particularly care."

I lit a cigarette and hung it out the window.

"Give me a drag," Styles said, turning into the blinding lights of High Street.

I handed her my cigarette.

"Take the whole thing," I said. "I have more."

She handed it back to me.

"You know I don't smoke," she said.

I sat back and studied her profile against the garish lights of shops and bars.

"So what's on the tapes you gave him?" I asked. "Were they blank?"

She flicked me an appreciative glance.

"I'm not that cheap," she said. "I copied some of the best

tapes in my cartoon collection. The one his client wants, or at least the one I think his client wants, is Bugs Bunny."

A hoot of laughter issued from the backseat.

9

"Aren't you just the teensiest bit curious?" Faye had asked Styles when our escapade was over. "About what's on the tape, I mean."

"Babe, life is not an Antonioni movie," Styles had replied. "You're not going to find a murder taking place in the background. Like I said before, chances are good you won't see anything, because you won't understand the significance of what you're seeing, and neither would anybody else. Somebody's just paranoid about something, that's all."

"Well, just 'cause you're paranoid, it doesn't mean they're not out to get you," Faye said.

"What's that mean?" Styles asked.

Faye shrugged. "I don't know. I'm just saying that somebody might, like, have a real reason to be paranoid. I want to look at the tape again and see."

"And I'm just warning you not to be disappointed," Styles said.

We were sitting in the lobby at the Paradise, drying out and drinking cappuccino made for us by another of my summer employees, Todd. Todd was a good-looking blond, a high school classmate of Duke's who aspired to be an actor. He was awed by Faye, and would gladly have carried her entire vanload of equipment fifty miles over hot sands in his bare feet if she'd let him. He'd settled for carrying her new editing deck to the second floor yesterday and helping her clean up one of the old dressing rooms over the stage.

"So you're not curious?" I pressed Styles.

"Sweetheart, you Liberties have enough curiosity to go around," she said.

She had a point.

By Tuesday, everyone in the family had a copy of the Channel Six newscast, and every Liberty had a pet theory about who or what gave this tape its theft appeal.

"It's that woman with the clipboard," my Aunt Gloria told anyone who would listen. "The one in the gray suit. Did you see the way she looked at those basketball players when she grabbed the mike? If looks could kill, they'd all be dead by now!"

"But looks *can't* kill, Gloria, that's the whole point," Clara would say. "I like the handsome man in the blue turtleneck at the back of the crowd. He shows up several times. I'll bet he's a jewel thief. If I were you, Gilda, I'd check with mall security to find out if any of the jewelry stores were robbed that day."

I was opening my mouth to ask why I'd been elected to take responsibility for any crimes that Natalie's camera had recorded for Faye's video, but my mother cut in.

"You've been watching too many Cary Grant movies, Clara," she scoffed. "I think it's probably much less dramatic—like the mother who slapped the kid for forgetting her lines. She's probably in the middle of a custody battle."

"I like the woman in the lace dress, myself," Uncle Wallace said. "I don't know if you noticed, Florence, but she's always wearing the most peculiarly blank expression. Some vampires I've known looked just like that."

My sister Betty said, "Maybe it has something to do with Smiling Sid."

"Who?" my mother demanded.

"Smiling Sid. You know, the car salesman with the bad toupee. He's on television all the time—plays the harmonica."

" 'Smiling Sid loves to make you smile,' " Uncle Ollie quoted. "I love that guy!"

"I knew he looked familiar!" Adele said. "He's sitting on a bench, talking to a tall young man, right?"

"But he's not doing anything," Gloria protested. "He's just talking."

"Ah! But who's the young man?" Wallace asked. "That's what we don't know. He could be a hit man or a drug dealer, or a professional arsonist."

"Surely he's too young to be any of those things," Gloria insisted. "He looks like a teenager."

My father laughed. "Where have you been, Sis? Hit men get younger every day!"

Even Lillian had seen the tape, and as family matriarch, she had, of course, formed her own opinion.

"That man you interviewed about his daughter," she said, narrowing her eyes in suspicion. "He reminded me of a beau I had once. No eye contact—that should tell you something. You should never trust a man who won't look you in the eye, Gilda. I learned that to my detriment."

I was opening my mouth to ask why she thought I needed romantic advice on the subject of men, since I was interested neither in romance nor men, when my Uncle Val spoke up.

"Tobias has a theory," he said, "about the man off to one side with the three kids. Remember him? Looks Hispanic, maybe."

Valentino's partner, Tobias Norton, nodded. "I think Florence is right about the custody suit," he said, "but that's my candidate. Every kid is drinking a soft drink and eating some kind of junk food. If you enlarged the frame enough, you could probably see the cavities forming in their teeth. If their mother got hold of that footage, his visitations would be cut back to once a year in the company of a certified nutritionist."

Ollie roared. "A certified nutritionist! That's good!"

Adele looked at both of them scornfully. Tobias might be a fiction writer by trade, her look said, but he had no imagination.

"I think you're all missing the obvious," she said. "This was a *cheerleading* competition, after all. Don't you remember that woman in Texas who tried to hire a hit man to bump off the mother of her daughter's cheerleading rival? Didn't you see the looks on some of those mothers' faces when their daughters didn't win?"

"All I can say is, it had better not involve the Buckeye State coach," my father observed. "Those coaches—especially Hale, the basketball coach, and Mower, the football coach—are considered gods in this town, and nobody would thank Faye for exposing any hanky-panky they were up to."

"You think Coach Hale was playing footsie with the woman judge under the table?" my sister asked.

"Probably not," my father said. "Poor guy still looks like death warmed over."

Ollie nodded. "They're hoping his ticker doesn't quit before the retirement banquet."

"Faye's seen the whole thing, not just the part we saw," Tobias reminded them. He turned to Clara. "What does Faye think?"

"She claims she doesn't see anything suspicious on the tape," Clara said. "Or if she does, she's not telling me." Clara looked at me pointedly, and everybody followed her gaze.

I didn't say anything.

Later, Faye called while I was doing some repair work at the theater. I was sitting on the floor in what was formerly the upper balcony, now our second theater, trying to reattach an armrest that always fell off in the middle of the quietest scenes. The portable phone beeped, and I answered it.

"Gilda! I'm totally freaked!"

"What's up, Faye?" I asked cautiously. After all, it wasn't as if before Faye had arrived in town, I'd been looking around for another wacko member of my wacko family to involve me in their problems.

"Last night, when I got home, I had this message on my answering machine from this guy I've never even heard of! So, I just called him back—well, actually, I called him back before, but he was at lunch. He works at some place called Alban, Gray and Associates. You ever heard of them?"

"No," I said patiently, superglue in one hand, flashlight in the other, phone wedged between my ear and shoulder.

"Me neither. I don't even know what kind of business it is. So, anyway, he calls back, and guess what?"

"What?"

"He says he wants to buy the tape! The Northstar Mall tape! He says if I leave it out of my film, give him the original and any copies I've made, he'll pay me a thousand bucks!"

I was so surprised, I dropped the phone and nearly glued it to my hand.

"Did he say why?" Now I was trying to read the superglue tube by the light of the flashlight, but I couldn't make out the Munchkin-size advisory about what to do if you glued your fingers together. They'd probably have to amputate a finger, I thought morosely, and I'd spend the rest of my life like Harold Lloyd, wearing a glove with a prosthetic finger.

"He wouldn't say. But I got the impression somebody else put him up to it. He slipped up once or twice and said 'we,' like he had a partner or something. He said a thousand dollars was a lot of money, and I could buy a lot of film for that. The way he said it, you could tell he thought I'd fall all over myself to take him up on the offer."

"What did you tell him?"

"I told him the tape had been stolen."

"Oh."

"I didn't tell him we'd gotten it back."

My cousin wasn't as ditzy as she sounded, I thought.

"What did he say to that?"

"He didn't say anything at first. I wanted to see if he'd say something like, you know, 'But it was the wrong tape.' Something like that. Then I'd know if he was the guy who hired Jake."

"But he didn't?"

"No, he just—well, I don't know. He seemed surprised. He got quiet a minute, like he was thinking, you know. And then he asked me when it was stolen, and if I'd reported it to the police and all. And I said yes, and he thought some more, and then he said that the offer would remain open, and either way he'd appreciate it if I'd give him a call if I recovered the tape. And I didn't want to tell him I'd already recovered it, because it wasn't any of his business, after all, and I couldn't decide what to do. And so I just told him I'd call if there were any new developments—that's how I put it, 'new developments'—and he thanked me and hung up. So what should I do, Gilda? Do you think I should call him back and, like, tell him I found the tape and want to sell it to him? I mean, I could arrange to meet him somewhere, and you and Styles and I could go gang up on him and make him tell us why he wants it."

"Bad idea," I said. I set the superglue down carefully on a section of newspaper. "In the first place, he could bring his friends, too, and in the second place, whether he's by himself or with his friends, he could have more firepower than we do. He may not have any intention of paying the thousand dollars."

"You mean he might just knock me over the head and take the tape?" Faye asked. "Yeah, I see that. But I could force him to meet me in a crowded public place, like back at the mall."

"I'd like to get a line on this guy first," I said. "You have a name?"

"Charley Drake," she said. "Sounds fake to me."

"How did his voice sound? Young? Old? Any accent?"

"Youngish, I guess. I mean, not as young as me, but not real old. No accent that I could hear. He just sounded—you know, average."

"But the person who answered the phone at this office, if it was an office, recognized the name. Did you look up Alban, Gray in the phone book?"

"No. Hold on. I got one right here. I was just so flipped out, I was, like, praying that I'd get hold of you, so you could give me advice. Wait, here it is! It's in the book! It's on Grandview."

"Does it say what they do?"

"No, just 'Alban, Gray and Associates.' "

"Okay. Let's figure out a really clever way to find out who he is."

"I can see if he's got his own Web site," Faye volunteered.

That was the voice of the younger generation. It would never have occurred to me that somebody who was clearly up to no good might advertise his identity on the Web, but what did I know? I'd read about people who were so hungry for fame that they set up cameras in their living rooms or bedrooms and let them run twenty-four hours a day with a direct feed to their Web site. You could tune in any time and watch them water their plants, trim their toenails, have sex, or clean up hairballs. I was carefully guarding this information so that my aunts wouldn't find out.

I thought for a minute.

"Do you think we should call in Styles?"

My own reaction surprised me. "I think we should be able to handle this on our own."

"Do you think this Drake guy is fronting for the woman we heard on Jake's answering machine?"

"We don't even know what she was talking about," I pointed out. "But we'd better hope that he or his cohort was behind the burglary, because if not—"

"Yeah, if not, there's more than one person after my tape," Faye said. "But how likely does that sound?"

"Well, if one person wants it because of what's on it, that means somebody else would probably want it, too," I said. "You know—like in the insurance case Styles mentioned, the guy who's claiming injury would want it, but so would the insurance company, so it makes sense."

"Yeah, but wouldn't the insurance company just come right out and ask for a copy?"

"Maybe they just did."

"But they wouldn't care if there were other copies out there," she insisted. "The guy would, but that leaves the insurance company to be the ones who hired Jake to get the tape. Even if they didn't, like, hire him to do something criminal, why would they need a detective?"

"I don't know, Faye," I admitted. "Maybe they couldn't track you down. Maybe that's what they hired Jake for, and the B and E was his own idea. Or maybe we're on the wrong track altogether."

"What do you think I should do?" she asked. "I mean, I feel like I should, like, stash the original tape in some train station locker, if there was a train station anymore, and mail the key back to myself, or something."

"I've got a better idea," I said. "Why don't you label it *The Lost World*, and ship it to Hong Kong? There'll be a million copies on the street the day after it arrives, and all efforts to keep it under wraps will be moot."

Instead, Faye decided to get the tape copied that afternoon and lock up the original in the wall safe at the theater. In the meantime, I promised to think of a way we could run down Charley Drake without his knowing it.

But I hadn't come up with anything by the time Faye arrived. Every plan I thought of was flawed.

"I'm coming up empty," I said. "Do you have any ideas?"

"How about this? I go into Drake's office, and I say that I hit a car in the parking lot, and I want to know if it belongs to anybody in the office, and so Drake comes out, and we identify him and his car, and then we, like, follow him—what?"

I was shaking my head. "Why would he come out? What kind of car did you hit?"

"Oh." She frowned. "I was too upset to notice?"

"I don't think so."

"Okay, so what about this? We get your mother to dress up and go in and say she's got this singing telegram for Charley Drake, and—what now? You don't think she'd do it?"

"In a Hollywood minute," I said. "And it's not bad, but who sent the telegram? And why?"

"It's anonymous," Faye said, squinting at the scenario she was building in her mind's eye. She was a Liberty, all right. "A friend sent it as a practical joke. The song could be kind of racy and embarrassing—well, as racy as Aunt Florence is willing to make it."

"And you don't think his suspicions would be aroused?"

"Well, let's hear your ideas!" she huffed.

"My ideas are as bad as yours," I confessed.

"Then Styles—"

"No," I insisted. "Our ideas will get better. We just have to think harder."

It was almost five when I dialed Alban, Gray, with Faye hovering in the background. When the female voice at the other end of the line asked "May I help you?" I said, with a nervous giggle, "I hope so. You see, I met this man, Charley Drake, at a party the other night, and we had a long conversation. He gave me his card, and I know I was supposed to call him about something. I distinctly remember that I was supposed to call him, and that's why he gave me his card, but I forgot all about it until I was changing purses this morning. Well, I'm just too embarrassed to call him up and admit how little I remember." I sighed deeply. "Anyway, I was wondering if you could tell me what business he's in. That might remind me what it was I was supposed to call about."

"It's happened to me a million times," she said sympathetically. "And the older I get, the more often it happens. Alban, Gray is a computer consulting firm. We help businesses set up computer databases, mostly."

"Oh," I said. "I'll bet it has something to do with my son's computer club, then. I think we were discussing a software problem. Tell me—this is really embarrassing, but now that I think back, there were several people in on this particular conversation. Is Charley on the short side, with kind of sandy hair and a moustache?"

"No, Charley's a redhead," she said. "And I wouldn't call him short. More like medium height is what I'd say. He has sideburns, but no moustache."

"The guy with the moustache must have been the one who worked for CompuServe," I said with relief. "And the older gentleman was from Chemical Abstracts. Listen, you're a life saver! Thanks a million!"

"Anyway," she offered chattily, "you can always tell Charley, even at a distance. He's the one wearing the bow tie."

If this were a cartoon, I would have reached through the phone line and kissed her.

"That's right!" I laughed. "I said to my husband, 'I haven't seen a bow tie in years. I wonder why they went out of style?' "

"Want to talk to Charley?" she asked.

"Not today," I said firmly. "I'd better talk to my son first and make sure I have my story straight. Or maybe I'll have John call him directly."

I thanked her again and hung up.

"Well?" Faye asked eagerly.

"Computer databases," I said. "That's what he does for a living."

She looked disappointed. "That doesn't sound very promising."

"I suppose even computer geeks can screw up their personal lives," I said. "Have messy divorces, sue for child custody, commit insurance fraud, stuff like that. On the up side, we found out that he's a redhead with sideburns and a bow tie."

"So now we case the joint," she said, and glanced up at the lobby clock. "Only it's too late to do that today."

"And besides," I said with emphasis, "you have some movies to project."

"You're going to have to project some time, Gilda," she said.

"Not if I can help it," I replied.

"If I work on it with you—you know, like help you learn it and all—will you crew for me again next week?"

"No."

"You know he's going to make you do it one of these days," she said.

I sighed. Faye would make me less nervous than Duke would.

"Okay," I said grudgingly. "But if I break the projector or scramble its brains, it'll be on your head."

10

Faye also wanted me to go with her to stake out Alban, Gray, but I managed to keep her tethered to the projector through Thursday. Even though I often thought I was more of a hindrance than a help to Duke in running the theater, he sulked if I left him on his own too much. He liked having someone around to share the responsibility with, and someone to commiserate with when things went wrong.

Styles showed no further interest in the case until early Thursday afternoon, when I was home catching up on some paperwork. Thursdays were often high-stress days in the movie business, because movies changed on Fridays. That meant you spent Thursdays waiting for the Friday film to arrive, calling the distributor if it didn't, worrying about what state it would be in when it did, and then making it up on the platters, which involved splicing the reels together. It could involve splicing pieces of film back together, or rewinding the film if it was on backwards. In the worst-case scenario, the reels arrived unlabeled, and you had to watch all or part of the film to ascertain what went where. The film we were showing in the main theater now, *Austin Powers: International Man of Mystery,* had arrived that way, and if we'd shown it the way Duke had first assembled it, Austin would have awakened in the past rather than the future. In theory, I had been trained to do this kind of assembly work; in a pinch, I did it. But happily we only had one film changing this week, it had arrived on time, and Faye was over at the theater making it up.

I liked paperwork. As a former insurance executive, I knew paperwork backwards and forwards. Doing paperwork made me feel competent and efficient—two things I never felt when I was struggling with the projector, the splicer, the popcorn machine, or the sound system. Reloading the ticket dispenser made me break out into a cold sweat. I'd finished the payroll and was studying the calendar. Would we get *The Lost World* or not? On the one hand, since the multiplex on the edge of town had burned down, we were the only theater in Eden. On the other hand, Columbus was close enough to make the distributor at least delay a booking in Eden. It was already playing in New York, and would probably open in Columbus next week. If they did send us the film, would they give us enough advance warning to advertise, so that our loyal followers wouldn't drive into Columbus to see it? The life of an independent theater owner is nothing if not suspenseful.

The phone rang, and I answered it, worried that Faye had hit a snag.

The voice on the other end was Styles's.

"Gilda, I need to see that video." She sounded tired.

"I thought you weren't interested," I said.

"Things have changed," she said.

"What do you mean?"

"Jake's been shot. From what I can make out, he was shot by the person he delivered the video to."

"Oh, no!" I cried. "Is he okay?"

"There were complications," she reported wearily. "He got shot in the gut, but the wound wasn't fatal. The shooting triggered a heart attack. He's still in intensive care. He'll probably pull through okay, but he looks like hell."

"Gee, I'm sorry, Styles." I didn't even know why I was sympathizing with her, but sympathy seemed called for. "Did the client find out that we switched the tapes? Is that why he got shot?"

"I'm not sure," she said. "Jake's not real coherent at the moment. I'm going back to Riverside now to see if he can give me a better account of what went down."

I checked my watch.

"Styles, how much sleep have you had?" I asked.

"What's today? Thursday?" She yawned into my ear. "I slept a few hours last night."

"When did this happen?"

"Late Sunday night," she said wryly. "Some time after we hit his apartment." She yawned again.

"He was shot *there*?"

"No, he was out. Somebody heard the shot, went to investigate, found him on the sidewalk around midnight. He's lucky he lives in Columbus, Ohio, and not New York or L.A."

"Yeah," I agreed. "Places like that, people just step over the body. Listen, I'll drive you to the hospital."

"No, no, I'm okay to drive."

"I'll be there in fifteen minutes."

She was still protesting when I hung up on her.

Then I realized that I didn't know where she lived. I rooted around in the desk drawer and came up with her business card. Her home number was scrawled on the back.

The phone rang once.

"Carlyle Street—one eighty-two," she said.

Styles's house was on the east side of town in an area I didn't know very well. Fundamentally, it was the kind of small brick bungalow they'd built in the thirties, but the architect's influences had been diverse. It had one of those pointed gothic arches over the front door, surmounted by stucco and topped off by a thin line of Victorian trim along the roofline, like a slip showing. It was unimaginatively adorned by low-maintenance yew bushes that probably hadn't been trimmed since Lassie was a pup. The lawn needed mowing. A rusty garbage can lay on its side by the curb like a lawn ornament. I was willing to bet it never went anywhere.

I surveyed the scene not only for what it would tell me about Styles, but also as a prospective house hunter trying to imagine myself living in a new space. It didn't tell me anything about Styles that I didn't already know, since I'd never pictured her as a happy homemaker. I couldn't even figure out why she lived in a house instead of an apartment.

Waldo bayed at me from the front door and pressed his stubby little basset legs up against the screen. His bloodhound snout was decorated with pink petals and pollen.

I wanted to tell Styles about Faye's thousand-dollar offer, but she justified my concern for her by sleeping all the way to the hospital.

I'm convinced she found the hospital entrance and the elevator up to the ICU on autopilot.

"I'm only allowed in for ten minutes once every hour," she told me in the elevator. "It takes me five minutes to wake him up."

As far as I knew, you had to be family to be allowed into the ICU—I would have thought immediate family. I wondered once again how immediately Styles was related to Jake.

But when we arrived at the intensive care unit, they told us that Jake had been moved to a semiprivate room.

"They must have needed his bed," Styles groused. "He looked pretty intense to me."

I hadn't expected to go into Intensive Care with her, but in my anxiety over Jake's condition and her obvious worry, I forgot all discretion and followed her into the hospital room.

The room was dimly lit, with shadows from the vertical blinds falling across the bed. The smell was starched and medicinal. But I thought we were in the wrong room. There was nobody here but an old guy. He was too old to be her ex or her brother, old even for a cousin. Too old, surely, I thought, to be a working private investigator.

But I trailed Styles to the bed, averting my eyes from the intravenous drip and the plastic bag clipped to the bedpost.

He had a full head of bushy white hair, high cheekbones in a tanned face, and a bushy white moustache. His jaws and chin were studded with three-day stubble. He opened his eyes.

"Sammy," he breathed, and reached out a hand for her. "Sammy." He closed his eyes briefly. "Long time, no see."

"You saw me two hours ago, Jake," Styles said, a little tartly.

He opened his eyes again. "I did? Damn! What do they put in that anesthetic?"

His voice was weakened by his condition, and hoarse, probably from the throat tube he'd had in the ICU.

His eyes shifted to me. I stepped back, uncomfortable.

"Who's that?" he asked. "Your girlfriend? Crank me up so I can get a look at her."

"You can see fine from where you are," Styles said.

"Afraid I might take her away from you, eh, Sammy?" he croaked. "Come over here, dolly. What's your name?"

"Her name is Gilda, she's not my girlfriend, and we need to talk about the shooting," Styles said severely.

His face puckered with emotion.

"If I ever get my hands on that dame—"

"Pull up a chair, Gilda," Styles directed me. As she sat down on the edge of the bed, she hooked the nearest one with her toe and pulled it closer. "From the beginning, Jake."

"Oh, no, Sammy!" he said. "I don't want you to fight my battles for me. I'll settle her score when I get out of here. You don't have to worry about that."

"Jake," she said sternly, "you stole a video from one of my clients."

It was the first I'd heard that she regarded Faye as a client of hers, but then this visit seemed to be full of revelations.

"Was that your client?" he asked in apparent surprise. "Ahh, Sammy, I'm sorry about that! I didn't know! You know I'd never—"

"In a heartbeat, if the money was right," she said.

I winced at the metaphor, but neither of them seemed as sensitive as I was.

"So let's cut the crap, Jake. Who hired you?"

He pulled feebly at his moustache, then shifted his gaze to me.

"I wonder, sweetheart, if you could hand me that water? That anesthetic they used really makes you thirsty. Not like my usual, eh, Sammy?"

Styles waited while he took a sip of water from the straw. Then he settled his head back on the pillow.

"Who hired you, Jake?"

"I wish I knew that, Sammy," he said. "All I know is this broad comes to see me—"

"A woman," Styles corrected. The correction seemed automatic. "Did she call first?"

"Oh, sure, she called. On Sunday, that was. So I met her at the office, and she tells me she wants this videotape, something about a local gal who was making this movie, only she—the broad, I mean—was in the movie without realizing it. And this broad—ah, she was a real looker, Sammy, and stylish, like you don't see much anymore, with all the broads wearing pants, like you—"

"What was the woman doing that she didn't want captured on film?" Styles asked bluntly.

"We-e-ll, she *said* she was out shopping with her boyfriend and didn't want the husband to find out." He coughed. "And then there was something about the boyfriend used to date her sister, yadda, yadda." He sighed deeply. "It was all bullshit, as far as I was concerned, but the money was right enough. In my racket, sweetheart," he continued, addressing me now, "you believe the money, not the client. The customer's never right, if you know what I mean, but the money might be. Trust the dough, not the Joe—that's what I always say."

"Did she give you the filmmaker's name? Or did you have to find that out?"

"No, she gave me the name. All I had to do was go get the tape. Shoulda been a piece of cake, Sammy."

"In a manner of speaking," Styles said dryly.

He looked blank, then realization dawned, and his grin turned sheepish.

"Well, you know how it is, Sammy," he said. "A man gets hungry when he's working."

"It was probably the cheesecake that added that last milligram of fat that brought on the heart attack," she observed. "So, did you contact this woman after you'd stolen the tape?"

He shook his head. "She said she was going to be out that night, and she'd call me. She left me a message on the answering machine Sunday night. I was down at Mike's for the games, but—" He closed his eyes and waved his hand, the one with the plastic hospital bracelet, in a gesture of disgust. "I don't suppose you caught it, Sammy. You see it, doll?"

He had to shift his head on the pillow to make eye contact with me.

"No, sorry," I said.

He huffed. "Don't be sorry! I'm sorry I saw any of it! You woulda thought they was all on drugs or something!"

His pale face flushed, and I looked around nervously for the nurse call button.

"I'm telling you, Sammy, they—"

"Yeah, yeah," she said, patting the gesticulating arm.

I worried that he'd start using the other instead, and dislodge the IV in the middle of the play-by-play. But he subsided.

"So, like I said, she left me a message, and I called her Sunday night, and she wanted me to meet her on this street corner. On a street corner, for chrissakes! Like we were in one of those private-eye movies from the forties. And I'll tell you something, honey," he said, shifting his gaze to me again. "She might have been a looker, but she was no Lana Turner, you know what I mean? And I don't know if you remember Sunday night, Sammy, but it was raining like a son of a bitch. So I'm standing on this fucking street corner, and it's raining buckets and pitch dark, and I'm thinking I might as well be in the belly of the whale, and here she comes, clickety-click up the street." He coughed.

"You're sure it was the same woman?" Styles asked.

"Oh, I'm sure, all right. So I go to hand over the tape, and she shoots me—bang!—just like that! And I'm just hitting the pavement when I feel the old ticker start to go. I'm telling you, Sammy, I thought for sure my number was up."

"She took the tape?"

"If the hospital didn't give it to you along with my other stuff, yeah, she took it."

"Mr., uh, Styles," I interjected. I glanced at Styles, but she didn't show any surprise that I knew his last name.

"Call me Jake, dolly," he said, leering at me. "All the girls call me Jake."

Styles rolled her eyes.

"Jake, why did you take all the tapes with you when you broke into Faye's apartment? Didn't you know which one you wanted?"

"Well, I knew I didn't want *Citizen Kane*, that's for sure. I took the ones that didn't have titles, but none of them said anything about Northstar Mall or any cheerleading contest or anything, and I knew that was the footage she wanted. Then, while I was eating the cheesecake, I got to thinking, and so I went back and checked the two VCRs, and found the one about the cheerleading contest. But I thought I should take all of 'em to be on the safe side. But, say, do you know those tapes didn't fit in my VCR? I thought I would take a look at one—"

"Just to see if it was worth more than she was paying you," Styles said.

He gave her a reproachful look.

"They're Betas, Mr. Styles," I volunteered, showing off my newly acquired expertise in documentary video. "Not the old kind of Beta, but something called 'Beta SP.' It's what TV news crews shoot with."

The nurse came in and made shooing noises. Jake's eyes were drooping.

"Well, if it's any consolation to you," Styles said as we stood up, "she didn't get the tape she wanted."

"No?"

"We broke into your place while you were watching the

game, took the tapes back, and replaced them with cartoons. I
think she got Bugs Bunny."

You could see he didn't quite know how to take this. Finally, he smiled, showing a full set of teeth so even and white,
I suspected they were dentures.

"No kidding? But you're going after her anyway, aren't
you, Sammy? Otherwise you wouldn't be asking all these
questions."

He grinned at her sleepily.

"Just wait'll I get out of here. We can work together. It'll be
just like old times, eh, Sammy? Just don't tell your mother.
Styles and Styles, me and my girl!"

"Don't count on it," Styles snapped, but I noticed she didn't
say it loud enough for him to hear.

"Do you think he was telling the truth?" I asked when we
got to the car.

"More or less," she said. "I've wanted to shoot him enough
times myself to know how tempting it is, but I think there
might have been more to that little episode than he's telling."

"Like what?"

"Well, he could've held out for more money, or he could've
made a pass at her. With my father, either is plausible, though
he doesn't usually make the pass until he's been paid."

She sank down in the seat until she was sitting on her
spine.

"Does he often get hired for burglary?"

She shrugged, and looked out the window.

"The thing about Jake Styles is he'll do almost anything
for money," she said. "I say 'almost' because as far as I know
he hasn't killed anybody yet. But he considers a conscience a
liability in detective work."

I wondered if he considered it a liability in parenting as
well, but I didn't ask.

"But Styles, don't you think it's a little too—too coincidental that the burglar who broke into my cousin's apartment
in Eden just happened to be your dad?"

"It's not as coincidental as you might think," she said.

"He's good at what he does—one of the best, in fact. In spite of present appearances, he doesn't make that many mistakes. So anybody who went shopping for a good, experienced, discreet detective without legal scruples—or moral ones either, for that matter—would be bound to end up with his name on a short list. He hasn't been shot for years, though, and this doesn't sound like the kind of mistake he'd make. A dark street corner, late at night? He'd smell a setup a mile away. But the cop who caught the call told me his gun was still in his shoulder holster. It doesn't make sense."

"Maybe this would be a good time to mention that someone called Faye today and offered her a thousand dollars for the tape," I said.

She whistled. "Could she hear Bugs Bunny in the background?"

"Nope, the guy was at work at some computer consulting firm."

I told her about Charley Drake.

"Faye thought Drake sounded surprised when she told him the tape had been stolen, for what that's worth. Maybe he was, maybe he wasn't."

"I'll see what I can dig up on Charley Drake," she said. "Meanwhile, we'd better take another look at that tape."

She squirmed in her seat and began massaging her neck.

"He looked better, though, the old man," she said, yawning. "Now I can go back to being pissed off at him without feeling guilty."

"You don't get along," I observed.

She sighed. "You were right about him—his whole life is as messy as his apartment. He misplaces wives, kids, and girlfriends the way he misplaces everything else. He's got the original Peter Pan complex—doesn't want any responsibility. I'm convinced Harry takes care of him more than he takes care of Harry. Speaking of which—"

She sat up and looked out the window.

"Do we need to go check on Harry?"

"Do you mind? Do you have time?"

"No problem," I said, and moved into the freeway exit lane to turn around and head back toward downtown.

"You know, Styles," I said.

She grunted sleepily.

"Let's suppose that whoever hired Jake has seen Bugs Bunny by now." I was thinking this out as I went along. "So maybe they figure Jake stole the wrong tape. Either they send somebody else to steal the right tape, or they decide on a more straightforward approach and call Faye directly and make her an offer. Are you listening?"

Another grunt from the shotgun seat.

"Faye tells them it was stolen," I continued. "But in any case, whether or not they were the ones—or one—who called Faye, they have to figure Jake has the tape. Are you with me?"

Her eyes popped open, and she turned to look at me.

I hit the accelerator.

This time Styles used a key to let us into the apartment, which made me hopeful we'd get to leave by the front door this time rather than by our more unconventional exit route. The door swung open, and I heard Styles's intake of breath.

"Holy shit!" she exclaimed.

I looked over her shoulder.

"Now that," I said, "looks like an apartment that's been searched."

Before us was a mess, but it wasn't the same mess we'd seen the last time we'd visited the apartment.

"Harry!" she called. "Yo, Harry!"

From my brief acquaintance with Harry, I could see why "here, kitty, kitty" wouldn't seem appropriate.

We made a quick tour of the apartment, calling the cat. But there was a hole in the window onto the fire escape that was bigger than cat-size, with a tuft of yellow fur stuck to one of the shards. I wasn't too worried. The condition of Harry's ears had clued me in that he had the run of the neighborhood. But Styles stuck her head out the window and yelled for him anyway.

"Now what?" I asked. "Do we call the police?"

She shook her head. "Jake would have another heart attack," she said. "We'd better look around and see if we can tell what they took."

I stared at her. "You must be kidding!" I swept the apartment with one hand. "I'll bet even Jake doesn't know what he had."

Her eyes met mine. "He had six hours' worth of cartoons on Beta format videos," she said. "Want to bet me twenty-five bucks he doesn't have them now?"

I was too smart to take her up on this bet, which was just as well. The videos were missing.

11

Harry showed up before we left. He appeared to be all in one piece and hungry, but not traumatized as far as we could tell.

"You never know, though," Styles said, stroking the cat's back as he chowed down on Little Friskies. "He's a macho man, like my dad. He could be holding in all his emotions."

Harry didn't deign to comment on this observation. It takes one to know one, I thought.

I dropped Styles off and went straight to the theater. I found Faye vacuuming the lobby without her customary vigor. Her eyes were suspiciously moist, and her nose ring quivered in a pink nose.

"What now?" I asked.

"Oh, Gilda, I'm such a dipstick!" she said. "I'm, like, totally four-oh-four! You know the copy I made of the Northstar Mall tape?"

I nodded.

"It's gone."

"You mean, somebody broke into your apartment again?"

I was beginning to think that either there'd been a run on burglars-for-hire, or one well-paid individual had had a very busy day. I wasn't as surprised as I should have been, but Faye didn't notice.

She said, "No! That's the worst of it! I invited him in!"

First things first. "Are the films set up?" I asked.

She nodded. "Duke's upstairs doing his homework. The concession stand's in pretty good shape. We made the tea and lemonade."

She followed me to the small office behind the concession stand.

"Okay," I said. "Tell me what happened."

"It was that guy I was telling you about—the sportscaster from Channel Ten. He came over today, and we talked about the project, and he seemed really interested, you know? He said he had a little sister who played soccer, and he just—I don't know, Gilda, he seemed so sincere."

"Who was this guy?" I asked. "I mean, what was his name?"

"His name's Hank Mann," she said. "And he's for real, Gilda. I called him up at the station afterward and asked him about my tape, but he said he didn't have it, and he acted, like, real surprised that I was asking him. But he *has* to have it! It was there in the VCR. I showed him part of it. And then after he left, it wasn't there."

"How soon after he left?"

"Jeez, I don't know," she admitted. "Couple hours, I guess. I mean, I went to rewind it right before I came to work."

"And in the meantime, you were where?"

"Well, I went for a run, but I locked the door and used the deadbolt. Otherwise, I was home."

"Take a shower?" I prompted.

"Well, after I ran, sure," she said.

"Was the deadbolt on then?"

"Well . . ." she said, and looked at me. "Jeez, Gilda. I'm not used to living in Fort Knox."

"You'd better get used to it," I admonished her. "Somebody shot Jake; that means somebody takes this whole thing very seriously. We're not just talking about a property crime anymore. I'm not saying this Hank Mann didn't take it. He may have. His interest sounds suspicious to me. And he'd know you'd never get anywhere with an accusation of theft against him. Even if the cops took you seriously, they'd never get a search warrant."

"It's my bad, Gilda. I let my guard down. But I won't do it again, not even for some hottie with the bluest eyes in the world who says he has a brother on the Oscar committee or that he's Leo Hurwitz's grandson. I mean, I'm just, like, incredibly relieved that the original tape is—" She broke off, glanced around, lowered her voice. "That the original tape is you-know-where. This whole thing is turning into such a trip. I'm afraid to take the tape out to finish logging it. I know I should make some more copies, but I feel like I should hire a Brink's truck just to take it out to get it copied."

"Take Styles with you," I suggested, "as soon as she's gotten her beauty sleep."

Faye laughed at this image of Styles, who was probably at this moment lying on a couch in her army fatigues with Waldo snoring on her stomach.

"Okay, Gilda, I'm chilling," she said. "The thing to do is, like, kick it and stay alert at the same time."

"I wouldn't know about that," I said. "But if it means we should take another look at the tape, I'm all for it."

12

I was outside having a cigarette during the second show that night when a sporty red Camaro pulled up to the curb, and a young man got out. I assumed he was headed for the bar across the street, but he made for the door of the Paradise. His step was jaunty, and he was whistling. I crushed my half-smoked cigarette under my heel and hurried inside.

I saw his back stiffen in surprise when he saw the lava lamps on the ticket counter. He looked around and his gaze swept the antiwar posters on the walls, the black light on the concession stand, and Sandy, wearing a miniskirt and platform shoes, crouching to wash the glass that fronted the concessions. Most theaters didn't go in for this kind of theme decor. But then, most theaters didn't have a set designer in the family.

"Can I help you?" I said to his back.

He turned with a smile and presented me with a pair of stunning blue eyes. He was on the short and stocky side, and muscular. He wore his blond hair neatly cut, and as the niece of a hairdresser I knew enough to guess that it was the work of a stylist rather than that of the corner barber. His eyes took in my tie-dyed T-shirt—my only concession to Adele's vision.

"I'm looking for Faye," he said genially. "Is she working tonight?"

"Who wants to know?" I asked, my suspicions aroused. I wasn't sure what a "hottie" was, but I had a feeling I was looking at one.

"My name's Hank," he said. "Hank Mann." He held out a

hand like an October politician. "I'm a sportscaster at Channel Ten. I went to see her today about her work."

I put my hand limply in his and let it lie there like a sweaty sock.

"You're the guy who stole her tape," I said evenly.

He drew his hands back in mock protest, but not until after he'd given my hand an intimate squeeze.

"I didn't!" he exclaimed, still smiling. "Honest! That's what I told her when she called, and it's the truth. But the more I got to thinking about it, the more concerned I got. Has she found it yet?"

"No," I said flatly. "Have you?"

"Not me," he insisted. "I'd know it if I walked out of there with a tape under my coat."

"Maybe you got it mixed up with some station footage," I proposed, offering him an opportunity to come clean.

"No way that could happen," he said. "I didn't take anything in with me when I went to Faye's, except my notebook. I really like her project. I wouldn't want to see it sabotaged. That's why I thought maybe I should offer to help recover the tape. I don't appreciate being cast in the role of chief suspect."

He seemed sincere. But I came from an acting family, so to me, sincerity was just another role.

"You're good," I conceded.

He threw up his arms in exasperation, but he was still showing his television teeth.

"Look, maybe I should just talk to Faye," he said.

You just want to remind her what big blue eyes you have, I thought cynically.

He didn't seem Faye's type, but then I was usually wrong about things like that. After all, I had thought that I was Liz's type, but she'd run off with a woman who rode dirt bikes on weekends and waited tables in a pizza parlor during the week.

"You don't need to talk to Faye." This was Duke, in his quiet but authoritarian voice—John Wayne without the boots and the stutter-step delivery. As a matter of fact, he was also wearing a tie-dyed T-shirt, this one featuring the Grateful Dead. He'd just come out of the projection booth, and he stood behind me in the lobby.

"Yeah, Faye's on to you, scumbag." This was Todd, similarly costumed, rounding the concession stand. "So why don't you just get lost?"

Sandy leaned against the glass she'd been washing and favored Mann with a hostile stare.

"Hey, what's going on here?" Mann asked, looking from one to the other. He opened his mouth and expelled a breath of air as he shook his head. "I thought Faye was just making a movie. Now I'm beginning to suspect she's CIA or something. Am I close?"

We did look like some kind of weird gang, a belligerent tie-dyed band of desperadoes who might off anyone who dared to wear black or white.

"Hank Mann!" Faye exclaimed in a surprised voice. She'd just descended from the balcony projection booth. She was wearing a red-and-black T-shirt that read IT'S TEN O'CLOCK: DO YOU KNOW WHERE YOUR MARINES ARE? She admitted it was slightly anachronistic, but her Woodstock T-shirt, featuring Janis Joplin, was in the wash. "What are *you* doing here? Did you bring back my tape?"

"I don't have your tape, Faye!" he said in a voice of exaggerated patience. "I'd swear on my mother's grave, but she's not dead. I don't know how else to convince you except to offer to help you find it."

"It's not lost, turd," Todd said. "It's been stolen."

"That's right," Faye reiterated. "We know where it is."

"Faye, be reasonable!" he pleaded. "Why would anybody want to steal your tape? Is there something you're not telling me?"

"Is there something you're not telling *me*?" she shot back.

"Look, Faye," I interjected. "I think you should take Hank up on his offer."

"I should?" she asked incredulously.

"Well, sure, why not? Maybe he can offer some insight into why anybody would take it in the first place," I pointed out.

"Well, I don't know about that," Hank said, and smiled at me gratefully. "I don't know why anybody would take it, except as a joke. But I'll help you recover it, Faye, if you want me to. I'd be glad to. Maybe I can clear myself."

Faye was frowning at me, puzzled.

"I'll have to think about it," she said.

"Will you call me tomorrow?" he asked. "I assume you still have my card."

"Yeah, sure," she said. "I'll give you a call."

"Great!" He beamed at her. "I'll be getting along, then." He smiled at all of us to show there were no hard feelings on his part. " 'Night, everybody."

"Peace," I said, and flashed him a V. He hesitated long enough to count the fingers, nodded, and left.

"Yeah, I'll call," Faye muttered, as the door shut behind him. "And I hope he holds his breath until I do." She whirled on me. "Gilda, what were you thinking?"

"Use your head, Faye," I told her. "You have two leads on this tape business, and he's one of them. Either he and Charley Drake lead to the same person, or they don't, but you won't find out if you're not speaking to him."

"Don't forget the mystery woman who shot Styles's dad," Duke put in. "She's in it, too."

"Sure, they could all be working for the same person, or they could all represent different interests," I said. "They at least represent different approaches. But I don't think you're going to be safe until you figure out what those interests are, and do something to resolve the situation—unless you want to just sell the tape to Drake and forget about it."

"No way," Faye said, hands on her hips. Her muscles flexed, and roused Wonder Woman.

"Yeah," Todd said, "and anybody who tries to break in here and steal that tape will have to come through me and Duke to get it."

Duke nodded.

"Me, too," Sandy said, and she brandished her squirt bottle of Windex as if it were a semiautomatic.

I gazed at them and Tiomkin's theme music for *The Alamo* swelled in my head. Maybe I should get bulletproof glass installed in the doors, I thought.

"So, what did you have in mind, Gilda?" Faye asked. "How am I supposed to weasel all this information out of Hank? Seduce him?"

Duke and Todd looked horrified, but I thought Faye looked a bit eager.

"I wouldn't rush into anything, though that's always a possibility," I said. "First, I think it's time we all had another look at that tape. By 'all,' I mean anybody and everybody you can think of who might have some insight into what's going on—everybody except Hank Mann. Hank's a sportscaster, so you'd better make sure some of your basketball player friends are there, in case that's relevant. Charley Drake's in computer database development, which seems less likely to be relevant, but you never know. Duke knows computers, so he should be there."

Duke frowned. "When can we do this, Gilda?"

What he meant was, we had a theater to run, and the weekend was upon us.

I sighed.

"Late Sunday morning?" I suggested.

"Won't people have church?" Faye asked.

"Tell them to go to the early service," I said. "We could use God on our side, so we don't want to piss Her off. Say, eleven o'clock, at Clara's? We could watch it on Grosvenor's video projection machine." This was one of the many gadgets my late uncle couldn't live without and couldn't take with him when he died.

"Too bad Jake's still in the hospital," I mused. "I think we should arrange to show him the tape, too, so that he can tell us if his mystery woman is on it."

"Will you ask Styles to come?" Faye asked.

"Yeah," I said. "She's mouthy, but she's got a good eye. And she's suspicious by nature, so she's not blinded by any prejudices regarding the fundamental goodness of humankind."

"Yeah," Duke said. "If Styles had been in the Garden of Eden, she would've skinned that snake for boots and cooked him for supper."

13

Faye went home at midnight and watched her apartment complex burn down.

My mother called the theater shortly after midnight and asked for Faye. When she learned Faye had already gone home, she broke the news. She and my father had spotted the fire on the way home from a dance program.

The night sky glowed over Eden. I could smell the primitive, familiar odor of burning wood as soon as I stepped out the door. I was on the scene by twelve-thirty. The perimeter of the complex was crawling with firefighters, and hoses crisscrossed the ground like tributaries on a topographical map. Tall fountains of water arced into the fiery core. The Eden cops were on crowd control, but most of the onlookers stood well back. Off to one side the shapes of satellite dishes mounted on vans stood out against the dull glow. The fire roared and snapped. As I approached, I heard a loud pop, then the sound of glass hitting pavement. The air was heavy with smoke.

The first person I spotted in the eerie illumination provided by fire department floodlights, television lights, and two-story flames was Styles. She ambled over.

"Business has been booming at the Eden Fire Department ever since you moved back to town, cookie," she observed.

I cut my eyes at her. "This," I said, "is not my fault. For that matter, neither was the other incident to which you are referring."

"Didn't say it was," she said. "Just making an observation."

I fumbled for a cigarette and lighter.

"Don't get too close with that thing," Styles said, eyeing the lighter. "They'll turn the hose on you."

"Styles," I said, "we don't think this is a coincidence, do we?"

I knew that she wouldn't be standing here if she did.

"They didn't succeed in stealing the tape," I continued, "so they're trying to destroy it."

"You'd better hope they don't find out where it is," she said, "or you'll be out of a job."

I looked at her.

"Duke sleeps most nights in the theater," I said.

"Is there a fire escape?"

"At the back," I said. "He sleeps at the front."

"He'd better sleep with a fire extinguisher," she said, "and one of those portable fire escape ladders."

"Did everyone get out of Faye's building okay?" I asked, turning anxiously to scan the scene.

"Far as I know," she said. "Your family's having a reunion in the parking lot, by the way." She nodded in that direction.

"Good," I said, breathing out a puff of smoke. "Let me have another cigarette in peace before I join them. Unless you're worried about secondhand smoke," I added, as a breeze blew smoke in our direction.

She flapped a hand in front of her face and coughed.

"The interesting thing about this," she said as the coughing subsided, "is that if it's what we think it is, it means somebody's content just to destroy the tape."

"You mean, as opposed to having the tape as evidence of something," I agreed. "Which also implies somebody else— a second party—would want the tape as evidence of something, don't you think?"

She nodded, took the cigarette from my hand, and put it to her lips.

"Whether or not the second party knows about the tape yet," she said, letting out a breath of smoke and passing the cigarette back to me.

"Oh, they must know, don't you think?" I asked, flinching as another part of the building caved in. "There are too many people involved already, aren't there? And they don't seem the same type." I counted on my fingers. "A burglar, a thief, an armed assailant, and an arsonist."

"Meaning some are packing guns, and some gasoline? Maybe what we have is one equal opportunity employer."

I noticed her eyes were constantly scanning the scene, and I followed her gaze. Was someone hanging around to make sure Faye's apartment was thoroughly destroyed? Whom should we suspect? The middle-aged couple eating ice cream cones? The guy in high-tops and a baseball cap, with a retriever on a leash? Someone in the crowd of teenagers who'd been told by the police to turn their boom box down? The family group sitting in the vintage convertible, watching the fire as if they were at the drive-in?

"Well, some aren't packing anything," I pointed out, "as far as we know, except cash."

"As far as we know," she repeated.

"Have you found out anything about Charley Drake of Alban, Gray?"

"Haven't had time."

"Did you get any more information out of your dad about his good-looking client? How is he, by the way?" I added the last a bit guiltily.

"Well enough to be either getting on the nurses' nerves or seducing them," she said. "About his client, he says that she reminded him of Madonna in *Evita*—a slick, polished blonde, could have been a model."

"Did he tell you if he made a pass at her?"

"We don't discuss my father's sex life, if I can avoid it," she said wryly.

I surveyed the crowd again. "I don't see anybody like that around here, do you?"

"Who knows what she looks like on an off day?" Styles grumbled. "But we should walk around and look."

I dropped my cigarette, and we started for the parking lot.

My relatives accounted for a good third of the crowd on hand.

Faye was standing with my cousin Clyde, who was an Eden city cop. He held his baby daughter, Harpo, asleep in his arms. His nephew, Groucho, dressed in diapers and a shirt, wobbled at Faye's feet, fists clenched around her index fingers. Groucho's twin sister Chico apparently had enough sense not to chase fire engines. Harpo's prospective sibling Zeppo, who would be the youngest in the pack, hadn't yet put in an appearance, and his mother Lisa was on bed rest until delivery.

Faye saw me, pointed me out to the baby, and they started in my direction, the baby rolling forward on curled toes. We met them halfway, and I swept Groucho off his awkward little feet. He rewarded me with a squeal of delight and a gummy poke in the eye.

"Can you believe this, Gilda?" Faye turned and swept the burning building with a dramatic gesture. The firefighters seemed to be getting the fire under control. "I mean, I feel like Typhoid Mary or something—or like Mrs. O'Leary's cow. I can't believe everything's so jacked up! I keep thinking how lucky I am that all my equipment and tapes and stuff are—" She glanced around uneasily, alarmed at the way her own voice carried. "Well, you know. But some of my neighbors are losing everything! It sucks!"

"Yeah," I said sympathetically. Groucho had discovered my earrings and was yanking on them to see if they were attached. They were, but I was less confident about my ears. "I'm really sorry, Faye."

"I mean, I guess I knew they were serious when they shot Jake." She glanced at Styles, who was still studying the crowd. "But then, Styles said that could've been Jake's fault, so I was, like, you know, maybe it wasn't really that dangerous. But I guess they're pretty desperate!"

"They're running out of time," Styles said, "and they know it."

"What do you mean?" Faye asked. "Time for what?"

Styles shrugged. "They know videos can be copied. It's been almost a week since they saw whatever they saw on the TV news. They must have hoped that nobody else saw it. By now, they've probably figured out that somebody did. So by burning down your place, they're hoping they took care of everything—not just the originals, but any copies you might have made." Styles spoke in a low voice.

"So does that mean I'll be left alone now?"

"Depends," Styles said. "Whoever did this ought to leave you alone, unless they find out that the tapes weren't here. But what's-his-face has a copy—"

"Hank Mann," Faye prompted. "At least, we think he does."

"Yeah, Hank, so they could go after him next, if they find out about that copy. And then there's Charley Drake. You told him the tape had been stolen. Maybe they'll figure out you told him that before Hank Mann boosted the tape, chances are they won't. If they do, they'll go looking for the blonde, or Jake, or both. In any case, you're in the clear as long as they don't find out about your stash."

"But which 'they' are we talking about here, Styles?" I said crossly. Groucho had mangled, stretched, dented, and bruised every vulnerable feature on my head and was now working on pulling my hair out. My eyes were smarting from more than the smoke, and I'd overtaxed my lungs. "And how many 'theys' are there? Jesus, the ones we've got all sound like they were named by the same agent! Hank Mann. Charley Drake."

"Hard to know at this point," she said. "I've got to do some background checking on Mann and Drake."

"At least the police will take more of an interest now," Faye said. "They'll want the guy who did this." She nodded at the building, which was now a smoldering ruin.

Styles surprised us both by laughing.

"Sweetheart, if you think the cops are going to buy a connection between this fire and a missing videotape, you've been watching too much television," she said.

"Well, well, why wouldn't they?" Faye sputtered. "If it's arson—"

"Cookie, there are plenty of motives for arson," Styles said. "Melting somebody's video collection is not high on the list."

"But if we tell them about Jake—"

Styles shook her head.

"Babe, allow me to point out that you come from a wacky family with a certain reputation among Eden cops," she said. "Ask Clyde if you don't believe me. This whole story sounds nuts to me, and I'm on your side. Coming from a Liberty, it sounds like a movie pitch or a publicity stunt. If we start babbling about a deadly blonde who looks like Madonna, they're going to think your aunt Adele designed the set and your aunt Gloria did the hair and your uncle Wallace wrote the script."

I had to admit she was right.

"Nor is your family a stranger to criminal tendencies," she continued, "arson among them. Which means, if I were you, I wouldn't be calling attention to myself during an arson investigation."

Faye opened her mouth to protest, but nothing came out.

"So where do we go from here?" I asked, shifting Groucho to my other hip so he could continue his depilatory activity on the other side of my head.

"I'd like to see that video," Styles said. "And I'd like Jake to see it. And I'd like Jake to see it in my presence, so that I can watch his shifty little eyes as he watches it."

"You think his blonde will show up in it?" I asked.

"Doubtful," she said.

"If there's a TV in his room, I can bring in a Beta deck tomorrow and show him the tape," Faye volunteered quietly. "I'm borrowing another deck from Natalie tomorrow so that I can copy the tape at the theater."

She and Styles made arrangements for the next day. Styles would serve as her bodyguard while she copied the tape in the morning, and then they would take a copy to the hospital for Jake to see. We also told Styles about the showing we'd set up at Clara's on Sunday.

"Make sure everybody knows to keep their traps shut about that," Styles said, looking pointedly at me. "It's not Oscar night; make sure they understand that."

"I get the picture," I said grumpily, swinging Groucho down to ground level so that he could practice untying my shoelaces. I wasn't mad at Styles for suggesting that my family couldn't keep a secret; I was mad at her for suggesting I take responsibility for their behavior. Arnold Schwarzenegger on the set of *Kindergarten Cop* had more control than I did.

"Meanwhile, there's the moral dilemma of Hank Mann," she mused.

"You mean, whether we should, like, gang up on him and make him cough up my tape and tell us what he knows?" Faye asked eagerly.

"I had in mind the other moral dilemma," Styles replied. "The one about telling Hank Mann that your building burned down tonight."

"I don't see why," Faye protested. "Let him fend for himself, the dog!"

"Good idea," Styles agreed affably. "And when we read in the paper that somebody's offed the bastard, we say good riddance! Hey, no skin off my butt! I watch Channel Six and ESPN, anyway."

Faye sighed in exasperation.

"Okay, okay, I'll call him," she said, "but you know what Mom always says—a good deed never goes unpunished."

"Agreed," Styles said. "And you can remind me a week from now when Mann's being a pain in the ass."

"Gilda!" My mother was bearing down on me. "What are you doing with that baby?"

I looked down. Groucho lay curled up on my feet, limp as a well-loved teddy bear, sound asleep.

She swooped down on him and picked him up, settling him on her shoulder. He didn't move so much as an eyelash. No doubt he was dreaming little baby dreams in which he mauled one grown-up after another. The cheek that was showing was black with soot from the ground.

"So, does that mean I should, like, call Channel Six and warn them, too?"

Styles and I looked at Faye.

"Channel Six has a copy of the tape?" I asked.

"Well, sure," Faye said. "I mean, news stations archive all their broadcasts."

Styles and I exchanged glances.

"You have a contact there?" Styles asked.

"Just a guy I've worked with a few times," Faye said. "He's not a friend or anything. But maybe I should pass the word, huh? Tell him to be on the lookout for a blond hoochie asking about the archives."

Styles blinked. "I think you should call him and make sure the footage is still there," she said, "and suggest to him that certain parties have taken an interest in it."

Faye's mother called her at that point, and she left.

I turned back to Styles.

"Do you think there's a difference between a 'hoochie' and a 'hottie'?"

"How would I know?" Styles said. "But if I were guessing, I'd guess a 'hoochie' is what Jake would call a 'tomato,' and a 'hottie' is what we used to call a 'hunk.' "

"You don't think a hoochie can be a hottie and vice versa?"

She shot me a look.

"I just think it's kind of interesting, that's all," I said. "Meanwhile, what are you going to do to protect Jake? He may be obnoxious, but he's also defenseless."

"Don't worry about Jake," she said darkly. "I've hired a private nurse. His name is Carmine, but he goes by Spike. I'd say he's definitely not a hoochie."

14

Clara's wide suburban street looked like a flea-market parking lot. My heart sank as I tried to imagine this many people keeping a secret. Try declaring *Titanic* a closed set.

Inside, the crowd was a mix of Liberties and tall, muscular young women who cut Clara's cathedral ceilings down to size. I recognized Berta Homans from Buckeye State and her basketball buddy from Eden College among them. Faye had identified the Eden player as Lee Patrick. They loomed over a buffet table where my cousin Greer and my aunt Adele had laid out a brunch catered by their hotel, the Studio Inn. They had basketball players' hands, ideal for demolishing a buffet.

I found Natalie standing at my elbow and said the first thing that came to mind.

"They sure look taller here than they did at the mall."

This was not the most perceptive remark to make to a cinematographer, but she nodded affably.

"Where's Faye?"

"I think she's hiding in the kitchen," Natalie said. "Your uncle's embarrassing her."

"Which one?" They were all capable of it.

"The one who came up to me and asked what would happen if he pulled my gold ring," she said.

"That would be Ollie," I said. I spotted him trailing Berta Homans. Even from this distance I could see his exaggerated reaction to the food on her plate and hear him exclaim "Don't tell me! You're a growing girl!"

"Wait till my uncle Wallace gets into the spirit," I told Natalie. That wasn't the half of it. With the least encouragement, my parents would re-create the song-and-dance number from their film *Alma Mater*. I saw Gloria eyeing several players with a professional interest; any minute now she would ask if she could undo their weaves to see how the hair was plaited.

Faye was sitting at the kitchen table, head in her hands. My sister Betty was emptying ice cube trays, and she gave me an amused grin over Faye's head.

"I have one word to say to you," I said in a low voice to Faye. "Just one word. Are you listening, Faye? Celluloid."

"Oh, God!" Faye moaned. "Another comedian! I totally can't stand it! Do you know what Ollie said to Sharifa Abdul? Do you? 'How's the weather up there?' That's what he said! Then there's Grams, who's holding court by the fireplace, gossiping about all the famous men she slept with. Adele's in a snit because Grams ordered her own flowers and didn't want to use this centerpiece Adele worked hours on—this basketball wrapped in film so it looks like an atomic model. I'm serious, I can't take the jive, Gilda. It's wack! Maybe I'll just jet and you can tell me what the deal is later."

"Oh, lighten up, Faye!" Betty said, laughing. "I'm waiting for Uncle Wally to pull his vampire act. I've got a bet going with Tobias for a KO on the first bite. I want to see Berta Homans flatten him."

Faye just groaned louder.

My sister and I exchanged smiles. We'd once been as mortified by our relatives as Faye, but age gives you distance from your family, along with sore muscles and aching joints.

My uncle Val popped his head in.

"Hey, kids, want to see me create a really keen strobe effect with Clara's track lighting?" he asked.

"Hey, cool!" Betty and I said at the same time that Faye cried, "No!"

"Jeez, Faye!" he said, winking at us. "Chill! This is, like, your premiere! Or maybe it's more like a preview. Well, party on, dudes!" And he was gone.

I was just about to ask Faye about Jake when the door swung open again and Styles ambled in. She was wearing drab beige parachute pants that looked like they were made out of somebody's pup tent, a man's white undershirt, and combat boots.

"I knew I'd find you here," she said to me. "I followed the smoke."

"Nice pants," I observed. "You run out of curtains?"

"Yep," she retorted. "I'll think about getting some new ones tomorrow. Say, Faye, this is some crowd. I didn't see Bill and Hillary, though. They out of the country?"

"Count your blessings," I said, to save Faye the trouble. "The West Coast contingent couldn't make it on such short notice."

"Point taken," Styles said. "How about the Men in Black? You getting them to come do their memory-erasing thing when this is over?"

"What I want to know is what Jake said when you showed him the tape yesterday," I said. "He see anything?"

"Nope," Styles reported. "Nothing. No hoochies or hotties that he recognized, not even a blond tomato." The corners of her mouth quirked up. "He's eager to meet this Carmine, though. He has a thing, he says, for brunettes."

Eventually, however, we were called into the living room, where everybody found a place to sit, stand, perch, or sprawl in front of Clara's mammoth video projection screen. The floor was swallowed up by legs.

"The first time through," Faye instructed us, "I'm going to ask everyone to remain quiet." She looked pointedly at Uncle Ollie, who mimed locking his lips. "No matter how excited you get, please don't say anything until the second time through. That way you won't distract anybody else from something they might see. Just pay attention, and try to take in as much as possible—background, foreground, whatever. Okay? Roll 'em!"

There was a brief buzz of excitement that died down quickly. The big screen really magnified the image, and I was impressed by the clarity. For once, poor old Grosvenor's snobbery was paying off, and he wasn't around to gloat. As the tape unwound before our eyes, I heard an occasional intake of breath, and once Uncle Ollie started to say something, but it trailed off in a yelp of pain, so I gathered that somebody had pinched him. When the tape ended, conversation flared up again.

"That was very nice, Faye," Lillian proclaimed regally, as if we'd been screening rushes. "You have some very good footage there—excellent camera work and sound."

Faye looked abashed, the way Mel Gibson might if his mother had shown up at the Academy Awards and started patting him on the head.

"Anybody think they see anything?" she asked.

Several of my family members started talking at once, all pushing their pet theories.

"What about you guys?" Faye was addressing the athletes sprawled on the floor.

They looked at each other.

Berta Homans finally spoke up.

"Yeah, we think so," she said. "Run it again, and we'll show you."

Faye complied. The tape proceeded like a rural bus, stopping often while various possibilities were discussed.

About five minutes in, one of the basketball players called out, "There! Stop it there!"

The scene froze before us. The contest hadn't started yet. Little girls were primping or practicing, their mothers retying bows, patting down cowlicks, fluffing out skirts. Kids were talking to each other, hanging out. Dads, grandparents, and siblings stood or sat around in various postures of boredom.

A dark silhouette walked up to the screen. It was Lee Patrick.

"Here," she said, pointing out a figure in the background. "This guy here. He's one of the hottest prospects in the country. He's from Hilliard. Name's Mike Falcone, so they call him the Falcon. He's not the tallest kid on the court, but he's got sharp eyes, quick hands, he's fast, and he's deadly."

The young man in question was sandy-haired, on the stocky side, and muscular, tall enough to stand out but more of a Magic Johnson than a Michael Jordan. He wore nondescript jeans and a T-shirt, but I noticed that his high-tops would fit Godzilla.

"He gettin' the kind of press Larry Bird got," somebody said from the players' section. "You know, 'Great White Hope' and all."

"Yeah, he the exception that prove the rule," somebody else said. " 'White men can't jump.' "

We heard the slap of hands from a high five.

"Are you sure that's him?" a player asked. "I didn't see him there."

"I didn't, either," Lee said, "but it's him, all right. My brother played him in the state semis last year. You get a better look at him a little bit later."

"But isn't that Smilin' Sid Green he's sitting next to?" I recognized Betty's voice.

The man seated next to Falcone was heavyset and bald on top, as if somebody had run a mower across his skull from the bridge of his nose. He wore a plaid sports coat.

"Hey, yeah! You're right!" This from the players' section.

There was a general murmur of assent, and everyone in the room tipped forward to scrutinize the image.

"What's he doing talking to Smilin' Sid?" a player asked.

"What you think he's doin', dipstick?" another replied.

"Well, I don't think he's buying a car at the shopping mall!" the questioner said, offended. Then she said, "Oh!"

"Uh-huh."

"He doesn't need to *buy* a car."

Another voice made an explosive sound of disgust. When it spoke, I recognized it as Berta Homans's.

"No, he don't need to *buy* no car. If you the Falcon, you don't need to *buy* nothin'! All you got to do is make your wishes known and shit materializes—like you had a genie in your hip pocket."

"But that's against NCAA rules," Uncle Wallace said sternly.

Berta gave another derisive snort. "Rules are made to be broken, don't you know that? If anybody comes around, askin' 'bout his new car, he going to have the paperwork. Don't worry about that. He going to produce a lease to prove he's payin' for the vehicle. Maybe he's payin' a dollar, or maybe he's a big spender and he's payin' five whole dollars, but if the NCAA comes after him, the lawyers'll get involved, and the Falcon be playin' in the NBA by the time they work it all out."

"Maybe they don't know each other," Gloria said. "Maybe they just happened to sit on the same bench."

Nobody said anything to that.

"Let's keep going," Faye said, and hit the pause button again.

If the two men were strangers, they must have hit upon a fascinating conversation topic. Mike Falcone, like many teen-aged males, didn't make eye contact with Sid Green as they spoke. He scanned his surroundings instead. But Green had a lot to say, and Falcone reacted with nods, frowns, and occasional subdued gestures. From time to time he made his own speeches, unsmiling. Once a young girl who had the same hair color as Falcone interrupted them to drop a canvas bag at Falcone's feet. He tucked it under his long legs and nodded at her. She was wearing a short full skirt, and when she turned around she gave us the benefit of a T-shirt studded with sequins.

"Looks like his sister's in the contest," somebody observed.

The arrival of the judges partially obscured our view of the two men on the bench. The camera captured a certain amount of ceremonial handshaking and chitchat at the judges' table, and then swung toward the stage for the contest.

We didn't see Falcone and Green again. The sister, if it was his sister, made an athletic but ungraceful cheerleader. We discussed other possibilities as they passed before our eyes, but many of the Liberties had withdrawn their candidates and gone over to the Falcone and Green camp.

My father wasn't completely convinced.

"How big a deal would it be if State were caught violating one of these rules?" he asked doubtfully. "Especially if there's paperwork to suggest a legal transaction."

"Okay, maybe we'd better explain that there's two things going on here," Lee said. "First, we're guessing he's been offered a car to sign with State."

"We're jumping to conclusions," my father said, "but okay, continue."

"Second, the whole contact is illegal."

"Because?"

"Only coaches are allowed to contact you for recruiting purposes," Lee explained, "and then only after July first. This is May. See, Falcone is just finishing his junior year; he's got a year to go. They're not allowed to send alums and boosters and other athletes to recruit you."

"But there's ways around that too, Lee," another player pointed out. "The rule doesn't apply to regular admissions recruiting, so all's a school has to do is say that this alum or whoever is part of the regular recruiting process."

"Yeah," Berta Homans put in. "It just so happens they got more car dealers and realtors contacting athletes than computer programmers and funeral directors. Go figure."

"Is that what happened to you, Berta?" my mother asked curiously. "Is that how you ended up at State?"

She laughed. "If you saw what I drive, you wouldn't ask that question. No, we talkin' here about the kind of perks they mostly keep for the boys. Not that I'm complaining—I got a full ride."

"I bet Sid Green wouldn't know what to say to a woman athlete," somebody said.

"He want to practice, he can practice on me," someone else retorted. "All he got to say is 'Porsche' and 'What color would you like?' "

This was greeted with laughter and the sounds of high fives.

"Can we run the first part of the tape again?" I asked. "I'd like to see the point where we first see Green and Falcone."

This time through it was my nephew Oz who spotted what appeared to be the initial encounter. Falcone, followed by his sister, found Green in the crowd, and the two men shook hands. Green gestured toward the bench.

"I can't see that!" Gloria protested, and turned to Ollie. "Can you see that?"

I couldn't see it that well myself.

"It looks pretty deliberate," Clara said, "but it's hard to tell. Too bad the figures are so blurry in the first few minutes."

"I was shooting telephoto," Natalie remarked. "And I wasn't shooting them, I was shooting the girls in the foreground."

"Well, that should be enough for today, anyway," Faye said. "You've given us something to think about. Thanks, everybody! If you think of anything later on, just give me a call."

Adele hopped up. "Dessert!" she announced brightly.

I found Styles doing a stretch with her arms extended behind her back.

"So, what do you think?"

She bent forward as if to pull her shoulders out of her sockets and gave me the benefit of a high-angle view of her dark curls. "I think your dad's smarter than the rest of your family put together." She straightened up. "Oh, you mean about the tape? I'm inclined to agree with your dad. I don't see anything there yet worth burning down a building for. I'm not taking the shooting into account right now, since I'm willing to entertain the possibility of a justifiable homicide attempt on that one."

"It's not hard to burn down a building, really," I said.

"It's hard to do it right," she countered.

"Okay, but lots of criminals do it, don't they? Not just buildings, but bodies, cars—whatever they're trying to cover up. And don't tell me fires don't destroy as much evidence as people might think they do. I know all about high-tech lab testing of trace evidence; I read *Newsweek*. But criminals panic, don't they? Even something like Faye's building—that could be a sign that whoever wants the video destroyed is in panic mode."

"Sure, but it doesn't take much thinking to realize that if you torch an apartment building at midnight, you're inviting a homicide rap. Even if the arsonist doesn't care about burning little babies in their beds—which stops more fires than we'll ever know—he has to care about a murder rap. Can you imagine a stupid recruiting violation being worth that?"

"You think it's something we've missed."

"Damned if I know," she admitted.

"So what do we do now?"

"Well, for starters, we could find out something about Hank Mann and Charley Drake," she said. "In Hank's case, I think Faye should show him the whole tape and see what he says."

"But he has his own copy," I objected. "He's already seen it. He's not going to tell us why he's interested in it, or he would have told us already, unless you think telling him a man's been shot over the damn thing will put him in a more collegial mood."

"I wouldn't bet on it."

"So what's the point? Are we going to watch for his pupils to dilate at the crucial moment?"

"No, but I'm interested in whether he'll identify Falcone or not," she said.

"You think Lee's wrong?"

"No," she said. "But if a local sportscaster won't tell us that he spotted the hottest recruit in college basketball, that will tell us something. If he does identify Falcone, then we might be back to square one. This whole business might or might not be about Falcone, we won't necessarily know. But if he doesn't, we'll know it is, right?"

I crossed my eyes at her.

"I also think Faye should contact Drake," she continued.

Out of the corner of my eye, I saw Ollie headed in our direction.

"Come on," I said, steering Styles by the elbow. "Let's go outside. I need a cigarette."

I closed the door on my family and lit a cigarette. Styles perched on one of Clara's ornamental pansy-filled urns, looking as incongruous as Rambo in Wonderland.

"So you think Faye should contact Drake," I prompted her. "And say what?"

"I don't know," she said slowly, "I have to think about it. Maybe she should just say that she got the tape back and is ready to sell. See what he says."

"Do you think he'll go for it?" I asked doubtfully.

"Again, it's a question of how much he knows about what's going on, and how much he's willing to let us know about how much he knows," Styles said. "It would be interesting to see what he has to say. It would certainly be remunerative if Faye can arrange to sell him a copy. A thousand clams is a lot of dough."

There was a surge of crowd noise as the door opened behind us.

"It would certainly be unfortunate if Faye got shot while handing the tape over to Mr. Drake," I pointed out.

"Great publicity for her film, though."

I grunted.

"I also want to know if Channel Six still has their copy," she said.

I felt something on my leg and looked down to see Groucho climbing my pants with a demonic gleam in his eye.

"And," Styles continued, "just in case I'm wrong about the Falcone thing, I think it's time we made an illegal contact of our own."

"You think Falcone's got a hoochie for a mother?" I asked, amused.

"I'm more interested in what he's got in his garage," she said.

15

"Come on, Gilda!" Faye whined. "You *promised*!"

"But what's the point?" I asked. "Styles can probably find out more about Charley Drake in five minutes on the computer than we can in five hours on a stakeout."

"Yeah, but I've never been on a stakeout," she said.

"Take it from me: They're overrated," I said. I'd heard Styles grumble about them often enough.

"But you *promised*!" she repeated, reverting to a childishness that was more Jane Withers than Shirley Temple. "You said that if I worked steady last week and last weekend, you'd go with me this afternoon to stake out Charley Drake!"

Her indignation suggested that I was paying her an allowance, not a wage.

"All right, all right!" I yielded ungraciously. "I'll go. But I'm not spending my night parked outside somebody's suburban ranch while they mow the lawn and watch prime-time television. And I've got to be back to close."

Faye picked me up in her mother's Oldsmobile.

"Look!" she said, brandishing a car phone. "If we catch him doing something illegal, we can call Styles."

"If we catch him doing something illegal," I said, "we'd better call the police." I started to say that the police had more authority than Styles, then thought better of it. Then I started to point out that Styles had other things she was working on, and that our case was a low-budget programmer compared to the big-budget megahits she was spending most of her

112

time on; we were Monogram, and she was working for Metro-Goldwyn-Mayer.

"We'll get more grief from Styles if we don't tell her what's going on," Faye said. "Check it out, Gilda: I've got a camera with telephoto and night vision in the backseat."

"This is not the French connection we're involved in here," I said crankily. "I assume you didn't pack any remote listening devices, since you didn't bring the van."

"No, but I thought about it. I'll bet Val could have rigged something up."

"Did you call your friend at Channel Six?"

"He doesn't work until, like, seven o'clock today," she said. "I'll call him later."

I put my foot down when she tried to park facing away from the modern brick building which housed Alban, Gray.

"That's how you're supposed to do it, Gilda," she insisted.

"I'm not straining my eyes by watching a stupid rearview mirror," I said, "or getting a crick in my neck from turning around. Just park across the street, will you?"

"Well, okay," she said. "But if he makes us and we get eighty-sixed or something, it'll be your fault."

Faye turned the radio on, which was okay with me. I've never had a high tolerance for boredom, and since my breakup with Liz, I'd developed a phobia about it. Whenever I sat for long periods without anything to distract me, I'd replay the soap opera of my life in the past year: the blissful ignorance, the Conversation—as I'd come to think of that Dear Jane moment when I'd been blindsided by her infidelity—the tears, the moment when she'd actually walked out, trailing three embarrassed kids. Worst of all was the moment when Paulie had turned back and flung himself into my embrace. I swallowed a lump like a boulder in my throat and looked out the side window to hide my face from Faye. Stealthily, I dug a handkerchief out of my pocket.

"Allergies?" Faye asked.

I nodded.

"It's a bad time of year," she said, "although I thought it was worse during Mae's funeral—remember? All the trees had just burst into bloom. I took these, like, industrial-strength antihistamines, and they really ragged me out."

I silently blessed the self-absorption of the young.

"Hey! Dig it! This is from Ani DiFranco's new CD!" She turned up the radio, beat percussion on the steering wheel with ringed fingers, and sang along.

I blew my nose and dabbed at the corners of my eyes.

Inconspicuous we weren't. On the other hand, nobody would ever guess we were on a stakeout.

"Check it out! Redhead with bow tie at eleven o'clock!"

She nodded at a figure carrying a briefcase. He had just emerged from the building and was headed for the lot on one side, his head down and his attention focused on his car keys.

"Killer!" Faye enthused. "He's going for his ride."

She started the car, put her left blinker on, and U-turned into the opposite curb.

When he exited the parking lot in a sparkling white Lexus, Faye was on his tail.

"A Lexus," she observed. "Dude's got a lot of K, huh, Gilda?"

"Either that or a relative in the car business." I said it without thinking.

Faye shot me a glance.

"What kind of dealership does Sid Green own?" she asked.

I thought a minute. I almost never watched television, making me the least qualified member of my family to answer that question.

"He owns several," I said at last. "I think Lexus could be one of them."

She handed me the phone.

"Call Betty and ask her," she said.

"Just because the guy drives a Lexus?" I asked. "Faye, I don't think—"

"Just call her," she insisted. "It's not just any Lexus. It's *this* Lexus."

I saw her point. The Lexus we were following was pristine—not a scratch or bird dropping marred its gleaming surface, even though he obviously parked it outside every day. It takes a special kind of arrogance, stupidity, or willed oblivion to drive a white luxury car, unless you're wealthy enough to afford a daily car wash. Or unless you have a generous relative who is a car dealer willing to give you access to a daily car wash.

I called Betty.

"That's an affirmative," I reported. "Smilin' Sid owns the Lexus dealership in Dublin."

"I can't believe it, Gilda! Look, the guy's going to Spagio."

Drake had turned into the parking lot of one of the hippest restaurants in Columbus.

"Good," I said. "I'm hungry. Let's go stake out dinner."

"I'll bet he's going to the meat market."

"Say what?"

"The bar," she explained. "I'll bet he's going to hang out in the bar. Hey, I thought you lived in Columbus! How can you be that clueless? The bar at Spagio is where rich dudes go to pick up women."

"I'm not exactly up on the swinging singles scene," I retorted.

"This is way cool, Gilda," Faye said excitedly. She parked the car, flipped the visor down, and began surveying her face in the mirror. She applied lipstick.

"Faye," I said cautiously, "I don't think you're his type."

"No," she agreed complacently, "but I can be."

She unclipped her nose ring, and stripped down to a bare minimum of jewelry. She handed me a fistful of rings, earrings, and chains.

"Here, hold onto these."

The jewelry was so heavy in my hand, I wondered how she could stand to wear it.

She tried to smooth down her hair. She looked at herself.

"Actually, Gilda, you're probably more his type," she said.

"Oh, right," I said. "I'll bet he really digs chubby forty-six-year-old lesbians."

"Is that how old you are?" She looked at me, surprised.

"Sean Connery is sixty-six," I countered. "Redford's pushing sixty."

She shrugged. "You're the same age as my dad," she said. "You always seemed—I don't know—like, younger. More hip. And you're not chubby."

"Thanks, kid." I decided not to point out that at her age, everybody seems more hip than your parents. My son John thought I was as hip as Lawrence Welk.

"Give me ten minutes," Faye said, opening the car door. "And then you come in, like we're supposed to be meeting there, and I'll introduce you, and—"

"No way," I said firmly. "I signed on for a stakeout, not the Dating Game. In ten minutes, I'm going in and ordering dinner. If you get hungry, you can join me. But you are not, under any circumstances, to go off with this guy on your own. For all you know, he may know what you look like, even if he acts like he doesn't. For that matter," I pointed out, "he may be meeting his wife here for dinner."

In ten minutes, I followed Faye into the restaurant. Sure enough, she had obviously inserted herself into a conversation that included Charley Drake. As I watched her, she said something to him, and he laughed. I asked the hostess to seat me outside in the sidewalk cafe so that I could keep an eye on the entrance.

My salad came and went, and then my pizza came. Spagio was the kind of place that ran to pancetta-and-goat-cheese pizzas, but I ordered the more traditional kind. Between people-watching and eating, I had plenty to distract me, so I didn't get maudlin again the way I had in the car. In fact, I sat there, sipping wine in the clear night air, a soft breeze rippling what hair Groucho had left behind, and thought that stakeouts weren't nearly as bad as they were reported to be.

I might even, I thought, take a stroll up the street after dinner and check out my competition. Not that I thought of the Drexel as competition for a theater located in a small town forty minutes away, but I had begun to get a vague impression that they thought of themselves that way. I'd occasionally and inexplicably lost a bid for a popular foreign or art film, only to hear Duke muttering imprecations against the Drexel. I couldn't understand it, though. They were up the street from Spagio, for crying out loud. I was around the corner from the Hamburger Heaven.

I took a trip to the dessert case and spotted Faye, tete-a-tete with Charley. She raised her eyebrows at me and stifled a yawn, but I wasn't about to go to her rescue. I smiled benevolently at her. Take your time, I thought, surveying tortes and tarts. I'm in no hurry.

Eventually, Faye came out with Charley Drake. They stood just outside the door and chatted a moment, then Charley made a gesture, and they walked off in the direction of the parking lot.

I looked from Faye's retreating back to my raspberry cream torte, and sighed.

"Don't let anybody touch that," I said to the server. "I'll be right back."

I spotted Faye and Drake as soon as I rounded the corner into the parking lot. It was only eight o'clock, and still light enough to see clearly. He opened her car door for her, she got in, and he closed it. He waved at her, and she drove off. As she passed me, she made a circling motion with her index finger. I watched Charley climb into his white Lexus. He was already on the car phone when he passed me. I went back to my raspberry cream torte.

Faye showed up as I was scraping the plate with my fork.

"What a wanker!" she said, dropping into the chair across from me. "Check this out: He's got a dent in his left ring finger where his wedding ring goes."

I handed back a fistful of her own jewelry.

"You should talk," I said.

"But I'm not hanging out in bars, flirting with women, and pretending not to be married when I am," she said.

"You're not."

"You know what I mean."

"And you introduced yourself as . . . ?"

"Effie. Effie Perrine." She made a face. "Like I said, he's totally clueless."

"He was on the phone on the way out of the parking lot," I said. "Either he was calling his wife, or he was reporting on you to the big boss, whoever that is."

"I know who it is," Faye said, eyes dancing. To the waitress, she said, "I want whatever it was that she had." She pointed at my plate, which sported a few crumbs and a bright red smear. "Raspberry something, from the looks of it. And whatever she's drinking. Fifteen minutes from now, I want to look as happy as she looks."

"Okay, so give," I said. "Who's the big boss?"

"His father-in-law," she said, leaning closer. "Smiling Sid Green."

"I thought he didn't have a father-in-law," I said.

She looked smug. "It wasn't easy to worm that out of him. But I got him to talk about cars, and then played on his ego until he couldn't stand not telling me who his father-in-law was. 'Course, he's separated from his wife."

I nodded. "Since about eight-thirty this morning," I guessed. "She probably doesn't understand him, either."

She giggled. "Gilda, that's so tired! No, what he said was that she had her own interests, and they had, like, fallen out of love, and decided to go their own ways."

"I don't suppose you asked him if he was interested in videotapes of local sports-related competitions involving young girls."

"Uh-uh," she said.

She polished off her cake and wine, and we returned to the car. She reached for the car phone as she was backing out. "I'm so psyched!" she said. "Wait'll Styles hears this!"

"I'll dial," I said, withdrawing the phone from her reach. "What's the number?"

"Card's on the dash," she said. "This is the bomb, Gilda! It's one of the reasons I like doing documentary video—it's a lot like investigative reporting, you know?"

I handed her the phone.

"Styles? Are you there? Styles, it's me, Faye. Pick up if you're there." She made a face. "She's not—oh, Styles? You're there. Check this out, Styles! Me and Gilda have been staking out Charley Drake, and guess who he's related to!"

To say that her face fell would be an understatement.

"Yeah, that's right. How'd you find out?" She listened a minute, then said, "Oh. Well, it's significant, don't you think? I mean—"

She broke off and listened.

"No, I haven't called him yet. Yeah, okay, I'll call as soon as I hang up. Yeah, I'll let you know what he says." She glanced up at me. "She's right here." She held out the phone to me.

"I don't approve of these things," I grumbled, half to her and half to Styles. "Either you talk on the phone or you drive. Green light, Faye. I'm sure they cause accidents."

"So does lighting cigarettes, babe," Styles pointed out in my ear. "Listen, Gilda, I have to go out of town for a few days on a case. You and Faye be careful, okay? If someone starts shooting, duck. If they burn the building you're standing in, duck—the air's cleaner close to the floor. And try not to screw things up. Oh, yeah, Jake gave me this weeping fig tree and this other plant, I don't know what it is. Could you stop by my office in the next day or two and see if they need water? It's on your way to the theater."

"You don't want me to screw things up, but you want me to take care of your plants?" I asked. "Why don't you just hand me a loaded gun?"

"Look, sweetheart, I'm going to kill them anyway, I just don't want them to see it coming," Styles said.

"Okay," I said, "but Styles, I, like, totally don't do plants."

There was a minute of shocked silence as we reacted to
Faye's voice coming out of my mouth.

"So how much water do I give them? Does the dirt have to
be completely dry before I water them?"

"How should I know?" Styles said irritably. "I don't do
plants, either. In fact, if you can find a good home for them
while I'm gone, I wish you would. I'll put the key through the
mail slot at the theater on my way out of town."

"Want me to check on Jake, too?"

She snorted. "He's a bit more out of your way," she said.
"Besides, I got Carmine sitting on him. So if you think you're
going to go over there and weasel out of him embarrassing
highlights from my childhood, forget it, cookie. He wasn't
there for them, anyway."

I hung up.

"How does she find this stuff out?" Faye exploded. "She
wouldn't tell me."

"Probably some database or other," I said. "It probably
wasn't nearly as much fun. Look at it this way—we ate at
Spagio, and she probably ate at Wendy's."

"Now dial Channel Six and ask for Byron Quant," Faye directed me. "Here's the number."

She handed me a business card.

"No," I said.

"What do you mean? Why not?" She looked bewildered.

"I'm not letting you make any more phone calls unless you
pull over." I hugged the phone to my chest.

"Gilda! This is a freeway!"

"My point exactly."

So she waited until we'd turned onto Highway 23 and she'd
pulled into a motel parking lot. She got through to Byron and
told him we were checking up on the tape she'd given him.

"Have you still got it?"

She listened.

"Would you check and make sure and call me back?" she
asked. "For some reason, a lot of people seem to be interested
in getting their hands on that tape since the news broadcast."

After a minute she spoke again. "Yeah, I know the general public doesn't have access to the archives. But just do me a solid and check anyway, would you?"

She hung up and handed the phone back to me.

"He doesn't have the copy I made him," she said. "They've already taped over that. But they have the newscast with the footage they used in the archives, or so he assumes. He's going to check and call me back."

The phone bleated at us just as we reached the outskirts of Eden—if a small town could be said to have "outskirts." Faye grabbed it off the dash before I could protest.

"Yeah?" Then, an octave higher, "*Yeah?* No shit!"

She sailed past our exit.

"What does that mean?" she said into the phone. "Can you find out? Yeah, yeah, okay. Okay, go for it. Later."

She handed me the phone.

"You can tell me all about it on the way to Marion," I commented.

"Oh, shit!" She hung a sudden left, and took the Big Boy parking lot on two wheels. "Sorry, Gilda!" she said, as we headed back to Eden.

"The tape isn't there," I guessed.

"No," she said. "They have this system, like a library, where if you take a tape out, you sign for it."

"Who has it?" I asked.

"The station owner."

"Uh-oh."

She scratched her head. "Do you think he's related to Sid Green, too?"

"He could be related to anybody," I said. "How good is the security system in the archives?"

"Well, Byron recognized the signature, if that's what you're asking," she said. "Of course, it could be a forgery, but Byron says that an outsider would never get past the door."

We were silent for a few minutes. Faye pulled into the theater parking lot and cut the engine.

"Okay," I said. "I think it's time for the direct approach."

"You mean, Sid Green?"

"Green or Falcone, either one," I said. "We think they're the principal players in whatever is going on. If it were my choice, I'd go see Falcone first. We know Green is involved in the attempts to get the video. We don't know that Falcone is. In fact, what's going on may not involve Falcone at all. But maybe he knows something, or saw something that day at the mall."

"I'm there," Faye said. "But do you think it'll be okay with Styles?"

"Styles just told us not to screw up," I said testily. "She didn't tell us to sit still with our hands folded."

I was damned if I was going to ask Styles's permission when she called back that night to ask about the station tape.

"Where are you?" I asked. "Vegas?" I shouted to make myself heard over the din in the background. "You sound like you're in the middle of the floor show."

"Des Moines," she said gloomily. "And yeah, there's a show going on, and it ain't Vegas. Imagine a convention of guys who own storage lockers."

I couldn't. Was this some kind of code?

"Are they Mafia?"

She snorted. "Sweetheart, if they were wise guys, we'd be in Vegas, not Des Moines."

"Hey, Sammy!" A man's voice came through loud and clear. "Come on, hurry it up! We need you for the conga line!"

Conga line? *Styles?*

"Styles, what are you wearing?" I asked curiously. I was trying to picture her in the kind of disguise that would encourage men to invite her to join a conga line and not having a lot of success.

"Well, it ain't a tutti-frutti hat, that's for damn sure," she growled. "About the tape?"

"Oh, yeah, get this," I said. "The station owner has removed it from the archives. I mean, he's checked it out, I guess. We don't know if he's planning to bring it back."

She muttered something I didn't catch.

"What did you say?"

"I said, 'Oh, shit!' " she shouted.

A man's voice said in the background, "Hey, Sammy, do you eat with that mouth?" This witticism was greeted with laughter.

Then the noise abated. I got the impression Styles had put something between her and the good-time boys.

"I don't like this at all," she said. "It means there are some heavy hitters involved in this thing."

"You mean the station owner? Should we check up on him?"

"Gilda, who has the clout to ask a station owner to remove a news tape from the station's official archives?"

"A major advertiser?"

"Possibly."

"Sid Green?"

"Possibly, but I doubt it. If an advertiser had that much power, station archives would probably be worthless. Who else?"

"I don't know, Styles," I said. "A judge maybe?"

"Who else?"

I was becoming exasperated. "I don't know, Styles! God?"

"And? Next to God?"

Next to God was Jesus, but she couldn't mean him.

"Think, Gilda! This is central Ohio!"

"Oh!" I exclaimed, light dawning. "A Buckeye State coach."

16

What a difference a day makes.

I was on my second stakeout in two days. My mood had been considerably soured by a morning showing of Kenneth Branagh's *Hamlet* to a horde of ninth graders. The kids had been relatively well behaved for ninth graders, but I wasn't accustomed to facing the world at ten o'clock in the morning anymore, and certainly not the teenaged segment of the population.

Faye was eating a single with Biggie Fries and a Biggie Drink.

"You're as bad as Jake," I said.

"I'm hungry," she insisted. "Besides, who got to eat a whole pizza last night, and who only got to eat dessert?"

"It's four in the afternoon," I pointed out. "What happened to breakfast and lunch?"

"Can't remember them," Faye mumbled through a mouthful of hamburger.

I knew I was bitter because she could eat like that and never gain a pound, whereas I couldn't eat a french fry without feeling like one of those balloon men in *Sleeper*.

We had already cruised the local high school gym, which had been taken over by drill team tryouts. We were parked in a relatively new subdivision of Hilliard, where all the houses looked like they'd been ordered out of the same mail order catalog and had just arrived last week. We were watching a blue-shingled, two-story house with a basketball hoop. There was no Lexus in the driveway, but there was a shiny late-model Jeep.

"So, assuming Falcone is home," I said. "What if he won't talk to us? He's probably been besieged by recruiters and reporters if he's that hot."

"He'll talk to me," she said confidently. I'd noticed she wasn't wearing her nose ring, and she'd left about ten pounds worth of jewelry at home. She was dressed conservatively, in a pair of jeans and a USC Film School T-shirt. The jeans were blue, and I realized that her hair was a duller shade of red than I remembered, and smoother.

"If this whole business is about a recruiting violation, who do we think is involved?" I asked speculatively, gazing out the window as the wind picked up and began tossing the trees around.

"Besides Sid Green, you mean?"

"And why is Sid involved?" I said. "Okay, he embarrassed himself by getting caught on camera making an illegal contact and probably an illegal offer of a car in exchange for a signed letter of intent down the road. But if Berta's right, the deal will be covered by a lease agreement, and it must take more than one recruiting violation involving one isolated alum for a school to be sanctioned by the NCAA. I suppose the kid could be sanctioned, but this whole thing seems bigger than that, with too many people involved, don't you think?"

"I don't know enough about NCAA rules, Gilda," Faye admitted.

"Me neither," I said. "If the coach or the school knew about the contact and set it up, that might be worse, but who could prove a thing like that? So, okay, maybe a thousand dollars isn't a lot of money to a Lexus dealer, and it would be worth that to Green to suppress the tape and get back on Coach Hale's Christmas card list."

"Or maybe State doesn't want an investigation because the NCAA would find more recruiting violations," Faye suggested.

"That's possible, even probable, given what Berta and Lee have told us. But meanwhile, Green's stock goes up in the Columbus community because three-fourths of the population bleeds scarlet and black, and they don't see anything wrong with a car dealer bribing players with free cars, as long as it gets their beloved Groundhogs to the Final Four. Green becomes a hero. So what's he worried about? That tape could be the best public relations gimmick to come down the pike."

She looked at me thoughtfully. "A minute ago you asked who's involved besides Sid Green."

"Well, unless Sid has a multiple personality, he doesn't seem to be behind all the attempts to get hold of or destroy the tape, does he?" I said. "Sid, through Charley Drake, offered to buy the tape. Now, that could have been his fallback position after Jake didn't come through for him, but do we really think he moved on to arson after that? And what's Hank Mann's role in all this?"

"Hank's a sportscaster," Faye said. "Maybe he's out for a story—you know, he could break the story about State's recruiting violations."

"If he breaks that story, he'll be out of a job," I pointed out.

"Yeah, but maybe he's got his sights set on something bigger than Columbus," Faye said. "Like CNN or something. It would really boost his rep if he broke this story. Maybe it's something he's been working on for awhile, and the tape is just additional evidence."

"You could be right," I conceded. "One measly alum contact doesn't seem big enough to build a career on."

"Well, who else?"

I gazed out the window. The street action was picking up—more kids home from school and out riding bikes, playing hopscotch, doing what kids do, more dogs liberated from solitary confinement to play with the kids.

"If this is about basketball rivalry—" I speculated.

"Don't tell me," Faye groaned. "Are we putting the whole NCAA on our list of suspects, or just Division One?"

"Maybe not even that many," I said. "Maybe we're just

talking about likely candidates for the tournament, or even the Sweet Sixteen. Or maybe we should only be looking at the Big Ten. You should talk to Lee and Berta, see what they say."

"For real?" Faye said. "Gilda, are you seriously suggesting that John Thompson or Bobby Knight or Lou Henson would shoot somebody to eliminate State from the playoffs? Or that State would burn down an apartment building to cover up one recruiting violation? That's totally wacked!" She shook her head. "You've been living at Liberty House too long."

I sighed. "You've got that right."

"Come on," Faye said, opening the car door. "Let's see if we can find out if Falcone knows anything."

This time I went with her. I didn't like the idea of her walking alone into a private home with gun-toting assailants and arsonists on the loose. I doubted that Jake's good-looking blond assailant was Mike Falcone's mother, but you never knew. Once mothers start killing over cheerleading rivalries, anything can happen.

The Falcon answered the door. He looked just like the picture from *Sports Illustrated* that Lee had dug up for us. He was a healthy-looking blond, with a sharp, prominent nose that suited his raptorial nickname. The nose seemed to exercise a magnetic force that pulled his brown eyes toward it, making him appear slightly cross-eyed. In one large hand he held a hunk of chocolate cake.

"Mike, I'm Faye McCadden," Faye said, and stuck out her hand insistently. She'd adjusted for the cake hand, I noticed, so he let go of the door and shook with the other one. I also noted that she could shift out of her youthful dialect when she wanted to and project a mature professional persona. "And this is my cousin, Gilda Liberty. I'm an independent film-maker, and I was shooting some footage at a cheerleading contest at Northstar Mall Saturday before last. Maybe you heard that I caught you on video?"

His face registered mild surprise, nothing more.

"Hey, no kidding? Come on in," he said easily, and stepped back to let us enter.

I could hear laughter and shouting coming from another part of the house. A particularly loud burst made him turn his head.

"My homeys," he said, waving the cake in the direction of the noise. "They're trippin' on my Sony PlayStation."

"You've got PlayStation?" Faye asked, as if impressed. Well, maybe she *was* impressed. I didn't know what they were talking about. "Cool!"

We followed him into a tastefully furnished living room done in pale greens and blues. It was so nice, in fact, that my mother would have cut my arm off if I'd carried chocolate cake into it when I was Falcone's age. Maybe the fact that he could slam dunk his mother cut him more slack than I'd had, though.

He stood. We stood. Having extended his hospitality this far, he'd either used up all his politeness or was reluctant to encourage any further intimacy.

"I'd offer you some cake," he said, grinning roguishly at Faye, "but I'm about to finish it."

With that, he shoved the remainder in his mouth and licked his fingers. I flinched as a shower of dark crumbs hit the carpet and spotted the telltale trail that led to the kitchen.

"So you were at the contest, huh? Did you film my sister?"

"Possibly," Faye said. "Was she wearing a sequined T-shirt?"

"That was her," he said, as if his sister had been the only girl at the contest who was wearing such an outfit. "That girl can really shake her butt. She's got some bad moves. They tied for third in her division, her and her friends."

Faye nodded. "I got a lot of nice footage of the contest," she said. "Plus, we filmed the demo, too, and some interviews afterward."

"Yeah? That demo really rocked," he said approvingly. "Those girls kicked some butt, huh? My sister was freakin'. She thinks Berta Homans is the bomb!"

"Yeah, well, Berta suggested I come talk to you about the video I shot that day," Faye said, which wasn't entirely accurate, but close. "See, they showed some of my footage on the news that night."

"Hey! My sister saw it! She was bummed she wasn't in it, though. I think she said you could see her elbow in one shot."

"The thing is, ever since that video got shown on the news, I've been having trouble," Faye continued. "Several people seem to be, like, after a copy of this tape, and I can't figure out why."

"No kidding?" he said, and turned his head toward another swell of sound from down the hall. "That sucks." He didn't seem concerned that we were being overheard, he just seemed distracted. He was missing all the fun.

"You met Sid Green that day," I said abruptly, playing bad cop. "You sat and talked to him—that meeting shows up on the tape. What we're wondering is whether he made you an offer—whether he offered you a bribe to go to Buckeye State. Maybe a car, maybe money. We're wondering if what we have is a tape of a recruiting violation."

That gained us his undivided attention.

"A what? A recruiting violation? What are you talking about?"

"Why did he arrange to meet you there?"

"We didn't arrange nothin'," he said emphatically. "I was there with my sister. I recognized the dude, he recognized me. I said, 'Hey, you're the guy on television!' And he recognized me 'cause he saw me play in the state championships last year. I was waiting on my sister, and he was just hanging out, so we sat down and talked. Sure, we talked about cars, and I asked him some stuff, but it wasn't a recruiting contact or nothin' like that. Anyway, what do I need a car for? I got my Jeep. There's guys around here that would kill for a ride like that."

"That's not the way it looks on tape," I said. "The meeting looks planned."

"Well, I can't help how it looks," he said. "That's what happened. Shyla did her thing, picked up her ribbon, and we came home. I said to Sid, 'Good to have met you, see you around.' That was it."

"Are you saying State hasn't made any illegal contacts?" I asked.

But he was smarter than I gave him credit for.

"I'm saying you don't have a tape of one," he said. "But yeah, that happens to be true, too. You can't have a tape of an illegal contact because they haven't made any. I got a letter from Coach Hale back in September, and I figure he'll call me some time after July first, but, hey, he wouldn't jeopardize the team's chances by pulling dumb shit like that. Especially not next year. You know how good they're gonna be?"

Faye shook her head.

"They're gonna be awesome, man," he told us gravely. "They got Richie Carter, they got Lionel Boseman—the Bossman— and they got Greg Jacoby. Plus, they got Jimmy D. in the back court. They're gonna be fuckin' killer, man, that's what they're gonna be. They're gonna go all the way."

"Does that mean you're leaning in that direction?" I asked. "By your account, there's a back court position open for you."

He stared at me. "Lady, I'm not gonna tell you that," he said. "I've still got a lot of thinking to do."

"Okay, suppose you're telling the truth, and suppose this encounter Faye captured on video was as innocent as you say it was," I said. "If it looks illegal, and it does, wouldn't State be upset? Would they try to suppress the video by buying it, do you think? Or stealing it? Or would they burn down an apartment building just to destroy it?"

He looked at me, then at Faye. He cocked a thumb at me, and spoke to Faye.

"Is she for real?" he said.

"Well," Faye said, a little apologetically it seemed to me, "all those things have happened since segments of the video were broadcast on the news."

"No shit? Whoa, that bites." He shook his head and lowered himself to a nearby sofa with the awkwardness of a kid accustomed to mistrusting the furniture. He might have been short on the court, but he made his mother's elegant living room suite look like it was designed for Lilliputians. "You sure you don't have a Mafia hit on that tape?" he asked.

"One of the people trying to buy the tape is Sid Green," I said.

"Yeah?" He continued to look puzzled. "Well, maybe he had a girlfriend sitting on the next bench or something. If he did, I didn't see her. Want me to ask my sister?" Then he bellowed, "Hey, Shyla!"

A voice from the back of the house called, "I'm on the phone!"

He grinned at us. "Well, get your butt in here," he shouted, loud enough to be heard over a sudden burst of enthusiasm from the PlayStation crowd. "You can talk to Missy any time."

A girl—the girl from the video—appeared in the door. She was a skinny kid of maybe nine or ten, with long thick hair the color of her brother's, and a less pronounced version of his nose and eyes. She had a jar of nail polish in one hand and a portable phone in the other. She pressed the phone to her chest.

"I'm on the phone!" she said, infusing her voice with as much irritation as was humanly possible. "God, you are such a prick!"

He turned his grin on her. "Hey, chill! I'm just thinkin' of your career. This is the lady that filmed the cheerleader contest. She says a bunch of bad-ass dudes've been trying to steal her film since they showed it on the news. You remember seein' anything weird? Like, if maybe that Sid Green guy I was talking to had a girlfriend hanging around or anything?"

She looked from him to us. Her face registered something, but I couldn't tell what. She hesitated, then said, "I didn't see anything like that."

I pressed her. "Did you see anything on the tape that you thought was odd or surprising, anything like that?"

"No," she said, and shot her brother a look. "Now, can I

please get back to my phone call? Missy's probably, like, totally fallen asleep by now."

Falcone turned to us and shrugged.

"I guess we can't help you," he said, standing up.

Faye shrugged. "Okay, it was worth a shot. Hey, can I use your bathroom?"

He looked only slightly taken aback, then pointed down the hall. "First door on the left," he said.

She disappeared down the hall and left Falcone and me to make polite conversation.

"So, you still have your senior year to go, huh?" I asked inanely.

He smiled broadly. "Yeah, it's gonna be killer."

"But I guess the recruiters will drive you crazy, won't they?" I asked. This time I was genuinely curious.

He humped his shoulders. "It comes with the territory," he said impassively.

"Aren't you worried about injuries?" I asked.

He looked away from me. "Nah," he said. "I never get injured."

"What do your parents think about all this?" I asked.

"They're cool with it," he said.

We stood in uncomfortable silence, as if in suspended animation, until Faye returned. He walked us to the door.

"Hey, I guess I'll be lookin' for your stuff on the big screen, huh?" he said to Faye when she offered her hand. "Like Spike Lee. I hear he's makin' a hoops movie."

"Probably not," she said. "I make documentaries."

"Oh, hey," he said, showing some enthusiasm. "You mean like *Hoop Dreams*? That flick was awesome! You making another *Hoop Dreams*? Well, let me know if I can help. You know, I got a lot of contacts."

He smiled ingenuously, seemingly impervious to irony.

I lit a cigarette on the way back to the car, then stood waiting for Faye to unlock my door. I gazed back at the house.

"I don't believe you did that," I told her.

"What?" she asked. "That wasn't lame, I really had to go. But I didn't even have to snoop around. He had this humongous bottle of creatine sitting out on the counter."

"Creatine? You mean like a steroid?"

"It's not really a steroid," she explained. "It's not even illegal in most sports. It's, like, this amino acid or something that builds strength. A lot of athletes swear by it, because it's got a reputation for being safer than steroids. But the thing is, nobody knows if it is or not. So the dudes who are taking it could be really screwing up their bodies big time."

"So the Falcon is a fake, is that what you're saying?"

"Well, not totally, I'm not saying that," she said. "It takes more than strength to play well and score—to make the j's, you know. But he might not be skying so high without creatine, that's for sure."

"So, to review, what did we learn about back there other than his questionable personal health habits?"

"God, this is frustrating!" Faye exploded. "It's my own goddamn tape, for crissakes!"

"Yeah, I know what you mean," I said. "What is it that a ten-year-old cheerleader can see in it that we can't?"

17

"Well, what if they burn down the theater?"

"They're not going to burn down the theater," I said. "They don't even know you have a copy of the tape."

"Everybody in the family knows I have a copy of the tape," Faye said. "We might as well take out an ad in the *Times*."

"You have a point," I conceded. "The safe is fireproof. The rest of the building, unfortunately, is not." I was busy tallying the evening's concession stand sales, so I was only half listening.

"Well, as far as I'm concerned, they could burn the flick we're showing upstairs," she said. "That thing is cheesy."

"I didn't have much choice, okay?" I retorted defensively. "Just keep your fingers crossed we get *The Lost World*—preferably before the millennium rolls around."

"So, anyway, I think I should have a talk with Sid Green," Faye said. "I know Styles wants me to, like, show the tape to Hank Mann, but I don't think I should do that until I've exhausted my other options, do you? I mean, just in case nobody knows I still have the tape."

"That makes sense," I said.

"He called, by the way."

"Who called?"

"Mann," she said. "Gilda, I think that's a three, not an eight." She was leaning over the counter next to me, pointing at the sales sheet.

"I can't read Duke's writing half the time," I grumbled. "I wish he'd let Todd fill these things out."

"Maybe you need glasses," Faye suggested.

"I have glasses."

"Maybe you need to wear them, then."

"What did Hank want? I thought you were going to call him."

She shrugged. "Not in the mood. He called just to say he hoped I wasn't still mad at him, and to tell me again he'd be happy to, like, help me anyway he can. I didn't talk to him. He left a message on the machine while I was out."

"Did he sound desperate?"

"No," she said thoughtfully. "He sounded like he was doing the play-by-play. That was a four."

I punched the CLEAR ENTRY button on the calculator.

"Aren't you supposed to be mopping the men's john?"

"I was just trying to help," she said in a huff. "So anyway,

Gilda, will you go see Smiling Sid with me tomorrow, and then to a shoot on campus at State?"

"How will you know where to find him? He owns several dealerships, you know, not just the Lexus one."

"Oh, I'll bet if I leave my name, he'll call me back," she said. "So, will you come?"

"Yeah, I guess," I said. "In for a penny, in for a pound."

"What?" Faye laughed. "Where'd you get that expression? Is that from back in the day?"

"Way back," I said. "Totally old skool. But, Faye, I really should be out looking for a place to live, not to mention doing all the paperwork I've got piled up around here." I was working at a small desk wedged in next to the ice machine in a little room behind the concession stand. I didn't work there often because the ice machine made the room hot, but the desk was piled with papers and unopened mail that had to be dealt with. "It's not like I didn't have a life until you showed up, you know."

It was bad enough that my family members, down to the last bit player, thought they had first claim on my time, but now other people's relatives were beginning to horn in. I had a phone message from Jake Styles waiting at home. I didn't have an answering machine there, though. I didn't even have a private line. What I had was a note written on the back of a supermarket receipt in Ruth Hernandez's peculiar scrawl.

"GILDA," it read, "old geezer name Jake called, says he is Styles's dad. True?!! What's the matter with him?!!!" And she'd written down a phone number. Then: "p.s. You can call late."

So I picked up the phone and dialed the number. He caught it on the first bounce.

"Gilda!" he said, in a voice that was both hearty and hushed. "How you doin'? Thanks for calling back."

"How are *you* doing, Jake?" I asked. "Are you supposed to be up at this hour? It's the middle of the night. Aren't you supposed to be resting?"

"No, no, I've been resting so damn much I'm growing

moss, know what I mean, dolly? I'll tell you, Gilda, I really dodged a bullet this time, I really did. I don't mean the bullet that hit me, I didn't dodge that one too good, did I? But the old ticker stopped, didn't it? So I'm doin' okay for a guy who was dead."

"That's good," I said, and waited.

"I guess you're a little lonely, what with Sammy out of town and all, eh, dolly?"

"Jake, Styles and I—uh, Sammy and I aren't—" I began.

"Yeah, I know how that goes. Of course, a little loneliness can be therapeutic, know what I mean? I could use a little loneliness right now myself." His voice dropped further. "I'll tell you something, dolly. This nurse Sammy hired—well, he's no Florence Nightingale. Christ! I've met cops and prison guards who were more simpatico, know what I mean?"

"Can I do something for you, Jake?"

It made me a little nervous, talking to Styles's father like this. I felt as if I were conspiring behind her back. Or if I wasn't, he was about to ask me to.

"Yeah, yeah, you know, dolly, I been thinkin'. Well, Christ, what else is there to do in bed, except a few activities I don't feel up to, right? So I been thinkin' about this whole business with the tape and the blonde, turning it over in my mind, you know? And I started thinking: What if the blonde wasn't blond on the tape? Huh? What do you think of that?"

I thought maybe he'd blown a head gasket during the heart attack. Had this possibility only just occurred to him, or was he suffering from amnesia, or was he having strokes now, or what?

I said, "I think that's a possibility, Jake, sure."

"Yeah, yeah, me too, I think so, too," he said eagerly. "And I'm wondering if maybe my brain wasn't working so good the other day when Sammy and Faye showed me the tape. Say, that Faye, she's a sharp one, huh? But, to tell you the truth, dolly, I don't get the whole nose ring thing. It must smart. Don't you think it hurts? Do you think it's supposed to be sexy?"

"I wouldn't know, Jake," I said.

"Yeah, so anyway, about the tape. I was thinking if maybe you could bring me another copy, I'd take another look at it, you know? Now that my brain cells have cleared, and I'm on my own turf, and all. Don't you think that would be a good idea?"

"I guess so," I said. "Sure. I'll have to find a Beta deck for you, too, though."

"I wasn't thinking, see? When Sammy and Faye came before, I shoulda had them leave me a copy, so's I could take another look. I mean, this broad could be anybody, right? Maybe even—" He lowered his voice further, and this time it seemed to be for shock value. "Maybe she don't even look like a broad on this tape."

"Anything's possible," I agreed.

" 'Course, I gotta tell you, dolly, it would take some doing for a looker like this dame to not look like a broad, know what I mean? Huh? But who knows? She could be the dame of a thousand faces, right?"

"It's possible, sure," I said.

"So, like I say, if you wouldn't mind bringing me a copy, dolly—I'd come after it myself, only Edith Cavell here won't let me out of the house."

"I could bring it to you tomorrow, early afternoon," I said.

"Hey, that would be great! You're a doll!"

"Will Spike let me in?"

"Oh, sure! He lets in all my lady friends."

Carmine, a.k.a. Spike, had a body that filled the doorway when I went to call the next afternoon. If he'd been a cartoon character, he would've taken the door frame with him every time he tried to walk through it. His muscles bulged out from under a teal shirt that must have been the latest fashion in nurse's uniforms. His pants and shoes were white, though, which was reassuring. His upper lip, jaw, and chin registered five o'clock four hours early, and I suspected it was five o'clock there twenty-four hours a day, except for the half hour after he'd shaved. He gave me a radiant smile, like a friendly Newfoundland puppy, and offered me a meaty paw to shake.

"Glad to meetya, Gilda," he said. He had the hoarse voice of someone whose larynx had been crushed one too many times and the confident grip of someone who'd crushed back. "Jake's in the can. Have a seat."

I looked around. Jake's apartment was unrecognizable. The first thing I noticed was that I could see the carpet. There was nothing on the floor except the customary lamp stands and furniture feet. The funky smell had been replaced with the slight hint of alcohol—the kind intended for external use only. And was there something else? I sniffed discreetly. Furniture polish? Murphy's Oil Soap? The upholstery on the furniture looked brighter, every surface gleamed, dust free. Even the doorknobs glowed, as if they'd been recently polished.

I whistled. "You've done wonders with this place, Carmine," I said in awe. "What did you do, have a Dumpster wheeled up to the fire escape and just throw everything out the window?"

"You can call me Spike," he said. He grinned at me in obvious pleasure at the compliment. This time I noticed the broken incisor. Like a damaged fang, it made him appear even less threatening. "Yeah, it looks good, huh? I guess you saw this place before, so you know what a pit it was." He looked around and nodded. "Yeah, I made him throw half the crap away, and the rest we piled in the closet. Old guy kept threatening to have another heart attack, but I told him I knew CPR and kept pitching."

I found Harry deep in a sofa cushion, paws up, fast asleep.

"I gave him some catnip a little while ago," Spike said, looking down at him as if we were discussing a patient across a hospital bed, "so he's kinda out of it. He don't know what to make of the place, now he don't have to walk through it like a maze, so he's been a little on edge, poor old guy. He don't hardly know what it's like not to live in fear a bein' crushed by stuff fallin' on top of him."

Harry opened one eye and looked up at him.

Spike squatted in front of the sofa, stuck out a hand like a concrete block, and began stroking Harry's head, gently.

"Yeah," Spike crooned to the cat, "you're a good old cat, aren't ya? You're Spike's pal, aren't ya? Me and you's buddies."

The open eyelid drooped. Harry yawned and squirmed, burrowing into Spike's hand.

"If you don't stop petting that cat, he'll go bald," a petulant voice said from the bedroom doorway.

"Ahhh, he's okay," Spike said, continuing to stroke the yellow head. "Aren'tcha, Harry?"

I could hear Harry's purr from a yard away. He didn't seem too concerned about losing his hair.

"Hey, dolly. How you doin'? Thanks for coming." Jake turned a smile on me. He looked pale and fragile. His hair was mussed, and his robe hung loose on a slightly stooped frame. He moved slowly, one hand on his stomach. He gestured toward Spike. "Can you believe this guy? He's got the whole damn place so goddamn clean I can't find anything." To Spike he said, "Where's my picklocks? What'd you do with my picklocks?"

"Middle desk drawer," Spike said. He continued to pet the cat. "Same place we put your minicamera, your little microphones, your handcuffs, and your channel cutters. Jake, I wish you'd pay attention when I tell you stuff."

"I do pay attention. It's that damn anesthetic," Jake retorted crankily. He tapped his temple with a forefinger. "It kills off your brain cells, dolly. Don't ever let them use that stuff on you if you can get out of it," he cautioned me. "Christ, I feel like I aged ten years in that joint."

"Should you be up walking around, Jake?" I asked anxiously as he tottered across the room and leaned heavily on the desk.

He grimaced. "Whole new way of thinking they got these days, dolly. They make you get up right away after you're operated on—unless you're dead, of course. That way they can squeeze more money out of you when you tear your stitches."

"What do you want your picklocks for, anyhow?" Spike asked, standing up at last. "I thought you was playing with that little voice-activated video camera Sammy gave you."

"Well, it's not going to do me much good to have a camera like that if I can't get in anyplace to set it up, now, is it? Besides, I gotta keep in practice." He retrieved a small case like a manicure set from the desk drawer, and said to me, "Come on back in the bedroom, dolly. I want to show you this camera Sammy got me."

"You got your meds in ten, Jake," Spike called after us.

"I'm tellin' you, Gilda, that guy's really gettin' on my nerves." He waved me into a straight-backed chair near the bed. "Sit down. Take a load off." He lowered himself slowly onto the bed, hand on his stomach again, and grimaced in pain. Then he craned his neck toward the living room. "He's probably in there now, wiping down your fingerprints and vacuuming Harry's fur. If that guy don't stop cleaning, he'll run me crazy."

"Harry seems to like him," I observed.

He snorted. "Harry's got the loyalty of a housefly," he said derisively. "He don't even hold out for tuna fish, like any self-respecting cat would do. No, the guy walks in here, starts petting him and talking baby talk, and right away Harry's making goo-goo eyes at him." He illustrated, batting eyelashes Harry didn't have, to my knowledge, then swatted a hand in Harry's general direction. "It's disgusting! He don't even hardly go out anymore! He just stays at home." He shook his head, then said resignedly, "Well, I guess all the lady cats are grateful for a little time off, if you know what I mean."

"Here's the tape," I said, placing it on the bed. I didn't want to discuss anybody's sex life—not Harry's, not Jake's, and not mine. Especially not mine.

"Hey, thanks! You're a doll. Yeah, I'll get right on that. I'm gonna look at that tape again tonight and see if I can't spot that broad. I'll bet she's there."

I'll bet she isn't, I thought. I didn't seriously believe that the tape had anything to do with her personally. But I didn't like to turn down a request from Styles's dad. At the same time, I was handing it over with some feelings of trepidation. I would have much preferred to have had Styles's permission on this one, but I hadn't heard from her.

He had already turned his attention to his new toy, and was explaining to me how it worked. It was a small camera, palm-sized, or if you were Spike, it was about the size of your pinky. You could set it to be activated by voice or motion. It was a nifty little piece of equipment, but my interest in mechanical devices had been eroded by years of my uncle Grosvenor's enthusiasms. Before I got out of there, he had to demonstrate it for me. First, he taped me, played it back, and sure enough, there I was, looking slightly bored. Then, after some arguing and negotiating over taking his medication, he had Spike go in the kitchen and call Harry, to prove that even Harry's voice would activate the video camera. I saw Harry as the silent type, but when Spike called him, he stirred sleepily, and gave a little interrogatory chirp. Again, the camera switched on and captured Harry, rolling over and eyeing the kitchen with a calculating look, then, hearing nothing, closing his eyes again with a sigh of contentment.

"That's great, Jake," I said.

"Yeah, it's something, all right," he said. "You never know when you'll need a thing like that."

On the way out the door, I crossed paths with a shapely, middle-aged, blue-black brunette, who gave me a suspicious glance.

"Hey," I said, hands up, "I'm just making a delivery. He's all yours."

Her face relaxed into a rueful smile.

"That'll be the day, sister," she said.

18

Smiling Sid gave us the benefit of a full complement of teeth as he crossed the showroom. You would have thought he was delighted to see us.

"Ladies," he said, and shook hands with us. Since we'd identified him on the tape, where he was a background figure, I'd caught a few of his television commercials. Up close and without his television makeup, he looked older, even though he'd recently had a close encounter with a tanning bed. There was more white in what hair he had left than I remembered, and the tan only emphasized the lines in his skin—not just the smile lines on his face, but the horizontal lines across his neck which betrayed a battle between body fat and dress collars.

He beamed at the car we were standing next to.

"What do you think?" he said, as if he'd caught us in a moment of undisguised auto lust. "She's a beauty, isn't she? But if I'm not mistaken, I believe you ladies wanted to test drive the Bonneville, isn't that right? I've got one waiting right out here, so if you'll just step this way."

He waved chummily at two of the salesmen standing chatting by the door, scanning their domain.

"Be right back," he told them.

He kept up the pitch so convincingly that I caught a glance from Faye. Did he have us confused with real customers? He held the door open.

"Which one of you ladies wants to drive?"

We looked at each other.

"I'll drive," I said.

He directed me to turn right out of the dealership and continued to point out the features of the car until he'd gotten us onto River Road, headed north—a four-lane winding road that followed the river up past the zoo.

"Why don't you turn left up here into the park, and we can sit a minute?"

The park was no more than a turnout that featured a few concrete picnic tables, barbecue pits, and a view of the river. The thought crossed my mind that he could shoot us both and dump us in the river, but that was the screenwriter in me; after all, I was a Liberty. I knew he wouldn't kill us. In the first place, there was plenty of traffic on River Road to witness any criminal activity on his part. In the second place, we had something he wanted.

Smiling Sid once again turned his smile on us. He had to bend one knee in order to screw himself around to face Faye in the backseat.

"Now, Faye, I believe you said something on the phone about a videotape?" he said easily. "What videotape would that be? See, I don't recall that I ever called you about a videotape, and I'd like this thing cleared up."

"Your son-in-law called me." I heard just a slight quaver of hesitation in her voice, as if she were beginning to wonder whether we'd been wrong about the connection.

Smiling Sid's brows furrowed over his smile. "Which son-in-law would that be, Faye?"

Maybe I'm an old-fashioned girl, but I hate it when people presume they're on a first-name basis with you without any encouragement on your part. Salesmen do this; also auto mechanics and other service people who want to put you in your place when you ask them why they didn't fix whatever you brought to them to be serviced. Increasingly, restaurants with pickup counters do it. It's supposed to make you feel like you're part of the family. That's probably how Smiling Sid wanted prospective customers to feel about him. But I had enough loonies in the Liberty family already to remake *King of Hearts*.

"Cut the crap, Sid," I said. "You know and we know that we have you on tape, making an illegal recruiting contact with Mike Falcone. You asked Charley Drake to offer a thousand bucks for that tape. We want to know who's interested besides you."

"Now, hold on a minute, Gilda," he said, swinging his head around to face me. "Let's say I did happen to meet up with that talented young man at the mall one Saturday while I was out doing a little shopping. What makes you think it was a recruiting contact? Did he say it was?"

"The grand you offered put a big dent in your credibility, Sid," I said, "if you're trying to tell us that all you talked about was the latest styles in sneakers."

"Well, now, Gilda, I know it doesn't look so good on tape," he said, spreading his pudgy hands. "That's why I'm willing to pay Faye here to leave it out of her movie. But I don't think Mike Falcone told you that we talked about college, because we didn't."

"I think you not only talked about college, Sid, I think you offered the Falcon a car in exchange for a letter of intent."

I reached for a cigarette. I was actually starting to enjoy this.

"Well, now, that's your opinion, Gilda," he said, hunching himself up to reach into a jacket pocket for a lighter. He wasn't fast enough. "But I don't see how you, the NCAA, or anybody else can prove that."

I leaned back and exhaled a puff of smoke.

"Ever hear of lipreading, Sid?"

I don't know why I said it; it came out of the blue. But as soon as it was out, Sid's million-dollar tan drained right down into his Italian leather shoes.

I was so shocked by the effect of my words, I nearly swallowed my cigarette, then covered my reaction with a smoker's cough.

"What do you mean, Gilda?" His voice was a ghost of its former self.

"Lipreading. You know, it's what blind people use."

"Deaf people." Faye corrected me softly from the backseat.

"Deaf people, that's right," I said. "They can read lips, which means they can tell what people are talking about by watching them. What do you think would happen if we brought in a skilled lip-reader to look at that tape?"

"It would have to be pretty sharply focused," he said. He was grasping at straws, and we both knew it.

"No problem, Sid," I told him. "You'd be surprised what can be done with video these days—not just freeze frame and enlargement, but actual image enhancement, too."

I had no idea what I was talking about. I was pretty sure I was lying, but at least Faye didn't feel compelled to correct me from the backseat.

Smiling Sid had stopped smiling. He ran one hand over his bald strip in a nervous gesture.

"I thought the tape had been stolen," he said, changing tacks.

"It had," I said. "We got it back. We don't exactly know who stole it, though. I mean, we know the thief, but even he doesn't know who hired him. That wasn't you, was it, Sid?"

"No, no," he assured us. "It wasn't me."

He turned his head to gaze out over the river. He was thinking. Take your time, Sid, I thought, watching him percolate.

"So, are you saying that Faye still has the tape? The only copy?"

I watched him closely. This would be a good time for him to pull a gun, if he was going to.

"The only copies," I amended. "Yes, she does."

"Well, except for the television station one," Faye put in. "I mean, like, the original newscast tape—"

I cut my eyes at her and she trailed off.

"The television station?" he echoed in a voice barely above a whisper. "They have a copy? Yes, I guess they would."

"In the archives," I said reassuringly, "which are restricted to station employees. The general public doesn't have access to those."

I glanced at Faye, and she shut her mouth, lips tight.

"I see," he said. "So, let me see if I have this straight. You're willing to sell the tape for a thousand." He checked my expression, obviously expecting me to up the ante.

"Could be," I said.

"And you have it here?" he asked. His eyes rolled over the seat back and dropped to Faye's capacious shoulder bag.

"Not here," she said. "That wouldn't be smart. I mean, how would we know you wouldn't be some heinous low-rent who would, like, jack us up and book it with the tape?"

His gaze shifted to me for a translation.

"We didn't bring the tape with us," I said.

"And if I paid money for it," he said, "how could I be sure that I had the only copy outside the archives? You could always keep a copy, or sell it to someone else."

"You think we'd do a thing like that?" I cried in mock indignation. "Do you really think we'd make a deal with you here, an honest-to-god, my-word-is-my-bond verbal contract, and then when you came back with your money tell you we didn't have exactly what you wanted? Maybe you think we'd raise the price or something? Show you a different tape, a more expensive tape? Sid! What kind of people do you take us for?"

He had the grace to squirm when I said it.

"Anyway," Faye said from the backseat, "we haven't concluded the negotiations yet. We aren't absolutely committed to selling. See, what we really want is for you to hook us up with the good word."

His eyes sought mine again.

"I think what Faye is saying," I translated, "is that we're more interested in the other parties who are after this video. Do you know of any other efforts to either acquire or suppress it? Have you talked to Coach Hale about it, for example?"

"Yes, I had a long talk with Creighton," he said wearily.

"He was very upset with me. He said that even if the contact was innocent, it looked bad for the program. I was—" He paused, then concluded. "—indiscreet. I should never have spoken to the boy."

"Is that what you told him?" I asked. "That the contact was innocent? You give him the same bullshit you gave us?"

"I told him that I met the boy by chance, and we had a general conversation about basketball, yes."

"Did he tell you he was going to try to get hold of the tape? Or destroy it?"

"I believe he said we needed to get it, yes."

"And what did you understand by 'we'? That he was leaving it up to you?"

"I thought he was," Sid said slowly, "but I may have misunderstood. You say someone was hired to steal it?"

"Yes, and someone tried to burn down Faye's building. That wasn't you, was it, Sid?"

He looked aggrieved. "Of course not! I made a legitimate offer for what I wanted."

"Through Charley Drake."

"Well, I didn't want to be involved directly, that's true," he said. "I'm a businessman. I didn't want attention drawn to me—yours or anyone else's. That's reasonable, isn't it? In any case, if you sell the tape to me, that will satisfy Creighton, I'm sure."

"How sure?"

"Creighton and I are old associates," he said. "He'd be pleased to have me take care of this."

I flicked my cigarette butt out the window.

"So, what's Hank Mann's interest in all this?"

I think the blood would have drained out of his face if there'd been any left. His eyes opened wide and he stared at me.

"Hank Mann?" he asked. "You mean, the sportscaster?"

I nodded. "Channel Ten, isn't it, Faye? He seems to want his own personal copy of the tape." I didn't tell Sid that Hank already had his own copy.

"Did he say why he wanted it?" Sid asked.

"He didn't say he wanted it at all," I said. "He expressed an interest in Faye's work based on the newscast he'd seen."

"What could he want with it?" Sid asked, frowning. "He couldn't possibly use it. If he did, he'd be fired. He can't intend to use it against the team, or even to blackmail Creighton. He'd never keep his job if he made trouble for the team or the coach. He didn't say anything about me, did he?" Sid asked this last question anxiously.

"I don't remember anything," Faye said cautiously. "But that's before we knew you were involved."

She was catching on.

"What do you care, anyway?" I asked. "Suppose you're caught bribing a recruit. Don't you think public sympathy would be on your side?"

He fumbled. "Well, I—I don't know. If the team were sanctioned, and if it were my fault, you see—I—I'm afraid I'd be blamed. You never know how people will react," he finished lamely.

There must have been something here we were missing, but I was damned if I knew what it was.

"Maybe we should, like, have a talk with Coach Hale," Faye said.

It was a brilliant move; I wished I'd thought of it myself.

"No, I don't think that's a good idea," he said, screwing himself around in the seat again to emphasize his point. "In the first place—well, he's a busy man. He's not—accessible."

"I'll bet we could access him," Faye said confidently. "All we'd have to do is mention the tape. He's not clueless, and I'll bet he's no derelict, either."

"He's not stupid," I translated. I was beginning to get the hang of Faye's speech.

"No, that's true," Sid said thoughtfully. Then, as if he'd just had an idea, he said, "I'll tell you what. Let me talk to him. I'll tell him what's going on. Maybe he has some insight into this Hank Mann business. Let me talk to him, and I can get back to you—say, tomorrow?"

Faye capitulated. "Okay," she said. "Meanwhile, we'll think things over, too, and decide whether we want to sell or not."

"A thousand dollars is a lot of money," he said, and I could hear that he was recovering some of his bonhomie. "It would make a nice down payment on one of these little beauties."

He tapped the dashboard affectionately and smiled at us.

I easily found Sid's dealership in the row of car dealers when we returned. It was the one flying an American flag as big as a minivan—and only slightly larger than the Buckeye State flag flying next to it.

19

"I'm not selling him the tape, Gilda," Faye said on the way home. "I might promise to leave out the parts he doesn't want seen, but that's it."

"Okay by me," I said. "And as far as I'm concerned, if that's worth a thousand dollars to him, you're welcome to that, too. I won't squawk."

Faye looked relieved.

"I got no problem with encouraging Sid to become a patron of the arts," I said.

"Really," Faye said.

My conversation with Styles that night was less harmonious. But then, conversations with Styles usually were.

She called at one-thirty, just as I was going to bed.

When I picked up the phone, I heard Ruth Hernandez's voice.

"She's tired, Styles," she insisted. "She don't need to be

talking to nobody at this time of night. She needs her beauty sleep."

"Ruth!" I cut in. And then we had a three-way discussion before Ruth finally hung up.

"How's Des Moines?" I asked.

"I wouldn't know," she said. "I'm in Little Rock."

"I envy you your glamorous life," I said.

"Doesn't everybody?" she said.

She asked about developments, and I told her about the interview with Sid.

"So now they know it still exists," she said. "Sweetheart, you better watch your back, you and Faye both."

"Well, it's not like I go around carrying a purse big enough to hide a video in," I said.

"Faye does," she pointed out.

"Okay, okay, I'll talk to her."

Then I told her that Jake had asked for a copy of the video, and I'd given it to him.

"Run that by me again," she said. "There's a car chase going on in the next room."

"I gave your father a copy of the video." I wanted to remind her that Jake was, after all, her responsibility, not mine.

"You did what?" Her voice rose. "Jesus Christ, Gilda, he's probably sold it to the highest bidder by now and been shot in the bargain. Have you checked lately to see if he's still alive?"

"He said he wanted to look at it again, maybe he'd remember something," I said crossly. "What was I supposed to do? He's *your* father."

"Oh, no," she said. "Don't pin this on me. Damn it, Gilda, I warned you about him. You can't trust him."

"What do you think, he sold it to the blonde who plugged him?"

"If she offered him enough money, you bet your sweet ass he did, especially if she's as good-looking as he says."

"Well, what was I supposed to do?" I reiterated childishly. "It's not like I could call you up and say, 'Mommy, may I?' "

"Jesus, Gilda, I have a pager, for crying out loud!"

"Do I have the number? Do I?"

"It's on my—no, hold on, you have one of the old ones. Okay, you win. But you didn't have to rush right over with it. You knew I'd call eventually."

I let this pass in silence.

"So, you saw the old boy, huh?" she said. "How's he getting along with Carmine?"

"He's not," I said. "But Harry wants Spike to move in permanently."

She snorted. "Who wouldn't? Last time I was there, Spike was whipping up some Italian fish delicacy he thought Harry would go for. I told him Harry would go for regular meals, and anything else was just icing. Did you check on my plants?"

I started guiltily. "No, I thought I'd do that tomorrow," I said. "That way, they'll really appreciate me when I come, and they won't be too particular."

"Good thinking," she said. "Well, that's about it, I guess. If I'm not back in a day or two, I'll call again. Watch your back. Liberty funerals are kind of like coronations—they're entertaining, but you don't want to sit through too many in one lifetime."

20

A faint glow lingered in the sky, and the moon was rising above the crab apple trees that lined Oak Street. The second showing was under way, and I was taking a leisurely stroll down to Styles's office on Main Street, about a block from the

theater. She had one of those unrenovated offices above a deserted storefront, the kind of office where dust blown north-
east from the original Dust Bowl was embedded in the cracks
of the hardwood floors. The night air still held the warmth of
the sun reflected off the sidewalks. I could smell newly mown
lawns, flowers in bloom—maybe even a lily, from the heady
sweetness of the scent—tar from a road patch somewhere,
and a faint hint of grease from the Hamburger Heaven. An occasional firefly flitted across my path. It occurred to me that
the tip of my cigarette might be stirring amorous interests.

The darkness inside Styles's building seemed total at first,
after the street. My sneakers made the wooden stairs groan
and creak like a fretful old man. I fumbled for the light at
the top of the stairs, feeling along the molding for the old-
fashioned button. Overhead, bare bulbs that could have arrived in the first lot Edison shipped cast a lambent yellow
light over peeling wallpaper, old paint, and scarred wood, as
if deferring to an aging diva's vanity.

"I'm glad you came. I didn't know if you would."

The low, breathy voice emerged from a shadow at the end
of the hall, where one of the lights had given up the ghost.

I dropped the keys I was holding. I bent down to pick them
up, and upside-down, head suspended over the floor, I got my
first look at her.

She was slender and blond, hair pulled back loosely to
frame a face as perfectly proportioned and arranged as a
Greek temple. Her hair was the same spun-gold color that
caused so much trouble for Rapunzel, but she was no Rapunzel. She was a Blonde. My instincts told me she was *the*
Blonde, and my eyes dropped to her hands, tipped in blood-
red. Then my gaze measured her handbag, an understated
clutch that was smaller than most of my pockets but large
enough to conceal a ladylike twenty-two.

She was wearing basic black—a tight-fitting little number
that showed off her figure as well as the dimples on her knees.
The neckline was low and square, no doubt out of deference
both to the season and to the whisper of cleavage it revealed.

Maybe it was a sundress, and if I behaved she'd take off the short white jacket and show me a plunge at the back. When the possibility occurred to me, I dropped the keys again. The hallway, which had seemed cool compared to the street outside, suddenly seemed warm, narrow, and close, the scent of her perfume heady. She smelled like gardenias.

Her eyes flicked upward, showing off a set of long, professionally-mascaraed eyelashes. "I couldn't find the light switch," she said.

Even in this light, I could tell that her eyes were green, the kind of luminous green that makes brown, black, and blue eyes seem pedestrian.

"Uh-huh," I said, again showing off the frizzled gray mixed with the brown on top of my head as I bent to pick up the keys. "You have to know where it is."

Silver-tongued in my romantic fantasies, I was instantly reduced to verbal clumsiness in the presence of a fantasy made real. I didn't know whether this one was a hoochie or not, but she was definitely what Jake would call a "tomato," or what my generation would call a "babe."

"I'm sorry about your father," the babe said, stepping closer and sending a wave of perfume my way. "As I explained to him, I was nervous and he startled me, and I was afraid he meant to—well, hurt me—and I panicked."

I considered dropping the keys again to give me time to process this speech, but there's a limit to the embarrassment I'm willing to suffer in the cause of clarity. Nevertheless, my razor-sharp deductive faculties concluded that one, she thought I was Styles, and two, she had spoken to Jake since she shot him.

I wouldn't want to be Styles all the time, I thought, but I wouldn't mind being her for the next half hour.

"Why don't you come in, Ms.—uh—" Damn! I thought. How much was I supposed to know? "Come on in."

I opened the door on the second try and ushered her into Styles's office. Her high heels made sharp little reports on the wood floor.

"Have a seat," I said generously, waving her into a curved-back wooden office chair that could have been acquired in an auction when *Black Mask* folded. I settled myself behind the desk and moved two listless plants out of the way so that I could see her. One of them—possibly the weeping fig—shed a few dry leaves in protest. The lights inside the office were marginally better than the ones in the hall.

She sat down and pulled the chair closer to the desk. She opened her clutch and extracted a cigarette. Holding it in two slender fingers, she leaned closer.

"Do you have a light?" she asked.

I fished my lighter out of my pocket, fairly certain that Styles didn't have one on the premises, leaned forward, and lit her cigarette. Then I lit one for me. I pushed Styles's New York World's Fair commemorative ashtray across the desktop.

"Actually," I said, "I didn't get your message. That is, I assume from what you've said that you left me a message asking me to meet you here. I've been out of town." That should cover any memory lapses, I thought.

"I see," she said. "Then I was just lucky."

We both were, sweetheart, I thought, simultaneously feeling appalled that I was beginning to talk like Styles, even to myself. Especially to myself.

She sat back and crossed her legs. I heard the whisper of stockinged calf against knee. Her eyes grazed the plants on the corner of the desk and passed on, dismissing them as inconsequential. They were going to be even more inconsequential if I didn't water them soon. Her gaze swept the battered file cabinets, the brass coat rack, the stained wallpaper, the computer on its venerable typing stand, and came to rest on the desk.

"Except for the computer, this office seems quite old-fashioned," she observed.

"I'm an old-fashioned kind of girl," I said.

"And do you keep a bottle of gin in your bottom drawer?" she asked, smiling faintly.

"It's bourbon," I said. "It's on the licensing exam."

Her smile lengthened on one side of her mouth.

"It's a good thing I'm not taking the test, then, isn't it? Do you have a gun there, too?"

I shook my head. "Top drawer, for quicker access. Better to shoot first, drink after. That's on the exam, too."

"I'll have to remember that," she said. "You see, I'm not very used to guns. Perhaps you can understand, then, how I came to shoot Jake."

"There's a lot I don't understand," I said, "but that one is a no-brainer."

I was enjoying being Styles.

"And now you're here," I continued, trying to jumpstart this conversation. "Are you going to shoot me, too, or did you just drop by to say howdy? Reason I ask is, I don't want to make any sudden movements that might be misinterpreted. Or if I do, I want to offer you a less vulnerable body part to shoot at."

"I deserved that," she said, looking down.

Good. She was on the same page of the same script I was on.

"No, the point is—" She paused to tap her ash into the World's Fair reflecting pool. "The point is that I'm still in the market for a copy of that tape—the one I asked Jake to get for me."

"Only one copy?" I said. "You're showing restraint. There's been a run on them, you know. I don't know what you paid Jake, but our top offer so far is a thousand."

"May I ask who made that offer?" she said, raising her eyes to mine.

"Sure," I said. "Ask away. But it wouldn't be good business for me to identify your competition. You and the other party might get together and queer the bidding."

"So you haven't sold to him yet—this other party?"

"I didn't say it was a 'him,' but no, we haven't reached an agreement with that party yet."

She studied me. She brought her left hand up to finger an earring. She was wearing a diamond the size of a runaway meteorite on her left ring finger. "It's difficult to know, you see, how much to offer for the tape," she said slowly. "Its value, to me at least, depends so much on its dissemination or suppression. In the wrong hands, it would lose all value to me."

"Then suppose you describe the nature of your interest," I said, "and I'll consider my options. You should keep in mind, of course, that the tape isn't mine to sell."

"But you know the owner, don't you?" she asked. "I understood you were advising her—Ms. McCadden."

"She doesn't always take my advice," I said. My own cigarette butt went to join hers in the reflecting pool.

"I haven't told you my name," she said after a minute. "It's Hale—Blanche Hale."

"Blanche—that's an old-fashioned name," I observed. Like Mae West, I thought, she'd probably been Snow White before she drifted. "Is Coach Hale an old-fashioned kind of guy?"

"Yes, he is," she said, gazing at me steadily. "That's why I'm divorcing him."

"Uh-huh."

"I don't think you need to hear all the intimate details, do you?" She sighed. "They're not very original. Neither are the scars. But I've finally gathered the courage to get away from him. And I need some security."

I looked at her. I knew an old, tired script when I heard one. Hell, some of my family members had written the originals. I resented the insult to women who had real problems.

"You hate basketball," I said.

Her eyes opened wider. Then she smiled. "As a matter of fact, I do," she said.

Even in the dull office light, I could see some tiny lines in the corners of her eyes like barely perceptible cracks in her otherwise perfect facade. Now, I like lines; I find them sexy. But I had a feeling these lines were doomed to be the subject of a serious discussion between Blanche and her cosmetic surgeon in the next few years.

"Do you have any idea what it's like to be a coach's wife?" she asked. "Do you? Preseason tournaments start in November, but the anxiety has been building since August when the boys arrive. From Thanksgiving to March Madness, I'm on tranquilizers. One of us has to be. Creighton doesn't believe in drugs so he takes out all his stress by shouting at me as if he could behave at home the way he does on the court. We have no privacy; I sometimes think I'll cut my wrists if I have to attend one more sports banquet or supermarket opening. Did you know people actually ask me for my autograph when I'm in line at the bank or getting my hair done? Then there's the recruiting—trips to every one-horse town with a really hot prospect he can't entrust to his assistants, late night phone calls, and more shouting when he loses something he wants. Creighton is not a good loser."

"But I understand that Creighton is retiring. Let me guess. I'll bet you're not much good in the sickroom, either," I said.

She shifted uncomfortably. "I'm not cut out to nurse a dying man, no," she said. "But Creighton was never pleasant. He always had a temper. And bypass surgery makes them worse. Did you know that?"

"You could start a support group," I said. "*Is* Creighton dying, by the way?"

"Not fast enough," she said evenly.

At that moment, the phone rang. We jumped. Maybe we both thought it was God.

It was not God.

"Gilda. Is she there?" Styles's voice was low in my ear.

"Mmm-hmm."

"Are you talking to her?"

"Mmm-hmm."

"Does she think you're me?"

"Mmm-hmm."

There was a pause.

"Really?" she asked. "Jesus, I can't believe you did that! I always saw you as the type of girl who thought her nose would grow if she told a lie."

"Let's leave my nose out of this," I said indignantly. "Was there something in particular you wanted?"

"Just checking on my plants," she said.

"Oh," I said, eyeing the limp foliage across the desk from me. "They're fine. I'd call them to the phone but they're having a bath in the rest room sink down the hall. I don't know if you can hear the splashing on your end."

The fig tree shed another dry leaf, and it hit the desktop with a loud click that made me cover the mouthpiece.

"Call me," she said succinctly.

I hung up. "I'm watching a friend's plants while she's away," I explained.

"What exactly are you watching them do?" she asked. The half smile was back.

"It's a botanical experiment to see if temperate-zone plants can adapt to global warming," I said. "But you didn't come here to talk about shrubbery. You were talking about security."

"Security, yes." She bent forward a little so that she could glance up at me through her long lashes. I was convinced that she did this for effect. It had probably slain all the boys in Toledo, or wherever it was she was from. She knew just how long to hold it, too—not long enough for it to seem conscious on her part. "Do you have any idea what it's like to fight Creighton Hale—here, on his home turf, in Groundhog country?"

"You need a good defense," I said, putting the accent on the first syllable.

She flicked me a rueful look and extracted another cigarette from her purse. This time I slid the lighter across the desk to her.

"I need the Virgin Mary and Mother Teresa playing guard," she said.

"And Maggie Thatcher, Winnie Mandela, and Madeleine Albright on offense," I said. "I get the picture."

"The referees are all Buckeye State alums," she said, "or they might as well be. You can bet they're season ticket holders."

"And if they're playing anything in court, it's the State fight song, not 'The Star-Spangled Banner.' "

"You see what I'm up against."

"And does Creighton know you're playing for the opposing team?"

She blew out a puff of smoke. "Not yet," she said. "He asked me to get the tape for him."

I nodded. She was a cool customer, all right, and I could tell she'd shoot me if I crossed her and never blink those nice eyelashes. I found myself wondering if Styles's gun was still keeping company with the whiskey bottle in the bottom drawer, or if she'd felt in need of protection from the locker men in Des Moines. I'd lied about the location of the gun to make Mrs. Hale think I was better prepared for her than I was.

"What is it you're trying to get out of him?" I asked.

"What's anybody trying to get in a divorce settlement?" she countered. "Do you have any idea how much Creighton earns in a year?"

"A girl's gotta live," I said.

She shrugged. "I need a whole new wardrobe, to begin with."

"Scarlet and black aren't your colors," I agreed.

She smiled. "You're very different from your father," she said. "But then, it's always easier to talk to a woman about these things. I wish I'd come to you first."

I was willing to bet the tournament that she expressed a different opinion when she was around men.

"So, Jake hasn't come through for you," I said. "That's surprising. He has a very good record."

"That's what Creighton said. But we seem to be having—a communication problem." She frowned slightly, and her well-formed eyebrows rippled like lazy inchworms. "I've given him two chances. I've even paid him. But it's possible he's holding the shooting against me."

"Seems ungenerous of him."

"I'm not asking for a refund."

"Very generous of you," I said. "Depending on what you paid him."

"I paid him well," she said. "I'm willing to pay you five thousand if you sell the tape to me exclusively. I believe the filmmaker is a friend of yours, so it should be less trouble for you. I'm not even asking for exclusive rights to all of the— what do you call it? The footage? I believe that your friend was interested in the cheerleading contest, and I don't object as long as she doesn't use anything that might incriminate Creighton."

"By 'incriminate,' you mean anything that could get him in trouble with the NCAA?"

"That's right."

"I'll have to talk to the filmmaker," I said.

"Of course," she said. "But I do hope you can appreciate the need to—let's say, reach an agreement expeditiously?"

I couldn't, actually. Was she that desperate to get away from the guy? She wasn't willing to make a move of any kind until she had some security?

"I'll do what I can," I said. "May I ask if you have other— well, resources? I mean, from what I hear, violations of NCAA rules must be commonplace among the top-ranked teams. Don't you have anything else?"

"I don't have evidence of this kind, no," she admitted. "In most of these cases, everything depends upon the willingness of witnesses to testify. And nobody wants to do that, not even if they sign with another school. It looks bad. And it might bring the NCAA down on their heads as well."

"If you released this tape," I mused, "there'd be a lot of hostility directed at you. Creighton must know that."

The half smile made an encore appearance. "Ah, but he can't be sure I wouldn't be willing to risk that. Besides, I don't have to live here."

"And Creighton does? Even though he's retiring?"

"Creighton wants to die here, surrounded by adoring fans. He wants his coffin draped in scarlet and black. He wants to be buried under the Buckeye State seal at center court."

She laid a card on my desk and tapped it with a shiny red fingernail.

"You can contact me at the number on the back," she said. "It's my private line. I'll hope to hear from you in the next two days."

She stood up. I stood up. We shook hands. She clasped mine warmly, held it longer than she needed to, and looked into my eyes.

"I so appreciate your willingness to help," she said, her voice low with sincerity. "And I am sorry about your father."

You won't need much of anybody's help, I thought.

I'd give her this, though. She was a tomato and a babe, all right, maybe even a hoochie. But she was an equal-opportunity seducer.

She left me in a cloud of perfume and cigarette smoke. She left me wondering why Jake hadn't delivered the tape he'd weaseled out of me.

21

"So do you think your dad's working for somebody else now? Smiling Sid, maybe? Or maybe Creighton's on to his wife's shenanigans, and Jake's playing both ends against the middle?"

I was still in Styles's office, my feet up on her desk, leaning back in one of those springy old wooden office chairs, talking to her on the phone. I'd given the plants a good drenching, but they didn't appear to have recovered from the shock yet.

"And making a bundle by collecting from both?" Styles asked. "It's possible. It sounds like him. Did she show you her gun?"

"She didn't show me anything," I said. "Not even the color of her money."

"Poor you."

"She did, however, let me light her cigarette. And she had that kind of thrilling, low, quavery voice that promised everything."

Styles snorted. "Try to collect, and she'll show you the little gun."

"So, where do we go from here?" I asked. "Can you call your father and find out what the hell he's up to?"

"Sure," she said. "I can call him. But considering the fact that he's a congenital liar, I don't think it would get us anywhere."

"Well, I wish you'd come home," I complained. "Things are getting weirder by the second around here."

"Golly, I'm touched," she said. "So what is it that appeals to you most about me? My ability to deal with weirdness?"

"That, and your training in the use of firearms."

"Ah."

"And your sartorial savoir faire counts for something, too."

"Oh, goody! I'd hate to think that all those hours at the army-navy surplus were wasted."

"So, back to the matter at hand," I said, glancing at my watch. The late show would let out in ten minutes.

"You haven't called Hank Mann back yet, have you?"

"Not yet."

"Try to set that up as soon as possible," she said. "With luck, I'll be back tomorrow night."

"Okay."

"And Gilda . . ."

"Yeah?"

"Say hi to the plants for me."

I hung up.

"Your mom sends hugs and kisses," I told the plants. "Big wet ones."

Back at the theater, the late show crowd was leaving. Well, to be honest, I couldn't really call them a crowd; they could have made an elevatorful of claustrophobics.

I held the door open for Philomena Muncie, who was dabbing at her eyes, pushing her glasses up and down her forehead. She smiled at me gamely, sniffled, and stumbled out the door. Duke was watching impassively from the ticket booth.

"Tell me she's crying because the movie was sad and not because she paid four-fifty for it," I said to him.

"She always cries at movies," Duke said. "Haven't you noticed? She probably cried when the shark bit it in *Jaws*. Wait'll she finds out the dinosaurs lose in *The Lost World*."

"You check the rest rooms yet?"

He nodded.

"That's where I found Justy Jerenovitch," he said. "He thought it would be cool to hide out in the theater overnight."

He shivered, and I guessed that he was imagining the threat of a six-year-old turned loose on our projection equipment. I wanted to point out that it was a lot like the threat of turning me loose on our projection equipment, but I refrained. I didn't feel up to a pep talk.

"Didn't his mother miss him?"

"I don't think she missed him," Duke said. "Whether she noticed he was missing or not wasn't real clear from our conversation. She sounded a little distracted. She said something about remembering to count noses more often, but I think she meant her, not me."

Jeanie Jerenovitch was one of those poor souls who had lost the baby lottery. After three boys, she'd tried one last time for a girl, been talked into taking fertility drugs, and wound up with male triplets. When they got older, they could form their own doo-wop group and earn money on street corners, but right now they were a handful. In school, Jeanie had been

as perky as Pollyanna on Prozac. Now, she and her husband
Tim dragged around town like extras from *Night of the Living Dead*.

"Faye around?" I asked.

"Upstairs."

After the apartment building fire, Faye had officially moved
in with her grandmother, Clara. The rest of the family had
worried about it, but Valentino had installed a new security system and checked all of the smoke detectors. Unof-
ficially, Faye was living upstairs in the Paradise with her
editing equipment. She told everyone it was probably safer
for Clara if she spent most of her time at the theater, but she
didn't say it when Duke was around.

I climbed the stairs, listening to my knees creak.

Faye was sitting in front of her state-of-the-art digital editing deck. She appeared mesmerized.

"Faye?"

"Hmmm?"

"Can we, like, talk?" I asked.

"Sure, Gilda," she said. Her eyes never left the screen.

"I mean, like, face-to-face."

"Yeah, sure."

"Faye," I said more peremptorily, "this is your cousin, but
also your boss, speaking. I want to see the whites of your
eyes."

"Yeah, okay," she said, in the same distracted voice. "Just a
sec." She pressed a key and the image disappeared. She turned
to me. "Sorry, I was floating. What's up?"

I told her about my evening's entertainment.

"Get outta here!" she exclaimed. "So this stone fox just
walks in and says she's sorry she shot your dad and then offers you money for the tape? So, what was she like? Was she
really raggin'? Did she, like, scam on you?"

"She asked me for a light," I said hesitantly.

"No shit!" She shook her head. "I wish I'd been there! And
she thought you were Styles the whole time! Right on, Gilda!

You go, girl!" She offered me her palm, and I slapped it—with less enthusiasm on my part than hers. "The way this is going, we'll collect from everybody and still have a copy of the tape. That'd be kick-ass!"

"Styles wants you to call Hank Mann and set up a screening," I said. "She still wants to know if he'll identify the Falcon."

She frowned. "I don't really see what difference it'll make," she said. "We know that's why everybody's after the tape, including Mrs. Creighton Hale. But if Styles wants me to, I'm easy. I'll call him tomorrow." She grinned at me slyly. "So, what do you think, Gilda? Would you like to, like, hook up with Mrs. Hale?"

"She's not my type," I said.

"Yeah, really," she conceded. "She's a leaver, and you already had one of those."

As if to underscore Faye's observation, I found a squarish, formal white envelope lying in ambush on the hall table when I went home that night. The handwriting was a familiar scribble, though I could tell from the elongated loops, uneven spacing, and darker ink patches that the writer had taken pains. The weight of memory crushed my heart as I picked up the envelope. It was an invitation to Paulie's eighth-grade graduation.

22

The next day, red eyed and hungover, I crewed for Faye as she shot some footage in the Buckeye State gym. Some of the Lady Groundhogs were playing a pickup game. The game looked pretty lethargic to me, but the pace intensified when the camera started rolling. The gym had that musty smell of well-aged gym socks and leather. I stood on the sidelines with a young woman wearing about twenty-five pounds of knee brace and leaning on a crutch. She introduced herself as AnneMarie Parnell.

We both kept our eyes on the game as we chatted, and she directed half of her comments to the players. Our conversation was punctuated by the squeak of sneakers on wood.

"So, you been doing this long?" she asked. Then, without missing a beat, she said, in a voice that started softly and built to a shout, "That's it, Danny, take it to the hoop! Go, girl! Go, go, go, go, go! Aww, no!" Her voice eased back down again. "Can't believe she missed that jam! She really skyed!"

"About three weeks," I said. "It's not a career opportunity."

"No?" she said. "What do you do?"

"I own a movie theater," I said.

"Whoa, Tonya!" she called. "You own that real estate, girl? Get out of the lane!" In a normal voice, she said, "Really? That's cool! So I guess you see a lot of movies, huh?"

"I see parts of a lot of movies," I said. "When you own the theater, you don't have much time to watch movies."

Just saying it made me anxious. What was I doing here? I had bills to pay, box office reports to fill out, orders to worry about. Hell, I still had to find a place to live where the answering service didn't screen my calls. How did I get sucked into every family project that came along? I looked across the court to where Faye and Natalie were filming under the hoop. Faye was proving to be a very expensive employee. But, I reminded myself, she can project.

Somebody went down hard. I heard the thud, the grunt, and the string of profanity that followed. A tall, powerfully built black woman I didn't recognize limped off the court and sat down on the bleacher next to us. She picked up the towel and whacked the floor a few times to vent her frustration.

"If that was your ankle again, you better put ice on it," AnneMarie told her.

"Yes, Momma," the injured player said. "Shi-i-i-it!"

I couldn't tell if she was mad at herself, mad at someone else, or mad at the basketball court.

"This really wasn't a good day for you guys to come down here," AnneMarie said to me. "Everybody's bummed about the trial."

"What trial?" I asked, looking at her.

"You don't know about that?" she asked. "Somebody finally got up the nerve to charge Jimmy DeGiulio with rape. Her lawyer even got another woman to come forward, but the fucking jury let him walk."

"Fucking judge threw out half the fucking evidence," the injured player said. "Shi-i-i-it!"

"Who's Jimmy DeGiulio?" I asked.

They looked at me.

"The biggest goddamn prick on the team," the injured player said. "Not literally," she amended, "though he acts like it."

"The men's team?" I prompted.

"You don't follow Hog hoops, do you?" AnneMarie said. "Jimmy D.—he's the star point guard on the men's team. One of their two leading scorers."

"In more ways than one," the injured player said. "Only Jimmy's such an ugly bastard—"

"And such a bastard, period," AnneMarie contributed.

"And such a bastard, period," the other continued, "that he doesn't score unless he uses force."

"He's got an attitude," AnneMarie said.

"Yeah, like a self-control thing going on, on and off the court," the other said.

"He thinks he's Dennis Rodman," AnneMarie said.

"Yeah, or Mike Tyson," the other said.

"Some of the guys live together in this house over on Tenth Street," AnneMarie said. "They call it Hog Heaven."

"More like a pigsty," the other muttered.

"Danielle used to go over there to study with Ben," AnneMarie said to me, nodding at the other in a way that suggested that my other informant was Danielle.

"And Ben is . . . ?" I prompted them.

"The only nonasshole on the men's team," Danielle said.

"Greg Jacoby, the team captain," AnneMarie said. "Most of these guys are majoring in, like, Phys. Ed. or something like that, but Jacoby's prelaw. Everybody expects him to be a judge or a Supreme Court justice someday. So they started calling him Obi-Wan Jacoby, because he was wise."

"And from there it got to Ben Jacoby," I said.

"She knows all about movies," AnneMarie told Danielle. "She owns a movie theater up in Eden."

"Cool," Danielle said. "You gonna give the whole team free passes when Spike's new movie comes out?"

"Sure," I said, "if we get to show it. Why not?"

I looked around guiltily just in case Duke was lurking under the bleachers.

"Yeah, so, anyway," AnneMarie continued, "this house where the guys live is like one big frat house. When they're not in training or in season, it's like anything goes over there. I could never figure out why Ben would want to hang out with those losers."

"He spends most of his time over at Jen's," Danielle said. "That's the only way he can stand it."

Shouts alerted us that two players were down at the other end of the court, but they both got up again. One stood for a few minutes bent over with her hands on her knees, breathing hard, but then she straightened and play resumed.

"So, anyway." AnneMarie picked up the thread of her story. "There's a lot of drinking going on over there when they're partying—"

"Which is most of the time, in the off season," Danielle put in.

"—and Jimmy D. gets drunk, and then he hits on a girl, and if she says no, he just doesn't let up. This latest one is, like, the fourth one I know of who got raped."

"Where does he find these girls?" Danielle slapped her towel angrily against the bleachers. "You'd think they'd have a clue!"

"Two of them at least were freshmen when it happened,"
AnneMarie said. "I don't know what class the others were.
Anyway, Danny, you know how they get when hot-shit Jimmy
pays attention to them."

"Weirded out is what I'd get, I know that," Danielle said.
"They probably went hoping to hook up with Richie or Ben."

"Whatever," AnneMarie said. "It's not their fault they got
raped, even if they were drinking. One girl told me he was,
like, waiting for her when she came out of the bathroom upstairs, and she couldn't get away from him. I think another
girl just passed out and woke up and found him on top of her."

"Talk about your worst nightmare!" Danielle shook
her head.

A ball slammed into the floor right in front of her, and before we could react, Berta Homans came diving after it.
Danielle put up her arms to shield herself and effectively de-
flected Berta's charge. Berta caromed off Danielle and fell at
my feet. When I looked down, I was holding her up by the
elbows.

"What you want to do, break my other ankle?" Danielle
cried in mock anger.

"I didn't even make you stop running your mouth," Berta
said as I righted her. "I ain't worried about your ankle."

She retrieved the ball and threw it in bounds in front of us.

"If there's been a trial," I said to my two informants, "that
means Coach Hale knows what's been going on. Doesn't he
care?"

Danielle made a sound of disgust and looked away.

"Ain't nothin' going on, far's Coach is concerned, just kids
screwing around," she said. "They drink, they get horny, she
wakes up embarrassed is all. And if she's got a few bruises,
well, hell, his boys're big and don't know their own strength."

"Yeah, you don't want to hear the one about how they're
trained to hold onto the ball," AnneMarie told me. "Now
that's just sick." She propped an elbow on one crutch and
pointed an index finger down her throat.

"And if she's *real* upset," Danielle said, "she gets a car."

"What?" I looked at AnneMarie for confirmation.

"That's right," AnneMarie said. "A car."

"From Smiling Sid Green?"

"That's right," she said again. "Is that bogus, or what? He's, like, this big-ass Groundhog fan—"

"Men only," Danielle reminded her.

"Yeah, okay, this big-ass fan of Groundhog football and men's basketball. That's why the men all got these killer wheels."

"Dude ain't even an alum," Danielle said to me. "Went to Michigan. Do you believe it?"

"Somebody offers women rape victims a car not to prosecute," I summarized, just to be sure I had this right.

AnneMarie nodded. "This one girl I knew, she said she took the car because they told her she'd never win taking a Buckeye State hoops star to court, and she figured they were right. She was, like, real intimidated by their lawyers, and her parents didn't have a lot of money, and she was freaking out about the whole thing anyway. She never even told her parents what happened, but then she dropped out of school 'cause she couldn't handle being someplace where she might run into Jimmy D., you know? She needed the car to get a job, and then later she told her parents that she bought the car with the money she was making at her job."

She paused to watch a nicely executed play that involved several quick passes and left a player alone, unguarded, right under the basket.

"That was sweet!" she exclaimed. Then she said, "At least she got something out of it, I guess—the girl, I mean."

"Lucky she didn't get AIDS," Danielle commented, "or rabies."

"But somebody finally said no to the bribe?" I asked.

"Yeah, girl name of Julie Stoebel," Danielle said.

"She's little, but she's awesome," AnneMarie enthused. "Her mom and dad really supported her, and we thought at last somebody was going to kick his butt."

"We just found out last night," Danielle said. " 'Not guilty.' "

"That sucks," I said sympathetically.

"Yeah," AnneMarie said. "It sucks big time."

There was a lull in the conversation while we all contemplated the whole depressing situation.

The game was winding down, and Faye was signaling me from across the court. I was trying to ignore her, still sore from hauling a hundred pounds of equipment into the gym. If she thought I'd move it all into the locker room, she had another think coming. If the news photographers could get away with one Insta-Cam, why couldn't she?

"Don't mind us," AnneMarie said at last. "We're still mad about it."

"Yeah," Danielle said. "And when we're through gettin' mad, we're going to get even."

23

We set up the Beta deck to show the tape on the big screen in Clara's living room. We'd planned out what to say to Hank Mann, depending on his reactions, but this was not your typical Liberty production. Clara was sworn to secrecy, and had complied for once. She didn't want Adele showing up to redo her living room, or Gloria showing up to restyle her hair.

I was there a little early on Saturday morning, yawning into my coffee cup and finger-combing my hair. I think I was still sporting a circular dent in my cheek from a button on my pajama sleeve. It complemented the bruise I'd gotten the day before when a tripod fell on me in the back of the Fast Flush van.

"What did you do to your hair, Gilda?" Clara asked, frowning disapprovingly.

"This morning? Nothing," I answered. "Why?"

Hank arrived with a bounce in his step that didn't disturb a single hair in his perfectly blow-dried do.

"Hey! I'm so relieved you got the tape back," he said to Faye, who would never win Miss Congeniality with the look she was giving him. "Who took it?"

"The less said on that subject, the better," Clara intoned. It was the only line we'd given her to say, and she delivered it with all the weight of a death announcement. It was intended to implicate some family member in the theft.

But if her performance was over the top, Hank didn't seem to notice, and I soon discovered why. He was a lousy actor himself.

Sixty seconds into Mike Falcone's first appearance on the screen, he raised a hand.

"Hey, wait a sec! That's—no, it couldn't be, could it? Yeah, it is!" He let the excitement build in his voice. He stood up, leveling an index finger and shaking it at the screen. "Well, I'll be damned! It's Mike Falcone!"

"Who?" Clara demanded, clearly not trusting us to deliver the line. She sat forward in her chair and frowned at the screen convincingly.

Faye glanced at me and rolled her eyes.

"Mike Falcone," Hank said. "High school basketball player. Plays for Hilliard. Really hot recruit."

"Well," said Clara nonchalantly, as if unimpressed, "I guess basketball players have to go shopping sometimes, too."

"No, but look who he's talking to," Hank said, approaching the screen and putting his finger on Smiling Sid's nose.

"Isn't that Smiling Sid Green, the car dealer?" I asked. I didn't want Hank to notice that Clara was the only one in the room on speaking terms with him.

"Yup, that's who it is, all right," Hank said with satisfaction.

"So the basketball player is buying a car?" Clara asked disingenuously.

"No, no, don't you get it?" Hank turned to face us, silhouetted against the screen. "They're offering him a car to sign with State!"

"Sign what?" Clara asked, playing her ignorance to the hilt.

"A letter of intent," Hank explained patiently. "See, schools recruit players to play on their team. When the player makes up his mind where he's going, he signs a letter of intent, and the recruiting is over."

"We know what a letter of intent is, Hank," Faye said irritably.

"But offering a college athlete a car to induce him to sign with a particular school, surely that's against some rule!" Clara protested. "I thought nonprofessional athletes couldn't be paid."

"It *is* against the rules," Hank said. "Maybe that's why somebody's trying to get their hands on this tape—or destroy it. Buckeye State could be charged with recruiting violations." He frowned at the screen and rubbed his chin speculatively.

"But is that common, offering high school kids cars to sign one of these letters of intent?" Clara asked. "Surely it's too expensive. After all, I just read that State had launched a new capital campaign, and the article talked about how the state government had cut budgets in the public university system. How can they afford to give away cars?"

"Let's see how this plays out, can we?" Hank said, crooking a thumb at the screen. "Then maybe I can explain it to you."

Faye rolled her eyes again.

She stopped the tape at the conclusion of the demonstration.

"The rest is just interviews," she said to Hank. "You don't want to see that, do you?"

"Well, if there's anybody in the background—" he demurred.

"No background to speak of," she said, "just a blank wall."

"Well, I guess not, then," he said reluctantly. "But I'd like to see it again—what we just saw, if that's okay. I may have missed something when we were talking."

While Faye rewound, Hank tried to answer Clara's questions.

"In the first place, Mrs. June, Buckeye State isn't giving away cars," he said. "A fan of Buckeye State is giving away cars on behalf of Buckeye State. In the second place, though he's giving away cars, he's probably got some paperwork to cover it—you know, like it's really a lease, and the kid pays a token amount."

"So a wealthy alum can literally buy a basketball team for his favorite school, and get away with it?" Clara asked.

"Well, yeah, pretty much," Hank said, "except Green's not a Buckeye alum, just a booster."

"But then what makes this tape so valuable," she said, "if the paperwork makes this look like a legitimate transaction?"

"Uh, well, that's a good question," he said. "They're probably concerned because there's a rule that nobody can contact a high school athlete till July first, the summer before his senior year, and we're not there yet. After July first, the coach can contact him, but boosters can't."

" 'Him'?" Faye echoed testily.

"What?" Hank said, looking at her. "Oh, well, him or her. Same rules apply."

"Same cars apply?" she asked.

He shrugged. "In some Division One schools, probably there are some cars for the top women recruits, too, along with the other perks the men get. But, yeah, the majority of the bribery and recruiting violations you see are in the men's teams. You know, Faye—the stakes are higher because the rewards are bigger. I'm just telling it like it is."

"By rewards, do you mean the game attendance and the—whatever you call it in sports—the box office?" Clara asked.

He shook his head. "It's much bigger than that, Mrs. June. The big prize is tournament money. The teams that make it to the Final Four are earning money from the NCAA's television contracts. Of course, the NCAA is making most of the money, but the schools get some of that, too. Anyway, a winning sports team—that brings in a lot of money in alumni donations, too. See? You've got to look at the big picture."

"If this was an illegal contact," I put in, "what do you think are the chances that Buckeye State would get suspended for that kind of violation? It doesn't seem very major to me."

"That's really hard to tell," he conceded. "It doesn't seem very major to me, either, but maybe it does to somebody. Let's watch it again."

I shook my head. "I'm outta here," I said to Faye. "I can run this thing in my dreams by now. I've got apartments to look at before the first matinee."

I'd made a desultory survey of apartment ads that morning in the Eden *Herald*. Sitting at my aunt Lillian's kitchen table with a notebook and a portable phone, I'd called and arranged to see a few places. I hadn't felt any particular enthusiasm for any of them, but I'd feigned a modicum of enthusiasm because Ruth Hernandez had been looking over my shoulder, clucking her tongue and pointing a flour-dusted, pastry-encrusted finger at each as I'd circled it.

"South Main Street? You don't want to live on South Main Street, Gilda," she'd said. "You're going to have a Wendy's on one side, a McDonald's on the other, and God knows who behind you."

"West Pearl Street?" she'd said. "I don't even know where that is. You got to watch out you don't end up living over a car repair place, you know?" As if I wouldn't notice before I signed the lease.

"Donovan Street? I know where that is," she'd said. "You move there, you're going to have dust all over everything, all the time. That cement place is on Donovan Street, and they move those big mixer trucks in and out all day, all day, stirring up the dust until you can't breathe. People die of emphysema living in places like that . . .

"Riverview Lane? Gilda, you're not going to call that one, are you?" she'd said. "That's a complex." Her voice held horror and contempt. "You don't want to live in one of those places, squashed on top of your neighbors like goldfish?" Despite her many years of speaking English, Ruth's figures of speech were often startling, familiar but unfamiliar, like a bent spoon.

She kept up her running commentary as I made my phone calls.

"Ask him can you smell the sewer plant from there."

"Ask him if he's the one got all those broken-down cars all over the front yard."

"Ask her do you get a garage."

"Ask her why the last people moved out."

"Ask him do they take pets. You should get a pet, Gilda, if you're going to live by yourself. A nice little dog to scare away burglars—someone you can talk to so you don't drive yourself crazy."

There were moments when silence and solitude appealed to me greatly; this was one of them.

The first place I looked at was small and laid out shotgun style, so that you had to walk through the kitchen to go to the bathroom. The second place, whose "quaint decor" had been touted in the ad, featured in the bedroom a dizzying wallpaper of pink and fuchsia cabbage roses that would give me floral nightmares, and in the kitchen row upon row of geese carrying baskets and trailing straw hats and bows. The third place was over a chiropractor's office, which might have recommended it if the chiropractor who showed it to me had been a bit less intense, his eager smile less unsettling. The fourth and last place, in an apartment complex, had been predictably sterile, as if catering to a transient clientele. I ranked it "tolerable if desperate." I wasn't desperate yet.

I was, however, depressed, and I arrived at the theater that way. I was still carrying the newspaper around with me, and I was looking over it again, hoping to spot some prospect I'd missed when Ruth Hernandez had been reading it over my shoulder. So I was looking down as I pushed open the door to the theater and met, just inside, with some soft but solid resistance. I looked up in confusion, as if the laws of physics had just gone on strike, and the air had turned to rubber. I had walked into something brownish green—a massive object that blocked my view and smelled of vinyl.

Still confused, I backed up. Maybe I'd opened the wrong door. I wasn't in the Paradise, I was in a parallel universe with massive trees constructed like inner tubes.

I backed up farther. Stretching from familiar floor to ceiling was a tubular object, with toes and claws at the base, I now saw. Above, hanging from the ceiling, was a second foot, which appeared poised to crush the ticket booth. I spotted Todd and Duke, Todd on the ladder tickling the thing's toes, and Duke on the floor, pulling on some kind of guide rope to help position it.

Duke grinned at me happily.

"Guess who's coming to dinner?" he said.

24

Todd went outside with Sara, another member of our summer staff, to paint giant footprints on the sidewalk in front of the theater. Duke gave me a word-by-word report of his conversation with our booker. You would have thought we'd won the lottery.

In a small, independent theater like ours, most films lost money. Some broke even. But every once in a while, you'd land a hit, often a sleeper, that would carry the theater for several months. Since being on the historic register didn't pay the light bills, small theater owners prayed for an error on the

part of the film distributors—either an error in judgment, or a
momentary confusion of a Paradise, Rialto, or Strand with a
Cinemark, General, or Sony theater—that would bring them
a first-run *Lethal Weapon* or even *The English Patient.* Since
the local multiplex had burned down, we had a better shot at
the big moneymakers, but we could still lose out to the suburban Columbus chain theaters. Snagging *The Lost World* was a
substantial triumph. Those lizards could pay a lot of light
bills.

With all the excitement, I didn't get a chance to speak to
Faye again about Hank Mann until the late show had started.
She had worked the second matinee and the early show, then
disappeared into her lair on the second floor.

The old dressing rooms over the stage had never been
soundproofed, and I wondered how she could work up here
with the noise from the soundtracks rising through the floor-
boards. As I approached the door of her editing room, there
was a sudden lull in the din from below, and I heard a man's
voice, not one I recognized, say, "I hope you've got good life
insurance."

"Faye?" I called, my heart picking up speed. "Faye?"

I pushed open the door. My eyes swept the room. Nobody.

She was sitting in front of a machine that looked like one of
those high-tech security monitors they have at nuclear power
plants—or what passed in Hollywood for a security monitor.
The room was good-sized for a dressing room, small for a
bedroom. It was lit by a bare bulb in a pockmarked ceiling, as
well as by a desk lamp she had clipped to the desk where she
was working. The paint on the walls was a dusky and discol-
ored beige that might have been white in its youth. Fissures
in the walls suggested bygone earthquakes, but I wondered
whether Sly Stallone and Arnold Schwarzenegger hadn't put
them there. I could feel the vibrations from the theater below through the soles of my sneakers.

There was a futon rolled up in one corner, two chairs, and
the editing table—a door supported by sawhorses. Otherwise, the room was crammed with equipment, so much equip-

ment, in fact, that I was taken aback. When had she moved it all up here? I had seen her lugging a camera and some tripods up the stairs one day, and I'd seen Todd staggering up the stairs with her editing deck, but where had all the rest of it come from? I'd been living downstairs from Sony TriStar, and I hadn't even known it.

She turned around in her chair, earphones draped around her neck.

"Sorry, Gilda," she said. "Was it too loud? I need a new set of earphones. These keep coming unplugged." She leaned over and wiggled the connector for emphasis.

"Who's that?" I asked, nodding at the man on the screen. In spite of myself, I was becoming interested in her work.

"His name's Murray Richman," she said. "He's a freelance sportswriter. He has a couple of books out on college sports. Want to hear?"

She reached for a nearby banana box labeled ELECTRICAL and dug out another set of earphones and a plug with a dual jack.

"Pull up a chair," she said.

The one available was a yellow vinyl and chrome tubing number from a kitchen in my past—Adele's, possibly, or Gloria's. I sat down and put on the earphones while she rewound the tape.

The image on the screen was Murray Richman's, but the audio included Faye's voice, asking him questions and making comments. Richman was a stocky man in blue jeans and a rumpled shirt with the sleeves rolled up. He had dark, curly hair, thick as Berber carpet and sprinkled with gray, and a broad grin under a full gray moustache. He had large hands, which he used liberally. Behind him was a desk piled so high with books and papers that it resembled one of those games in which you see how many blocks you can remove from a structure without making it fall. The whole tenuous construction appeared to be in constant danger from his flailing hands.

"Okay, look," he said, "you gotta understand the scam.

These guys—the athletic directors and the coaches—they want you to think they're making money hand over fist for the colleges, not to mention building school pride, yadda, yadda. That's how come they earn these ridiculous salaries—they want you to think they practically pay themselves, see? Did you know that there are at least a hundred Division One basketball coaches earning ninety to a hundred thou a year? Think about that the next time your dear alma mater puts the squeeze on you!"

Faye's voice responded: "But they do earn money for the school, right?"

He leaned forward and pumped an admonishing finger at her.

"That's what they want you to think," he said. "Ticket sales? Forget it. They're not letting that money outside the athletic department—no way! Franchises for team T-shirts, sweatshirts, souvenir mugs, funny hats, baby pants, et cetera— ditto. You think that, say, the French department or the psych department ever sees a dollar of that money? Not a chance." He made a sweeping slash with his hand that began just under his chin and ended just shy of a box of floppies perched on top of a pile of books.

" 'Aha!' you're thinking, 'but what about all that scholarship money?' Because at the end of every game you've watched on television, they name MVPs, and Chevrolet or State Farm or somebody donates a thousand dollars to the general scholarship funds—the general scholarship funds, mind you, not the athletic scholarship funds—of their respective schools." He gestured in the direction of the desk behind him, as if he had a television there. Maybe he did, hidden under all the other junk.

"You're supposed to get all choked up about it—you're not supposed to sit down and calculate how much scholarship money has already been invested in bringing you this televised event. It's part of the myth that television underwrites college sports to a significant degree, or that revenue sports underwrite the athletic programs as a whole, keep it afloat so that colleges can continue to turn out Olympic swimmers and runners and shot-putters. Do you know how much money it costs to light and heat the gyms and fieldhouses and stadiums, build and maintain them, keep them secure, provide water for the locker rooms, not to mention the grass on the football field, launder towels and uniforms, provide and maintain equipment for training, and probably a lot of other stuff I'm not thinking of at the moment? And every home game adds to the university's utility and general maintenance bills, and every away game costs them a fortune in travel. Fortunately for the athletic departments, most of those expenses—utility bills, especially—never show up in a separate budget for the athletic department."

He leaned forward, elbows on his knees, and began ticking things off on splayed fingers. "Plus, you got your salaries for trainers and assistant coaches, recruiting expenses for coaches to go there, recruits to come here. You got your coaches' salaries, which I've already mentioned. Athletic directors are in the same ballpark, often higher. It's obscene!"

"Doesn't alumni giving increase when the school has a winning season?" Faye's voice objected.

"Believe it or not, there are studies that show that there's no relation between win-loss records and alumni giving," Richman said. "Alums tend to be interested in academic programs, not athletic programs. Now boosters are another matter. Boosters aren't alums. But then, boosters don't give money to the academic programs; they just want to see the team win."

"What about televised bowl games and tournaments? They bring in money, don't they?" Faye's voice asked.

"Yeah, but not as much as you might expect, because the school's usually splitting the dough with the NCAA or with other teams in the conference. But you're right—that's the big prize. So every school is investing a fortune on the chance that they'll make the Rose Bowl or the Final Four. You may think Rose Bowl fever around here is all about status and glamour. But to some people, it's about raises and bonuses and renewed contracts. Bottom line?" He sketched a line in the air in front of him. "Only a handful of college athletic programs make money. Only another handful break even. The rest are losing money—a lot of money." He raised his hands, palms forward. "It's all smoke and mirrors," he said. "Smoke and mirrors."

"So the whole setup is ripe for an exposé," Faye's voice said.

He grinned. "If you can get anybody to listen to you, I hope you've got good life insurance. You understand, there's a fortune being made here, and people don't give up that kind of money gracefully."

The screen went white. I glanced at my watch and removed my headphones. Faye followed suit.

"So what does he think should be done?" I asked. "Does he want college sports abolished?"

"No, he says not," Faye replied. "He thinks smaller schools like Eden College maintain a good balance between academics and athletics. He just thinks we should stop pretending that schools like Buckeye State **are** engaged in amateur athletics. He says that at that level, college sports is, like, professional entertainment, and we ought to pay the athletes. And he doesn't think they should try to play and go to school at the same time. He thinks they should do one and then the other. Or just go play, if that's all they want to do. A lot of these guys could care less about college."

"Well, he's very articulate," I said. "You have some really great footage, Faye."

"Yeah," she said gloomily.

Surprised by her tone, I said, "What's wrong?"

"I don't know, Gilda. It's just that I started out to make a half-hour film on gender equity and sports. Now I have all this really great footage, but it's, like, all over the map." She sighed heavily. "I have footage of women playing basketball and soccer. I have a tape from a baton-twirling school. I have interviews with coaches and players and kids on street corners. A friend gave me a tape of the Kilgore Rangerettes. Oh, yeah, and you missed the part on the Richman tape where he talks about college athletes and rape. He knows somebody who's doing this study, and it seems to be showing that a disproportionately high number of rapes on campus involve male athletes assaulting women."

"Really? That's pretty amazing."

"Yeah, right, but what am I going to do with it all? I started out to do a senior project, and what I've got is *The Civil War*. I'm so bummed."

"Well, at least you don't have to worry about financing it," I pointed out.

"Yeah, but . . ." She trailed off in obvious frustration.

"Maybe you do have more than one film," I said. "That's okay, isn't it? You just need to figure out what goes best with what."

"I guess."

"Anyway, what I came up here to ask was, what happened with Hank after I left?"

"Oh, that's another thing." She sat up straighter. "It was so weird. He tried every way he could to get me to admit I had more footage somewhere that I wasn't showing him. He didn't come right out and say that, but that's what he meant."

"Other footage?" I felt my brow crease. "You mean, the Hi8 footage I shot?"

"But how would he know about that, unless somebody who was there saw you walking around with a camera?"

"And anyway, there were other people walking around with video cameras that day," I said. "Moms and dads who were taping their kids' performances, remember? Why would somebody remember me in particular, unless they watched us long enough to associate me with you? I don't get it."

We sat in silence for a minute or two.

"Why do I get this feeling, like we're standing at center court at tip-off?" Faye asked.

"Yeah," I agreed, "and everybody heard the whistle but us."

25

"He says he gave it to her."

"He says what?" I shouted into the phone. "Styles, I can't hear you."

"Hold on," she shouted back.

I heard what sounded like disco music in the background. Then it faded, only to be replaced by loud voices and other sounds I couldn't identify.

"Styles?"

"Hang on, I'm in the kitchen."

The noise died down, but I could still hear it.

"That's better," she said.

"Where are you now?"

"Out back by the garbage cans, so we'd better make this quick."

"I didn't know disco music was that big in Little Rock."

"It's not. I'm in Dallas. I'm bringing you a T-shirt: *I Shot J. R.*"

"Oh, goody."

"About the tape—Jake says he gave it to her."

"What?" This time it was disbelief I meant to express.

"He says he gave it to her," she shouted.

"I can hear you, I just can't believe you," I said crossly, rubbing my ear.

"He says he gave it to her, she paid him, and everybody was happy. He doesn't know what she's complaining about."

"She didn't shoot him? Like in the head?"

"Spike says no. Says he didn't hear any loud noises, and he checked Jake for new bullet holes. Nada."

"So you're sure he's telling the truth, then? Why would he admit to you that he betrayed us by lying, stealing another tape, and selling it?"

"Because we both know that I know he's a louse," Styles said. "And because his professional pride was hurt when I told him she'd come to me—well, you—to get what he apparently couldn't give her."

I stared up at my bedroom ceiling. This made no sense.

"You're sure you gave him the right tape?" she asked.

I didn't deign to answer this question.

"I mean, was it in your possession and under your control at all times?"

"Styles," I said, "you've been flying too much."

"Tell me about it."

"Hank Mann thinks we showed him the wrong tape, too," I reported.

"He does? Does he say what's wrong about it?"

"No, he just thinks we have some footage we're keeping to ourselves."

"Of what, for chrissake?"

"Beats me," I said. "I did shoot some Hi8 footage that day—"

"Wait a minute," she said. "Somebody just dropped a tray of dishes. I thought you said you shot some footage."

"I did." I realized what she was implying, and said indignantly, "Hey, I can aim a camera and push a button as well as the next bozo."

"Sorry, sweetheart, but you're not exactly known for your mechanical aptitude."

"Well, I'm not a complete washout," I said sulkily. "I can use a phone."

"So where's the footage you shot?"

"Faye has it, I guess. But who would have seen it? Nobody. So how do they know they want it?"

"Maybe because they watched you film it," she said. "Maybe because they looked up and spotted you at just the wrong time."

"Such as?"

"Well, if this is about that basketball player—"

"Falcone."

"Yeah, if it's about him, then maybe Sid Green handed him an envelope."

"You mean a payoff?" I asked. "But I didn't see anything like that, and I sure don't think I filmed it."

"How do you know?" she said. "It could have been taking place in the background while you were filming some kid's splits. The point isn't what you saw, it's what they think you saw, or might have seen, and especially what you might have filmed."

"So we should go back and look at the Hi8 footage? Faye's seen it, and she says there's nothing on it. But I guess we can take another look. Damn, Styles, I'm going to know this film as well as she does by the time she's finished with it."

"Maybe she'll thank you in her Academy Award acceptance speech."

"Maybe," I said. "But she'll call me 'the bomb,' and nobody over twenty-two will know what she's talking about."

26

"You got a new girlfriend, Gilda?"

Ruth Hernandez woke me up with the portable phone clutched to her chest.

"What?" I mumbled, half asleep.

"You got a new girlfriend?" She waved the phone at me,

her hand over the mouthpiece. " 'Cause if you do, you better invite her for dinner sometime. Ask her does she like spicy food. If not, I got this new fish recipe I want to try, but you only get fresh fish on Fridays, so I got to plan ahead. She sounds like she likes spicy food, though. She sounds real sexy, Gilda." She raised an eyebrow and gave me a knowing smile.

I blinked at her. She handed me the phone.

"I *do* like spicy food, as a matter of fact." A silky voice spoke low in my ear.

"I don't," I said flatly, as if she cared. I rested my eyelashes on my cheeks. I could think better with my eyes closed, especially in the fog of interrupted sleep.

"Does that mean I'm not invited?" she asked coyly.

"You'll have to talk to Ruth about that," I said. "I'm never home for dinner." In my opinion, Ruth needed to have her feminine intuition checked if she thought Blanche Hale was a good prospect for me.

"Is your name really Gilda?" she asked. "I thought your first name started with an *S*."

"It does," I said. "Gilda is a family name."

"Does it have anything to do with that old Rita Hayworth movie?" she asked.

"They had trouble keeping me in winter gloves when I was a kid," I said. "I was always taking them off and leaving them somewhere."

I could hear her smile over the wire.

"What about my proposition?" she asked.

"The filmmaker wants to meet you before she decides," I said. "She met with the other interested party, and she thinks it would be only fair to meet with you."

Faye and I had agreed on this course of action in hopes of buying time to figure out what the hell was going on.

"All right," she agreed. "What did you tell her about me? I'm curious."

"I told her that you were bigger than a breadbox," I said. "What did you want me to tell her?"

"You told her I was offering five thousand?"

"Oh, that. Sure, I told her."

"Did you tell her why I wanted the tape?"

"Lady, I'm not sure I know why you want the tape, but I told her what you said about it. I probably didn't do it justice, though. I kind of stumbled over the bid for female solidarity."

"Then I'd better tell her myself, hadn't I? Say, tomorrow at seven?"

"I work nights."

"That's right. I suppose you do. Nights and days, both. Suppose you suggest a time."

"Let's say, Tuesday at eleven?"

"In your office? So I can see the progress of your botanical experiment?"

Damn! The plants! I'd forgotten all about them! Well, it had only been three days. Either they'd died, or they'd recovered. I couldn't be expected to run an ICU ward for recuperating plants.

"My office," I confirmed.

I looked in on the plants on my way to the theater. The weeping fig stood leafless. The other plant, whatever it was, though green, trailed languid arms over the side of its pot. This would have been okay if it had been intended to be a vine, but it had the disconcerting appearance of a military officer with a spinal cord injury. I drenched them with water from the rust-stained basin down the hall.

I yawned as I pushed open the theater door and dodged the dinosaur foot. This made two relatively early mornings for me, and I wasn't sure I'd make it through the day. I yawned three more times between the front door and the projection booth, from which issued soft but heartfelt singing. Maybe this wasn't a good day for a projection lesson, after all.

Faye was plugged into a Walkman, so I had to hammer on the wall to warn her of my presence. She turned and slid the headphones down to her neck.

"Hey!" she said with enthusiasm. "We're all set!" She peered at me more closely. "You look wasted."

I raised one eyebrow.

"You know," she said. "Tired."

"The anticipation kept me awake all night," I said.

"Gilda, you need to chill about this stuff," she said. "It's not that hard."

She dragged the small stepladder over to the tall steel contraption that fed the film to the projector. It consisted of three platters the size of small satellite dishes mounted on top of each other like those animated rings that surround the automaton in *Metropolis*. I already knew how to load the film onto the platters from the makeup table off to one side and thread it through the circular frame at the center of each platter, but beyond that I had never ventured—not even through the series of rollers inside the frame.

"That's the brains," Faye said, standing on the stepladder and poking a finger at the rollers. "That's what keeps the film taut and turned around in the right direction and all. It regulates the tension as the projector pulls the film through." She tugged at one end of the film where it passed through a slit in the frame. "This is all scrap on the end of the film—you know that, right? You can't damage the film if you, like, tear or bend this part or anything."

Sez you, I thought.

"So it goes through here like this." She looked down at me, then sent me for one of the stepladders from one of the other booths.

I stood on it and watched her.

"So, like this," she said, and demonstrated, threading the end and pulling it through. "See? Now you have to do it right, or else you, like, scramble the brains. And even if you do it right, you can get static electricity that screws things up, or if the film isn't put together right, so that everything's aligned and all, that screws things up, too."

She said this matter-of-factly. I felt my pulse quicken.

"Well, what do you do when that happens?"

She made a wry face. "Call me or Duke," she said, "and let

us handle it, until you figure it out. Anyway, the static problem hasn't been so bad, according to Duke, since we installed this humidifier unit." She had moved on to another set of rollers mounted on a frame to one side. "Then you thread it through this cleaner, which cleans a lot of the dust off it, and over to the projector."

But instead of going on to the projector, she turned the platter with her hand, and I watched the film come unthreaded, slipping through each roller in turn like a receding memory.

"Now," she said, straightening, "you do it."

I sighed heavily, and traded places with her. I stared down into the brains as if into the heart of darkness.

"Come on, Gilda!" Faye encouraged me. "Just do it! I won't let you screw up and, like, trash the thing."

Fumbling, I managed to get the film threaded through the brains and the cleaner. I took a swipe at my sweaty brow with the back of my hand.

"That's good!" Faye exclaimed, beaming at me. "Very good, Gilda!"

My sense of portending doom was unshaken. The worst was yet to come, and we both knew it.

"Here," she said, reaching up to retrieve something taped to the wall, "you can read this in your spare time."

She handed me a photocopied sheet. At the top, in Duke's scrawl, were the words "READ THIS!" They were underlined three times. The flier was entitled "Troubleshooting Platter Brains."

"I don't have any spare time," I muttered to myself, "since my cousin came to work for me."

She ignored me.

"Now," she said, with the air of a driving instructor preparing to release the emergency brake, "you bring the film over to the projector, and you find the beginning of the film. You know what to look for, right?"

"Numbers."

"Right." She nodded. "There's a lot of scrap on the end,

more than you might think, but you just, like, go through that and look for the numbers, which count down to the start of the film. Now, this is where you have to be really careful, so you get everything lined up right."

I shuffled in close. She opened the projector door.

Something flew out at us. Instinctively, I closed my eyes and threw one hand across my face. I felt a liquid spatter my face and hand. Belatedly, I heard a loud pop.

"Jesus Christ!" Faye exclaimed.

I heard a crash and opened my eyes to see her falling backward. I was too far away to catch her.

I abandoned the projector to its fate and kneeled over her, where she lay on the floor, cussing. This time, I had no trouble understanding what she was saying.

"Goddamn it!" she swore. "Goddamn it!"

"Where are you hurt?" I asked anxiously.

She sat up.

"Ow! I think my ankle's broken." She moved her leg and flinched. "Ow, ow! Shit, Gilda, it hurts like hell!"

"Did you get hit with anything?" I scanned her for blood, but didn't see any.

"I don't think so," she said, then put a hand to her face. "Just this stuff." She ran a finger down one cheek. "Ew, gross! I think I got some in my eye." She winked at me, her eye watering. "What *is* this stuff, Gilda?"

I put a tentative finger to my own forehead, then rubbed thumb and forefinger together. I sniffed my fingers.

"It feels like glue," I said uncertainly.

"Glue?" Faye exclaimed, sniffing her own fingers. "What would glue be doing in the projector?"

My own defensiveness rose and cut through my panic like a shark's fin.

"Well, *I* didn't put it there!" I said. "Don't look at *me*!"

Her mouth twitched, and she suddenly burst out laughing. This made me angrier.

"What?"

"Gilda, I promise—not to—look at you," she said between gasps of mirth, "if you won't—look at me!"

"It's not funny," I said grumpily, wondering if I looked as bad as she did. My scalp contracted at the thought of all that glue in my hair.

"I know it's not!" she gasped. "Ow! I'm the one with the broken ankle! I tripped over the damn stepladder!" She gave it a petulant kick, which earned her another cry of pain.

I stood up to survey the damage to the projector. Faye sobered instantly.

"Oh, Gilda! How bad is it?"

I couldn't answer at first. I didn't know much about projectors, but the sight of all that glue sickened me. It was oozing down the side of the metal frame that surrounded the aperture, dripping from there onto the rollers that I knew had something to do with sound, and then dropping from there into a puddle at the bottom.

"It's bad," I said at last.

"Better call Duke," Faye said.

"Duke, the police, the ambulance—"

"The glue removal squad," Faye put in. "Gilda, I hate to mention it, but I think this stuff is, like, hardening up. Do you think you could help me down to the rest room to wash up?"

"I don't think it's a good idea for you to walk on that ankle," I said.

"I don't think so, either, but if I don't, I'm going to look like I had plastic surgery," she pointed out. "Besides, athletes usually limp off the field if they can. It's not that far to the bathroom."

"Okay," I said, "I'll help you." I bent down and put a hand under her elbow as she struggled to her feet, crying in pain and cursing. "But what if we get stuck together?"

That set her off again, and she was laughing through her tears all the way to the bathroom.

We took one look at our faces in the mirror, and chorused, "Ew-w-w! Gross!"

"Let's hope it comes off with water," I said, ripping paper

towel after paper towel from the dispenser and handing them to Faye, who was leaning against a sink for support. "You'd better take all your jewelry off." I refrained from pointing out that she wouldn't want to have her nose ring surgically removed.

She filled the sink with water, then dunked as much of her face as she could manage. She came up sputtering and cursing.

"Those bastards!" she said viciously. "This was totally uncalled for!"

I was underwater myself when she said this, but I agreed wholeheartedly. The only thing keeping my anger and outrage in check was the prospect of calling Duke to tell him what had happened.

A bellow of rage from beyond the rest room door told me I didn't have to.

The door flew open and hit the wall with a resounding crack.

He stood staring at us, quivering, speechless either with rage or astonishment.

"Glue bomb," Faye said succinctly. "The bastards put a fucking glue bomb in the projector."

He nodded once and turned to go. I was sure his mind was racing ahead to the cleanup. Then he paused and looked back at us guiltily.

"Anybody hurt?" he asked.

"Faye tripped over the stepladder," I said. "She thinks her ankle's broken."

He took a step toward her.

"Never mind me," she said. "Go work on your projector."

"Did you call the police?" he asked.

I shook my head, peeling a strip of glue off my chin. "We came in here first, to wash the glue off before it hardened."

I saw the flash of horror in his eyes. He snatched a fistful of paper towels from the dispenser, turned, and ran.

I trailed him to the scene of the crime.

"You know, Duke," I said hesitantly, "if we call the police, they'll want us not to have touched anything."

He was already engaged in open heart surgery.

"They can't always have what they want," he said testily. "Hand me that bottle of solvent on the shelf behind you."

"Duke's right, Gilda." To my surprise, Faye was at my elbow. How she'd made it across the lobby I didn't know. She was standing on the top step of the short flight of steps that led up to the projection booth. She was clutching the stair rail for support. With her red hair flat against her head, and stripped of her jewelry and makeup, she looked like an otter. Unconsciously, she reached up, grabbed a bottle off the shelf, and handed it to me. "The projector's our first priority, 'cause without it, we got no show. If we even have to cancel one movie tonight, they will have, like, won, and we can't let them do that."

Again, I heard theme music swelling in my head. Faye stretched out an arm, and both she and Wonder Woman flexed their biceps.

"Help me over to the projector, Gilda," she said. "I'm going to help Duke."

"With a broken ankle?" I said. "Don't you think we should take care of that first?"

Even as I said it, I was helping her move in the wrong direction.

"You can bring me some aspirin," Faye said, wincing as she eased herself down to the stepladder, her left leg stretched out stiff in front of her.

"I'm gonna take this thing apart and clean everything," Duke said.

I wanted to ask if he'd ever done that before, but my caution was running against the tide.

"I'll sit on the floor," Faye offered. "You can hand stuff to me, and I'll clean it."

"Are you sure?" I said, wincing myself at Faye's grimace when she lowered herself to the floor.

"Why don't you get her some ice out of the bin?" Duke

suggested, eyes focused on his work. "And Gilda," he added, as I turned to leave, "maybe you should wait to call the cops. I don't want them getting in the way."

"Well," I said. I peeled another strip of glue from my nose. "Okay."

I had a thought.

"Duke," I said, "can I take pictures?"

He scowled. "You want to take pictures of me cleaning the projector?"

"I want to take pictures of the crime scene, before you clean it up."

"Well, okay," he said grudgingly. "But hurry up."

27

Detective Sergeant Dale Ferguson, my high school class-mate and former lab partner, was not amused. His attitude said Monday morning. But I was functioning on five hours of sleep myself, and I could match him snarl for snarl. His sandy hair, freckles, and boyish good looks belied his transformation into Mr. Hyde.

He glared at the small can of 35-millimeter film I'd laid on his ink blotter, then looked up at me.

"What the hell am I supposed to do with that?" he said. "Run it through an enlarger until I can see the fingerprints?"

"It's evidence," I said testily. "If you don't want it, fine."

I reached for the film, and he grabbed my wrist. Our eyes locked across the desk.

"Who took the pictures?"

I narrowed my eyes at the implied challenge. "I did," I snapped.

"You did," he echoed. "Gilda, do you remember the pictures you took at the senior picnic? Or the ones you took at the junior prom? Remember?"

"Well, cameras were harder to operate in those days than they are now," I said huffily.

He released my wrist. "You still have to remember not to put your fingers in front of the lens," he said tiredly. "Gilda's 'finger studies' we called them, remember?"

"Well, there's nothing wrong with these," I said. "I hope."

He began lecturing me. "Gilda, you know better than this," he said. "If the crime scene's contaminated, there's nothing much we can do."

"Duke and Faye wore gloves," I objected.

"Even so," he said. "They introduced all kinds of hair and fibers, and smudged any fingerprints we might have found. We probably wouldn't have found any, but who knows? Now, even if we did find something, we'd never get a conviction. Chances are we'd never even get an arrest, because everybody would know it would be a waste of time."

"Fine," I said, and stood up. "I understand. I just thought you'd like to know. Have a nice day."

"Gilda," he said placatingly. "I'm going to investigate, all right? I am. But I want you to know up front how little chance there is that anything will come of it. Now." He nodded at my voluminous shoulder bag. "What else you got in there for me?"

I handed him a Baggie containing bits of plastic.

"And this would be . . . ?" he asked, squinting at it skeptically.

"The bomb," I said. "At least, Duke can't identify them as anything that belongs on the projector."

He sighed. "Did he get the projector fixed on time?"

I nodded. "With twenty minutes to spare, in spite of an emergency trip to Columbus for parts. I ran Faye over to the hospital to get her ankle X-rayed and taped, and he staffed the ticket booth till I could get back."

He studied the plastic fragments through their protective plastic and cocked an eyebrow at me. "You're sure somebody didn't step on the film canister when you loaded the camera?"

I didn't deign to respond. I handed him a smaller Baggie.

"Glue," I said. "That's what was inside the bomb."

"If I'm not mistaken, I could get a sample of that from your left earlobe."

I clapped a hand to my ear in consternation and peeled away another piece of glue as he grinned at me.

"It's not funny!" I protested. "You know what my aunt Gloria said to me last night? She said, 'You're looking radiant, Gilda. What are you using on your skin these days?' "

He laughed. "Well, look on the bright side. At least it hasn't tamed your hair."

"That was so funny I forgot to laugh," I said, reverting to an old standby.

"That was a compliment!" he said. "I like your hair wild. It suits your personality."

From most men, this would sound like a come-on. But Dale had turned his natural quickness, attentiveness, and charm to good use on the police force. Unlike most men, he gave compliments without embarrassment, and they were backed by a scrupulous honesty. He felt equally comfortable delivering a criticism.

"So," he said, leaning back in an upholstered desk chair that was color coordinated with the relatively pristine carpet on the floor. "You want to tell me why somebody is hiding bombs inside your projector, or do we have to go down to the basement and get out the phone books and thumbscrews?"

I sighed. At least somebody's mood was improving. I'd already decided to tell him everything I knew, but I didn't expect him to believe me. I wasn't sure I believed myself. I told him.

Sixty seconds in, he asked me if he could record me. I signed a release and started over. He was taking notes.

"So that's all I know," I summarized at the end. "And no, I don't have any kind of evidence for any of this, except the tape."

"Which is locked in the safe at the theater?"

"Which is locked in the safe at the theater."

He tapped his pen on the desk blotter.

"Okay," he said abruptly, standing. "Let's go look at what's left of the crime scene. I'm just warning you up front—" His hand dropped to his stomach. "—I may have to investigate some of those Milk Duds."

"How'd the guy get in and out?" he asked as we approached the theater.

I shrugged. "The doors are open all night. Anybody can walk in. We don't always have somebody staffing the ticket booth, if the shows have started. Sometimes nobody's watching the front. The kids who staff the concession booth can study or read at one of the small tables while the shows are in progress. Somebody might be in one of the storerooms, the rest room, another projection booth, whatever. This is a small town operation. We trust our customers to pay just like we trust them to come tell us if the film's out of focus or the sound's too loud."

He frowned. "Maybe you'd better take this warning to heart, and keep a closer eye on people's comings and goings." Reading my dismay, he added, "Just for now."

"Maybe I'd better keep a Luger on top of the free passes under the ticket counter," I said.

"Not if you value your kneecaps," he said.

He followed me to the projection booth. I opened the door on the projector, but that was as far as I was willing to go.

"Now don't you get fingerprints on it," I admonished him. "If you drop so much as a pencil shaving in there—"

"I know, I know," he said. "I'll have Duke to answer to." He whistled. "He took all this apart and put it back together?"

"He's happy in his work."

"No shit, Sherlock," he said. "He do VCR repair?"

"He'd consider it aiding and abetting the enemy."

Dale was poking around with his ballpoint pen in a way that made me nervous. Finally, he shut the door.

"So, who's your prime suspect for this little escapade, out of the characters you described to me? And please don't say 'Creighton Hale.' I've got a ways to go yet before retirement."

"He's the only one we haven't talked to," I said, "so I don't know how involved he is. He's certainly connected to several of the parties who are involved, I just can't tell if any of them is really representing him."

"Okay, so we'll skip him for the moment." He paused and watched me fidget. "Need a cigarette?"

I nodded. "Can we go outside?"

"Better anyway," he conceded, "in case they planted a bug while they were at it."

That shot a jet of ice water up my spine, and my thoughts stumbled all over each other like day-old puppies as I tried to remember what had been said in that room.

We stood on the sidewalk and leaned against the building. In the flower shop next door, Penny Georgakis was arranging a graduation display in the window. As I turned away from the breeze to light my cigarette, I spotted it. I felt the instantaneous tug at my heart that I always felt when something reminded me of my former family. Paulie's graduation, I thought dully. I need a graduation present, and soon.

"So tell me about Mrs. Creighton Hale," Dale was saying. "I gather she's a bombshell, but is she a bomber, do you think?"

"I don't really think it's her style," I said, trying to keep the quaver out of my voice. Dale was more perceptive than Faye, and I didn't want to discuss my emotions right now—or ever. "She might chip her fingernail polish."

"But she could have hired someone," he proposed.

"That," I agreed, "would definitely be her style. She likes to hire people."

"And can afford it," he said. "I'm guessing a high school basketball player can't—at least, not yet."

I looked at him in surprise.

"You consider Falcone a suspect? What's he got to lose?"

"He could be sanctioned by the NCAA as well, I'd guess," he said, "maybe lose a year of eligibility. I'll have to check on that." He wrote a note to himself.

"Let's face it," I said. "Anybody could have hired somebody. Sid Green could have—he's not much of a do-it-yourselfer, either. And he's got the money."

"But Hank Mann probably doesn't have the money," Dale said. "I don't think local sportscasters earn that much."

"Maybe he saved up for a rainy day," I said. "Anyway, I think he's after a story. I'm guessing that he wants this whole business made public, and I think he wants to be the one to do it. That's just a hunch, though."

He nodded. "Sounds plausible." He turned to look at me. "I hate to ask you this, Gilda, but do you think Jake Styles could pull a stunt like this?"

I took a long pull on my cigarette.

"Do you know him?" I asked.

"Only by reputation."

"Oh." So Styles hadn't been exaggerating about that.

"Funny, I never connected him with your Styles," Dale said.

"She's not *my* Styles," I objected. "As for Jake, I certainly wouldn't put it past him on ethical grounds, Dale, but he's not well enough. He looks like death warmed over, and he's confined to his apartment. More importantly, he's being babysat, or maybe just sat on, by a male nurse named Spike who has the muscle mass of concrete."

"So if you're right about what's behind all of this, and unless there's a player you don't know about yet—"

"Which is perfectly possible," I put in.

"Which is perfectly possible," he agreed, "we're looking at somebody, maybe more than one somebody, who has the money to hire out the dirty work. Bombers—even glue bombers—don't come cheap. Arsonists don't, either."

"Dale," I said, squinting into the sun as I turned to face him, "could an amateur have set up that bomb?"

"You mean, somebody who got hold of *The Anarchist's Cookbook*, or downloaded instructions off the Web?" he said. "Well, *you* couldn't have done it," he said, grinning.

"All right, all right, this is no time for chemistry jokes at my expense," I said crabbily. "Could *you* have done it?"

He gazed into space. "I doubt that I would have tried—not that particular type of bomb, anyway. The trigger mechanism would have been set so that the circuit closed and the bomb detonated when the door was opened. I don't think the mechanics are that complex conceptually, but you'd have to be pretty confident to walk into a crowded theater and do it under pressure. Projectors probably aren't all alike, either, are they?"

"They all have doors," I said. "And the bomber could have practiced."

"Now there's a thought!" he said enthusiastically. "We could go looking for a perp with glue on his face! I like it!"

He reached over and peeled a small patch of glue from just under my jawbone. I reached up self-consciously and ran a hand along both sides of my chin.

"Forget it," I said. "I'll keep my suggestions to myself."

"No, seriously, Gilda," he said, fighting to get his smile under control, "you're right. An amateur could have practiced until he could do it quickly and smoothly. But he'd have to have nerves of steel to get it right under pressure. Why'd you ask about amateurs?"

"Oh, I don't know," I said. "Maybe because both coaches and car dealers seem to be surrounded by a retinue of lackeys. Coaches especially. I mean, suppose the coach said to his players, 'Boys, we're in deep shit if this tape ever gets out. I'd sure like to put the fear of God and the Groundhogs into those women!' I could see something like that happening."

"Was the late-show audience taller than usual last night?"

"Not that I noticed."

"What did you notice? Any suspicious types?"

I made a face at him. "We're showing that Bruce Willis

film in the side theater," I said. "Everybody in the audience was a suspicious type."

"And I don't suppose you noticed anybody lurking in the lobby, waiting for all of you to disappear?"

I shook my head. "The only person who stands out is Mrs. Moss," I said. "And she comes to the theater to have somebody to talk to at night. If the bomber hired her to make us disappear, they're even smarter than we thought. No, I hate to say this, but it's the video all over again—everybody has a favorite suspect or two."

"Then I guess we'd better talk to everybody, and get descriptions," he said, putting his notebook away. "And it sounds like we should talk to Mrs. Moss as well."

"How much time do you have?" I asked wryly.

Styles had her own helpful questions to contribute when she called that night.

"What did the bomb look like?"

"How the hell should I know what it looked like?" I retorted. "All I saw was glue coming at me—or something coming at me that turned out to be glue. All that was left afterwards were some pieces of plastic and wire—and a shitload of glue."

My second and third winds had come and gone. I was lying on my bed with my eyes closed, and there was a good chance I'd be asleep before Styles hung up.

"And I don't suppose you caught it on tape," she said.

"No, Styles," I said with acerbity, "it never occurred to me to install a security camera in the projection booth at the Paradise."

"Maybe you should think about it, babe," she said. "Paradise ain't what it used to be, and there were snakes in the trees even in the old days."

28

Sounds bounced off the walls and echoed in the cavernous building. Outside, another thunderstorm was throwing trees around and beating its fists against the sides of buildings, but in here, the sounds of thunder were faint and distant. The darkness outside made the inside light seem more artificial. The air was thick with humidity and acrid with the odor of human exertion.

Near us, a group of men—young, middle-aged, and old—was playing an intense game of basketball. Their shirts were soaked through and sticking to their bodies. Their breaths came in gasps. They grunted and chattered, ran, lunged, spun, and danced. The ball thunked against the wood floor or slapped against open palms.

Between them and us lay the track, where people of all ages and both sexes, in various states of dress and undress, were running or walking. Some appeared to be college athletes, some were women in polyester pants and sneakers, and some were older men in gym shorts, sauntering or striding purposefully, arms pumping.

Beyond the basketball game, a volleyball game was in progress. This game was coed, and no less intense than the basketball game. Shirts were wet, hair was wet, and the court was slick. The ball made a satisfying thwack against the server's hand.

In spite of the artificial brightness, Faye and I were conscious of danger. We were deep in enemy territory, ground zero in Groundhog country: the Buckeye State gym.

Beside me, Faye shifted uncomfortably on her crutch. I hadn't wanted her to come. She would be a handicap if we had to make a run for it. But she'd insisted, demonstrating how quickly she could turn the crutch into a weapon of surprising range.

"Anyway, what can they do with all those people around?" she'd asked.

I'd swung my hands to her throat.

"Oh, that," she'd said.

"Dale thinks it has to be someone with enough money to hire bombers and arsonists," I'd said to Styles last night. "And according to Murray Richman, Faye's sports expert, these guys are rolling in dough. They're making twice the salary of the average professor, and God knows how many times the salary of the graduate students who teach most of the introductory classes at Buckeye State. But that's not enough. They want to sign the best recruit, so they can win the NCAA or the Rose Bowl or whatever, so they can make even more money! And they're willing to risk lives and destroy property in order to do it! That's so fucked up!"

"You're right, babe," Styles had agreed. "And the bomb itself—"

But my outrage had run away with my tongue, giving me a brief resurgence of energy. "The fucking bomb just goes to show how fucking arrogant they are! They expect to waltz into a crowded theater, set a bomb in place, and get away with it! And glue, for chrissakes!"

"You would have preferred shrapnel?"

"No, but *glue*!" I'd screamed in her ear. "They screwed up our equipment, they scared the shit out of us, and they probably thought it was funny! I swear, Styles, right now, at this minute, I understand the death penalty. Somebody's going to pay for this, big time." Even to my own ears, I'd sounded like a poor imitation of Rambo—maybe an Italian dubber.

"Just make sure the somebody isn't you," Styles had responded mildly. "And remember, Gilda, they weren't born arrogant. One way or another, they earned that arrogance."

I hadn't understood what she was getting at until we'd passed the trophy case in the hall. Here, too, the walls were hung with reminders of victories past: Rose Bowl, 1983, 1984, 1997; NIT champions, 1980, 1995; NCAA champions, 1978, 1986, 1992. The last of these dates was too distant to satisfy a greedy, ambitious head coach, I thought. Now Creighton Hale had been forced to retire. I wondered if that banner had galled him every time he looked at it.

Headed in our direction along the perimeter of the track was a straggling troupe of muscular young women wearing short skirts and wielding field hockey sticks.

"Excuse me," I said, as they approached, "can anybody tell me where to find Coach Hale?"

"He's probably in his office," said a young woman with dark curly hair pulled back into a ponytail. "Have you looked there?"

"You're not from his doctor, are you?" another young woman asked.

"No, why?"

" 'Cause I heard he wasn't supposed to come in," she said, grinning, "but he can't stay away."

"Aw, he's addicted to the smell of gym socks," another said. "They'll have to carry him out of here feet first."

"Fine with me," put in a redhead. "I'll help carry him out." They all laughed.

"His office?" I asked.

"Oh," the first one said. "You go through those doors and down that hallway and turn left, and go up the stairs there, and then he's, like, the second or third office on the right."

"Don't worry," someone reassured us. "You'll hear him."

We followed their directions, Faye taking the stairs at a hop, and resting halfway up. Luckily, the occupants of the offices were identified by signs posted to the right of the door. A rumble of thunder reminded us of the storm outside, but it wasn't loud enough to drown out the sound of the coach.

"This is the third time I've called today! The third fucking time! I could be dead by the time he gets around to returning my calls!"

His door was open, and he was on the phone. He listened, but not for long.

"No, I'm not having another heart attack! I know goddamn well what a heart attack feels like, and I'm not going to the fucking emergency room! But I got a million pills to take, and I still feel like shit! So you tell him this is not working, understand?" There was a brief pause. "No, I haven't stopped taking anything, but if you ask me, it's these fucking pills that are killing me!" A briefer pause. "You just tell him to call me back, and I don't mean two hours from now! I know goddamn well he's sitting on his ass in the goddamn doctors' lunch- room! And you can just get up off *your* sweet ass and go down there and tell him what I said!"

The phone came down with a crash.

"Fucking morons!" he was muttering around a pill in his teeth. "Stupid shits!"

In person, even close up, he was smaller than his voice—a man of medium height, a stocky man deflated by illness. He glared at us over the rim of a mug the size of a tankard. Printed on the mug was *I* ELECTED ME GOD!

We stood in the doorway and watched. Before him on the desk was a row of pills, six or seven of them in a staggered line like drunken soldiers. One by one, he snatched them up furiously and tossed them down his throat, taking a noisy gulp from his mug each time. He kept his eyes on us as he completed this drill.

"Coach Hale?" I ventured, seeing that he didn't intend to make this easy. I also noticed that my comrade in arms, who got us into this mess in the first place, was bringing up the rear.

"What do you want?" he demanded. He set his mug down, put his hand to his chest, palm spread, and rubbed gently, grimacing.

"Are you all right?" I asked apprehensively. This was a bad time to remind myself that I needed to learn CPR.

"What do you think?" he asked belligerently. "I'm popping pills like fucking candy, and I might as well be swallowing air for all the good it's doing me."

"She means if you're, like, having chest pains or something, maybe we should call an ambulance." Faye's tentative voice floated over my shoulder.

"Do you have nitroglycerin tablets?" I asked, hoping he'd tell us where they were before he collapsed.

"Since when is my health any fucking business of yours?" he asked. "Who the hell are you to come in here and ask nosy questions about me?" He rose, apparently in an attempt to intimidate us, but either he was shorter than he remembered, or his recent illness had undermined the impressiveness of this gesture.

His attitude reminded me how pissed off I was at him. I walked in and helped myself to a chair, a cheap affair made out of fake wood and real plastic upholstery textured to look like cloth.

"Fine," I said. "Go ahead and die. Don't let us stop you." I folded my arms across my chest.

This move increased his fury, and Faye, suddenly finding herself out in the open, hobbled for cover behind my chair.

"Who the hell do you think you are, barging in here?" he bellowed.

I was only marginally reassured by the apparent genuineness of his bewilderment. He truly didn't seem to know who we were, not even Faye, who had appeared, however briefly, in the original news broadcast of the cheerleading contest. But then, maybe she looked different with a crutch. Maybe we both looked different since we'd been burgled, burned, and bombed.

"We're the people who own a videotape of the Northstar Mall cheerleading contest," I said.

He rounded the side of the desk and came after me. Instinctively, I blocked his frontal approach by raising my legs, bent at the knees, to kick him, saying a silent prayer to the Amazonian goddess of female combat to prevent me from having to kick the ailing Buckeye State head basketball coach and bring on another heart attack. I'd have a limited future in the state of Ohio if I took out Creighton Hale.

Of course, I looked ridiculous. He could have just grabbed my ankles and started a tugging war while I held onto the flimsy plastic chair for dear life. Instead, he approached from the side and took hold of my arm.

"Get out!" he commanded, yanking me to my feet and propelling me toward the door. "Get out!"

He moved toward us again, but now Faye was standing on one foot, wielding her crutch like a baseball bat.

"Don't even try," she told him, "or you're history!"

He stood his ground and pointed to the door. "Get out!" he roared.

"You know, I can't believe this!" Faye expostulated. "This is so lame! I mean, we're the ones who've been taking all the shit! Everybody's so schizzed out about this tape, and we come down here to talk about it, and we're the ones getting yelled at! This is so bogus! Come on, Gilda! We're outta here!"

"I don't know what kind of scam you bitches are trying to run, but it won't work on me!" he thundered. "And if you ever come near me again, I'll break you both in so many pieces, your mothers won't know you good enough to identify the bodies! And if you ever show that tape again, I'll sue you for every goddamn penny you're worth!"

We more or less backed out the door, with Faye anchored by my hand on her elbow as she hopped backward and waved her crutch at Hale. He slammed the door behind us.

Our troubles were not over. I backed into a chest like a cement wall, surmounted by a head that towered a foot above mine. I was a foothill to his Alp.

He was a white kid with black curly hair and a face that gave stupidity a bad name. He had a basketball wedged between biceps and rib cage.

"You botherin' Coach?" he asked.

His sidekick had seized Faye's arms, pinning them to her side. I had an impression that the sidekick, who was black, was shorter, but it was hard to tell from down near the floor, where I was standing.

"Nobody bothers Coach," the sidekick instructed us, in a quiet voice that took power for granted.

I again heard a rumble of thunder overhead.

"Hey, chill out, will you?" Faye said, wriggling free. Her captor must have loosened his grip, but he'd probably left dents in her flesh that would turn purple overnight. "Jesus! You try to do somebody a favor, and all you get is grief!"

I hadn't seen our visit in the light of a favor we were doing, but I wasn't about to contradict her.

"Coach is a sick man," the first one said. "You come around here again, you got us to contend with." He grabbed my wrist and twisted until I yelped. "Understand?"

A loud crack resounded through the hallway. The lights flickered and went out, plunging us into a premature dusk relieved only by an exit sign glowing red down the hall. The pressure on my wrist released. Before I could react, Faye had swung her crutch and slammed it into my assailant, pushing him into hers.

"Run, Gilda!" she shrieked.

She recovered the use of her crutch quickly as the two went down, and took off down the hall at an uneven gallop. I raced after her, followed by curses. There was no way we'd outrun a pair of basketball players, even off season.

"In here," Faye said, and tugged at my elbow.

I got a brief glimpse of a triangle with a circle on top as I skidded through the door. Faye threw her shoulder against the door and shot home a small bolt.

I eyed the latch skeptically, panting. Like the latches on most women's rest rooms, it was intended as a polite indicator that the occupant preferred solitude, not as a serious defense against assault.

"I don't know, Faye," I said. "I think we're one kick away from dog meat."

"So look for weapons," she countered, her ear against the door.

I surveyed the dim room in dismay. What light I had to search by was coming through a thick, barely translucent window that hadn't been cleaned in years. "Weapons?" I echoed. "What do you think? We're going to pelt them with toilet paper? Force soap down their throats?"

"Shh!" She waved me to silence.

I supposed we could break the mirror, but that seemed to me a poor choice. In the first place, it would produce an overabundance of sharp objects, which could be used by our opponents as well. In the second place, the way my life was going now, I couldn't afford seven more years of bad luck.

I found a hot pink plastic hair clip on the narrow, polished-steel shelf under the mirror. I held it with its plastic spikes turned up and went to stand behind Faye.

"I'm ready," I said.

"I think they're gone," she said.

"How much are you willing to bet on that?"

"Well, jeez, Gilda," she said. "I mean, they can't really afford to beat up two women, can they? I mean, right here, in the Buckeye gym, in front of everybody?"

"I didn't notice everybody," I said. "Where were they standing? And what colors were they wearing? If they were there, they were probably with the home team."

"You don't seem to be taking this very seriously," she observed.

"That's because I basically share your opinion," I said. "But I'd hate to be wrong."

"Get ready," she said. "I'm going to open the door and look."

"So soon?" I asked. "I haven't even had a chance to use the facilities."

She cracked the door open. No large male bodies came hurtling through the opening. No loud voices berated us. She looked out.

"The coast is clear," she said.

"How can you tell?" I asked. The hallway was even darker than the rest room. I peered over her shoulder.

"I don't hear anything, either," she said. "You know how much noise they make in those size-twenty high-tops."

"Maybe they went off to lurk in the stairwell," I suggested.

"Then we, like, bypass the first stairwell, and take the next one," Faye proposed reasonably.

We made it down the stairs and dashed to our car in the downpour. I offered to retrieve the car and pick Faye up, but she was unwilling to be separated from me, and I conceded her point. We didn't see anybody during the course of our retreat. Or rather, we saw everybody except the three people we were avoiding. Everybody was wearing scarlet and black.

"What are *our* colors, Gilda?" Faye asked as I slid wetly behind the wheel.

I glanced down at my arm. "Black and blue," I said.

"It seemed weird to me that Hale didn't even want to talk to us," she said. "I mean, he obviously knew about the tape, but he didn't even want to discuss it. Everybody else is falling all over themselves to get hold of it."

I nodded, checking the rearview mirror for thugs in the guise of basketball players.

"He threatened to sue," she continued. "That was weird, too. You don't think he really thinks he'd get anywhere with a suit, do you? I mean, he could, like, screw up my senior year big time with a lawsuit, but he wouldn't win."

"Maybe he thinks he would," I said. "After all, he's Creighton Hale."

"Huh," she said dismissively, leaning forward to clear a space as the window began to fog up. "He may be Creighton Hale, but he's totally N-C-double-A."

I shot her a look.

"No class at all," she translated.

29

Tuesday departed without so much as a smoke signal from Mrs. Creighton Hale, whose divorce I was warming up to as a cause worth supporting. I had made it to Styles's office around eleven, and hung out, shooting the breeze with the plants, until eleven-thirty. I wondered whether she'd heard about our visit to her husband and was suspecting that my loyalties were at best divided and at worst for sale to the highest bidder. The way I'd presented myself to her so far, I didn't think that should come as news to her, but you never knew. She might put as much faith in her good looks and flirtatious charm as Creighton Hale did in his status as head coach of the Groundhogs.

I spent the late morning and early afternoon on Wednesday with my friend Peachy Gower. She went with me to look at a few apartments. The first one was really a small house. Peachy made a sound of disapproval as soon as we stepped inside the door.

"Unhhh," she said, shaking her head. "A pussycat lived here, and from the smell of it, she was one pissed-off kitty."

"No wonder," I said, slapping at my ankles. "She had fleas." We beat a hasty retreat.

At the next place, Peachy said, "You want to tell me why they put a bathtub in the kitchen?"

"They had to put it somewhere, I guess." I sighed. "Maybe they're going for a rustic retro feel."

"Uh-uh," she said. "They want to put a Jacuzzi in here,

that would be one thing. But nobody wants to be that rustic anymore."

The next place had burnt-orange shag carpet from the sixties. It had kind of a sticky feel to it, and a mystery padding that sounded like disposable diapers when you walked on it.

"Well," I said, "at least it's not fake retro."

"No," Peachy agreed, "it's the real thing. You look down deep, you probably find some love beads in there."

"Maybe I should reconsider the complexes," I said disconsolately. "They're probably filled with divorcées. We could start a support group."

"That would be one way for you to meet some new women," Peachy said.

I made a face. "At the moment," I observed gloomily, "I have one more woman in my life than I can handle. And I can't even fire her, because she's family."

"Why don't you buy yourself a nice little house?" Peachy asked.

"Because I've also got one more piece of real estate in my life than I can handle," I said. "I can barely keep up with the maintenance on the theater. I don't want to be one of those people the neighbors take to court for turning the front yard into a preserve for endangered weeds."

From there we went to Northstar Mall. Peachy was shopping for a dress to wear to her niece's wedding.

"I'm used to buying funeral attire," she told me as we strolled the mall. "I'm not sure I know what to wear to a wedding. Funeral directors don't get invited to too many of those."

"And you brought *me* along as a fashion consultant?" I looked down. I was wearing baggy white shorts, an oversized New York Film Festival T-shirt, and sneakers.

Peachy was dressed in a linen pantsuit with a silk blouse, and her purse matched her shoes. I'd long since resigned myself to the study in contrasts we made when we went out together, and not just because she's tall, slender, and black and I'm short, dumpy, and white. She's in a business that demands that she always look good to prospective clients, I reasoned. I'm not. Most people don't even notice what a ticket seller looks like.

"I brought you along to zip me up," Peachy said.

"Thanks, Peach," I said wryly. "I can always rely on you to boost my self-esteem."

She looked momentarily contrite, and a little wary. "Nothing wrong with your self-esteem," she said, putting her arm through mine. "You just need better taste in women."

"There's nothing wrong with my taste in women," I said, patting her arm, "as long as I don't sleep with them."

"Honey, you can sleep with them," she said. "Just don't move in with them."

"No kidding," I said ruefully.

We were approaching the center of the mall, where the cheerleading contest had taken place. I slowed my steps, musing over the scene as it was now and remembering it as it had been that day when all the trouble started.

"Hey!" I said, startling myself as much as Peachy.

"Hey, what?" she asked, turning back.

I stood still a moment and looked. In my line of vision were a group of teenagers, passing just in front of us; a pair of women with baby carriages, standing together some six or seven yards away; and in the distance, an elderly man sitting on a bench, talking to someone I couldn't see because of the two women.

"Natalie was using a telephoto lens that day," I said. "What if . . . ?"

"What?" Peachy asked, looking around to see what I was looking at.

"I just figured something out, maybe, that's all," I said. "Maybe I know why people think they're looking at the wrong tape. I think we've been looking at the wrong tape, too."

Peachy put a hand on her hip. "Does that mean we have to stop shopping?" she asked.

I laughed. "Certainly not," I said. "Your dress is the top priority right now."

In the end, she found a fluid, peach-colored, drop-waist dress that looked as if it had been made for her, and I returned to Eden eager to try out my theory on Faye. I stopped at Clara's to see if Faye was there. But she had gone off to shoot some playground footage with Natalie, according to Clara.

"When will she be back?"

"Don't ask me," Clara said. "I'm not her housemother. I hope she's out having a good time, but young people don't seem to know how to do that anymore. The ones who are trying seem to think that having fun means drinking until you pass out. The ones who aren't, like Faye, are always working. Now, when I was her age—"

"Clara," I interrupted. "Do you still have that news broadcast on tape—the one about the cheerleading contest and Faye's movie?"

"I never had it, Gilda, don't you remember?" she said, then added bitterly, "I could never get the damned VCR to work. Adele and Gloria and your mother all have copies, though."

I called my mother from the theater.

"Gilda, have you heard the news?" she asked, before I could say anything.

"What news?"

"Creighton Hale died."

I was stunned speechless. That was my first reaction: shock. It was quickly followed by guilty apprehension.

"Are you still there?" my mother was saying.

"Mom, when, exactly, did he die?"

"Just this afternoon," she said. Her voice swung away from the phone. "Douglas, what time was it when we heard the news? Gilda wants to know when he died."

I heard the distant rumble of my father's voice, then my mother's close to my ear.

"We were eating a late lunch, around two, and watching CNN," she reported. "The local news comes on just before the half hour. Douglas says we heard the report at two twenty-five or so. He'd only been dead about an hour. What, dear?"

The rumble came closer, but I still couldn't make out the words.

"Oh, your father says the press must have caught him on the first bounce when he dropped," my mother said. "He thinks he's being funny. But they did find out awfully quickly. I suppose either they located the next of kin right away—Mrs. Hale, I guess—or didn't bother waiting because it was too important."

It was probably Mrs. Hale, I thought, who could have caught him on the first bounce, except that she would have let him bounce.

"What, Douglas?" I heard my mother saying. "She can't turn on her television right now, she's at the theater, aren't you, Gilda? He wants you to see all the fans outside the gym. All these people have turned up—grown men in business suits, weeping, and elderly women in red-and-black jogging suits, and women with their kids, and students. And somebody's passing out red-and-black armbands—they're making them, right there, ripping up cloth. And there was this man carrying around a basketball, autographed by some Groundhog team or other—I think they must've won a championship that year. Anyway, he's talking about a candlelight vigil tonight. The whole thing is ridiculous, Gilda. He's hardly Mother Teresa, or even Howard Metzenbaum!"

My mother had been a longtime supporter of Ohio's most liberal senator, now retired.

"What, Douglas?" she was saying. "No, I certainly wouldn't take off work to go cry outside Howard Metzenbaum's office if he died. What? Oh, your father says it's more like Rudolph Valentino's death. Well, I wouldn't have taken off work for him, either. Who? Well, all right, I would take off work for Jimmy Stewart, but then I know Jimmy, don't I? The way these people are carrying on, you'd think the pope had died."

"Mother," I said, "do you still have a video of the news broadcast about the cheerleading contest and Faye's movie?"

"Yes, I'm sure it's around here somewhere," she said. "You

know, Gilda, he didn't look good that day, the coach. He was obviously not well. No, Douglas, it didn't have anything to do with color adjustment. Your father is lobbying for a new TV now that he's seen Grosvenor's—well, Clara's—big screen. But, anyway, Creighton Hale looked like he already had one foot in the grave."

"Could you find that tape for me, Mom?" I said. "I'd like to borrow it, if that's okay."

"When are you coming?"

"Tonight, after the theater closes?"

"We'll be up," she said.

30

"She killed him," I said to Faye, when she came dragging in that night.

"Are you sure we didn't?" she asked dejectedly. "He was pretty red in the face when we left."

"That was almost twenty-four hours before he died," I objected. "And he was red in the face when we got there. You might as well accuse the nurse he was talking to on the phone."

"I guess."

"Faye, the man was a bastard," I said. "Get over it."

"You know what it is, Gilda?" she said. "I think I'm kind of feeling guilty that I'm glad he's dead, you know? I mean, now I don't have to worry about whether he or his goons are going to come after us, right? And you're right, he was a bastard. And he, like, let his players run wild and made excuses for them and threw his weight around, and when a player fucked up some girl's life, he just basically didn't give a shit. So basically, I'm glad he's dead."

"Good," I said. "Then I hope you feel up to projecting, because I sent Duke upstairs to write his history paper."

"Whatever," she said agreeably.

"She killed him," I said to Styles when she called the theater during the late show that night.

"What do you care?" Styles said. "Sounds like you should throw her a party. Anyway, the guy was on his way out. Sooner or not much later, he would have kicked the bucket. What difference does it make if she gave him a nudge?"

"It doesn't, really," I said. "Except that she's dangerous. Look at Jake."

"Mmmm," Styles said. "You think she used him for target practice, found out she couldn't shoot straight, and moved on to a different method."

"Well," I said, "I didn't see it quite like that. But I still don't like to think of her running around with her little toy gun in her clutch."

"Point taken," Styles said. "So how did Hale die? The news said a heart attack after lunch."

"According to the paper, he had lunch with the athletic director, a guy named—I forget what. Turk somebody. They ate somewhere in the campus area. He drank a couple of bourbons, even though, according to Turk what's-his-face, he— the A.D.—told him he shouldn't. He washed down his pills with his bourbon."

"There's your answer right there," Styles commented.

"They walked to lunch, and walked back," I continued. "Only they didn't make it back, or at least, Hale didn't. He collapsed on the street and died in the ambulance on the way to the hospital."

"Did he strike you as the type of man who wouldn't follow his doctor's orders?"

"He struck me as the type of man who hadn't followed an order in his life."

"There you are, then," Styles said.

"I don't like it."

"You don't have to," she observed mildly. "No autopsy, right?"

"Why do you say that?"

"Guy had serious heart problems, dropped dead from a heart attack," she said. "What's to find out? Besides, he's got a grieving widow and thousands of adoring fans who think his body is the next most sacred object after the host. They're not going to cut it up if they don't have to."

"It wouldn't be that hard, would it?" I said. "To give him that nudge."

"Piece of cake," Styles agreed.

"And she's going to get away with it," I said.

"Probably," Styles agreed again.

"Styles, if she did it, how do you think she did it?"

"Hey, cookie, this is your script, not mine," Styles objected. "How do *you* think she did it?"

"Well," I said slowly, "the guy's taking a whole fistful of prescription drugs. I'm betting it wouldn't take much to screw up his system somehow. He probably has to be careful about the dosage, maybe even about mixing them with other drugs—you know, like allergy pills or whatever."

"And alcohol," agreed Styles.

"Hey, that's right!" I said.

"Which lets your blond babe off the hook, since she wasn't at lunch to urge him on."

"Yeah," I said, deflated. "Unless she increased his dosage or something. Maybe she told him what to take, and he took it. You know, now that I think of it, she said she took tranquilizers during the basketball season every year. What if she slipped him some tranks?"

Styles sighed. "Even if she did, you'll probably never prove it."

I took this in silence, recognizing the truth in what Styles was telling me. Then I said, "Okay. Suppose you want to look for evidence that she did it."

"I don't."

"I said *suppose*, Styles. For crying out loud, if I can pretend to be you for a few hours, you can pretend to be me for a few minutes."

"Is your family part of this fantasy?"

I ignored her. "What would you do?"

She sighed. "You won't like the answer," she said.

"Well?" I asked. I thought she was going to stonewall me.

"Garbage," she said enigmatically.

I thought. "Oh," I said.

"Look on the bright side, babe," she said. "You've got experience. But you'd better hope today wasn't garbage day in Mrs. Hale's neighborhood."

"How do I go through her garbage without being conspicuous?"

"Come on, Gilda," she chided me. "You come from a family of actors. Improvise! Carry a clipboard. Clip some kind of photo ID to your pocket. Rent a baby buggy. Whatever. But remember, what you find in the garbage and turn over to the police probably won't be admissible in court. They have to find it, and in order to find it, they have to go looking for it. That means they need enough basis for suspicion to persuade a judge to issue a search warrant, unless they wait till it's been put out by the curb."

"So you think it's a waste of time, right?"

"I didn't say that," she said. "It's more fun than sorting socks. I just don't want you to get your hopes up and expect it to lead to anything. And it does strike me as a shift in focus. But you don't have much choice on that."

I sighed. "And to think that just this afternoon, I thought I figured something out about that damned videotape."

"Sorry, sweetheart," Styles said, "Hale's death makes the whole thing moot—as dead an issue as he is."

"Why do you say that?" I asked. "Maybe Mrs. Hale doesn't need the videotape anymore, but it's still evidence of a recruiting violation."

"Babe," Styles said with an air of exaggerated patience, "who, in the wide world of sports, is going to kick a grieving Groundhog when he's down?"

31

I picked up the newscast tape from my mother that night. My father waved me into the den to watch live coverage of the candlelight vigil. I stashed the video in a book bag, along with some paperwork from the theater, and promptly forgot about it.

I was startled to see Hank Mann, microphone in hand, on a screen behind a polished woman I recognized as one of the news anchors. Hank looked as if he hadn't been off duty since Hale had died twelve hours earlier.

"That's right, Tina," he was saying somberly. "We'll be here all night, sharing in the experience of this great tragedy, and bringing it to you at home. We know you're here in spirit, and that your prayers join with ours for the brokenhearted team members, and for the widow, Mrs. Hale."

"Hank, I understand Mrs. Hale is at home right now, resting," the anchor said. "Is that right?"

"Yes, we understand that Mrs. Hale is under a doctor's care, but that she is resting peacefully at home," Hank said.

I'll bet, I thought. She's probably drinking champagne.

"She apparently relayed a message through a friend that she wished she could be down here with all of us, but, as I say, she isn't well enough," Hank said.

"It looks like it might be starting to rain," the anchor said. "Is that right?"

"Yes, Tina, we're getting a—oh, I'd say kind of a drizzle now," Hank said, looking around. "As you can see, people are covering their candles with their hands. It's quite a moving sight, Tina. It's as if the heavens were weeping at the passing of this great man."

Oh, please, I thought.

My mother called me from the doorway.

"Faye's on the phone," she said. "She wants to talk to you."

"Gilda," Faye said excitedly, "this is just too good to pass up! Are you watching? Natalie and I are going down there to shoot. Want to come?"

I was physically exhausted from a day of apartment hunting, shopping, and work. I was mentally exhausted from trying to figure out what was going on. I was emotionally exhausted from the tug and release of fear, anger, and worry. I felt like an old piece of film that had been fed through the rollers one too many times.

"Sure," I said. "I'll come."

I carried the light kit and a case full of reflectors; Natalie, the camcorder and a portable battery; and Faye, a clipboard of release forms and a bag of mikes. Even with all this gear, I knew we were traveling lean out of deference to Faye's injury, and I was thankful.

"Will there be enough light?" I asked.

Natalie shrugged.

"We'll see what we get," Faye said. "This is a low-light camcorder, and all the news stations will be using lights." She handed me a poncho.

"That's okay, thanks," I said. "I have a slicker in the back of the car."

It turned out that my gratitude was misplaced. "Your slicker won't cover the equipment," she said. "Put this on."

The scene outside the Groundhog gym was a bizarre mix. Off to one side were the news vans, with their crisscrossed umbilical-cord cables. This area was well lit and looked a little like the landing strip in *Close Encounters*. The main crowd of people stood in front of us, a dark mass of bodies lit by the firefly glow of candles. The light from the candles reflected off hundreds—perhaps thousands, I was no judge of crowds—of hands and was softened by a fine mist that was coming down. On the opposite side of the crowd from the news trucks was a band—or at least a group of people playing instruments. They played an off-key dirge, each musician following his or her own inclinations with regard to time. I didn't recognize the tune, but Natalie seemed to think that it was the Buckeye State alma mater.

"Need an armband and a candle?" I was asked by a young woman with red eyes and swollen cheeks.

"I've kind of got my hands full," I said. "But I'll take an armband, thanks."

She tied it around my upper arm and gave it a loving pat.

"He was a great man," she said, as if it were part of a litany.

"Yes, he was," I intoned, hoping that would do for a response.

She sighed deeply and moved on.

In front of us stood a middle-aged couple wearing shorts and Buckeye State T-shirts. They had their banded arms wrapped around each other, and they were sobbing.

"Follow the light!" Faye shouted over the music, which had changed to the Buckeye State fight song, a number more readily recognizable to nonalums like me. We headed for the lighted area, skirting the crowd. As we approached, we were suddenly flooded with light, as if from an arriving angel. Maybe God sent an emissary, I thought, to report on the coach's progress. But the crowd parted for a young black woman whose hair and makeup matched her stylish red suit. She was holding a microphone and trailing a cameraman.

"You know, Bob," she said, turning to face the camera, "this is really incredible! I've seen many Buckeye State crowds in my day, but I've never seen one as subdued as this one. And I'd like to point out that I haven't seen any drinking in this crowd—not a can of beer in sight! Some people might think that's remarkable, but these folks have come down here to mourn and express their love for a man they will sorely miss. They didn't come here to party."

She thrust her microphone at a college-age young man wearing a T-shirt that commemorated Buckeye State's 1992 NCAA championship. He had outgrown the T-shirt in the five years since its creation, and it rode up to flash skin above his jeans when he gestured. I heard Natalie's camera whirring behind me.

"What's your name?" the reporter asked.

"Rick," the young man answered, glancing shyly at the camera. "Rick Futrell."

"Tell me, Rick," the reporter said earnestly, "what's it like to be down here tonight?"

Words failed him. Tears filled his eyes. He looked over the crowd.

"Oh, man, I don't know," he said in a choked voice. "This is really incredible! To be down here tonight, and to feel all the love that everybody has for Coach Hale—it's just—"

"Incredible," the reporter supplied at last.

"Yeah," he said. Then, looking straight into the camera as if it were a pipeline to the afterlife, he said solemnly, "We're gonna miss you, Coach!"

Personally, I doubted that there were television sets in heaven, but it wasn't past imagining that hell kept a goodly supply of fuzzy black-and-whites and discarded color sets with no color adjustment or vertical hold knobs. They'd probably play the same five *Gilligan's Island* or *Lawrence Welk* reruns over and over.

The reporter had moved on to an elderly man wearing a red golf shirt with the Buckeye State logo embroidered over his heart, plaid polyester pants, and a sporty red porkpie hat.

"Sir," she said, "can you tell us what brings you down here?"

"Young lady," he said, grabbing hold of her microphone hand and leaning forward to speak into it, "I graduated from this university in nineteen and forty-two. That was during the war, you know. And except for that time I was in the army,

I haven't missed a single Buckeye State home basketball game."

Someone cleared their throat behind him, and a sweet-faced woman with curly white hair put a hand on his elbow.

"Well, there was that time you had the surgery dear," she corrected apologetically. "Gallstones," she stage-whispered to the reporter. "They won't wait until after March, you know. He was fit to be tied."

"What about you, sir?" The reporter turned to a man in a business suit who was holding a candle awkwardly between thumb and forefinger while trying to brush candle wax off of his pants. "What brings you down here?"

"Well, Audrey, I'm not an alum," he said. "You might say I'm an immigrant to Columbus. But I adopted the Ground-hogs when I adopted the city, and I always had a tremendous respect for Coach Hale and his program. He was an outstanding coach and a fine role model for the young men who played for him. We'll all miss him."

"I think I'm going to be sick," said a voice in my ear, and I turned to find AnneMarie Parnell at my elbow, accompanied by some other Lady Hogs I recognized.

"Is Berta with you?" I asked. I didn't see their star player.

"Huh," somebody grunted. "She boycotting this circus."

"You're not, though," I observed.

AnneMarie shrugged. "We just wanted to see what was going on."

"Yeah, but Berta was right," the other player said. "We shouldn't never have come. It just makes us madder than we already are."

"Yeah, Audrey," AnneMarie said in a louder voice. "Why don't you talk about the times Hale's players have raped women, while Hale looked the other way? Huh? Why don't you talk about that?" She raised her crutch for emphasis, and the crowd backed off, either glaring at her or looking apprehensive.

Audrey threw AnneMarie a nervous glance, and then, turning her back, walked off. The cameraman shrugged at us.

"*I* think it would make a good story," he said, as he followed his leader.

We found Hank Mann checking his hair and makeup in the rearview mirror of the Channel Ten van.

"Hey!" he said. "Look who's here! Shooting more footage?" He nodded at the camera Natalie was carrying, then gestured toward the crowd. "Makes great material, doesn't it?"

"Yeah," Faye agreed. "But I don't know how you can stand up there and go on and on about what a great man that jerk Hale was."

He made a face. "I know, I know. Believe me, it isn't easy. But it's all part of the game."

"So does this mean you're not going to break the story about recruiting violations at State?" I asked pointedly.

He licked his hand and patted a small cowlick into place, his eyes shifting to the mirror as he did.

"Bad timing," he conceded. "I'd be crucified."

"Does that worry you?" I asked.

"What, are you kidding?" He laughed ruefully. "Crucifixion is not my idea of a good time. Besides, the guy's dead. What's the point?"

We heard somebody calling him.

"One minute," he answered. "Speaking of crucifixion, Faye, what happened to you? You didn't run into any more burglars, did you?" His forehead creased in a good imitation of concern.

"I tripped over a stool in the projection booth," she said succinctly.

"Oh. Well, hey, you take care," he said paternally. "Gotta go. Catch you guys later."

A young woman in a cheerleading costume stood before us. She held a large white plastic bucket filled with money. I heard Natalie's camera whir behind me.

"Would you like to make a donation?" she asked. "It's for a commemorative statue of the coach. They'll probably name the new arena for Coach, and it'll go out in front."

"I only give to academic scholarship funds," I told her.

"Could you hold the bucket up," Natalie said behind me, "so that I can get a shot of the money?"

The cheerleader obliged. "Is this, like, for the news or something?" she asked. She dimpled into the camera lens.

"It's for a documentary film," Faye replied.

"About Coach Hale?" she asked. "That's so cool!"

"Not exactly," Faye said, but the cheerleader was busy smiling through her tears for the benefit of the camera.

Someone bumped into me from behind. It was a young woman in a long black dress. She had long purple hair. She was apparently with a group of six other women, also dressed in black to their ankles. She carried a hand-lettered sign that read TAKE HEED! COACH HALE WAS BE-WITCHED!

"What does your sign mean?" I asked curiously.

"Creighton Hale was not a good man," the young woman said earnestly. "It's no accident that he died on Friday the Thirteenth."

This *was* Friday the Thirteenth, come to think of it; I hadn't thought of that before. I encouraged her to say more.

"Thirteen is the witching time," she explained. "It's the hour when witches are most powerful, because it's outside of time, you know? It also represents the unknown."

"So are you saying that witches killed Coach Hale?" I kept my voice down, because I didn't want these women to get mugged. They were a little dotty, to my way of thinking, but their hearts were in the right place.

"We did our best," she whispered modestly.

"Nice going," I said.

The fine mist had grown heavier, and a few of the more practical, and presumably less grief-stricken, mourners had raised umbrellas.

"Up front, Gilda," Faye said, nudging me. "We're going to shoot the flowers. If we really book it, we can use the television lights."

Natalie was already deftly clearing a path through the crowd like a guard setting up a moving pick. We followed.

The crowd had assembled at the base of a short, wide flight of steps leading up to the main entrance of the Buckeye State gym. Now, the steps were strewn with flowers. Here and there among the flowers, like Japanese beetles in a rose garden, were odd bits and pieces of Groundhog memorabilia. As we moved closer, I noticed a few glassy-eyed stuffed groundhogs poking their heads up through the carpet of flowers.

Hank Mann was already on the scene. He was making a conscious effort to ignore the rain that was taking care of his cowlick for him. He reached for a stuffed groundhog, but it was a stretch, and his foot must have slipped, because he went down in the flowers, cursing. It was a Kodak moment, and Natalie captured it on film.

He resurfaced clutching the groundhog by its stubby tail.

"I hope to Christ we weren't live on that," he said to the cameraman, who just grinned at him.

He stood up and swiped at his pants.

"You all right?" the cameraman asked mildly.

"No, I'm not all right," Hank said irritably. "Knee hurts like a son of a bitch."

"Here we go," the cameraman said, unconcerned. He counted down with his fingers.

Hank's disgruntlement disappeared from his face, and he smiled sadly. "Tina, I'm standing here at the entrance to the Buckeye State gym, and as you can see behind me here, thousands of flowers have been laid here on the steps to pay tribute to the fallen coach." Hank swept an arm over the floral display. "Many of these flowers have personal messages attached—the ones I've read are mostly simple, heartfelt outpourings of grief and gratitude. Some of the most moving are the ones written by children." He held up a wilted bouquet of pansies, with a note attached. "This one says simply, 'I love you,' and it's signed 'Patty, age five.' As you can see, Tina, many of these flowers are homegrown."

"Yo, Hank," a male voice called from somewhere to my right, "looks like you got some poison ivy in there, bro."

Hank almost dropped little Patty's tribute. He fumbled it, but caught it on the way down. Anger flickered in his face, but he faced the camera again with determination.

"And this, Tina, is one of many groundhogs scattered among the flowers—another poignant tribute to the man whose name will always be synonymous with Groundhog hoops."

He hoisted the groundhog up for Tina and the television audience to see, and realized that he had it by the tail in an unflattering pose. He hastily righted it and cradled it in the crook of his arm. Its close-set eyes made it appear cross-eyed, and its nose looked out of joint. The camera zoomed in for a close-up.

I was looking around to see who Hank's detractor was when my eyes met another set of eyes only a few yards away in the crowd. The eyes locked on mine and narrowed. Their owner yanked on a nearby sleeve.

I did the same.

"Faye," I said. "I think it's time to go."

"What are you talking about?" she said. "We're getting great stuff here!"

"You know that guy you hit with your crutch?" I asked.

That got her attention. "Where?" she asked.

"Three yards due north and closing fast," I said, already moving in the opposite direction.

She touched Natalie's back. "Nat, trouble," she said, proving that she could be succinct when she wanted to be. "Let's jet."

"I'm there," Natalie said.

I faded back to let Natalie take the lead out of deference to her superior blocking skills. I also felt obligated to take up the rear position in order to protect the injured Faye, though memory suggested that she was better armed than I was. She could always use her crutch, after all, whereas if I threw the light kit at anybody, Faye would never speak to me again.

Natalie was retreating in the direction of the parking lot.

"Head for the lights!" I shouted urgently. "The lights!"

She heard me and changed course.

They caught up with us just as we reached the first of the television trucks. This one was the size of a large RV, apparently decked out to permit coverage of sieges, prison riots, and Groundhog candlelight vigils.

I felt myself caught by the shoulders, dragged backward, spun around, and slammed up against the television truck. The truck was solid, and I felt the air rush from my lungs and heard a ringing in my ears. My head was pounding, and I realized that that was because someone was dribbling it up against the side of the truck. I couldn't make out what he was saying, garbled as it was by volume and fury, but it had a lot of "fucks" in it.

I had felt the heavy case of reflectors fly from my hand when I'd been turned. I was holding on to the light kit, though, with a death grip. I couldn't drop it on his foot; something would break.

So I kicked him.

You'd think men, especially athletes, would know better. You'd think that it would occur to them to protect their most vulnerable area in a fight. But this guy—the tall white kid with black hair—probably hadn't thought of this as a fight. He'd thought of it more as an assault: He was supposed to beat me up, and I was supposed to offer little resistance. He'd made a serious mistake.

He folded, right in front of me, hands buried in his crotch. I couldn't resist the target: I clobbered him with the light kit. He dropped like a slam dunk at my feet.

His buddy from the day before, the black kid, was getting the worse end of Faye's crutch. He'd raised his arms to protect his head. She was now advancing on him, furious—obviously too angry to feel any pain in her ankle as she hobbled. He backed away from her, tripped on a cable, and fell backward into a crowd of astonished mourners. A candle ignited one of his sleeves, but someone beat it with a stuffed groundhog until it went out.

"The bigger they come," Faye observed, resting at last on her crutch.

Natalie, for her part, was filming the whole scene, as were three television news cameras.

32

I slipped the tape into the VCR.

"Styles is probably right about this," I said. "What's on here is probably irrelevant now. But I still want to know."

"I don't get it," Faye said. I'd pulled a chair close to the television for her to sit in. I sat cross-legged on the floor.

We were at Liberty House instead of Faye's editing room because we were watching my mother's tape of the original news broadcast containing Faye's footage, and we needed a VHS deck instead of Faye's Beta. Lillian's living room was arranged to accommodate television viewing at a comfortable range. But I didn't want to miss anything, so we were sitting about two feet from the TV screen.

"I thought you were a film student," I said.

"What's that supposed to mean?" she asked.

"It means that everything depends on editing," I said. "Didn't you study the Russian formalists?"

"Hmm," she responded thoughtfully. "Were they those guys that hung out with Eisenstein? The ones who did all those experiments on perception?"

"That's them," I said.

Light dawned in her eyes. "So you think—?"

"I guess we're about to find out," I said, and pushed the

play button. "I'm going to turn down the volume, because I think the commentary will just distract us."

We watched in silence. We saw cheerleaders, we saw Creighton Hale, we saw Mike Falcone and Smiling Sid Green. We saw Creighton Hale talking to Mike Falcone.

I heard Faye catch her breath. She reached out and hit the pause button.

"Holy shit!" she expostulated. "Did I just see what I thought I saw?"

"No," I said. "You didn't. That's the whole point. What you saw and what you thought you saw were entirely different."

She smacked herself in the forehead. "I don't believe it! Have I been a total crackhead, or what? I must be from Chicago! Jeez, Gilda, if they ever find out at school, I'll never live this down! They'll probably, like, withhold my degree or something!"

"Look, we just didn't think of it, that's all," I said. "We weren't looking at this tape."

"Yeah, but you'd think it would have occurred to me. I mean, it's not like I've never edited film before." She hit PAUSE again, and then REWIND. "I've got to see this again," she said, shaking her head.

She played it again. And again, we saw a shot of Coach Hale, standing and talking animatedly to someone on his right who was out of the frame. Next, we saw a crowd shot. On the right-hand side near the edge of the frame, the Falcon could be seen. He nodded once, then spoke to someone on his left. In the next shot, both Hale and Falcone could be seen, just behind a dimpled cheerleader in the foreground. They appeared to be talking. The whole sequence had lasted no more than thirty seconds.

Faye froze the image on the screen.

"There's Sid Green," I said, pointing to a sliver of color like a shadow behind Hale's shoulder. "But you can barely see him because Hale is blocking our view of him."

"And Natalie was shooting telephoto," Faye said excitedly, "so that created a shallow depth of field. They look like they're standing a lot closer together than they really are. If you look at it, you can see that Falcone is blurrier than Hale, but you don't notice really, because he was in better focus in the last shot, so you already know who he is."

"Especially if you have a vested interest in keeping the Buckeye State Groundhogs eligible for the NCAA," I pointed out.

"Or not eligible," Faye said.

"Right," I assented.

"Gilda, I feel like the stupidest person on the planet right now," Faye admitted. "But at the same time, this is so totally cool! I mean, it's, like, this textbook example of all those fundamental principles of filmmaking."

"Isn't there some kind of psychological principle about believing the first thing you see?" I asked.

"The primacy effect," Faye said. "Yeah, so even if Hale and Falcone are shown talking to other people in other shots, it wouldn't matter, right? Because your brain's already registered them talking together. It also kind of reminds me of this other guy, André Bazin. French guy. You ever read any of his stuff?"

"Sounds vaguely familiar," I admitted.

"Well, he talks about this one movie set in Africa, where this kid is being threatened by a lion. And first you see the kid, then the lion, then the kid, then the lion—all separate shots, right? But then finally you see the kid and the lion in the same shot. Bazin says that's when you really get scared for the kid, because you know it's real. Of course, now you can add anything to a shot you want, but you couldn't in those days. So, anyway, what I'm saying is that maybe it makes an even bigger impression on somebody who knows Falcone and Hale, and is worried about recruiting violations, when he finally sees the two of them together in one shot."

"Faye, you don't think your friend at Channel Six did this on purpose?" I asked. "Edited the tape this way, I mean."

"I don't think so," she said. "He's not a big sports fan, he's into music. And this wasn't a sports story, remember? It was just a regular news story."

As we played the tape through, we saw Falcone and Green in the background from a slightly different angle. It was clear they were having a discussion, and in this shot, Hale was nowhere in sight. The entire segment on the cheerleading contest lasted less than four minutes.

"So, Gilda," Faye said, as the tape whined, "what are you thinking? That none of this was about Sid Green after all? Or some of it was?"

"I have my own theory about why Sid Green got involved," I said. "But as for everybody else, whoever they are, yeah, I think they thought they'd seen evidence of a major recruiting violation by the Buckeye State head coach."

"And when they got their hands on one of our copies of the tape, they thought some of the footage was missing," she continued, "because they believed the first thing they saw."

"And believed it so strongly that they didn't recognize the same footage, unedited, when they saw it," I finished. "After all, they probably didn't remember the details."

"But who are we talking about here?" Faye asked. "Mrs. Hale? Sid Green? Not Hank Mann, if he wanted to break the story. The other two don't seem like bomber types. I mean, I haven't met Mrs. Hale, but I have trouble picturing the woman you described building a bomb or torching a building. Oh, wait, she wouldn't have torched the building, anyway, even if she could hire someone. She wanted a copy of the tape. Hale could have done it, I guess."

"It's possible," I conceded, "but unlikely, I think. After all, he knew he hadn't talked to Falcone that day. He might have been the only person, besides Falcone, who could be sure of that. But since he *was* sure, he probably didn't feel threatened by the tape. Remember how he treated us?"

"Like we were scum," Faye recalled.

"Like we were photographers for the *National Enquirer*, or whoever it is that puts together those bizarre composite cover photos you see in supermarket checkout lines." I ejected the rewound tape and held it in my hand. "No, I think we're looking for someone else whose job and income are tied to a winning season and a trip to the Final Four—someone who couldn't be absolutely sure that Hale was telling the truth."

"The athletic director!" Faye stared at me, open-mouthed. "Turk what's-his-name! The guy Hale had lunch with right before he kicked the bucket!"

"Makes you wonder, doesn't it?" I said.

33

By the time the weekend was over, we knew a great deal more about Boris "Turk" Turkovich. We knew he'd ruled over the vast fiefdom that was the Buckeye State athletic programs for ten years. We knew that he was twice divorced and that he lived at an upscale address along River Road. We knew that he was a ladies' man, a fashionable dresser, and a frequently photographed man-about-town. We knew that he pulled in a staggering six-figure income likely to astonish the average taxpayer, if our own outrage was any indication. We even knew that he didn't like to be called "Boris." It's downright astonishing what you can find out at the library about a public university employee and public figure.

"I can see why he wouldn't want to be called 'Boris,' " Faye said. "But I wonder if the name 'Turk' is any reflection on his temperament."

"If it is, we can't tell by his press clippings," I said. I held up a bad photocopy of a newspaper photograph. "I guess he looks Turkish. And his grandparents immigrated from Georgia, near the Turkish border."

By then, we also knew more about Hale's death, which the press had covered in nauseating detail: how the two men had dined at a small pub several blocks from campus; how Hale had insisted upon drinking, despite Turkovich's protests; how the coach had made some prophetic remark about dying happy if he was going to die; how Hale had collapsed in the street on the walk back; how Turkovich had desperately searched the dying man's pockets for nitroglycerin tablets, and come up empty. The coach had been D.O.A. at the Buckeye State Hospital.

"There goes your murder theory," Faye had said at one point. "The asshole was ripped. No wonder he bought it."

"And he wasn't carrying any nitroglycerin on him?" I asked skeptically. "Come on, Faye. Think about the guy we overheard on the phone. Did he strike you as a man unconcerned about his health? He was complaining about all the pills he was taking, but he was taking them."

"Well, maybe he had too many pills to keep track of," she suggested.

"Listen," I said, "if you've just had open heart surgery, and you've been told you're a prime candidate for another heart attack, I don't think you leave home without nitroglycerin, and I don't think you forget which pocket you put it in."

"So you think Turkovich is lying? You think he killed Hale just to prevent a recruiting scandal and an NCAA sanction?"

I sighed. "I don't know. The missus is still my favorite candidate for murder, but if she did it, I doubt we'll ever prove it."

"It's worth a try, though, Gilda," Faye said encouragingly.

As the weekend had worn on, my enthusiasm for another clandestine garbage raid had waned. I felt sure that Styles had been right: We wouldn't find anything, and whatever we found would be inadmissible in court. Faye's enthusiasm, however, had remained high. But then, given her injury, she wouldn't be the person skulking around a strange backyard.

We scouted the Hales's neighborhood early Sunday afternoon, before the matinee. There wasn't a single garbage can lying empty by the curb.

"Good," Faye said. "That means that Friday wasn't garbage day around here."

"Either that, or we're in a neighborhood so upscale that no one would dare to leave their garbage cans out after garbage day," I pointed out.

The Hales lived on an unusually large shady lot tucked back off a short street in Upper Arlington, not far from River Road, where the athletic director lived. The house was modern and showed the hand of an architect in details such as an undulating brick facade and protruding wood beams beneath the roof.

Faye whistled. "Some house!" she said.

She was busy admiring the front garden, with its small pond and miniature waterfall and lush foliage. I was noting the security company sign posted by the driveway.

"Jeez, Gilda, maybe in this neighborhood the garbage truck drives right up to your back door, and the sanitation guys take care of your garbage without anybody having to drag the cans to the curb," Faye said.

"Well, one thing's for sure," I said gloomily. "I'm going to stick out like a sore thumb, no matter what I wear."

"That's why you're coming tomorrow," Faye said reassuringly, "when nobody's around to see you."

I rolled my eyes. "Faye, look around! These are the kinds of households that employ maids and nannies. Some of the wives are probably at home planning their social lives, and some of the husbands and wives are probably both retired and living off their stock dividends. I'll never get away with stealing something, not even garbage!"

She shook her head at me. "Gilda, we've got to do something about your attitude."

We drove past Turk Turkovich's house for good measure. It was even more daunting, given the distance from the road to the house, the imposing appearance of the house itself, which bore a resemblance to an ancestral manor house, and the two large boxers lying in the drive.

"As long as we're collecting garbage—" Faye began.

"Don't even think about it," I cautioned her.

"This was your idea to begin with," Faye reminded me.

"I can have stupid ideas from time to time," I said. "I'm allowed. The important thing is to recognize them before they become fatal."

"Hey, chill out!" Faye said. "We can do this! We just need some strategy, and maybe some help."

In the end it was Uncle Val whom Faye recruited to join in our little expedition. Natalie's father needed the plumber's van, so we couldn't use that, but Val borrowed an electrician's truck from a friend. We also borrowed two work shirts; his had "Steve" stitched over the pocket, and mine had "Slim."

"Where's the verisimilitude?" I grumbled. Nobody had ever been tempted to call me "Slim" in my entire life.

Clara insisted on doing our makeup, and when Gloria found out about it, she insisted on doing my hair.

Over my protests, she cut it short and put a dark rinse on it.

"If Mrs. Hale is home, she'll recognize you, Gilda," Faye said.

"And the jig, as they say, will be up," Val agreed. At seventy-four, he could pass for a much younger man; he could keep up with my father, the former dancer, on the racquetball court, with energy to spare. I'd always thought him handsome enough to be a matinee idol, and the photographs of him as a young man had strengthened this impression. But he claimed to have always preferred to work behind the camera, addressing himself to the intricacies of the gaffer's art.

Clara added a pair of round, tortoiseshell glasses to my own disguise, and I barely recognized myself.

"I wish you'd given us more notice, Gilda," Gloria clucked, fussing with my hair. "We could have done wonders with you."

Clara ignored Val's protests that electricians weren't auto mechanics, and rubbed grease into our fingernails, and smudged a little black eyebrow pencil down one of my cheeks. We wiped it all off in the van.

We arrived at the house in Upper Arlington at around ten-thirty—late enough to miss the exodus to work, early enough to miss the home lunch crowd. Val pulled the van into the Hales' driveway. I took a deep breath, snatched a clipboard from the seat beside me, and followed Val to the back of the van, from which he extracted a toolbox and a white plastic bag full of garbage from his own house. I eyed it skeptically. Val had assured me that nobody pays enough attention to their garbage to spot a substitution, and we had a collection of garbage bags, and even paper bags, in case we needed to make a change, but I still wasn't convinced that this plan would work. Faye was perched on one of the built-in tool-boxes in the back.

"Now, remember," he told her. "Anything suspicious—anything at all—you hit that button."

"That button" was the play button on a tape deck wired to the van's speakers. If Faye played the tape, we'd hear one of those obnoxious car alarms go off and make a run for the truck. You would have thought we were collecting garbage from the Pentagon.

"Roger," Faye said, finger on the button.

The actual burglary was anticlimactic. Nobody spotted us, as far as we could tell. Nobody stopped us. No dogs barked, no cats attempted blackmail. We were back in the van within five minutes, carrying a single tidy white plastic bag bulging with garbage. We'd left the other bag in its place.

We drove to a convenience store and parked the van. Faye spread a plastic sheet on the floor in the back, then soberly handed us each a pair of plastic gloves, to preserve any significant fingerprints.

Val dumped the trash bag, and we inspected our booty. We sorted it into piles: three medicine bottles, a pile of miscellaneous paper and mail, and the usual household detritus—some steak and chicken bones, some empty boxes and wrappers, some wadded tissues and napkins, a McDonald's bag and a Burger King bag, a measuring spoon that appeared to have had a close encounter with a disposal, two lemon rinds, some grape stems, an empty milk carton, an empty wine bottle and five beer bottles, three filters full of coffee grounds, a name tag that read HELLO, MY NAME IS CREIGHTON HALE, a lighter, and a ballpoint pen.

"Sorry, Gilda," Val said. "No tins of nicotine-laced wasp poison."

"No, but this stuff is really revealing, though, don't you think?" Faye said.

"What does it reveal?" I asked. "That she doesn't recycle?"

"Well, for one thing, it reveals that he was probably still drinking, doesn't it?" Faye said.

"If you think Mrs. Hale couldn't drink a bottle of wine and five bottles of beer all by her lonesome," I said, "think again."

Val held two of the bottles up and scrutinized them. "No lipstick marks, though," he said. "She too classy to drink from the bottle?"

I shrugged and picked up a Twinkie wrapper and an empty macaroni and cheese box. "I'd say it was a nutritionally chal- lenged household," I observed. "No wonder the guy had a heart attack."

Val wagged a finger at me. "Don't assume. Unless we run the fingerprints on those, we have to entertain the possi- bility that Mrs. Hale was the only family member to con- sume them."

"I'd still say her brand of choice was Godiva, though," I said, "not Hostess."

"Check out the junk mail," Faye said. "Some of these underwear catalogs are scary."

"Leather?" Val asked, peeking over her shoulder. "B and D?"

"I think she means ugly," I told him. I was reading through the scraps of paper, trying to ignore the oily bits of lettuce and coffee grounds that clung to them.

"Here's a phone number with no name," I said. "The hand- writing matches these other notes. Looks feminine to me, so

I'd guess it's Blanche Hale's. The number is probably her dentist's number, but I suppose we could check it out."

"This must be Hale's writing," Val said, holding out a scrap of paper half transparent from a butter smear. "It's barely legible. But look, Gilda. Doesn't this say 'Falcone'?"

I took it by one corner and squinted at it.

"Something about a Barbara Falcone?" he suggested.

"No, I think it's 'something re. Falcone.' 'Call Bob,' maybe? Call Bob re. Falcone?"

Val pulled his head back and looked down his nose at it. "That's it. You're right. Call Bob re. Falcone."

"Who's Bob?" Faye asked.

"Is Turk's real name Bob?" Val asked.

Faye and I shook our heads. "Boris," I said.

"Boris," Val said thoughtfully. "And he never anglicized it to Bob?"

"Not that we know of," Faye said.

We gazed at the slip of paper in silence.

"Well," Val said at last, "it proves he was interested in Falcone."

"Big duh," Faye said. "Val, everybody's interested in Falcone."

"And Sid's name is Sid, and Hank's name is Hank," I said, throwing up my hands in frustration. "So who the hell is Bob?"

"He's probably some assistant coach or something," Faye suggested.

"Yeah, you're right," I said. "It probably doesn't matter at all. Anyway, as far as Hale's death is concerned, I don't see anything incriminating here."

"What were you hoping for, Gil?" Val asked.

"I don't know," I said. "Maybe a full container of nitroglycerin tablets with her fingerprints on it, so we could prove that she removed them from his pocket and pitched them. Pretty unlikely, though, right?"

Val put a hand on my shoulder. "Well, we knew it was a long shot."

"Anyway," Faye said cheerfully, "we still have Turk Turkovich's garbage to search."

"Uh-uh." I shook my head emphatically. "No way. I'm not waltzing in there to ask those boxers if I can please borrow their garbage."

"Come on, Gilda." Faye smacked my arm. "Maybe they'll be locked up in the house. Where's your sense of adventure? We brought along another full garbage bag." She patted a reserve bag we'd taken from Liberty House.

"Excuse me?" I said. "Who just risked life, limb, and a clean record to steal a bag of garbage? God, listen to me! Do you hear how nutty that sounds?"

"Val?" Faye turned to him.

He sat back on his haunches. "I'm game."

"Do you have sadistic fantasies about being eaten by a large animal?" I asked.

"No, I have a roommate who lives vicariously through me and my family," he said. He climbed out of the back of the van and stretched. "Come on, Gilda. Do this caper with me and I'll bake you a Decadent Chocolate Cake."

I weakened. "They won't let me eat it in intensive care," I said. "Or in the pokey either, if it comes to that."

He got into the driver's seat and started the van. "Let's go, Slim. I want to stop at Kroger."

"What for?"

"Dog repellent."

When we turned into the driveway leading up to Turkovich's house a short while later, things looked quiet enough. There were no dogs in sight. But we heard the two boxers as we approached the house. Sure enough, they were pressed up against a tall fence that surrounded most of the backyard, barking furiously. Just outside the fence was a short walkway to the back door. Between that and the driveway was a concrete slab on which sat a metal cart with two garbage cans. They were the raccoon-proof kind with double-lock lids.

"Thoughtful of them to clear a path to the back door," Val observed, putting the van in park.

I didn't get out. "I think it's intended to give us a false sense of security," I said. Val was farther away from the dogs than I was; I could see the whites of their eyes. I was willing to bet they could break the fence down if they put their paws to it. "They'll be out before you can get the lid off the first can."

Val got out of the van and approached the fence with his Kroger bag.

I rolled my window down a crack. "What are you doing?" I asked urgently.

"You never know," he said, "when you might need a friend or two."

He held out the bag with the steaks.

"Don't be a lunatic!" I admonished him. "I told you in the checkout line, this only works in cartoons."

The dogs continued to bark frantically and hurl themselves at the fence. Val stood still on the other side of the gate and spoke to them in a low, soothing voice.

"Maybe they're vegetarian," Faye offered from the back.

I grunted. "We should be so lucky."

"Why don't you jump out and get the garbage, Gilda?" Faye suggested brightly.

"Why don't I? Because I'm paralyzed by terror, that's why."

But now the dogs had stopped barking. They were making snuffling sounds. Val unlatched the gate and stepped inside.

"Oh, God! I can't look!" I covered my eyes. "Tell me when it's over."

"Aww, that's so sweet!" Faye said. "Look, Gilda, they like him!"

Whether they liked him, or whether they'd decided to tolerate him for the sake of his offering from the Kroger meat department, I wasn't prepared to say. But he emerged grinning and in one piece.

That's when the door opened.

"Can I help you?" A middle-aged woman in polyester pants

and a large shirt stood in the doorway. She was wiping her hands on a dish towel, and wet patches at her knees suggested we'd interrupted her cleaning.

Faye ducked out of sight.

"I hope so," Val said easily, flashing her his most winsome smile. "Does this household recycle?"

"Who wants to know?" she said, suspicious but with just a hint of flirtation.

He laughed. "I'm sorry. Steve Liberty, with Ace Electric." He gestured toward the van. "The young woman cowering in the front seat is my niece." He leaned forward conspiratorially, shaking his head and laughing. "She's not much of a dog person. I keep telling her that if she wants to go on service calls, she's got to get over her fear of dogs, but it's taking a little longer than I expected."

She was looking puzzled, still a bit suspicious, but intrigued. "About the recycling?"

"Oh, yes, we're looking for households that don't recycle who might be willing to donate their garbage to a worthy cause. It's a project sponsored by the electricians' union." He smiled modestly. "It was my idea, really. We were trying to come up with a way to raise money for charity. We pick a different charity every year, you see, and this year it's Children's Hospital. Anyway, I said that there was money in recycling— you know, cans, glass, newspaper. I said that I'd noticed, getting around like I do, that a lot of folks don't recycle. You know how they are—they have good intentions, but they're busy or preoccupied or whatever. I said that a lot of them would probably be willing to give us their recyclables, if we took care of everything for them—that is, if they didn't have to do anything different than what they normally do. Electricians spend a lot of time driving around in their trucks, and it doesn't take that much more time to make a few stops every day and pick up a few garbage bags. We could even save people the bother of lugging their cans out to the curb. Then, every week at the union meetings, we could sort while we talked. To tell you the truth, most of those meetings are pretty boring anyway, and a little garbage might liven them up."

He flashed her another dazzling smile. I don't know whether she believed him, or whether, like me, she was simply dazed by the intricacy of the lie. The dish towel hung limp in her hand, and she was staring at him.

"How'd you come to choose this house?" she asked.

He grinned at her. "Maybe I just liked the looks of the place," he said. "We come by here all the time—got a job right up the road at the Thomases." He jerked a thumb over his right shoulder. "You know them? Jean and—oh, heck, what's his name? Slim!" he called out, making me jump. "What's Mr. Thomas's name?"

"Val," I said. It was the first thing that popped into my head.

"That's it—Val. You know them?"

"I'm just the housekeeper," she said. "I only know the neighbors on either side. It's not like a real neighborhood, you know, this road."

"Yeah, you're right," Val said. "I guess they don't have block parties around here, huh? So, anyway, what do you think? Will the owners be willing to participate in the recycling project, do you think?"

"I don't know," she said hesitantly. "I'd have to ask."

He nodded, satisfied. "Sure, that's no problem. Tell you what I'll do. I'll write down my name and phone number." He took a pen from his pocket and turned around. "Slim, I need the clipboard."

As I handed it out the window to him, I crossed my eyes at him.

He laughed. "Yeah, Slim here, she's deathly afraid of dogs. Some people are like that. I don't know why. Me, I love dogs." He wrote on an Ace order form as he talked. I wondered what his pal at Ace would say when they got the call about garbage recycling. "Do you?"

"Some dogs," she conceded, glancing through the fence at the boxers. "These dogs scare most people. I'm actually surprised they calmed down like they did. They don't usually take to strangers."

One of the boxers had his nose pressed between the vertical slats of the wooden fence. Val reached out and rubbed the nose affectionately. The boxer gave a little snuffling sigh of contentment.

"I guess they know a dog lover when they see one," he said shamelessly. The boxer was trying to lick his fingers.

"So this is you, Ace Electric?" the woman asked, studying the work order he'd handed her.

"That's us," he affirmed. He pointed to the sheet of paper. "I wrote down there 'recycling project' so you'd remember what it was for."

"Ask for the garbage," Faye whispered loudly from the backseat.

What the hell, I thought. My life didn't seem to be in imminent danger.

"Uncle Steve," I called. "Ask her if we can have the garbage."

"Oh, hey, would you mind?" he asked her. "Some of the guys down at the local, they're not convinced we can collect enough recyclable stuff this way. They're all hot to sell chocolate bars again." He shook his head at the hidebound conventionality of his fictitious colleagues. "Me and Slim, we want to prove them wrong. But if we bring in our own garbage, they'll think we loaded it up with cans and bottles."

"Well—" She hesitated.

"Think of it as an early garbage pickup," he suggested. "Garbage day is when?"

"Wednesday," she said. "I put the cans out tomorrow night."

"There you are," Val said. "We'll save you the trouble."

"Well, okay," she said. "I guess I can't see any reason not to. Go ahead and take it if you want."

"Thanks! That's great!" He whipped the covers off both garbage cans and returned to the van carrying two bags of garbage. Faye scrambled to get out of sight and out of the way when he opened the back doors and tossed them in. He climbed into the front and started the engine. He waved jauntily out the window. "Bye, now!" he said to the woman. "Bye, boys!" The dogs gave a few friendly barks, and we were gone.

He backed out onto River Road and headed for home, whistling. When he turned to look at me, we both burst out laughing.

"God," I said, "are you ever a Liberty!"

34

We went back to Liberty House, where we could spread out our haul on the floor of one of the unused garages. I couldn't see Clara or Faye's mother welcoming our piles of garbage with open arms. Turkovich's garbage was long on sports magazines of all types and descriptions, and short on food-related items.

"The guy must not eat," Val said.

"Hey, I thought he lived alone," Faye said, holding up a lipstick-smudged tissue.

"Well, just because he lives alone doesn't mean he sleeps alone," I pointed out. "What does it smell like?"

Faye sniffed it. "It's pretty faint."

I sniffed it, too. She was right. I caught the faintest whiff of perfume, but it wasn't strong enough to be identifiable under the cloying scent of the tissue.

"Take a look at this," Val said. He handed me a note on a small piece of notepaper.

It said, "6:30 Thursday, Leonardo's." The handwriting looked familiar. I sniffed at it. Gardenia, definitely gardenia.

"Where are the handwriting samples?" I asked.

Val passed me the notes from the Hale house.

"It's hers," I said. "Look."

"Maybe they're just good friends," Val proposed suggestively, waggling his eyebrows.

"And maybe Mrs. Hale is moonlighting as a dogsitter," I said wryly. "I don't think so."

"Sweet!" was Faye's comment. "So she hooked up with Turkovich and got him to bump off her husband."

"Maybe, but how?" I continued to sort, pushing aside a rolled-up, empty toothpaste tube, a container of nasal spray, a *Sports Illustrated*, and several pieces of used dental floss. I was glad I was wearing gloves.

Faye pounced on something in the pile I was sorting. She held it up: a pantyhose wrapper.

"How kinky do you think this guy is?" she asked.

"Cafe au lait," I read. "I don't think it's his color."

"This isn't, either," Val remarked. He was holding up a loose ball of light blond hair. "Tisk, tisk."

I was unwrapping a ball of newspaper I'd found. I would've tossed it aside, but it was lumpy, as if something had been wrapped up inside it. I stared at the contents. I thought at first that I was looking at someone's craft project and tried to remember the ages of Turkovich's kids. They lived with their mother, according to our information, but I supposed they visited from time to time.

"What've you got there, Gil?" Val asked casually as I smoothed out the newspaper. "A schedule of ships arriving in Central Ohio today?"

Wrapped inside the newspaper were a prescription medicine bottle, half full; a small, thick square of some light yellow substance, soft and crumbly and faintly smelling of something that was a mix of Play-Doh and paste; a plastic wrapper; and a half dozen small yellow tablets. I opened the bottle, which was unlabeled, and shook several pale yellow tablets out into my palm. I held them out to Val and Faye.

"What are these?" I asked.

Val poked at them and lifted one between gloved thumb and forefinger. It had a heart-shaped hole in the middle.

"Looks familiar," he said slowly. "Wait, it'll come to me."

"That's Valium," Faye said. "Grams got a prescription after Grosvenor died. Remember what a space cadet she was at the funeral?"

"That's right," Val confirmed.

I picked up one of the loose tablets that still lay scattered on the newspaper and held it up next to the one Val was holding. No hole.

"Does Valium always come with a heart-shaped hole punched in the middle?" I asked, my voice tight in my throat.

"I think so, Gil," Val said. "All the ones I've seen have. I think the different dosages come in different colors, but the hole's still there."

"How do you know so much about tranks?" Faye asked him.

"I worked in Hollywood, remember?" he said. "Everybody was on something."

"Except you," she said.

He smiled back at her and let it go at that.

"So if that one's Valium," Faye said, pointing, "what's that one?"

"A Valium with a good makeup job," I said.

"What?" she said.

"Some clever little craftsperson figured out a way to make Valium look like something else," I said. I smoothed out the plastic wrapper and showed it to them. "They used Fimo— the modeling clay used to make beads for jewelry."

"Get outta here!" Faye exclaimed. "And they used that to kill Hale?"

"Can you think of any other good reason why somebody would go to the trouble to fill in all the holes in these Valium tablets?" I asked.

"They were embarrassed to be taking medication with little hearts in the middle?" Val offered.

"I said a good reason."

"No, but what's the deal with the Valium?" Faye asked. "I mean, it's not usually used to, like, bump somebody off."

"Doesn't Lillian have a *Physicians' Desk Reference* around?" Val asked. "I thought I saw one somewhere."

"I'll go see," I said, unfolding myself and standing up.

In the library, tidier and better organized since Mae had died and Lillian had become its sole librarian, I quickly found what I was looking for. The book was red, and heavy enough to sink a small rowboat.

Back in the garage, I handed the book to Val. He opened it, found the entry under "Valium," and ran his finger down the page.

"Sorry, kids, I can't translate most of this," he said. "But there is something about not combining it with alcohol. That's the only thing I can understand that's relevant."

"And Turkovich went to lunch with Hale and watched him drink. So that means Turkovich killed him, then," Faye summarized.

"Or Turkovich and Mrs. Hale together," Val said. "Remember the blond hair and the pantyhose."

"I wonder," I mused. "Why go to the trouble to remove the prescription label from the Valium bottle? And I'd still like to know about the nitroglycerin. It seems kind of a chancy way to kill someone. How did they know he wouldn't have any nitroglycerin on him whenever he took the Valium?"

"Ah," Val said. "That's why you brought a senior citizen with you on this caper. We know more about prescription medications than you kiddies."

"Such as?"

"That nitroglycerin doesn't just come in tablet form," he said, and rummaged in my pile of discarded paraphernalia. "It also comes in a sublingual spray."

Triumphantly, he held up the small plastic bottle I'd taken

to be a nasal spray. He shook it. We heard the soft click of liquid against plastic, signaling that the bottle was full.

35

"It has to go back," I said. "All this stuff has to go back."

"What do you mean?" Faye asked.

"She means, so that the police can find it," Val told her.

"But they're not looking for it," she said reasonably. "How are we going to pass the word without getting arrested?"

"We're not going to get arrested for stealing Turkovich's garbage," Val pointed out. "The housekeeper gave it to us. The bigger question is how to convince the cops to go looking for it."

"But then we have to put it back," Faye said.

"Val can do that when he goes back to give the dogs their dessert," I said, standing up awkwardly. I bounced two tablets in my gloved hand, one doctored and one undoctored, then slipped them into one of the small plastic bags we'd commandeered from the kitchen for evidence bags. "I think I'll keep two of these. Maybe I'll go have an unofficial chat with Dale Ferguson. Anybody want to come?"

Val shook his head. "Much as I'd like to see the expression on his face when you've finished your story, I can't. I promised Tobias we'd go bicycle shopping while I still had the van."

"That's okay, Gilda," Faye said. "I've got to get back to work on my film. But if he doesn't believe you, he can call me." She pulled off her gloves with a snap, and the movement flexed Wonder Woman's muscles.

"Why don't I think that will reassure him?" I said.

"You really want to put this stuff back, Gilda?" Val asked. "I can do it, but garbage day is Wednesday. That doesn't give the cops much time."

"Well," I said, "if we need it again, we'll know where to find it."

When I called Dale, he proposed a late night meeting over beer at Oscar's, since he was staying late to catch up on paperwork anyway. He looked tired in his rolled shirtsleeves, with his collar open and his tie on the table next to his mug of beer. In the middle of my story, he closed his eyes, and kept them closed. I wasn't sure if he was awake and still listening.

I finished by saying that Val had already called to confirm that the Turkovich garbage had been returned without incident. The boxers had apparently been left home alone, and they had enjoyed their dessert very much.

Dale opened droopy bloodshot eyes and looked at me.

"You know what I say whenever people ask me if a cop's life is dull in a small town like Eden, Ohio?" he said. "I tell them about the Liberties and reassure them that as long as the Liberties are in town, there will never be a dull moment."

"If you don't want me to report murder," I said, "just say so."

"Oh, I want you to report murder," he said. "I just don't want you to report it to me."

"You're the only police detective I know," I said humbly.

He rubbed his eyes. "Gilda, you may find this hard to believe, but every day thousands of people report crimes to police detectives they don't even know."

"And what would be my chances of getting a Columbus homicide detective to listen to my story and take it seriously?"

"Touché. I'm only listening to you because you're buying the beer. You *are* buying, aren't you?"

"Look," I said, "do you know if they performed an autopsy on Hale?"

"No, I don't, but I'd be real surprised if they did. And I'd be bowled over if they exhumed the body on the basis of your cockamamie story."

"I realize that," I said. "And I doubt they'd get a search warrant, either, to search the Hale house or the Turkovich house. But tell me this: Do they need a search warrant to search garbage that the garbage collectors have already collected? I mean, if they had the sanitation department's permission, could they search a bag once it had been deposited in a sanitation truck?"

Dale licked at a moustache of foam and sat back. "They can search it as soon as it's left out on the curb," he admitted.

"So it all depends on whether a Columbus homicide detective could be induced to take an interest in the contents of the athletic director's garbage," I said. "That's where you come in."

"Uh-huh. And who should I tell this detective gave me this hot information?"

"A reliable anonymous source."

Dale emitted a bleat. "I should be so lucky," he said.

36

"Turkovich wants to see me," Faye announced on the phone the next morning in a doomed voice.

I was still half asleep and a little hungover.

"Is he mad about his garbage?" I asked in confusion. "We put it back."

"He didn't say anything about his garbage," she said. "He says there are one or two matters about a certain videotape that need clearing up. I asked what matters, but he said he preferred to discuss them in person. He wants me to go to his office tonight after nine-thirty."

"Whatever happened to regular business hours?" I complained.

"He says he's booked solid, and that he has a baseball game to attend at seven-thirty. He also says I should appreciate the need for privacy in a delicate matter."

"He must think we're idiots!" I said, offended.

"Actually, he doesn't seem to know anything about you, Gilda," Faye said. "He thinks I'm an idiot, I could tell."

"Well, you're not going by yourself," I said firmly. "And you're not going tonight. Put him off till tomorrow night, in case we get the Columbus cops to look at his garbage."

"Will Duke let you off work tomorrow night?" she asked.

I greeted this with silence. I didn't look forward to Duke's reaction. I might get a lecture about my priorities, or worse, a whole evening of tacit disapprobation. It didn't even matter that I was supposed to be the boss; everybody knew who really ran the Paradise.

"He'll have to, I guess," I said weakly. "And Faye—tell Turkovich that we expect to see Mrs. Hale and Mr. Green at this meeting, too. Tell him that we won't want to reach separate agreements with all of the parties involved."

"Not Hank Mann?" she asked.

"No, I think Hank's a lone wolf," I said. "But the other three are definitely connected."

I called Dale Ferguson. "I'm going down there this afternoon to talk to a friend of mine in the Columbus P.D.," he reported. "But you owe me big time, Gilda. This could make me really unpopular."

Tuesday was blessedly uneventful. I heard nothing from Styles. For all I knew, she could be hot on the trail of some storage locker scam in Timbuktu. I figured I'd see her when I saw her.

Late in the day, Dale Ferguson called to say that his friend would check out the Turkovich garbage.

"He's doing it on a bet, though, Gilda, so he'd better find what you said he'd find," Dale threatened.

"What are you betting?" I asked, suddenly nervous.

"Groundhog season tickets."

"Don't worry," I said with feigned conviction. "It'll be there."

Wednesday shaped up quite differently. From breakfast onward, it made its intentions clear.

My aunt Lillian was eating lunch while I ate breakfast. She was reading the local paper.

"Gilda," she said, "what's this about a major construction project on Oak Street? It says here they're planning to tear up the street to lay new sewer lines."

My eyes popped open.

"What?" I said, putting down my spoon. "Where?"

"Here." She pushed the paper toward me and tapped it with her finger.

The item was short and seemed deliberately vague. There was no map adjoining to clarify its import, so there was no way to tell whether the section of Oak Street the city planned to pulverize corresponded to the section that ran past the Paradise Theatre.

At that moment, the phone rang. Ruth Hernandez answered and handed the receiver to me.

"It's Duke," she told me. "I can't understand what he's saying. I think he's a little upset."

This proved to be an understatement; my business manager was beside himself. "Did you see that story in the paper about some stupid sewer improvement project, Gilda? Do you know what they're planning to do?" In the background, I could hear the dull roar of a high school cafeteria, where lunch was in full swing.

"I just saw it, Duke," I said. "I don't know anything about it."

"They can't get away with this!" he sputtered. "We can't let them! We'll need to get every single Liberty down there to picket the next city council meeting, Gilda. And every movie-goer in the city of Eden. Hell, we'll get every moviegoer in Eden County! Start spreading the word."

"Maybe we should—" I began.

"Apart from the whole question of access, do you know what all that construction dust will do to our equipment? Do you know how many film breaks we'd have?"

"Film breaks?" I echoed in horror.

"Wait, there's Tony now." Tony was the mayor's older son. "If he thinks he's going to eat his lunch in peace, he's got an-other think coming!" On that peremptory note, my business manager hung up on me.

"Lillian, if you got some time this afternoon, you should water those new plants we put in on the side of the house," I heard Ruth saying. "They look droopy."

Plants? I thought. Oh, hell!

"Gilda, your mother called this morning to remind you about Oliver's birthday tomorrow," Lillian said. She looked at me over her reading glasses. "Did you remember?"

"No," I said miserably.

"She said she saw a boxed set of P. G. Wodehouse down at the bookstore, in case you were interested."

"Thanks, Lilly," I said, relieved.

"Don't thank me," she said. "It was your mother's idea."

I smiled a little to myself. There were a few—a very few—advantages to living in the bosom of my family again.

I sat in the room I still considered Mae's study and made a few phone calls. Ferguson was in court, so I left a message. Yes, one distributor informed me, I could get a print of *Mrs. Doubtfire* for a kids' film series this summer, but I'd have to preview it.

"See, there's only two prints left," said the voice on the other end, "one good, one lousy. You won't know which one you have till you look at it."

"Aren't they marked?" I asked incredulously.

"Like I said," the voice responded, unperturbed.

"How can you only have two prints of *Mrs. Doubtfire*?" I asked.

"You want it or not?"

I stopped off at Styles's office to give the plants a decent burial and found one of them clinging to life. For all I knew, the weeping fig could have been clinging to life, too, but I couldn't tell because it had lost all its leaves. I doused them and left them sitting in saucers of water to make up for my past neglect.

When I arrived at the theater, I found the front walk littered with broken beer bottles. In the lobby, one of the dinosaur feet had unaccountably deflated and lay in a green vinyl puddle on the floor. The ice machine was making strange noises, and one of the lights in the women's rest room was blinking like a strobe. That was before the sky blackened, the thunderstorm rolled in, and the electricity went out. When Duke arrived, still in a lather about the threatened construction project, I was reading the owner's manual for the ice machine by flashlight.

When the lights came on again at five-thirty, Duke enlisted me in an attempt to patch and reinflate the dinosaur foot. I was up to my earlobes in green vinyl when Dale Ferguson called, so he left a message on the answering machine saying only that he was collecting his Groundhog season tickets from an irate Columbus detective, who hadn't yet decided what to do about what he'd found. Todd arrived, soaking wet and muddy; he'd fallen from his bike on the rain-slicked street. Faye appeared and raced upstairs to unplug all of her equipment, though the worst of the storm seemed to have passed.

The rain, which had let up, turned back into a downpour about ten minutes before the early show started. A handful of intrepid souls turned up, shedding water on the lobby floor like retrievers. Todd mopped for the third time as I gathered my courage and told Duke we were going out.

"Out?" he asked. "In this?"

"We have an appointment to see a guy about a video," I said. I told him where we were going and why.

"You're not going by yourselves, are you?" he asked in alarm, glancing at Faye.

I shook my head. "Valentino's going to drive us."

Duke looked skeptical. "Does he have a gun?" he asked.

"Come on," Faye said. "What do you think—the dude's going to eighty-six us right there in the middle of the Groundhog athletic complex at nine-thirty at night?"

"Yeah," I said. I snorted half-heartedly. I still had a ways to go to work up to Faye's level of confidence.

The place looked safe enough, though, when we arrived. It was well lit against the black of the cloud-heavy sky. As we cruised past, several men carrying gym bags were making their way down the flower-strewn steps, talking and laughing.

"I suppose they could have machine guns in those bags," I observed.

"And stun guns in their gym socks?" Val asked.

Tobias was riding shotgun. He already had his notebook out. "Can I come listen at the door, Gilda?" he asked.

"No," I said.

"Please?" he pleaded. "I wore my Buckeye State T-shirt and my gym shorts."

"He's got a portable phone in *his* gym bag," Val told me.

"Well, okay," I said. "But you can't be conspicuous."

"I still think you should have told Ferguson you were coming," Val said.

"I couldn't reach him. He was in court all day, and when he called back, I was in the middle of plastic surgery," I said.

Val parked, and everyone got out. The rain had faded to a drizzle, but lightning was still flickering in the west.

"I think I'll go hang out by the elevators," Val said. That's when I noticed he was wearing his Ace Electric shirt again. He retrieved a toolbox from the trunk.

"Okay, Steve," I said, "but the same goes for you: Lie low."

Faye and I took an elevator to the third floor. Faye leaned on her crutch, humming to herself. She was wearing a full complement of silver jewelry. Her hair blazed bright red like an artificial sun.

"Maybe it's a ruse," I said. "Maybe that wasn't Turkovich who called you. Maybe those two guys set this up, and they're planning to jump us and beat the shit out of us."

Faye shrugged. "We've already won two rounds with those dipshits. It's their funeral." As she hobbled down the hall, she added, "Remember, now, Gilda. You're Styles."

I stopped in my tracks. I'd forgotten I was Styles, and now the reminder worked on me like magic. I found myself grinning. When I walked on, it was with Styles's steely determination in my step.

The office door was open. The outer office, which was deserted, had not had the same decorator as the coach's office downstairs. Here, polished wood and brass gleamed in the soft glow of several lamps. No doubt intended to impress the boosters and recruits, the elegance was spoiled by a scarlet-and-black rug, which took up most of the generous expanse of floor. In the middle of it was the cartoon figure of a fighting groundhog.

A backlit figure appeared in the doorway of the inner office.

"Miss McCadden?" he said. He crossed the rug to us and extended his hand slightly, looking from one of us to the other. He was a handsome man, with thick dark hair, heavy eyebrows, and dark eyes to match his tanned skin. His hair was showing white at the temples, but it was difficult to guess his age. He looked as if he were in his fifties, but given his position, he might have been much older. He was in his shirtsleeves, but his tie was still firmly knotted at his throat.

"That's me," Faye said. "Wow, that rug is scary."

"I'm glad you like it," he said smoothly, shaking her hand. "Turk Turkovich. And this is?"

"My cousin and my attorney, Gilda Styles," Faye said.

We shook hands. My fingers emerged bruised by a large signet ring he was wearing.

"I shouldn't think we'll need the services of an attorney," he said, smiling cordially, "but you're welcome to sit in anyway."

"You never know," I said.

"She's not an attorney," said another voice, "she's a detective."

This time I recognized the silhouette in the doorway as that of Mrs. Hale.

"Don't worry, Mrs. Hale," I said. "I know my way to the courthouse."

"Please, come in." Our host waved us into his inner office.

This office was even larger and more elegant than the outer office. It featured tasteful draperies woven in scarlet and black and a more tasteful rug with the Buckeye State logo in collegiate letters. A small groundhog was relegated to one corner. Standing on its tail and shuffling his feet nervously was Smiling Sid Green.

"I believe you've met Mr. Green," Turkovich said.

Smiling Sid gave us a sickly smile. Whatever was going down tonight, he didn't want to be here for it, that much was clear. I realized when I saw him that I'd been introduced to him before as Gilda Liberty. But if he was puzzled by my multiple identities, he didn't mention it.

Turkovich closed the door to the outer office. It shut with the soft whisper of a well-trained servant.

"Please, sit down," Turkovich said. "I'm afraid my secretary isn't in, or I'd offer you some coffee."

I considered pointing out that any moron could run an electric coffeemaker these days—even I could do it—but I kept my opinion to myself.

"I do have a bar, however," he went on. "May I offer you a drink?"

I spoke up for both of us. "No, thanks," I said. I might not have been a trained detective, but I'd seen enough detective movies to know that you don't accept a drink from an enemy.

We sat. Sid Green sat. Turkovich leaned against the front of his mammoth mahogany desk, which was surprisingly clean for an athletic director with a six-figure income. Maybe, I thought, today had been garbage day. Mrs. Hale stood to one side of the desk, just outside the circle of light cast by its lamp, and smoked a cigarette. She didn't offer me one.

Turkovich smiled at us. "I appreciate your willingness to talk."

"You're a man who likes talking to a man who likes to talk," I quoted. He didn't look anything like Caspar Gutman from *The Maltese Falcon*, but I pegged him for a man with Gutman's avarice.

He didn't get it. "You could put it that way," he said. "Now," he continued, still speaking genially, "I think we all know what this is about. You, Miss McCadden, have a certain videotape that could prove damaging to the basketball program here at Buckeye State. We hope to persuade you to destroy that tape, or at the very least, to erase those parts of it which might render the Groundhogs vulnerable to an NCAA sanction."

"I'm glad we're having this talk," Faye said. "So far, I like it a whole lot better than the fire and the glue bomb."

I stole a look at her out of the corner of my eyes, once again impressed at how articulate she could be when she wanted to be.

"Sorry," he said politely. "I don't know what you're referring to."

We let that go, for now.

"The tape you have implicates our late basketball coach, Creighton Hale, in an illegal recruiting contact with Mike Falcone," he went on.

"Implicates" seemed like an odd word to use if he thought we'd caught the guy red-handed. In any case, we weren't about to explain to him that we hadn't.

"Of course, it may or may not also suggest that another illegal recruiting contact was made on the same day by Mr. Green, but I'm not concerned with that here. Athletic programs can't always control what their boosters do, and I doubt that the NCAA would come down on us too hard as a result of

Mr. Green's misguided attempt to help us out. No, I'm only concerned here with the contact made by Coach Hale.

"Miss McCadden," he said, hands on his knees, "I think most people recognize that Coach Hale's health was extremely precarious after his surgery. He was taking quite a bit of medication, which may have affected his judgment. He may even have realized that he was dying and was worried about the future of the program after he was gone. He may have risked making this contact in the spirit of ensuring the future welfare of the program. Isn't that right, Blanche?"

He half turned to her.

"Of course," she said, and I could hear the irony in her voice. "Anything for the Groundhogs."

Turkovich didn't permit himself to be ruffled or deterred. "And there's no doubt whatsoever that this young man, Mike Falcone, could guarantee us a national championship—maybe more than one national championship—if he signed with Buckeye State. So the coach was acting in the best interests of the school, as he saw it, when he spoke to the young man. What's more, it was a purely unselfish act on his part—he had nothing to gain from it."

Mrs. Hale made an incoherent noise and turned her head to blow smoke at the wall.

"He wouldn't even have had the opportunity to coach Mike Falcone," Turkovich continued. "His only reward would have been seeing his beloved Groundhogs take another national title."

He leaned forward and gazed at Faye intently.

"Now, I put it to you, Miss McCadden," he said quietly, "what good would it do to release that tape now? It's doubtful that the NCAA would take any action, given the state of Creighton's health at the time, and the magnitude of his contribution to college basketball. I expect they'd see it as water under the bridge. Now that he's gone, we all want to celebrate his achievements, not publicize his mistakes. As for the Groundhog fans . . ." He gestured eloquently. "I don't want to be misunderstood here, Miss McCadden, but I'm tempted to say that I'd fear for your safety if you released that tape. Unfortunately, our fans can be—"

"Violent," I supplied. "Mean-spirited, unsportsmanlike, drunk and disorderly, and destructive of property."

He raised his hands. "You're speaking of a small minority, Miss Styles, but yes. They're not under my control."

The door to the office flew open and slammed against the doorstop, shuddering like a knife-thrower's blade. The man who stood there took up most of the doorway, blocking our view of the outer office. He was tall and muscular, biceps straining at the fabric of his navy blue blazer. His nose had been broken at least once in his twenty-odd years. A protuberant forehead overhung small, recessed eyes, and he was going bald prematurely. His expression was truculent, but he avoided eye contact with anyone in the room. He looked like a thug, but he wasn't a thug I recognized. This outfit seemed to run to thugs.

"What is it, Mark?" Turkovich asked, with only a slight edge of impatience in his voice.

Mark hunched his shoulders in an elaborate shrug, and I heard a seam rip. Then I heard a voice I recognized.

"Some people like suspense," it said. "Me, I'd just as soon have all the guns in the hands of the good guys."

Mark, apparently prodded from behind, advanced several slow steps into the room. From behind his bulk appeared, like a small bird on the rump of a rhinoceros, S. Styles, private investigator. She was wearing loose cotton pants, a khaki shirt, a loose-fitting cotton jacket, and white cowboy boots. In one hand, she was carrying a boxy leather briefcase, as if she'd come straight from the airport. In the other, she was holding a gun.

"May I ask who you are?" Turkovich inquired.

"I'm with the visiting team," Styles replied. "I'm her lawyer." She nodded at Faye.

"I thought Miss Styles here was her lawyer," Turkovich said, raising his formidable eyebrows.

"Also," Styles said. "I take the really hard cases."

"I see," he said, frowning. "And your name is . . . ?"

"Styles," she said. She nodded at me. "We're related."

He looked from her to me, and back again. "Very well, Miss Styles, you might as well come in and sit down. I can assure you that our intentions here are perfectly honorable, and that Mark carries a gun only for protection."

"What's he lift weights for, to attract girls?" Styles said.

"And, if it makes you feel more secure, you can hold on to the gun," he said.

"Gee, I was hoping you'd say that," Styles said. She sat down in a high-backed leather chair that made her look like Jiminy Cricket. She set the briefcase down flat on a polished walnut table as if she might be about to produce a set of legal contracts in triplicate. "I'd like Mark to stay, too," she added pleasantly. "He made me nervous, hanging out in the hallway, playing with his piece."

"All right," Turkovich conceded. "Sit down, Mark."

"Keep your ears open, Mark," I told him, "and you might win a car."

Everyone ignored me except Mark, whose gaze shifted to Smiling Sid. If there were cars going around, he wanted to be in line.

"Now, where were we?" Turkovich returned to his former position, leaning against the desk. I presumed this was a pose calculated to keep him taller than anyone who was seated.

"You were at the part where schizzed-out fans were, like, mauling us for releasing the video," Faye reminded him. "Although personally, I'd prefer a little straightforward mauling to the random, totally wack shit that's been going on lately."

"Well," Turkovich said, apparently impervious to accusation, "as I said, I doubt that the release of the video would achieve anything positive. I wonder if it would even be legal to release video footage of someone who didn't know he was being taped." He smiled slightly at Faye.

"Don't go there," she warned. "I've got a signed release form. All the judges signed them."

His smile evaporated. He stood up, walked to the window,

and looked out. He did it casually, but I knew the movement well. My father had made the same move in at least three movies I could think of. Blanche Hale sat down on a couch, looking bored. I wondered if she had her little pistol buried under a cushion. Sid Green, who sat nearest her, threw her an apprehensive look and edged his chair away.

"What is your alma mater, Miss McCadden?" Turkovich asked, turning his gaze vaguely in her direction.

"I'm still in school," Faye said. "I'm at USC."

"Ah," he said, as if pleased. "A very good school. Miss Styles, your alma mater?" He was looking at me.

"UCLA."

"I see. A Bruin. Miss Styles Number Two?" He angled an eyebrow at Styles.

"Buckeye State," she said, surprising me. She'd never mentioned where she'd gone to school, but then again, I'd never asked.

"Really? What year?" he asked.

"Two years after they shut the place down," she said. "Two years after Kent State. So don't ask me if it was a Rose Bowl year. I wasn't really paying attention."

He tilted his head back slightly and studied her.

"Let me ask you this, Miss McCadden," he said, his eyes still on Styles. "Is there some particular reason why you don't want Falcone to play for Buckeye State? Do you have an interest in seeing him go elsewhere?"

"I don't really care jackshit where he goes," Faye said. "Any of the places he's likely to go are probably just as corrupt as this place is."

"So you have something against college athletics, is that it?" he asked.

"I don't have anything against college athletics generally," she said, leaning forward in her chair. "But I got a whole shitload of complaints against Division I men's athletics, starting with your salary as Top Hog. You want to hear the rest of 'em? How much time do you have?" Her nose ring quivered with emotion, and Wonder Woman leapt to life on her forearm.

"And while we're at it, is this the office you bring all the rape victims to when you offer 'em one of Sid's cars not to prosecute?"

A light seemed to dawn in his eyes. "You're one of Julie Stoebel's friends."

Mark apparently felt compelled to speak up from his corner. "Listen, that girl was pissed! And she gave Jimmy the come-on, I don't care what she says now!"

Turkovich made a quelling gesture with one hand.

"I never met Julie Stoebel in my life," Faye said angrily, "or any of Jimmy's other victims, for that matter. But they're just one sign of what's wrong around here. This whole program is rotten to the core!"

"Miss McCadden, please!" Turkovich looked pained, as if compelled to reprimand a naughty child. "Suppose you just tell me what you hope to accomplish by releasing this tape."

"I thought you'd never ask," Faye said. "All I want to do is finish my movie, without the building burning down around my ears, and preferably without any more injuries. And I don't want anybody fuckin' telling me what to put in and what to leave out! This is a senior project, for crissakes! I'm the producer, the director, and the editor! I want to do documentary so I don't have to listen to everybody telling me what to do. Jesus, if I wanted censorship, I'd go right to Hollywood!"

"I see," he said. He'd returned to his favorite position in front of the desk. He was looking down on her paternally. "So this is a matter of principle for you?"

"That's right."

"And you intend to use the incriminating footage?"

"I really don't know."

He blinked at her a few times. She looked back at him. You could almost see the wheels turning behind his eyes.

"When will this project be finished?" he asked.

"By January, I hope."

"You say it's a student project. Do you plan to distribute it nationally?"

"I hope so."

"Sometime after January."

"Realistically speaking, after I graduate in June."

"I believe you've had some offers to buy the footage in question."

"It's not for sale," Faye said, glancing at Sid Green. "If somebody wants to buy a copy of the finished film, I'd be happy to sell it to them."

"I believe when your film was described on the television newscast, it was described as a film about gender equity in sports. Is that accurate?"

"Yes."

"So the recruiting contact isn't directly relevant to the subject of the film?"

"Not directly, no."

"Well," he said, smacking his knees with his hands and standing up, "maybe that will have to content us."

"Maybe it will," Faye said.

"You seem like a nice young woman," he said. "I'm sure you'll come to accept that it would be needlessly cruel to drag Coach Hale's memory through the mud—cruel to his family as well as his fans."

Blanche Hale had the faintest of smiles on her lips. She didn't look like she cared, one way or the other.

"As far as I'm concerned," Faye said, "Hale's memory belongs in the mud. But I'm not about to go on a crusade to put it there. I've got better things to do."

He opened his arms. "Then I suppose our business is finished."

Sid Green bobbed up, and so, after a short pause, did Mark the thug. Mrs. Hale shifted about on the couch and reached for another cigarette. Turkovitch extended a hand to Faye.

"Not quite," I said.

37

"There's a small matter of crime to be dealt with," I said. "Several crimes, in fact."

I flicked a glance at Faye. "You go, girl!" she said.

I looked at Styles. She waved the gun languidly, and said, "Have a seat, guys. We could be in for a long night."

Everyone who had been sitting sat. Turkovich folded his arms across his chest like a stern parent.

I was still being Styles. It didn't deter me in the least that she was sitting in the room. I took a deep breath, but before I could speak, we heard a small noise from the outer office, like a suppressed sneeze.

I sighed, got up, went to the door, and opened it.

Tobias was crouched on the floor, holding a handkerchief to his nose. "Sorry, Gilda," he said, "I couldn't help it."

I waved him in. "Take a pew," I said.

He pocketed his handkerchief, ambled over to the couch, and sat down. "Tobias Norton," he said, extending a hand to Blanche Hale. He had a pen stuck behind one ear and a small notebook in the other hand. "Don't worry, I write fiction."

She shook reluctantly.

"I don't see that we have any more to discuss," Turkovich said, a little peevishly. "I don't know what you're talking about when you talk about crime."

"Arson, assault, destruction of property, murder," I ticked them off on my fingers.

"Murder?" That uncrossed his arms. He laughed and shook his head. "Really, Miss Styles—"

"Have I left any out?" I asked Faye.

Styles spoke up. "There could be a manslaughter charge to go with the arson. There's one old guy in the hospital for smoke inhalation. He still in there, Faye?"

"I think he got out on Monday," she said.

"Okay, so you dodged a bullet there," Styles said to Turkovich. "Better hope he doesn't have a relapse."

"I don't have any idea what you're talking about," Turkovich said, throwing up his hands.

"I don't know what they're talking about, either," Sid Green put in.

I turned to him. "That's because you don't have a devious enough mind, Sid," I said. "Oh, you're devious, all right, but you're not in their league. At least when you saw you were in the soup, you tried to buy the tape. You were pretty clumsy about it, but you didn't break any laws or pay anybody else to break any. Of course, you knew you were going to catch hell from Turkovich and Hale for making an illegal contact and being stupid enough to get caught on tape doing it. Why *did* you pick that place and time, by the way? You knew Hale was going to be there."

"He wasn't supposed to be," Sid protested. "The arrangements had been made before he got sick, and he'd canceled afterward. But then he was feeling better, so he called them the night before and said he'd do it after all. He wasn't supposed to be there."

I nodded. "That makes sense. That was puzzling me, because I don't think you really did talk to Falcone about signing with Buckeye State."

From across the room, I could see his face glistening with sweat.

"You're a big Groundhog booster, aren't you, Sid?" I asked. "You have to be, if you want to do business in Columbus. But Buckeye State isn't your alma mater, is it? If I remember correctly, your alma mater is that school up north, Buckeye State's archrival, Michigan. That's why you panicked when I mentioned lipreading. You weren't talking to Falcone about signing with Buckeye State because you were talking to him about signing with Michigan, am I right?"

"No," Sid croaked.

Mark the thug, who was sitting closest to Sid, leapt out of his chair as if he'd just learned he was sitting next to a plague victim. He retreated some distance, backing away and eyeing Sid Green with disgust.

I glanced at Turkovich. "I can see that Mr. Turkovich isn't surprised by my accusation of disloyalty, but then, I think he already knew. He claims he can't control the fans, and that's true, but I'm willing to bet he exercises considerable control over his boosters, so when he saw you on the tape, he knew you weren't representing the dear old scarlet and black. I'm sure he gave you a hard time about it, and I'm betting that in the long run, it will cost you a lot of cars, starting with his."

"How 'bout it, Turk?" Styles asked. "You driving a Lexus these days?"

Turk didn't deign to comment.

"But Gilda," Faye said, "if the fans find out that Smiling Sid was recruiting for Michigan, they'll boycott him. His business will take a megahit, and he won't have any more cars to give away."

"Yeah," I said. "Ain't that a shame?"

We all contemplated his misery in silence for a moment.

"Well, Turk couldn't afford to waste too much of his valuable time on you, because he had a bigger crisis on his hands," I continued. "You were a small-time criminal, speaking from the perspective of the NCAA, but Creighton Hale was another matter. One of the most recognizable coaches in the NCAA had gone after the hottest recruit in the country before July first, the date when recruiting season officially opens, and he'd been caught on camera doing it. If the NCAA got its hands on that tape, the Groundhogs would be out of the tournament before the season ever started. In fact, the association might be so outraged that it might sanction the Groundhogs for more than one season, the way it did with

UNLV. And the person who would ultimately take the heat for that would be you. You'd be out of a six-figure job."

"He'd lose this cool office, too," Styles observed.

"He'd be history," Faye concurred with satisfaction.

Turkovich gave Faye a cold stare, then returned it to me.

"There were two copies of the tape," I said. "One presented no problem. I'm sure you know the CEO at the station, you two probably swap drinks and sports stories at the Groundhog Club. You explained the situation, in more or less detail, and he arranged for the station's copy of the tape to disappear. That left one copy. You had to destroy that tape. But you were smart enough to know that if you tried to buy it, the way Sid did, you'd make Faye wonder why it was so valuable. She might find out what she had. So you hired Jake Styles to steal it. Or rather, you asked Mrs. Hale, who has a way with men, to hire Jake Styles to steal it. From our brief encounter with the coach, I'm guessing you couldn't convince him of the gravity of the situation. I suspect he flatly denied that he'd made any contact with Falcone." I raised my eyebrows at Turkovich.

"He did," Turkovich confirmed tightly.

"He probably forgot," Faye said, "being so sick and all."

"What's one more rule violation?" Styles said. "After awhile, you hardly even notice."

"Mrs. Hale had her own fish to fry, as you know," I said. "She wanted out of her marriage, but she wanted out with a good return on her investment, which she didn't figure she'd get from any judge in Groundhog country. She wanted her own copy of the tape to ensure that Hale would sign off on any financial agreement she offered him. But she didn't get the tape, and she called attention to herself by shooting Jake Styles."

Turkovich's eyes shifted to Blanche Hale. This, I guessed, was a sore subject.

"He frightened me," she said evenly, looking at me. "You know how he is."

Styles spoke up. "Randy bastard, isn't he? But I don't think it was sex he wanted from you, cupcake—at least, not till he'd been paid. His rules are pretty inflexible: money first, then sex. If you'd paid him before you shot him, you took it back. He didn't have enough money on him when he was found. He says you didn't pay. Of course, he could be lying about that, he often is. But when it comes to lying, you're no slouch yourself. And you don't strike me as a babe who frightens easily."

Mrs. Hale fingered a string of pearls at her throat and gazed back at Styles levelly. She didn't speak.

"If she'd really been frightened of Jake," I put in, "she wouldn't have gone back to see him later. But that's getting ahead of the story, right, Turk? Because when Blanche didn't get the tape for you, you handled the crisis the way you always do, I bet. You hired somebody to take care of it for you. Their job was to get rid of the tape, and you didn't care how they did it."

"Call me conservative," Styles put in, "but burning down a whole apartment complex to destroy one measly little video-tape seems like overkill, doesn't it, Turk?"

"She's a renegade Groundhog, Turk," I said to him. "She doesn't understand that we're talking about a national championship here, maybe even as many as four national championships, right? Unfortunately, that little escapade, expensive though it must have been, didn't succeed any better than the first one. The fire burned up everything except the master video. You didn't know that at first, but you found out."

"How'd he find out?" Styles asked.

"I don't know," I admitted. "Maybe Smiling Sid told him after we paid Sid a visit."

Styles nodded and picked up the thread of the story. "Meanwhile, your shapely sidekick here was pursuing her own game plan. She had the nerve to go back to Jake, whom she rightly pegged as a guy who could forgive anything if the money was right. He agreed to try again, did, and failed again." She shot a glance at me. "But you figured, what the hell? Third time's a charm, and you had charm to spare, so you went after

Jake's daughter because by then you knew she was involved somehow."

Turk was staring at the floor, frowning. I guessed he didn't like what he was hearing.

"Listen," Styles said, "you should just be grateful we're clearing the air now, before you do anything you'd really regret."

"Jake's daughter," I continued, "told you that Faye was considering an offer from your old buddy, Sid Green, who was off doing his own thing. Like I said, maybe you knew about that, maybe you didn't. You weren't really worried about it, because you had a long-standing alliance with Sid, and you knew that it wasn't in his interest, either, for the video to get a public airing. Anyway, Blanche doesn't get quite the reception she'd hoped for from Styles Junior, so she starts casting about for another way to accomplish her goal, just in case this one fizzles."

"I bet she was a Girl Scout when she was a kid," Styles said. "Can't you just picture it?"

"You, meanwhile, decide to pursue another course of action yourself," I said to Turk. "You decide that maybe Faye missed her cue when her apartment building burned down. Maybe she thinks it was just an accident. What she needs is an unambiguous threat—something that will indicate the power of the forces she's up against. You know she works as a projectionist at a movie theater; maybe Jake passed that little tidbit on to Mrs. H. So you withdraw a little more cash, or if we're lucky, you write a check, and somebody sneaks into the projection booth and plants a bomb. Not a big, bad, dangerous bomb, just one that will gum up the machinery and scare the bejesus out of whoever's standing nearby when it goes off."

"You think he's got a whole team of pyrotechnicians on retainer, or what?" Styles asked.

"Yeah, I don't like to rag on anybody's friends," Faye said, "but he's got some real wankers in that crowd."

"And then, what happens? Poor old Creighton Hale, God rest his soul, kicks the bucket." I paused. Mark the thug jumped up from his chair, face flushed, fists clenched, and took a belligerent step in my direction. Turkovich waved him back. "Outside the Groundhog sports complex, all hell breaks loose, as inconsolable Groundhogs gather to mourn their fallen leader. But inside, up on the third floor, peace reigns for the first time in two weeks. You've already articulated all the reasons why the video is probably moot, but it all boils down to a general reluctance to speak ill of the dead."

"Kick a dead Groundhog," Styles muttered.

"Even Hank Mann won't air that video now," Faye observed.

"So, your troubles are over, or so you think," I summarized, "and you invite Faye here in a kind of mop-up operation. You explain to her the likely consequences of releasing the video now, she departs chastened, and that, as they say, is that."

Turkovich laughed. "Well, I certainly didn't expect such an entertaining account of recent events." He crossed his arms and smiled at me. "Did you three think this up together, or did your writer friend make it up for you?" Turkovich pointed an elbow at Tobias, who'd been writing in his notebook nonstop since he'd sat down.

"Oh, we had lots of help," I said.

"Well, I hope you don't expect me to throw myself at your feet and confess," Turkovich said, eyes twinkling.

I decided that they'd just twinkled their last twinkle at our expense.

"No, I don't," I admitted. "So we'll be going now. But I did have something I wanted to give you."

I approached him, and he looked quizzically at me, still amused.

"Hold out your hand," I instructed him.

He did. I dropped the two little yellow tablets in it, the one with the heart cut out of the middle and the one without, onto his palm.

"What's this?" he asked, laughing.

"Better ask your girlfriend," I advised him.

"My girlfriend?"

I could see Blanche Hale stirring on the couch. From where

she was sitting, she couldn't see what I'd given him, and that made her nervous.

I leaned in closer. "Confidentially," I said in a low voice, "I'd find out what she did to the last husband before you tie the knot." I gave him a slow wink.

Now, he was beginning to look a little confused, even apprehensive.

Blanche Hale couldn't stand the suspense, though whether she'd heard the last thing I'd said to him wasn't clear. "What is it, Turk?" she asked.

"Yellow tablets," he said. "Two yellow tablets." He sounded puzzled.

"Valium," I said. "One doctored, one undoctored."

He looked up at me then, and I could see him taking it in.

"You probably saw Hale take some just like that one,"—I pointed at the doctored tablet—"not long before he died."

He studied my face. "Where did you get these?" he asked.

"I'm glad you asked," I said. "I found them in your garbage."

The implications of that hit him, and he turned to stare at Blanche Hale.

"Well, boys and girls, I guess that about wraps things up," I said, stepping away from him. "Time to go. Don't bother," I flapped a hand at Mark as he stood up. "We'll see ourselves out, thanks just the same."

"It's been real," Styles said, backing toward the door with the briefcase in one hand and the gun held casually in front of her with the other.

"Ciao," Tobias said.

Faye paused at the door, leaning on her crutch, and turned back.

"Hey, Turk," she said. "Shit happens, y'know?"

38

Valentino was waiting for us in the hall.

"Take the stairs," he said, pointing the way. "I've disabled the elevators."

At the top of the stairs, he swept Faye up in his arms and carried her. Tobias followed with her crutch. Styles brought up the rear, watching the stairwell behind us. But no one came after us.

"I think they really have a lot to say to each other," Faye declared, her voice bouncing.

"No shit," Styles said. "Worst case scenario, they're making a deal."

"Best case scenario?" I asked breathlessly. I had reached the first floor landing and was putting my head cautiously through the doorway from the stairwell to check out any action in the foyer. "Coast is clear," I reported.

"They're fighting like cats and dogs," Styles replied.

"Or like Fighting Groundhogs," Val amended as we passed the trophy case and crossed the foyer to the front doors. Beneath our feet was a Fighting Groundhog frozen in linoleum.

"But how do you know she won't go home and destroy evidence?" Tobias asked as we reached the car and stood for a moment, catching our breath. The rain had stopped, but the moon wasn't visible through the clouds overhead. I noticed that Styles was still holding the gun as she scanned the parking lot. I also recognized the pickup truck parked next to us as Styles's.

"What evidence?" I asked. "She planted it all on him, just

in case there were any questions. The cops aren't stupid; it won't take them long to find out who had a prescription for Valium and who didn't."

"What about Hale, though?" Tobias asked. "Couldn't he have had a prescription?"

I'd lit a cigarette and was inhaling in between gasps. It hadn't escaped my attention that I was more winded than anyone else, including the seventy-four-year-old who had carried more than a hundred pounds down three flights of stairs. I was really going to have to quit.

"She said he didn't like tranquilizers, or didn't believe in them, something like that," I said, wheezing.

"Say, I hate to be a party pooper," Styles interrupted, "but could we change the venue of this discussion? We're sitting ducks out here if somebody decides to stage a drive-by shooting."

The parking lot wasn't exactly deserted, but there were few cars near us, and the flickering light overhead seemed more like a beacon advertising our location than a source of security.

"Yeah," Faye said, "plus, I have to pee."

Val and Tobias looked at her a little askance.

"We could go to Jake's," I proposed brightly.

"We can go to Bob Evans," Styles pronounced. "I'm hungry."

So she followed us in the truck through the wet streets, and we all watched our backs.

Bob Evans felt like a haven in the dark, foreboding night. The smiles there may have been no more genuine than Turk's, but at least you didn't expect your biscuits and gravy to be booby-trapped.

"What if Turkovich has a prescription for Valium?" Faye asked when she returned from the rest room.

"Then the cops will have to work it out," I said, "assuming they decide to pursue the case. I guess we'll find out if they have the guts to exhume the body."

"Maybe they'll find the stone rolled away at the entrance to the tomb," Val speculated. "Then we'll know for sure that God is a Groundhog."

"You really didn't think he knew, did you?" Styles asked me.

"About her? I was just guessing," I confessed. "And I think he was complicit to a certain extent. But his style is the indirect approach. He doesn't like to get his hands dirty. He'd rather pay someone else to do it. See, if I were Blanche—"

"Instead of Styles," Styles put in.

"Here's what I would've done. I would've read up on Valium, the way we did, in the *Physicians' Desk Reference*. I might've read up on some of his heart medications, too."

"He had plenty of those," Faye said.

"I would've made up the substitute tablets, and then arranged for them to be the last ones in the container. Maybe he was almost out and asked her to get him some more, and that's what gave her the idea. Or maybe she just threw the real ones away. Either way, I'd want him to take all of the doctored pills so that there wouldn't be any questions afterward, if the medical examiner looked at what he had in his pockets."

"Then, just for good measure, she took away his nitro," Faye said.

"Well, she couldn't risk him keeping it," I said. "If he used it, he might survive the attack, and she'd have to go back to the drawing board."

"You said Turkovich was complicit," Tobias said. "How was he complicit? He looked pretty surprised to me, or was that just a good act?"

"Again, I'm just guessing," I pointed out. "What if she suggested the lunch? What if she said, 'Why don't you ask him out to lunch tomorrow?' Maybe she even said, 'It'll be a nice day. Why don't you walk over to that restaurant you like on Fourteenth?' I'm betting she at least said, 'Don't discourage him if he wants to drink. Maybe we'll get lucky, and he'll drink himself to death.' "

Styles nodded. "He'd have top-notch emergency cardiac

care five minutes away at the Buckeye State Hospital. She'd have to hedge her bets somehow."

"Speaking of cardiac care," I said, as the server set down a plate of scrambled eggs in front of her.

"It's quicker than lung cancer, sweetheart," Styles said, admiring a slice of bacon.

"Hey!" Faye exclaimed. She pointed a fork at Styles. "How did you know where we were?"

"I stopped at Jake's on the way home from the airport," Styles said, "and called the theater. When Duke told me what was going on, I didn't want to miss all the fun, and I was practically in the neighborhood."

"There's one thing *I* want to know," I countered. "What was in the briefcase?"

She grinned at me. "Like it? That was Jake's voice-activated video camera. You don't have to be a Liberty to be in the movies, you know."

"You had a camera in the briefcase?" Faye asked, astonished.

"I thought it might be too conspicuous under my ten-gallon hat," Styles said.

"But Styles," I protested dryly, "you didn't get any of those folks to sign a release form."

"Oops," she said. "Silly me."

39

"But I still feel bad for Julie Stoebel. I mean, I feel bad for the other rape victims, too, but I especially feel bad for her because she had the guts to take that Jimmy D. asshole to court, and she lost. That sucks!"

That was the last thing Faye had said at Bob Evans that night. And I'd replied, "Well, maybe we can do something about that."

Now, she and I were in a basement weight room in one of the Buckeye State dorms. We had a reluctant Duke and a sulky Styles in tow. We had to move fast, because this was Thursday of finals week at Buckeye State. The dorm already seemed half empty, and quieter than any dorm had a right to be.

The equipment around us looked old and well used. Berta Homans was explaining that the Lady Hogs liked to use this weight room sometimes because they didn't have to share it with the men's teams.

"Down here," agreed a thin, muscular young woman I now knew was Sharifa Abdul, "we got some privacy."

"The guys got Hog Heaven, but we got Hoggy Bottom," Berta said with a conspiratorial wink.

"Yeah," Danielle said. "You need to dish some dirt on somebody, you know where to come."

"We got spies everywhere," said a lanky brunette who'd been introduced as Martha.

"That's good," I said, "because we have a plan to set up Jimmy D., but we're going to need a lot of help."

Ignoring rumbles of discontent and even outbursts of rebellion from my teammates, I explained what we had in mind. It didn't help that my two detractors weren't getting along, either, ever since Styles had asked Duke if she looked twenty-one, and Duke had told her he thought she could pass for the midtwenties. Most people want to look young, but most women who are petite get tired of having their heads patted, in my experience, and Styles wanted to look her age. So just now, Styles's youthful look was all shot to hell by her belligerent scowl.

"Styles, we've been over this and over this," I told her for the hundredth time. "It has to be you. You can take care of yourself, and you're not intimidated by the prospect of prosecution."

"I wouldn't mind if I could just bash him in the nuts as soon as he lays a hand on me," she complained.

"That's only a temporary deterrent," I explained patiently. "You know that. Besides, you look like his type, right?" I turned back to the players.

Martha cocked her head to one side and studied Styles. She pressed her lips together. "Mmmm, she *looks* all right, I guess, but she's kind of—"

"Hostile," I supplied. "I know. We're working on that. What about Jacoby?" I asked. "Will he help?"

"Jen's talking to him now," Sharifa said, "but I think she'll talk him into it."

"He knows what a loser Jimmy D. is," Martha said.

"Yeah, but you know that male code of honor shit," Berta said. "It's hard for them to get over that."

"We don't have much time, do we?" I ventured.

"He'll be around for another week," Berta said. "The guys are all doing a basketball camp for kids."

"Which they're getting paid big bucks for," Sharifa said bitterly.

"Yeah, so they'll be partying Saturday night after finals," Danielle predicted.

"Even more than usual, she means," Sharifa explained.

Just then the door opened to admit a young woman with a reddish brown ponytail and an unhappy-looking young man, who was holding her hand. He traded a glance of misery with Duke.

"He'll do it!" the young woman announced.

So late that afternoon, Faye and Todd stood on the sidewalk in front of the theater, slapping Duke on the back and wishing him luck. We'd fended off Gloria's attempts to "update his look," as she called it, by telling her that he didn't have time for a permanent, couldn't see through any glasses other than his own, and needed to feel comfortable in whatever he was wearing. And, we said repeatedly, this was no time for him to start living his life as a Scandinavian blond. Adele, the former set designer, plied him with questions he couldn't answer about the bar where Ben Jacoby was taking him. We'd offered him a fake ID, only to learn that he already had one.

"Everybody does, Gilda," he said, red-faced. "It's just something to have. It's not like I use it or anything."

That was undoubtedly true; when did he have time?

Everyone, from Lillian down to Clara, tried to give him tips on acting.

"Keep him laughing, Duke," Uncle Oliver told him. "That way, he won't notice what's going on."

"Be mysterious," Uncle Wallace advised him. "That should pique his interest."

"Just remember, Duke," Aunt Clara said, "whatever emotion is called for, think of a time and place when you felt that emotion, and let yourself go there imaginatively. You can't miss."

Even my parents had advice. "Follow his lead," my father said.

"That's right," my mother agreed. "Be sensitive to changes in his moods, and adjust your approach accordingly."

"You're all just making him nervous, for heaven's sake," objected his great-grandmother, my aunt Lillian. "Duke, dear, just remember to speak up and enunciate clearly so that the tape will pick up the conversation."

Val was going to drive him, since Val had his own role in the script we were writing, and he needed to scout the location.

At the last minute, I took Duke aside, faced him, and put my hands on his shoulders.

"Are you going to give me advice, too?" he groaned.

"Yeah. Forget what everybody told you. Be yourself." I grinned at him. "Remember, he's the asshole, and you're the stand-up guy. Go get him, tiger!"

He looked over at Styles, who was leaning against a No Parking sign.

"Don't *you* have any advice?" he asked.

"Sure, kid," she said. "Don't forget to turn the camera on."

As they were driving off, Duke stuck his head out the window and shouted something.

"What's he saying?" Faye asked, waving her crutch.

"I think it was something like, 'Clean the film gate!' "

Dale Ferguson stopped by around six to tell me that his detective friend from Columbus homicide was going for an exhumation order based on what he'd found in the Turkovich garbage and what he'd learned from his medical consultants, but he wasn't sanguine about the possibility of obtaining one.

"He says the only chance he has is to push the wife as a suspect, not the A.D.," Dale said. "Nobody's keen to go after Turkovich, who's got friends in high places on top of several hundred thousand Buckeye State fans in Central Ohio. I gather that the wife, on the other hand, was not especially popular."

"No kidding?" I said. "What a surprise."

Dale studied me with narrowed eyes. "You wouldn't be sitting on any other evidence I should know about, would you?"

"Who, me?" I said.

"Ahh, forget it!" he said, with a dismissive wave of his hand. "If you had anything else, it would be even weirder than doctored pills in somebody's garbage, and I wouldn't want to know about it."

Duke returned in high spirits some hours later, with a flushed face and beer on his breath. The early show was running, and we were all checking our watches and trying not to worry when he walked in the door, trailed by a smiling Val. He stopped, leaned casually against a reinflated dinosaur leg, and proclaimed, "Damn, I was good!"

We held our curiosity in check for the most part, though, until after the late show let out. By then additional Liberties had dropped by, not wanting to seem too curious but dying to hear Duke's story. We trooped upstairs to Faye's workroom, where Styles had set up a special viewer.

Duke sat on one of the worktables, and everybody else

stood or sat. I smiled to see how his success had transformed him. He was a Liberty, too, after all, and he was thoroughly enjoying his moment in the spotlight.

"Okay," he began, "so me and Ben Jacoby are sitting there in the bar, and I'm fooling around with the camera. And Ben goes, 'Here he comes!' And this big guy comes up to the table, and Ben introduces us, and he sits down. Ben tells him we're waiting for Jen—that's Ben's girlfriend. And I turn the camera in Jimmy's direction, and say, 'Smile! You're on *Candid Camera*!' And he goes, 'Yeah, right!' Like that. And then Ben laughs at him, and says, 'No shit, Jimmy! Duke's got this amazing camera that does all kinds of cool tricks.' After that—I can't believe how easy it was! I rewound the tape and showed it to him in the little viewer window. I explained how it was voice-activated, and turned it on, and set it up on top of the jukebox. Every table has one of those little mini-jukeboxes, you know? And pretty soon, he's asking me where he can buy one. And then—" He seemed to experience a sudden attack of modesty, like an Academy Award winner in front of the microphone. "Well, maybe we should just watch the tape."

We crowded around the viewer, which had a screen the size of a small computer monitor. We waited patiently through the beginning, which featured a brief shot of Ben Jacoby and Duke, sitting in a booth at a bar, looking nervous. They both had beers in front of them, but neither appeared to have drunk anything.

After that cut off, we heard the end of Duke's sentence: "—on *Candid Camera*!" I was surprised to recognize the face on the screen. Jimmy D. was the tall white kid who, along with his black pal, had chased Faye and me twice with clear intent to inflict bodily harm.

"Look, Gilda!" Faye said excitedly. "It's him! I hope those are crutch bruises on the side of his face."

"How much does a machine like this cost?" Jimmy was asking avidly.

Duke grimaced. "A lot. This one belongs to my dad. Why? You interested?"

"Yeah, sure! Why not? This thing is cool!"

"Come on, Jimmy!" Ben protested. "What do you need a camera like that for? You've got a regular video camera."

"No, no, this is really cool!" Jimmy protested. He'd picked it up to examine it, apparently forgetting that it was still running. We got a low-angle close-up of his nose.

"Oh, that's attractive!" Faye said.

On tape, Duke was delivering his lines like a pro. "Some guys like to set 'em up in their rooms. You know, someplace inconspicuous." He sounded both embarrassed and titillated. "Then, when they have a girl in, they have, like, a record."

"That's dope!" Jimmy enthused. We were getting a blurry, dizzying, high-angle view of his crotch and of something, presumably beer, that he'd spilled in that region.

"I know some guys who have, like, a whole library of tapes like that," Duke went on, his voice lowered confidentially.

"That's awesome, man! That's totally awesome! I could really get into that," Jimmy said.

"You could?" Duke asked, as if impressed.

"Shit, yeah," Jimmy said. "Just think—a whole library of ladies, and my sexual exploits. That would be one totally hot show!" He shook his head in appreciation of his own prowess.

"Well, I don't know," Duke said. "If you really want one, my dad distributes them. He has this company that sells all kinds of security electronics. I could probably get you one. But they cost around two thousand."

"I could do that," Jimmy said. "That's not a problem."

"So you'd really like to have one of these cameras set up in your room like that, so you could tape yourself having sex with your dates?" Duke asked, a measure of awe in his voice as if this were a level of masculine audacity he'd really only heard about before.

"You find me one of these little guys," Jimmy affirmed, and turned a thumb up in front of the camera. "I'm there!"

We laughed, hooted, applauded.

"Okay, Styles," I said, "there's your release."

"Yeah, yeah, okay," she said. "Looks like Jimmy's about to be in pictures."

I put a hand on her shoulder. "Just remember, Styles. It's Jackie Chan who always comes out on top."

"Babe, I never forget who belongs on top," she said, and grinned at me.

40

The trouble with a Liberty production, any Liberty production, was that however small it started, it always ended up with a cast of thousands. If this particular production had been budgeted, it would have been over budget faster than you could say Erich von Stroheim.

There was, as I kept pointing out to anyone who would listen, a much simpler way to do things. Why don't we just ask Ben Jacoby to call us when Jimmy D. was out of the house and Hog Heaven was relatively quiet? I said. Why don't we ask Ben to let us in? I said. But no, that was too easy. Nor did it provide enough parts. I gave in without much grace when Faye pointed out that Ben, having stuck out his neck this far for us, preferred to know as little as possible about what we were doing.

So on Friday morning, my mother called the house in her most efficient secretarial voice. She informed the young man who answered the phone that his landlord, who we knew from Ben to be a well-known property owner in the campus area and a major Groundhog booster, would be sending over an electrician that afternoon to check the wiring in preparation for an upcoming city inspection. She confirmed that someone would be home to let him in, thanked him for his cooperation, and hung up. She was off the phone in less than sixty seconds.

"That was fast!" Faye exclaimed.

"An actor in a supporting role never calls undue attention to herself," she said sententiously. She glanced sideways at Clara and Adele, who were sitting on a nearby sofa and rehearsing their own roles. "I should say, a good actor," she amended.

Adele had never acted, but since she had her heart set on participating in our little production, and since there were no sets to design and none we'd let her decorate, we'd caved in and given her a speaking part. Since Gloria got to do both Adele's hair and Clara's, she was content. Val even let her color his gray. Lillian, Wallace, and Oliver were given walk-ons, and my father said that he would just as soon ride along in the van. I wanted to point out that the back of the van was getting as crowded as a *Titanic* lifeboat, but I didn't have the heart. In the end, we needed two vans, the Ace Electric one and the Fast Flush Plumbing one—or if we didn't exactly need them, we used them, one for Val and one for the director and the backup troops.

Wallace drove his own car with Lillian and Oliver riding along, and Adele and Clara took one of Lillian's antiques—a 1939 Buick, with its humped fenders, running board, and well-defined snout above its front grille. Each of the men had written his own character to play. Wallace was dressed rather formally, in a suit that was tasteful, if outdated. Oliver was wearing bright green polyester pants, a red-and-green-plaid polyester golf shirt, and a cap. Lillian was playing her favorite role of dowager empress and was wearing a midcalf georgette dress appropriate to a tea dance at the Ritz-Carlton. Clara and Adele were both dressed more eccentrically than usual. Clara was wearing a long skirt, a prim white blouse with a Peter Pan collar, and a pair of glasses on a black cord around her neck. Draped around her shoulders was a sweater fastened to a sweater guard, which kept getting tangled in the black cord. Her slip hung down a half inch below her skirt. Adele, whose hair Gloria had miraculously toned down from tawny tangerine to a light ginger, wore a frumpy suit accessorized with a loud floral scarf and a gaudy pin. She had a run in one stocking, of which she was very proud.

"It's the details that count, Gilda, when one is striving for an authentic effect," she told me.

"Is that what we're striving for here, authenticity?" I said to Faye in an aside. "I thought we were doing a geriatric version of *Revenge of the Nerds*. If Jimmy D. swallows this, he's stupider than even I give him credit for being."

Faye sighed. "Well, you know things always get out of hand once the family's involved. But look how happy they are. We've just got to chill, I guess, and if this whole thing gets really crazed and like, falls apart, we'll just have to come up with something else, that's all."

"Something else?" I echoed. "Jesus, Faye, I don't think I could go through this again."

Val finally got them all into their respective cars, but not before Adele had asked brightly, "Shall we synchronize our watches?"

"Let's!" Oliver had responded enthusiastically.

I climbed into the driver's seat of the Fast Flush Plumbing van with a cast of thousands in the back. I felt like I was driving the Keystone Cops.

The house known as Hog Heaven was located on a car-choked narrow street on the south edge of campus. Val had already scouted it the evening before, and working with Ben Jacoby's information, he had identified Jimmy D.'s car: a shiny, new, silver Saab 9-3 convertible parked in the street two doors down from the house.

"What kind of idiot leaves a Saab convertible parked on a crowded street like this?" I complained.

"The kind who knows where he can get another one," Styles pointed out.

"You have a point," I conceded. "This street is suspiciously dense with high-priced sports cars."

I cruised slowly down the street, worried that I might actually hit one of the Nissans, Saabs, or Lexuses that crowded in nose to tail with Honda Civics, Geos, and older Fords and Chevies. The other two Liberty cars had been in front of us, but they weren't looking to park.

"What if I don't find a parking place?" I asked.

"Pull into a driveway and wait for something to open up," my father suggested.

"I have a better idea," I said. "We could go home. We don't need to be here, you know. This is a simple, straightforward operation; it isn't *The French Connection.*"

Nobody gave any sign of having heard me. Like a miracle on Tenth Street, a car pulled out in front of me, between Hog Heaven and Jimmy D.'s car and on the opposite side of the street. I parallel-parked the van. It only took me four tries.

"Val's right behind us," Faye reported. "He's turning in."

They were watching through the van's tinted back window. I watched in the rearview mirror. Taking his time, Val sat in the van, fiddling with a clipboard full of papers. A born actor, I thought again, just like all the other Liberties. He climbed out of the van, opened the back doors, and removed a large tool kit. Inside, I knew, was the palm-sized, voice-activated camera.

The house itself had the seedy, neglected look of student housing. The porch sagged, the gutters sagged, and the roof was furry with moss. Some kind of woody vine had climbed up one side of the porch and across the front before giving up the ghost. It reminded me of the plants in Styles's office, which she hadn't mentioned to me since she'd returned from her trip.

Val climbed the wooden steps up to the porch and knocked on the front door. He looked down at his papers again. Somebody must have opened the door, because his posture changed and he was talking. Then I saw a screen door open, and Val disappeared inside.

"He's in," Faye said, then added, "Now remember, give him at least five minutes." I knew she was speaking into a walkie-talkie to the other actors in our little drama. I heard a muffled, "Roger, unit two. We copy."

I glanced at my watch. There was no way they'd restrain themselves for a full five minutes, I thought. But they did.

In fact, it was nearly ten minutes before the gray Buick pulled up next to Jimmy D.'s Saab, angled in toward it, gave it the gentlest of taps on its rear bumper, and stopped dead. I heard Adele's shriek. In fact, I was willing to bet that if, as Ben had predicted, Jimmy D. was sleeping off a morning final, he'd just awakened. Adele and Clara were on.

Clara hopped out of the car on the passenger's side and ran to examine the damage. Adele, her whole attitude suggesting that of a woman whose nerves had been shattered, stumbled out on the driver's side and stood gazing at the contact point, her hands covering her mouth. An argument apparently ensued, and Adele looked increasingly flustered. The two of them looked around at the houses. About this time, another car came up the street, only to find it blocked by the Buick. Clara went to talk to the driver, who, sufficiently discouraged, backed down the street.

Clara said something to Adele, and then left her standing by the car as she marched up the steps of the house in front of which the Saab was parked. She must have struck it lucky because a young woman carrying a baby came out on the front porch and pointed at Hog Heaven, nodding. Clara apparently reported to Adele and made the kind of gesture you use when you want a dog to stay. She trooped up to the front door of Hog Heaven and rang the bell. She seemed to get a quick response, and then she stood on the porch talking for awhile, arms flying expressively like a heroine of the silent screen. Then the door opened, and she disappeared.

"What's happening?" I heard Wallace bark tinnily on the walkie-talkie.

"She's gone inside," Faye reported. "No, wait, she's coming out! She's got him!"

In the rearview mirror I watched Clara come down the steps followed by two tall young men. One of them, the one who was tucking his shirttail in and finger-combing his hair, was our old nemesis, Jimmy DeGiulio.

Another car drove up, playing loud rap music. Its bass rattled the van. The new car honked several times, but Jimmy's sidekick, whom I didn't recognize, gestured for them to go around. A shouting match began, and for a minute there, I thought perhaps Wallace, Lillian, and Oliver would never get to play their parts, but at last the new car ground into reverse and shot backward and out of sight.

Jimmy D. bent over to inspect the bumper. He reached out to touch it. Then he made a gesture toward the Buick, but Adele vehemently shook her head. Clara appeared to remonstrate with Adele, but Adele held her ground. If Jimmy D. wanted the Buick backed up, he would have to do it himself. Finally, he made placating gestures and climbed into the car. And there he sat, stymied by the 1939 controls. He called his friend over, but his friend just stood laughing at him.

Now Wallace's cream-colored Ford appeared on the scene. Instead of backing up, Wallace got out to see what the trouble was. He listened to the explanations and examined the bumper himself, squatting to get a good look at it, before turning to address himself to Jimmy's problem. He stood by the driver's window and began to gesture and point. But at this juncture, Oliver got out of the car. Wallace interrupted his instructions to Jimmy to explain the situation to Ollie. Ollie went around to the passenger side of the Buick and got in. Gradually, Wallace's voice rose, and his gestures became more impatient. Jimmy's two advisers appeared to be giving him contradictory advice.

Lillian stuck her head out the window of the Ford and asked something. Wallace abandoned Jimmy to Oliver and walked back to the Ford to confer with her.

"He's out," Faye said behind me, and I glanced in the rearview mirror. Val had come out of the house and was un-hurriedly returning his tool kit to the back of the van. "Okay, Lilly, you're on."

In front of us, Wallace opened the door for Lillian, and she got out. Making stately progress with her cane, she advanced on the agitated little group and spoke to Jimmy through the car window. He got out, and she got in. Adroitly, she turned the car on, put it in gear, and reversed it several feet. She emerged with dignity, while Jimmy, his friend, Adele, Clara, Wallace, and Oliver examined the bumper. Jimmy was shak-ing his head. By now, Val had backed the van out and was idling next to us, watching the proceedings and whistling.

Adele reached out and touched Jimmy on the shoulder. Enough, already, I thought. I would have said less is more, but Liberties never dealt in less, wouldn't know less if they tripped over it. Clara made her exit speech and got into the Buick. Wallace opened the driver's side door and helped Adele in. He, Lillian, and Oliver made their way back to the Ford. Adele inched down the street. Wallace followed. Val followed him. I waited until the boys had reentered the house before pulling out and following Val. When last I saw the boys, Jimmy D.'s friend was still laughing.

41

The Liberty men had all tried to help Styles prepare for her role in this production, and they had the bruises to show for it.

"Sorry," she'd mumble as they departed in search of ban-dages and ice. "I just wasn't cut out for this."

In fact, I had serious concerns about whether our whole scheme would survive Styles's portrayal of a coed, which had the quality of Sly Stallone playing Tinkerbell. And I was having second thoughts about asking her to go through with it. Maybe it wasn't fair to set anyone up for rape, even knowing that she could handle herself, that help would be within call, that she wouldn't have to face the emotional upheaval of a trial. But just when I was about to suggest that we call the whole thing off, she experienced a breakthrough in her acting. It was Todd, the drama student and the only unbruised male in the near vicinity, who was responsible.

Todd had Wallace, who was usually half-potted anyway, play the drunken Jimmy D., and Todd played Styles's role. They were both good, especially Todd in the role of a reluctant but tipsy coed. The way he played it took into account Styles's own personality. He wasn't passive or giggly or awestruck, just determinedly polite. Politeness was a stretch for Styles, but suddenly it became possible to imagine her in the role. The next time around, Todd played Jimmy D. to Styles's coed and emerged unscathed. After a few more rehearsals, she was ready.

Val and my father brought her by the theater on their way to Columbus, and Faye and I were stunned. Gloria and Adele had gotten her into a black Spandex miniskirt, tight but flexible for easy movement. She wore a low-cut black knit top and black Mary Janes, apparently because she had vetoed anything she couldn't run in. Slung over one shoulder was a black purse, small but large enough to hold a walkie-talkie. Around her neck she wore a locket that concealed a one-way mike, which transmitted to a portable unit inside the van. Gloria had tamed her unruly curls. They had even managed makeup and perfume.

She stretched her lips in a red smile. "Babe," she said to me, "I feel like a new woman."

I groaned. "Don't tell me: You feel pretty."

"I was never lovelier," she agreed. Then she sneezed. "But this goddamn perfume has got to go."

"Now, remember," I said one last time as we put her back in the car.

"I know," she said. "I come out on top."

I told Duke to pick his jaw up off the sidewalk, and we went inside to wait.

Styles was going to the Hog Heaven party with Ben Jacoby's girlfriend Jen. She would be introduced as Samantha, a friend of Jen's older sister who was visiting from out of town. We hoped that this explanation might cover Styles's age, if she seemed older, and distance her slightly from Jen, just in case Jimmy D. had any scruples where a teammate's girlfriend's friend was concerned.

"He might not try anything," I pointed out. "After all, his last escapade landed him in court."

"No stress, Gilda. In the first place, we don't know if it was his last escapade," Faye argued. "Plus, check it out, he *won*. He's going to figure he's, like, totally unstoppable. I bet he'll try something. And if he doesn't try it with Styles, at least she'll be there to stop it."

"What if he hooks up with a girl who wants to be hit on?" Duke asked.

"According to Ben, there's not much chance of that," Faye said. "He's got a really bad rep."

"You don't think he'll look in her bag, do you?" Todd asked anxiously. "And find the walkie-talkie?"

"If he does, she'll clobber him with it," I said.

The last late show let out at eleven forty-five. Duke, Todd, and I cleaned up, and Faye went upstairs to work on her video, but she didn't last long.

"I'm too nervous to work," she admitted.

For my part, I was chain-smoking in the lobby right under the No Smoking sign.

At twelve-fifteen, Tobias joined us with a bottle of merlot. We drank wine and tried to keep from talking about all the things that could be going wrong. Two by two, the Liberties drifted in, pretending to be casual about it, not anxious or even

particularly curious, just interested, they said. Someone—
probably Clara—brought a pitcher of Tequila Sunrises, so we
were a pretty noisy group by the time Val and my father
brought Styles back at one-thirty.

We cheered her while we examined her anxiously for signs
of violent struggle, but she looked pretty much the same way
she had when we last saw her, except that her makeup was
smudged and her hair ruffled.

"Well?" Faye asked, as soon as the cheering died down.

Styles looked at us seriously. "I broke his wrist," she reported. Then she smiled. "I think I took the slam out of his
dunk."

While Jimmy had been downstairs putting ice on his wrist,
Styles had retrieved the camera. We all went upstairs and
crowded into the small room again to watch the tape on the
viewer.

At first we saw only a shaft of light and heard a voice,
Styles's voice.

". . . the bathroom," she was saying, complaining.

A light came on, and we saw a room typical of a college
male—bed unmade, clothes on the floor, a few dirty dishes
lying around, and a pizza box next to the bed. Actually, it reminded me a lot of Jake's apartment, except that there was a
life-size Michael Jordan poster on the wall over the bed. I
couldn't discern any signs of serious study.

"No," Jimmy D. was saying. "This is my room." He grinned
at her boozily. Both of them were holding plastic cups.

"Jimmy," Styles reproached him, in a voice that came closer
to a whine than anything I'd ever heard out of her mouth.
"You spilled beer on me. I've got to go wash it off."

"Come here," he said, yanking on her wrist to bring her
closer. "Where'd I spill it? I'll clean it up."

"No!" Styles said, making a good show of trying to pull
away. She was trying to fend off his hands.

But now her top bulged with a groping paw. We shifted uneasily about. I glanced at Styles, but she just looked curious,

not embarrassed. We'd wanted evidence, and we were getting it. We hadn't quite reckoned, or at least I hadn't, on its impact on us.

"Where's the beer?" Jimmy asked, pulling up her top. "I like beer."

"No, Jimmy," Styles said, this time with an edge of steel.

"Hey, no bra! That's nice." Jimmy leaned forward, tongue lolling, trying to lick her bare midriff.

She pushed his head away. "No, Jimmy!" she said sternly.

If he had been sober, he would have backed off. Anyone would have. If he'd only been half-smashed, her voice would have sobered him up. But he was too far gone to notice or care.

"At this point," my father interrupted, "we were on the front porch, Val and I. Another three minutes, and we would have gone in."

But it didn't last that long. Suddenly Jimmy rushed her, picked her up, and threw her on the bed. "Come on, baby," he said. "I got something tastes even better than beer." We could only see his back, but the elbow we could see told us all we needed to know.

"No, Jimmy," she said clearly, one more time, before he pounced on her.

It was hard to make out what she did to him from our angle, but we heard a crack. He yelped and fell back, holding his wrist. In profile now, his mouth hung open. She shut it with her knee, and he fell to the floor.

"I said no, Jimmy," Styles repeated calmly, standing up. "No means no."

Then, after a moment's pause, punctuated by moans from the fallen Jimmy, she glanced up at the camera, twiddled her fingers at us, and mouthed, "Hi, Mom!"

42

We waited a few days until Dale Ferguson informed me that the body of Creighton Hale had been quietly exhumed, and that a murder investigation was under way. Then Faye and I paid one last visit to the Buckeye State gym.

We didn't see Jimmy D., but we spotted Ben Jacoby and some of his teammates performing for a group of boys as we looked in on one of the basketball courts.

"Basketball camp," Faye said, lifting her crutch slightly to point. "All boys."

We sighed and took the elevator up.

Outside the athletic director's office, the traffic was heavy. The door was open, and several secretaries were busy in the outer office. Everyone looked harassed. I was willing to bet they were having a bad week.

I handed the package to Faye. "You take it in," I said. "It's really your film. I'll wait for you downstairs."

"Are you sure?" she said, glancing nervously into the office.

"You go, girl," I said.

If she was lucky, Faye would not even see Turk Turkovich. She didn't need to. We'd written down our list of demands. We wanted Jimmy D. removed from the roster of Buckeye State players, with the understanding that if he transferred in order to play on another team, the tape we were enclosing from the party at Hog Heaven would follow him not only to his new school, but to the local media. We wanted him told that if he ever assaulted a woman again, a copy of this tape would be sent to the Columbus media, and that the young woman it featured would make herself available to any woman wishing to prosecute Jimmy DeGiulio on a rape charge.

We noted that if Turkovich didn't meet our demands, copies of another tape, also enclosed, would be provided to the local news media and to the National Collegiate Athletic Association. That second tape, the one from our meeting with Turkovich, wouldn't have provided evidence of any criminal activity, but it would have been embarrassing at the very least to both Turkovich and to Buckeye State, and it might have had a deleterious effect on Turkovich's career at Buckeye State and elsewhere. We noted that should Turkovich leave his position at Buckeye State before our demands could be met, he should instruct whomever had power to act upon them to do so.

Finally, we enclosed one final tape—a copy of the infamous cheerleading contest footage that had started all the trouble in the first place. We explained to him how he had been misled by chance editing and a telephoto perspective into believing he was witnessing something that had never taken place. His mistake had caused him to risk lives to protect something that wasn't worth protecting.

As for the rest, we were leaving it in the hands of others. The police would either find enough evidence against Blanche Hale or they wouldn't; if they were lucky, they might succeed in getting Turkovich to testify against her. But that presumed that Turkovich had anything concrete to add, and I doubted that he did. Blanche Hale was a very careful woman. Similarly, Mike Falcone would either play for Buckeye State or he wouldn't. In the overall scheme of things, given the state of men's college athletics today, it didn't much matter. When the time came, he'd undoubtedly pack up his creatine, or whatever the latest performance enhancer was, and head off to the highest bidder.

Downstairs I found myself standing in front of the trophy case. What did it mean, all that metal, that so many people were willing to invest their lives in collecting it? Standing this close, I could see the tarnish and dust in the nooks and crannies of the metal statues.

Then I noticed Faye's reflection in the glass.

"What are you looking at?" she asked.

"The stuff that dreams are made of," I said.

A NOTE ON
THE MALTESE FALCON

John Huston's directorial debut made movie history in 1941. Huston was a contract screenwriter at Warner Bros. when he was given the opportunity to direct as well as script the third film version of Dashiell Hammett's novel, *The Maltese Falcon*. Seven years later, he would win Oscars for Best Director and Best Screenplay for *The Treasure of the Sierra Madre*.

Huston's debut also made several careers. Humphrey Bogart, who had played a series of gangster roles at Warner Bros., landed the role of Sam Spade when George Raft, unwilling to work with a novice director, turned down the part; this role, along with a role similarly acquired in *High Sierra* the same year, vaulted Bogey to stardom. Mary Astor acquired the role of Brigid O'Shaughnessy as a castoff from Geraldine Fitzgerald; it would result in her most famous performance. The portly Sydney Greenstreet made his screen debut as Caspar Gutman, and would continue to be paired with Peter Lorre, a Hungarian actor best known to film aficionados for his role as the child murderer in Fritz Lang's *M* (1931). Bogart, Greenstreet, and Lorre would reunite in *Casablanca* (1942).

Many historians agree that *The Maltese Falcon* launched a cycle of films now known as *film noir*, or "black film," from a French description of American films of the forties. Critics debate whether *film noir* is a genre or merely a visual style, but these films are typically crime melodramas featuring an antihero, usually the detective, as protagonist. They are set in urban neighborhoods filled with dark, wet streets, neon signs that illuminate shadowy interiors, tawdry rooming houses and motels, and unadorned office buildings. The night-for-night cinematography creates a darkness that both reflects and contributes to a confusion of motives and a cynicism regarding human nature. These are films about mystery, and at the center of the mystery, like a spider at the center of a web, is a woman—beautiful, seductive, powerful, and dangerous.

Women in Film

ACROSS

2 Mae West said, "___ that a gun in your pocket, or are you just glad to see me?"

5 One of the pioneers of feminist film criticism, author of FROM REVERENCE TO RAPE.

11 26 across designed these for Mae West, Audrey Hepburn, Dorothy Lamour, and Grace Kelly.

14 Script direction for a shot that is filmed from the opposite point of view from the previous shot (abbrev.).

15 The pronoun Miss Piggy uses to refer to herself.

16 One of a trio of acting sisters, she played Camille and DuBarry in the silent era (initials).

18 Where Dorothy met Glinda and the Wicked Witch of the West.

19 Julie Andrews played in the 1966 Hitchcock thriller, ___ CURTAIN.

22 The first African American woman to win an Academy Award.

26 For more than sixty years, her

name was synonymous with Hollywood film fashion.

28 Suffix for a language or dialect; Clara Bow lost popularity in the sound era because she spoke Brooklyn-____.

29 Screenwriter and producer nominated for Best Screenplay Oscars for SILKWOOD (1983) and WHEN HARRY MET SALLY . . . (1989) (initials).

32 Australian director best known for MY BRILLIANT CAREER (1978).

34 Katharine Hepburn and Judy Holliday teamed up in ADAM'S ____ (1949).

36 The place where Celeste Holm might have mailed A LETTER TO THREE WIVES in the 1949 film (abbrev.).

37 Brenda Fricker won her Best Supporting Actress Oscar for her role in the 1989 film, ____ LEFT FOOT.

38 First and last initials of the German director who made THE LOST HONOR OF KATHERINA BLUM (1975).

39 Julie Dash's 1992 historical drama about a Sea Islands family migrating to the mainland, ____ OF THE DUST.

43 A possible nickname for Lamour and Arzner, not to mention the girl who went over the rainbow.

44 Nicknames for Field, Struthers, and Potter.

45 Brazilian director Susana Amaral's 1985 film of a Clarice Lispector novel is called THE ____ OF THE STAR.

46 First and last initials of the union to which Brianne Murphy was admitted as the first woman member.

48 Eleanora Rossi Drago plays the wife of this famous biblical character in John Huston's 1966 film, THE BIBLE.

49 A former stage actress, she won an Academy Award for the title role in DRIVING MISS DAISY (1989).

50 Her films include A RAISIN IN THE SUN (1961), ROOTS (1979), DO THE RIGHT THING (1989), and JUNGLE FEVER (1991).

51 Jean Arthur met Mr. Smith there, Bogey and Bacall went there with the Committee for the First Amendment, and Barbra has been there for the inaugural ball.

53 First two initials of the Vietnamese filmmaker who made REASSEMBLAGE (1982) and SURNAME VIET GIVEN NAME NAM (1985).

54 A word frequently paired with "gossip," it might be used by some to describe the talk in THE WOMEN (1939).

56 Animator Ayoka Chenzira's 1985 film "for Nappy-Headed People."

59 Abbey Lincoln plays Denzel Washington's mother in Spike Lee's 1990 film, ____ BETTER BLUES.

60 Mary Pickford was one of the four founders of this distributing company for independent productions (abbrev.).

61 Viennese actress who appeared in films as diverse as BOCCACCIO 70 (1962), THE TRIAL (1962), and WHAT'S

NEW, PUSSYCAT? (1965) (initials).

62 Where Bette Midler lives in DOWN AND OUT IN BEVERLY HILLS (1986) (abbrev.).

63 Actress who appeared in THE LAST OF THE MOHICANS (1992), THIS BOY'S LIFE (1993), and THE AGE OF INNOCENCE (1993) (initials).

64 Sigourney Weaver played Dian Fossey in the 1988 biopic, GORILLAS IN THE _____.

66 She owned one of the best-equipped of the early production facilities, claimed to have made the first narrative motion picture, and experimented with synchronized sound in the teens.

71 Metro-Goldwyn-Mayer translated its studio motto, "_____ for art's sake."

72 Rosalind Russell was really Cary Grant's star reporter, not _____ GIRL FRIDAY (1940).

73 She won an Honorary Oscar in 1991 for her lifetime achievement (first name only).

DOWN

1 Scarlett asks Rhett, "Where shall I go? What shall I _____?"

2 Clara Bow was the "__ Girl."

3 Logo for Solax, the production company owned by 66 across, or A RAISIN IN THE _____ (1961).

4 Katharine Hepburn's autobiography.

6 Screenwriter, editor, and the best known of the Studio Era women directors, she made CHRISTOPHER STRONG (1933) and DANCE, GIRL, DANCE (1940).

7 Acting coach who taught the Stanislavsky Method to Marlon Brando, Robert De Niro, Warren Beatty, and Harvey Keitel (initials).

8 Clara Blandick played this famous auntie.

9 What Georgy Girl would call a rest room.

10 The actress with the violet eyes (first name only).

11 Simone Simon and Natassia Kinski both starred in horror films called _____ PEOPLE.

12 A Depression-era genre which showcased strong women, including Claudette Colbert, Katharine Hepburn, Carole Lombard, Rosalind Russell, and Irene Dunne.

13 Television production company owned by the actress who received an Academy Award nomination for her role in ORDINARY PEOPLE (1981).

17 Actress, director, and producer Marshall.

20 Rosalind Russell played the leading role in the 1967 film of the Arthur Kopit play, _____ DAD, POOR DAD, MAMA'S HUNG YOU IN THE CLOSET AND I'M FEELING SO SAD.

21 Angle designation for an eye-level shot as calculated according to the height of the average cameraMAN (abbrev.).

23 In the 1985 Susan Seidelman film, Rosanna Arquette and Aidan Quinn are _____ SEEKING SUSAN.

24 She played Brigid O'Shaughnessy in THE MALTESE FALCON.

25 Bette Davis and Ann Baxter might have been told to break one in ALL ABOUT EVE (1951).

27 Same as 39 across.
30 Among her editing credits are E.T. (Academy Award nomination for Best Editing, 1982), THE BIG CHILL (1983), and BELOVED (1998).
31 Before EVITA (1997), The Material Girl starred in TRUTH __ DARE (1990).
33 Prolific Italian actress who played in LA DERNIERE FEMME (THE LAST WOMAN, 1976), LA VITA E BELLA (LIFE IS BEAUTIFUL, 1982), and SWANN IN LOVE (1982) (initials).
35 An actress turned director, she made THE BIGAMIST (1953) and THE TROUBLE WITH ANGELS (1966), among others (first name only).
38 The state where everyone is supposed to meet Judy Garland and her family for the World's Fair (abbrev.).
40 Famous singer with the Jimmy Dorsey band, she appeared with them in several films, including THE FLEET'S IN (1942) and I DOOD IT (1943) (initials).
41 Carmen Miranda was known for her ____ frutti hat.
42 Gloria Swanson, Joan Crawford, and Rita Hayworth all played this notorious Somerset Maugham protagonist (first name only).
43 Editor Allen; her legendary cutting of BONNIE AND CLYDE (1967) revolutionized film editing.
44 Tinkerbell's light dims when she's feeling this way.
47 Statuesque dancer who danced

with Gene Kelly in SINGIN' IN THE RAIN (1952) and Fred Astaire in SILK STOCKINGS (1957) (first name only).
52 Fay Kanin was the first to hold this title for the National Film Preservation Board.
55 What Katharine Hepburn finds on Humphrey Bogart after he takes the plunge in THE AFRICAN QUEEN (1951).
57 Leslie Harris's 1992 film was about JUST ANOTHER GIRL ON THE _____ (abbrev.).
58 Michelle Pfeiffer shares one with George Clooney in ONE FINE DAY (1996) (pl.).
60 Actress Thurman; she learned THE TRUTH ABOUT CATS AND DOGS (1996) so that she could play the Cat Woman in BATMAN AND ROBIN (1997).
63 What Ruby Keeler wears on the bottom of her shoe.
65 Joan was one (abbrev.).
66 A costume for Hilary Swank in THE NEXT KARATE KID (1994).
67 Country which has the most extensive history of women filmmakers, counting the immigrants (abbrev.).
68 Humbert Humbert's nickname for the nymphet played by Sue Lyon and Dominique Swain.
69 A small, extremely portable camera often used by documentary filmmakers is a ____ 8.
70 Known to most Americans as "Our Miss Brooks," she was nominated for Best Supporting Actress as Joan Crawford's sidekick in MILDRED PIERCE (1945) (initials).

SOLUTION

Notes on Women in Film

ACROSS

14 reverse angle
16 Norma Talmadge, sister of Constance and Natalie
29 Nora Ephron
36 post office
38 Margarethe von Trotta
46 American Society of Cinematographers
53 Trinh T Minh-ha
60 United Artists
61 Romy Schneider
62 Los Angeles
63 Tracey Ellis
73 Sophia Loren

DOWN

 7 Stella Adler
10 Elizabeth Taylor
21 neutral angle
33 Ornella Muti
35 Ida Lupino
38 Missouri (*Meet Me in St. Louis*)
40 Helen O'Connell
42 Sadie Thompson (Francine Everett also played her in 1946 as *Dirty Gertie from Harlem*)
47 Cyd Charisse
65 saint
67 United States
68 in *Lolita*
70 Eve Arden

Don't miss the first
Movie Lover's Mystery:

FADE TO BLACK

by Della Borton

Published by The Ballantine Publishing Group.
Available at your local bookstore.

PETER BOGDANOVICH'S
MOVIE OF THE WEEK
52 CLASSIC FILMS
FOR ONE FULL YEAR

Director, producer, screenwriter, author, actor, and film critic, Peter Bogdanovich knows movies. Now, in this unique new book, Bogdanovich shares his passion with a connoisseur's insight and delight by inviting the reader to join him for a year at the movies.

52 WEEKS
52 FILMS

A FRONT-ROW SEAT
TO A YEAR'S WORTH
OF MUST-SEE MOVIES

Published by Ballantine Books.
Available at your local bookstore.